"Carcasses," Sweetsea said with admiration.

"Explosive carcasses. Floating bombs, torpedoes, catamarans."

Justice let his eye run over these appalling novelties as Sweetsea rattled off their names.

There were carcasses that looked like pairs of barrels joined by a bridle of chain. There were square boxes covered in lead and coffin shapes in sheeted copper. There were globes and cylinders, boxes with floats and boxes with anchors.

"Do you see, sir?" Sweetsea spoke respectfully. "This is new, Mr. Justice. New since I was last here."

As Scorcher helped the crippled squire drag the curious object into a better light, Justice saw that it was a gun.

It was the simplest and most menacing weapon of them all. With such a gun the *Pandora* could drive a line into the side of any ship and pull a hundred-pound carcass of powder home against her hull.

No ship would be safe against such an instrument of war . . .

"Lively adventure"
—PUBLISHER'S WEEKLY

The Pandora Secret

A CAPTAIN JUSTICE STORY

ANTHONY FORREST

A JOVE BOOK

For Michael Berry

This Jove book contains the complete
text of the original hardcover edition.
It has been completely reset in a typeface
designed for easy reading, and was printed
from new film.

THE PANDORA SECRET

A Jove Book / published by arrangement with
Hill and Wang

PRINTING HISTORY
Hill and Wang edition / September 1982
Jove edition / January 1984

ISBN: 0-515-07394-6

Jove books are published by The Berkley Publishing Group,
200 Madison Avenue, New York, N.Y. 10016.
The words "A JOVE BOOK" and the "J" with sunburst
are trademarks belonging to Jove Publications, Inc.

PRINTED IN THE UNITED STATES OF AMERICA

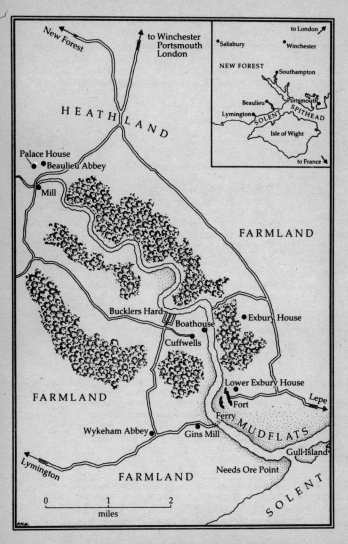

Sketch of Sir George Lilly's map of the Beaulieu River 1804

~❧1❧~

JUSTICE HEARD THE sharp crack of the guns as he and Scorcher came to the edge of the woods, and the sound puzzled him. It was too late in the day for anyone to be shooting birds, for the clear frosty sky of the November afternoon was fading fast, and the first wisps of mist were already drifting along the banks of the river. In any case, a party of sportsmen would fire raggedly, as each man took his chance of a shot, and this was disciplined shooting.

As the second volley flashed yellow through the trees, Justice felt his horse tug nervously at the bridle, and he swung himself out of the saddle to calm the animal.

Thirty seconds, near enough, between one fusillade and the next. So these were not regular troops, trained to fire at a steady three rounds a minute, come what may, but recruits or militia. All the same, they were keeping good time. Justice had so often watched marines at target practice that, out of habit, he found himself counting through the drill. One. The pans were open and each man would have a blue paper cartridge in his hand. Two. They would be pushing the hard paper between the teeth and tearing it open. Three. Shake a few grains of powder into the priming pan and close it. Four. Ground the musket, pour the powder down the barrel. Five. Insert the ball and drive it home with the ramrod. Six. Make a wad of the cartridge paper and drive that down, too. "Present! Ready! Fire!"

It was not quite the welcome he had expected at Cuffwells after a three-day ride across Sussex and Hampshire. He was chilled, tired, and very hungry, for he and Scorcher had pressed on all day with nothing but brief stops to water their horses and take a tankard of ale for themselves, hoping to reach George Lilly's house before nightfall. A winter journey on horseback was seldom agreeable, and he had been thinking more of a warm fire and an early supper than of military exercises on the banks of the Beaulieu River.

"Look, Cap'n," said Scorcher, who had looped the horse bridles over a low branch and joined him as another row of flashes lit the water.

Justice stared through the dark towards a boat coming round the bend of the river, the oarsman bent low and pulling hard against the running tide, while his companion tipped casks over the stern like a run of lobster pots, bobbing and rocking away in the stream.

"Buoys?" Scorcher suggested.

"Marks, more likely." Justice scarcely had time to wonder why landsmen should be firing at the kind of target the navy regularly used for exercising its guns. Before he could say more, a file of green-coated Volunteers pushed through to a clearing on the edge of the water, kneeled to make sure of their aim, and fired again.

"They shoot better than marines," Justice said admiringly as a cluster of balls splashed round one of the casks.

"If you're married to Mistress Roper, you can't see straight." Like most sailors, Scorcher had little liking for the stiff-stocked marines who served as a ship's marksmen in a fight and its harsh policemen between times.

Justice let the contemptuous remark pass. At sea his servant knew his place too well to make such a gibe, or even to speak without asking leave. He had to take his turns and chances with the rest of the crew. But ashore he had the licence of a familiar. There was a gritty independence among the short-shanked and thickset people who were raised in the dyked sheeplands of Romney Marsh, and John Valcourt Justice, of Hook Manor, Appledore, gentleman and captain in His Majesty's navy, had long ago come to peculiar terms with Fred Scorcher, sheepherder, smuggler, and sailor, bled with him, saved his life, and been saved by him. Between such men there was a bond of blood that was even stronger than ties of family, rank, or discipline.

It was puzzling. Why should a squad of local Volunteers be out firing at such a time and place? The government, as Justice and every other ship's officer knew from hard experience, was a mean master, and he'd heard that few of the thousands who had joined the Volunteers had ever fired a shot at the King's expense. Even at the end of 1804, when Boney had been threatening an invasion for months on end, most of the companies had to be content with pike drill, patrols, and parades to raise their spirits. If England had to depend on them to save her, if Boney's fleet should one day slip past the weathered squadrons that blockaded his ports, the French grenadiers would face more puff than powder as they marched inland from the beaches.

Yet these seemed to be well-trained men, and there was clearly purpose to their practice. Someone had brought them out in this miserable light, and paid for their ammunition, and Justice was fairly sure that it was George Lilly's purpose and purse that provided the explanation.

They were finished now, for he saw the oarsman swing his boat round and pull to where they stood chatting on the bank, saw the man in the stern lean out to call to them, saw almost the last of the light catch his long face.

"Eli Dunning." Justice spoke the name quietly, remembering. If Dunning was here, Lilly would not be far away, and there was secret work in hand.

Justice knew that the sad-featured evangelical, who larded his speech with biblical texts and could have passed for one of Wesley's wandering preachers, was employed by the Society for the Distribution of Improving Tracts for Seamen. He also knew that this high-sounding enterprise worked in mysterious ways for Lilly as well as the Lord.

It had been Dunning who had hastened down to Appledore in July, breaking into a cricket match to summon him to Richmond Terrace, just off Whitehall, where Lilly had promptly enlisted him in the clandestine service of the Board of Beacons, Bells, Buoys, and Mercantile Messengers, and packed him off on a perilous journey to Verdun and back.

"Aye, it's him all right." Scorcher gave a snort of indignation, for he had harboured a grievance against Dunning for months after the man had whisked his master away and left him to nurse a leg wound at Hook. "Because I growed on the marsh, he took me for a sheep," he said bitterly.

THEY HAD JUST TURNED to mount when there was a rush of hoofbeats, and a rider came off the frost-hardened track, saw the two men blocking the way, with trees on one side of them and water on the other, pulled violently at the reins as the horse skittered on wet leaves and pitched sideways, then hit

3

the ground at their feet with an oath of surprise.

Justice had been sent stumbling as the horse lurched to regain a foothold, but he came back quickly to look at the prone figure, dressed simply in short jacket and breeches, glaring at him from the ground.

"Damn it to hell! Shouldn't be out if you can't look after yourself."

Uncertain whether this was self-reproach or a complaint, Justice put out a helping hand to the youth, scarcely noting the pitch of the voice until the gentler grasp told him that it was not a man who had run into them but a young woman, hair cut close like a boy's. She scrambled to her feet, dusting stiffly at her clothes, and as she stared at him as if she had run into an apparition, he stepped back in embarrassment.

"I'm sorry," he began, and stopped as she spoke at the same time.

"What the devil are you doing here?" she asked, and then seemed to be aware of some mistake or discourtesy, and gave him an apologetic smile.

"Well." Justice didn't feel he owed an apology, and this excuse seemed lame. "I'm sorry," he said, and left it at that.

"Oh, Squire Sweetsea's sharpshooters." She glanced past Justice at the Volunteers, now chaffering happily like men with their duty done. "The pride of the Beaulieu River and the terror of the French. The thought of them must make Boney shake in his imperial boots!" There was something more in her voice than gentle sarcasm at the expense of clerks and countrymen in uniform, though she let the thought go as she came to her question.

"Were you coming to Wykeham?"

"To Wykeham?" Justice felt like a schoolboy repeating a query to gain time, but her sudden appearance had distracted him.

"Yes." She sounded irritated, as if he should have known what she meant without asking. "Wykeham Abbey. My father's house."

Justice hesitated. Lilly no doubt expected him to arrive discreetly, though secrecy was out of the question. One had only to ride through villages like Beaulieu and Bucklers Hard for everyone to know that a naval officer had arrived—and for the younger men to start looking for their protections in

4

case there was a press gang at his heels. The woman was already giving a knowing glance at his shoulders to see whether he wore one gilded epaulet or two.

"A captain, then," she said with certainty, carrying on as if bent on forcing an introduction out of him, and he felt so much at a disadvantage that he jerked out his name as reluctantly as though he had just been made prisoner by the French.

"John Justice." He paused for a moment, wondering what to add where another officer would have given the name of his last ship, and decided to say nothing.

"Harriet Romney," she replied, surprising him by the way she held out her hand in a mannish fashion before she turned to glance at Scorcher, who was busy checking the saddle girths and stirrup leathers of her horse.

He touched his forelock, mumbled "Captain's servant, ma'am," and went on whistling in a groom's soothing falsetto, running a hand down the stallion's lathered and quivering withers before he looped the reins together and handed them to her. He expected her to mount and ride on, yet she took them almost absentmindedly, standing her ground, looking so hard at Justice that it seemed she must be sizing him up and trying to decide whether he was a booby or a bravo.

Justice was equally unsure what to make of this abrupt encounter. "We are bound for Cuffwells," he said, assuming that was enough of an answer.

"Then you have gone too far." She had a husky voice, and spoke more firmly now that he had broken the awkward silence. "This is the old road, that served when our land ran clear to Beaulieu Mill. Now Mr Lilly . . ." She stopped to catch up her error. "Sir George, of course, since the summer. Now Sir George has bought that part of the property and built himself a fine new house on it. You must take the first fork after Bucklers Hard to reach his drive."

The Volunteers had broken into two small groups, and Harriet pointed to them as they began to move away. "The Exbury lot," she said, nodding at a party setting off down the river with a lantern carrier and a boy drummer at their head. "They cross on the ferry from Gins Mill." The remaining men were less organised, strolling away quite casually, and Harriet gestured towards them. "From Cuffwells and Bucklers Hard.

If you follow them, you will see the house before you, standing back from the water." She hesitated. "Do you stay?" she asked.

"I believe so." At the moment Justice had no idea what Lilly planned for him.

"Then Saturday," she said. "Come to my hedger-and-ditcher, if you've found your land legs by then." She brought her horse round, swung herself into the saddle, touched her heels to its flanks, and was gone before Justice could ask what she meant.

Scorcher untied the horses. "It's always a fresh wind as takes you aback," he said under his breath, and found that he had to nudge his master to take the reins.

MOST MEN WHO ENLISTED in the Volunteers were content if they were given any kind of musket, and counted themselves lucky indeed if they could lay hands on the familiar Brown Bess, reliable, sturdy, and deadly at short range. But as Justice followed the party heading upstream, he was astonished to see that these men carried longer weapons, Brunswicks by the look of them, like those issued to the new rifle regiments.

He now understood why their fire had been so controlled and accurate, why Harriet Romney had called them sharpshooters. A skirmisher could drop a man at three hundred yards with one of them, and with such guns in their hands these countrymen would be a very different proposition from the Sunday soldiers one saw in most towns and villages.

He could only tell that there must be something more to protect on this tidal backwater than the slipways at Bucklers Hard, where Mr Adams had long been building fine ships for the navy—Nelson's *Agamemnon* years ago, Blackwood's *Euryalus* last year, the *Swiftsure* this past summer. He had read about them all in the *Naval Chronicle*, seen some of them come into the service, and as he and Scorcher had threaded their way through the stacks of timber in the wide village street, he had looked with interest at two new ships on the stocks at the bottom of it.

It must be something very important if Lilly had raised his own company of Volunteers to protect the river approaches, some kind of vessel for certain, if the proximity of Bucklers

Hard meant anything. There were skilled men here, and anything that went into the water below Beaulieu could easily reach the Solent and the Channel beyond.

A vessel. But what kind of vessel could interest Lilly so much that he would be building it on his own account and in the privacy of his own estate?

Justice stopped himself running on with guesses as some of the men kept on past a boathouse and a cluster of sheds, while the rest turned away towards a house where the windows flickered bright with candles.

Cuffwells. Behind those windows one of the most powerful men in England was waiting. The man who dined with the King and was the Prime Minister's closest supporter, who sat in the House of Commons and on the Board of Admiralty, and was the master of so many secret enterprises.

Waiting with some impatience, no doubt. Sir George did not easily bear delays, and though the message the mud-spattered Admiralty courier had brought to Hook five nights ago had been brief, its tone had been urgent. "Come soon," Lilly had written, "and come prepared to stay."

This was no casual invitation to spend a week chasing duck with a fowling piece. Less than a month after a French dragoon had half killed him with a blow from a sabre hilt, Justice knew he was being called back to the war.

EVEN IN THE GLOAMING, Justice was surprised and charmed by the house. On that July morning at Richmond Terrace, when Lilly had casually said that John Nash had lately built a country mansion for him in Hampshire, Justice had imagined that Cuffwells would be something in the pillar-and-pediment style, so popular these days for gentlemen's residences. This rambling white building, all towers, turrets, and little battlements, with rows of pointed windows and a curious-looking gazebo at one end, seemed more like a fairy-tale castle, and such an unlikely place for Lilly to live that Justice thought for a moment they had again lost their way.

Yet here, at the first sound of their horses on the gravel, was a footman opening the door, a groom hastening forward to show Scorcher the way to the stables, and Lilly himself coming out, all cordiality, and saying "Pretty bobbish, thank'ee" to

Justice's polite enquiry about his health.

"They call it Gothick, you know." There was a note of pride in Lilly's voice.

Justice did not know. No follower of architectural fashion, he liked a house like his own home at Hook, which had grown higgledy-piggledy over the centuries and was warmed by the passage of time. So he stood amazed in the elegant entrance hall, acutely aware that his muddied boots were leaving trails across the black and white marble floor, and generally so tired from the journey that he was scarcely able to keep up with Lilly's explanation. He had noticed before that the great man had a disconcerting habit of beginning to talk as if he had just been interrupted, or was already halfway through a thought, and it always took some moments to catch the drift of what he was saying.

"Everything up to the minute," Lilly went on, more like a middle-aged man of quality showing off his domestic novelties than like the head of the most confidential branch of the Admiralty receiving a trusted agent. "Piped water. Bramah closets. Bristol glass in the conservatory. Bellpulls in every room." He glanced at the footman who was waiting to conduct Justice upstairs. "Very convenient." Lilly had a characteristic way of tipping his head back and looking down the bridge of his nose when he wanted to convey a hint. "Discreet, too. No need to have flunkeys standing about everywhere waiting for one's whims."

It was neatly put, Justice decided, as he followed the footman. In anything that bore upon the secret activities of his Board he had found George Lilly the epitome of caution, eking out information in such a miserly manner that Justice suspected that even Hatherley, his chief assistant, was not told everything he had in mind or in hand.

And yet, Justice thought as he looked down from the arched gallery that ran across the head of the stairwell, in normal conversation Lilly could be as blandly loquacious as any other man of affairs, concealing his true feelings behind an agreeable flow of talk. His host was still standing there, trim and vigorous for all his sixty summers, and dressed as sharply as though he were about to leave his London house in Clarence Row to attend a royal drawing room in St James's Palace next door. It was remarkable that he should be so equable and self-possessed, showing almost no signs of the strains he bore, the confidences he kept, the great decisions in the making.

Justice had heard people gossip about him. They said that from humble beginnings George Lilly had done well by his country but even better by himself. That he had spent thousands to buy his parliamentary seat in Cornwall. That his rich cronies in the City had spent ten times as much to put Pitt back in office. That a word from him could tip one man out of a well-paid sinecure and slip another man into it. That this, that, and the other thing, and so on.

It was mostly true, Justice believed. That was the way of the world. Nothing, not even the waging of war, could be done in England without influence or reward.

Yet, for all that, Lilly was doing as much as any man to keep Boney's so-called Army of England standing idle on the cliffs above Boulogne, and to hold the country firm to its purpose through the long years it might still take to topple the Corsican Ogre.

"The *Superb*, sir." The footman had lighted a candelabra at the top of the stairs, and as he led Justice along a windowed corridor he paused before a pair of watercolours which Justice knew would have the initials G. L. in the right-hand corner. He had already seen something of Lilly's gift as a painter of ships. The man lifted the candles higher. "And the *Pelican*. Sir George served in them both."

The way the man spoke, and the manner in which he planted his feet apart, braced as if the floor might suddenly rise or drop beneath him, told Justice that he would have been more comfortable in a blouse and slop trousers than in the tight blue livery in which Lilly had suited him.

The footman grinned, noticing that Justice had marked him for a seaman. "Joslin, sir. Tom Joslin. Paid off the *Lynx* in July." He bent to open the door and then stood straight to let Justice pass into the room. "Came aboard like the rest of us when Sir George read hisself in."

The familiar naval phrase came so pat that Justice almost missed the incongruous notion of Lilly commissioning his house like a captain reading out the orders which made him master of a new command, and arbiter of life and death for all those who served under him.

Yet it was oddly apt as well. "Old winds take a long time to die," Scorcher was fond of saying about people with ingrained habits, and a man who had first shipped as a midshipman on the *Infernal* in '58—"four wars and more ago," Lilly had reminded Justice that summer—well, such a man might well feel more comfortable if he ran his house like a ship and staffed it with sailors.

Joslin certainly knew his domestic duty, and what the weary traveller wanted. He lit the sconces on each side of the blazing fire, put a decanter of brandy on a small table beside it, and was about to close the curtains when Justice dismissed him and went across to a window that looked down to the river. He could see nothing except the faint gleam of a lantern by the boathouse.

It was all quiet and peaceful, the thin mist clearing as the frost came down. Too peaceful. At the edge of his mind he felt the nagging instinct, for it was never more than that, which he had sometimes felt at sea in the presence of unseen danger.

Before a storm had struck suddenly off Tortuga, and caught him five minutes after he had gone to bare poles.

Before a French gunboat had crept out of the darkness when he was becalmed off St Malo, and found his guns already loaded with grape.

It was the kind of night on which he would chide himself for fussing, and then put his best men to watch, fore and aft, with two more amidships to make doubly sure.

Men such as Joslin. He wondered how many prime seamen Lilly had brought to serve him here. Four as footmen, perhaps. Two or three in the stables, and more in the gardens and grounds. There could well be a boat's crew of carefully chosen men in and around this house.

As he has chosen me, Justice said softly to himself, turning back from the window towards the fire and catching a glimpse of his trim figure in the long cheval glass, noticing the fuzz of new hair beginning to grow where the surgeon of the *Monarch* had shaved and stitched his scalp, putting his hand up to untie the knotted scarf which hid the older scar that ran so near to the crease of his throat.

Lilly had not yet said what he wanted. He had simply been the courteous host. But the sight of Joslin had somehow told Justice that Lilly's summons was not the prelude to another mission to France. He was wanted here. Cuffwells was a place for seamen turned gamekeepers.

Or for a spy turned watchdog.

●　　●　　●

JUSTICE STRIPPED AND sponged himself in the nearby bathroom, which was one of Lilly's pleasing novelties, put on fresh smallclothes, chemise and stock, a dark blue vest under the high-necked coat, a pair of white kerseymere breeches and silk stockings to match; and then, as the clock on the carriage house outside struck six, stretched himself out on the fireside chair. "We may have to wait until seven for supper," Lilly had said, giving the impression that another guest was expected, so that there was time to doze over a glass or two of brandy and let his mind run free over the images that shimmered before him like fragments of a half-remembered dream.

So much had seemed like a dream since he came back from France that he felt his head injury must have played disagreeable tricks with his memory. There were things about those weeks of difficulty and danger he could no longer recall, things he could not easily forget, like the black comedy of his escape from Verdun, which he saw over and over again like a scene from a play; and as he dozed, the flickering firelight brought back the gun flashes as Admiral Keith's ships began to bombard Boulogne, and he woke to a crash and a flurry of sparks as a log rolled against the brass fender.

He pushed it back with his foot, sipped at his brandy glass, and found himself thinking of golden autumn days at Hook, with the apples showing red as the leaves curled and fell from the trees, and the shepherds driving their flocks off the marsh to market. There had been mornings with Scorcher, with his "Look at this, Cap'n," and his "There, sir," noting all the changes that had been made in the months he had spent in France, and afternoons idly chatting to Mrs Roundly in the kitchen, watching her boil the hams that would hang all winter from the beam above the inglenook. These were the times when he thought there was nothing he would rather do than spend his days farming at Hook, or even on some part of his French mother's property at Recques, beyond Boulogne, if peace should ever come.

Then one filthy night Lilly's courier had come hammering at the door, and by noon next day he and Scorcher were out of Kent, taking the muddied roads that would lead them across the Weald and onto the rolling chalk ridges that carried them clean to Portsmouth. It had been a cold and blustery journey, with good, bad, and indifferent beds—the worst a wretched beer house near Arundel, where they ate charred rabbit and stale bread, and slept fitfully on the taproom benches.

Justice was awake now, as the stages of that long ride came fresh to his mind, and the most curious of all its incidents pushed the rest to one side.

The last morning had dawned fresh, and the hoar frost was white on the grass as they breasted Butser Hill, pausing to look down at the little squares and triangles of the sails dotted all across Spithead. Justice was still wishing that he was hurrying down to Portsmouth to take up his own command, when they had crossed the familiar road from London and headed for the bridges that would take them over the Itchen and the Test.

They had been on a track meandering through the water meadows between the two rivers when Justice heard the first scream, and Scorcher came up alongside to point at the gypsy woman running from behind a barn and screeching as she came.

She was running like a wild thing, Justice recalled, stumbling only a few paces ahead of a roughly dressed man who was lashing at her with a flail and getting more than one savage blow home across her rump and shoulders. Justice spurred his horse to come up to them, hearing the farmer swear over the woman's shrieks, catching the words "evil eye" as Scorcher realized the woman was a gypsy. "Turns milk sour," he said, taking the reins as Justice swung out of the saddle.

"Rubbish." Justice had no time to say more as the woman flung herself past him, a streak of blood from her face showing where a fist had opened her cheek, her black hair adrift, and a shawl clutched across the heavy breasts that fell from her torn shift.

She was gabbling at Scorcher in a frightened rush of Romany and English, but Justice could not catch what she was saying. The man was upon him, stopping short when he saw the glint of buttons, coming close enough all the same for Justice to see the veins in the grog-blossoms on his face and smell his breath foul on the clear air.

"You be beyond your bent, master." The man's voice was thick with fear and anger. "Do 'ee let un pass at t'witch or 'tll be the worse for 'ee." Justice had thought the fuddled wretch had found the gypsy sheltering in one of his byres and lunged at her, but he now saw that Scorcher's guess was right. He had heard terrible stories about the way some farmers treated gypsies they found on their land—beatings, even brandings and pitchfork murders, and no one willing to swear anything before a magistrate.

"Cut away with you." He spoke curtly, hoping a sharp word would bring the man to his senses before he swung the flail again. An attack on a uniformed officer could get him sent to Botany Bay for the term of his natural life, even if he was lucky enough to escape a morning dance on the gallows.

Scorcher muttered something he did not hear and slipped past him, leaving the woman to hold the horses and the farmer to shout a few more obscenities at them all before stamping away in his rage.

The gypsy cried after Scorcher and stopped her mewling when she saw him carrying a small ragged bundle out of the barn. Then Justice understood. She must have been feeding her baby when the man found her and drove her out, and like a bird flying away from its nest, she had run off to distract him. He fumbled with cold fingers for his purse, to find a shilling for her, while Scorcher held the wailing child like a clumsy godparent at a christening; and, giving her the money, he felt her seize his wrist, turn his hand over, and look up from the palm straight into his eyes.

"Over water. Under water," she said in the singsong speech of her people. "Brother's face and hangman's halter." She took the baby from Scorcher, ignoring his outstretched hand, and set off walking without another word to him.

Scorcher looked after her for a moment, shook his head, and pulled himself up on his horse. It was all over and done with in a matter of minutes, and it might have been no more than a casual encounter along the road if Justice had not found himself so oddly affected by the gypsy's rhyme.

He was not a credulous man like so many sailors, prone to believe in curses and warnings, but he could not forget the hard look the gypsy had given him after she had read his hand. He wished she had told Scorcher's fortune instead, and so did Scorcher, who nursed a grievance for the next two hours, riding silent a few paces behind his master. It was only as they left Marchwood, skirting the edge of the New Forest and turning south towards the river crossing at Beaulieu, that Scorcher grunted, "Black's the white of her eye, all right," and shrugged off his annoyance at the gypsy's refusal to tell him what fate had in store for him.

13

· · ·

THE GYPSY. Then Lady Harriet. Justice was thinking of the two women who had so suddenly come on him that day, when the clock struck a quarter and he knew it was nearly seven.

There were voices below the window, and he roused himself to go over and look down into the stable yard, where a couple of lanterns hung on brackets and he could just see Scorcher talking to a large man who stood with his feet wide apart and his hands on his hips. Another seaman, to be sure, who turned away as he heard a clatter of hooves, and an ostler ran to receive a horseman. The newcomer was instantly recognisable.

Hatherley. Of course it would be Hatherley that Lilly was expecting. If Dunning was here, and a posse of seamen, and now Mr Hatherley, well . . . Justice doused the candles and stood for a moment in the firelight before going down to his supper. In that case, Sir George had very serious business in hand at Cuffwells.

2

"CHINESE CHIPPENDALE." Lilly's words were so offhand and unexpected that Justice felt as if he were being introduced to one of the odd-looking chairs before being invited to sit on it; and he took his time, testing the flimsy-looking frame to see whether it would really take his weight, but found it surprisingly comfortable when he did so.

While there had been something about Lilly's office in Richmond Terrace which reminded Justice of a captain's cabin running clear across the stern of a ship, he saw that he was now inside a room that had been built quite deliberately to give a nautical impression. It was obviously the curious gazebo he had noticed as he rode up to Cuffwells in the twilight. A set of windows ran the length of the longest wall, pitched outwards and gently curving under beams so dark with age that he supposed they must have come from a wreck or a ship-breaker's yard. At one side there was a rosewood secretary topped by a latticed bookcase, its shelves empty except for a sextant, a box which probably contained a pair of matched pistols, and a pocket bring-'em-near so green with salt and age that it must have gone back to the time when Lilly was a skinny and shivering midshipman scanning the horizon from the masthead of a frigate.

In the centre of the room, the four curious chairs were drawn up to a chart table. The table itself was bare, except for two belaying pins that would serve as weights on an unrolled chart, and a small brass orrery, with the sun and planets ingeniously connected and balanced to make a revolving carousel which Lilly flipped, setting the gleaming spheres spinning about each other.

"We could almost be afloat here."

"With no charts, Mr Justice?" Lilly smiled, so that Justice guessed he was remembering the last time the two of them had sat thus together. But that had been in Richmond Terrace

15

when Lilly had spread the sea charts of the Straits of Dover on the table and so courteously, and yet so crisply and precisely, given him the orders that had taken him on the dark road to Verdun.

Orders. No mistake about that. He was now Lilly's man, and though Lilly might put his wishes as polite requests and reasonable suggestions, they would bind him as firmly as though they came from Secretary Marsden himself by the hand of an Admiralty messenger. If Lilly despatched him to find the terrible passage through the tangle of ice and islands north of Hudson's Bay, or to rescue the Pope from Napoleon's clutches, he would have to go, and do his best. In the confusions of war, duty was the only course a doubting man dare follow.

"No charts," repeated Lilly, then seemed lost in his own thoughts for a moment. "But I fear we cannot roll them up yet. We are so desperately pressed that we must take any means we can to delay and harass Bonaparte. One serious miscalculation, one unfortunate change of wind, as you well know, can deny us control of the Channel long enough for him to throw thirty thousand men onto the beaches of Kent. Or fall upon Cork and raise all Ireland against us. The peril has by no means passed."

Lilly paused, judging the effect of his words before he continued. "Let me put my case in strong and simple words, Mr Justice. What happens here, what I am going to ask you to do here, is of great importance to our country. No less important than what you did at Boulogne . . ." He stopped again, his expression drawn and serious. "Suppose Boney could sink any of our squadrons at a single blow, stop up the Thames to our trade, close Portsmouth or Plymouth to our ships—"

Justice stared. Lilly's words were rarely fanciful. But the extravagance of what he had just been saying seemed to have an end-of-the-world ring to it.

"Or suppose we might do the same to him," Lilly went on more hopefully. "Destroy his fleets at Brest and Rochefort and Toulon. Sink the vessels that creep from port to port around the coasts of France. Make all the ships he has collected to carry his army over to England as useless as if all the water had been drained from the harbours of Boulogne, Calais, Dunkirk . . ." He pushed the decanter of brandy forward like a man staking a pile of guineas. "You see why I spoke of gambling, Mr Justice."

"They are very great odds, sir," said Justice, for some words seemed called for after Lilly's striking speech. Hyperbole was not a mode of speech that Justice used himself, and if any other man in England had spoken so glibly and dramatically, made naval war sound so easy and so all-or-nothing, he would have called him fanciful.

Only, if there was one man in England who was not given to such fancy it was George Lilly, he thought, pushing the decanter back and noticing the third glass, which stood empty on the tray beside it.

Lilly had caught his glance and nodded. "Mr Hatherley will join us in a moment. He has gone to fetch certain files that relate to the business on which we must speak." He paused, with such a hesitation in his usually forthright manner that Justice wondered if it was truly Hatherley and his files that he was waiting for, or whether there was something in his story he was unsure how to come at. "It is also important that you see the picture of what I have to tell you, broad. Hatherley, I believe, sees some aspects of it too narrowly. Not been in this part of the world before?"

"As close as Portsmouth, sir."

"It's interesting country, and there's some interesting creatures as neighbours. And it's safer with some, perhaps, to know their habits and their lairs."

Justice looked up, surprised at the suggestion that there could be anything or anyone threatening in the smiling, peaceful countryside.

Lilly waited a few moments, gathering his thoughts.

"There were once two abbeys on this stretch of land between the New Forest and the Solent," he began at last, taking up one of the brandy glasses and placing it well away from him on the table. "There's Beaulieu. You'll have seen what's left of it as you came by. You may also have noticed that the river's quite deep and tidal all the way up to the ruins, so there's always enough water at the Hard to launch a frigate or a first-rate even in a dry summer."

He slid the bottle over to mark the village. "There." He put the second glass down close to it. "Cuffwells." He moved the third glass some distance away. "Wykeham. Two miles downstream and fairly close to the mouth." He gave Justice a sharp look as he often did to register a detail. "There's no bar, in case you find yourself running in or out one day without a chart. Just keep to the obvious channel, and well away from the spits on falling waters." He paused, while Justice made a mental note to be up to look at the chart before the day began. "Wykeham was always the richer of the two foundations. Been in the Romney family since Henry the Eighth robbed the monks and rewarded his friends."

"Romney?" Justice looked up. "I met the daughter," he said, going on to describe the surprising girl who had so suddenly ridden up to him and Scorcher at the river's edge and so brusquely invited him to Wykeham.

Lilly gave a shrewd smile. "She's a game 'un to be sure, as you'll find for yourself if you go a-chasing with her. Rides as though she were racing the devil to the gates of Hell."

"And her father?"

"Old Lymington? The Earl's a strange creature. A cousin to Mr Pitt on the mother's side." Lilly paused. "Which might be an embarrassment, though it isn't: the Pitts have got used to the odd streak in the family by now. The elder son's governing some place in India in his own peculiar fashion, and Lord William, who's here most of the time—well, let's say he's as *unusual* in his own way as his father and sister."

Lilly rarely emphasised a word, and Justice guessed he had just done so to catch Hatherley's ear as his assistant came in with a thickish file of papers tied with the faded red tape of Whitehall. "Not here yet?"

Hatherley shook his head. He was an original, Justice had decided the first time he clapped eyes on the man—a smart Cockney who had come up in the world, had perhaps worked in a commercial house in Paris or been a courier for some milord on his travels. And had slipped into confidential work for Lilly when the war had started years before. "Have you . . . ?" He had the habit of asking questions without committing himself to the subject.

"No. Not yet."

Justice wondered who could be awaited with such concern, for there were few members of the government, let alone public servants, who would have dared to keep Sir George Lilly on tenterhooks.

"We were speaking of the Romneys, first," Lilly said, and turned back to Justice. "Mr Hatherley has his own opinions of that family and its friends."

18

"They are all of the levelling kind, Mr Justice." When Hatherley spoke like that he would purse his lips and look down under hooded eyelids, weighing his judgments like a grocer watching his scales.

"It's a strange thing to say about persons of such good family." Lilly sounded slightly aggrieved by a fact which he could not explain. "They certainly belong to that body of energetic men and women, enthusiasts I should say, who consider themselves to be the friends of all mankind, and of the American and French varieties in particular."

"Are they Jacobins? Bonapartists?" All through the war, Justice was well aware, there had been a strong peace party in England—men and women who had rejoiced as the French armies had tramped across Europe, who had sung the *Marseillaise* and proclaimed the rights of man as loud and clear as any Frenchman.

"Neither, in a strict sense. Yet as Mr Hatherley says, they're a levelling lot, strong for liberty and equality. I'd say fraternity as well, if Lymington wasn't such a contentious sort of fellow."

Lilly stretched out a pair of fingers to set the orrery spinning again. "Now, mark you, we all have our place in the scheme of things," he said to the spinning globes as they winked in the candlelight, "but that doesn't mean keeping every man in his station all his born days. We are coming to live in a different world, Mr Justice, and I can see that this war hurries us on towards it. I am not upset to see the advancement of a man who in earlier times would never have come near a lord except to hold his horse or to bow to his orders."

JUSTICE ASKED HIMSELF what might be the purpose of all this talk of levelling and novelties and the Romneys, for it seemed so far from the point of anything like Lilly's usual concerns. Was it even possible that Lilly was also wondering about Justice himself, testing to see what sympathy he might have for the Romney causes? Not that Lilly would doubt his loyalty or his courage . . . but there were radical cranks in the Navy as well as the most crusted bigots, men who actually admired Bonaparte, however much they could be trusted to do their duty in a sea fight.

"The Earl of Lymington." Justice was slightly relieved that

19

Lilly had come back to his point. "I was going to say that he has ambition, talent, energy, all of them gifts a man needs to play his part in the nation's business. Yet he seems perverse, bent on using them to go down in the world rather than to rise in it." Justice caught the touch of sarcasm. "Citizen Romney, he took to calling himself at one time, painting out the arms on his carriages, letting his gardeners and grooms harangue him on any subject they pleased, talking of going off to live in Philadelphia one minute and Paris the next, hobnobbing with Dissenters and Yankees and that crowd of halfhearted Frenchie democrats who came over here when the Terror got too hot for them."

He broke off as a footman knocked and entered. "Beggin' pardon, sir. For Mr Hatherley. A message."

"Pray excuse me." Hatherley got up with such a sour expression on his face that Justice wondered if it was all the talk of the Romneys' radical ways he found so distasteful. There was no Tory so high, he thought, as one humbly born who had improved his station.

"Hatherley has much business to finish before I go in the morning." Lilly said no more, though it was the first Justice had heard of his plans to leave so soon; but as Hatherley's footsteps faded down the corridor, he passed the decanter and spoke in a confidential tone.

"There's something private to say—something that concerns you."

Justice waited. Lilly's conversation seemed to be taking odd turns this evening, and he wondered again what all the talk of Romneys and radicals could have to do with the lurid prospects of maritime war.

"We have had some news from France. You will not expect me to tell you its origin, or how it came to us, but we have heard . . ." Lilly stopped, and went on gently. "A French agent," he said. "Dead in some scuffle on a beach in Normandy."

"And known to me?" Justice was well aware that Lilly would say no more about the circumstances; but he wondered which of his old antagonists it could be. The man who sometimes called himself Schulmeister, and was said to be the best of all Fouché's minions at disguise? O'Moira, the blind Irish doctor? The earnest young Sergeant Ritter from Alsace? As a man who had come and gone on French beaches so often at the risk of his own life, he was glad of anything that evened the score. And yet, as a man, he was sorry for anyone who daily risked his life to serve his country in the shadows, in the work for which there was neither praise nor pardon.

"Known to you." Now Lilly's voice was gentler still, as if he knew how the name would clutch at Justice with an icy claw. "Your cousin."

"Luc?" He had half known since Lilly had begun to speak.

"Just so. Luc de Valcourt."

Luc. So Luc was dead. Luc. His cousin on his mother's side, and brother-in-law as well, for he had married Justice's sister Fanny two years before she died of a stillborn son. And as well she had, Justice had often thought. For Luc had come to England. Had become one of the most trusted of the royalist agents. And then gone back to France to play a shameful part in the betrayal of Georges Cadoudal, the Breton leader who had plotted to kill Bonaparte.

The renegade Luc. A wanted man if ever he came back to England.

Yet it was not that Luc he remembered now, but the Luc with whom he had spent boyhood holidays before the wars began, fishing and swimming in the river Course where it tumbled past the mill at Recques—running wild through the great estate at Valcourt, his mother's family home near Boulogne. The Luc who was so close to him that when people commented on the family likeness between the two cousins they fancifully said that it was some trick of nature.

"By us?" Luc had lived to dishonour the family name, and he hoped he had found some touch of honour in his death.

"The fortune of war," Lilly said tersely, and came back to his subject without a word of regret. He was a hard man, Justice knew, because he had hard decisions to make. Every day.

"Lord Lymington," Lilly went on reflectively. "As you may gather, Hatherley and I do not see eye to eye about him. To my mind he's a political simpleton, not a knave or a traitor. No, it's not Lymington that troubles me so much as some of the company for whom he seems to keep open house." He seemed to run over a register of doubts in his mind.

"And Lord William?" Justice went back to Lilly's own word. "Unusual, you said."

"William Washington Romney." Lilly grimaced. "Only Lymington would have given his son such a name, nigh on thirty years ago now. Might have called him Franklin Romney or Lafayette Romney or some other fol-de-rollery while he was at it. Doesn't seem to worry Lord William, anyway. He's as odd and enthusiastic as his father, though he spends his time dabbling with gases rather than windbags, and trying to improve machines rather than human nature. Been to Paris often enough, though that may mean nothing."

Justice was catching only the half of what Lilly was saying, for through the windows he had seen a flicker of light which was like the brief gleam of a lantern he had seen from his window.

Someone moving at the water's edge? Or only the reflection of one of the candles?

He was moving his head from side to side, looking through different panes of glass to be sure, when Hatherley came back.

"Not at Wykeham, either," he murmured so low that Justice barely caught the words.

Whoever was expected could have been at Wykeham. And all the talk about the Romneys was very much part of Lilly's business . . .

Then the thought was gone, for he saw that the light was no reflection. It was brighter, getting brighter all the time. Turning from yellow to orange, with a deeper red at its centre. Lilly and Hatherley caught his stare and turned to follow it as the windows rattled with the explosion of a charge of powder.

Lilly was across the room in three quick strides, tugging at a bellpull beside the fireplace.

"Here, Mr Justice." Hatherley was offering him one of the belaying pins from the table. An odd weapon for fighting a blaze, Justice thought, but took it, knowing it was habit rather than thought which sprung him into action.

He was out of the casement window with no idea what lay beneath it, then stumbling through soft newly dug earth onto the lawn, running towards the flames that were now rising high enough to light him to the river.

Behind him a man was shouting. It could be Scorcher. Then the voice was lost as the bell on the carriage house began to toll, quickly, irregulary, like a tocsin.

ᴲ3ᴃ

As Justice raced towards the boathouse, he ran into the smoke that was eddying in folds of lurid red, dancing yellow, and utter darkness, catching pungently at his eyes and throat, making it impossible to see anything distinctly. Dried brambles catching at his legs, he realised he had blundered into a copse that ran down towards the river.

The flickering light seemed to touch a figure frozen against a tree, perhaps another, so hidden that he caught only the white blur of a face. And then he heard a shout close by and turned to glimpse a man coming at him like a charging bull, head ready to butt and arms spread to grab or pummel him.

He had no time to decide whether the man was a surprised poacher, an incendiary, or simply a guard doing his duty. In that part of a second, as the light flared and failed, he could only twist sideways to lessen the impact and make sure of his grip on Hatherley's makeshift club.

The man's shoulder caught him on the hip, bringing them both down in a dogfall. Bruised and winded, for the man was powerfully built, Justice felt strong hands scrabbling at his back to fasten him in a bear hug, and smelt rum on the man's breath as a savage sideways jab of the head just missed his jaw.

His legs were useless, for his right ankle had doubled under the left as they slithered to a stop. Yet both his arms were free, and he knew what he must do as the man again pulled his shoulders back to butt him. Grabbing the stout wooden bar at both ends, he forced it under the man's chin, levering his head back, making him loosen his hold or risk a broken neck.

There was no time to call for help, though in the smoky darkness he could hear men calling to each other and the bell still tolling in the carriage house, for he could feel his assailant drawing up one knee to make the agonising thrust in his crotch that would finish the fight in a moment. He tensed himself, aware that the ground under his back would give him leverage and that the man's hands were pinned useless beneath him.

Suddenly, with a grunt, the man pushed himself away, releasing the pressure and the pain on his neck, and scrambled free. To forestall a wild kick, Justice struck out with his bludgeon. He felt the swing make contact—a glancing blow on heel or toe, he guessed, from the flat sound of wood on leather, but hard enough to knock the belaying pin out of his hand and to evoke an oath as the man toppled backwards.

Justice, on his feet again, started to go after him, then stopped as he saw the folly of it. He had lost his weapon, and in such a vicious game of blindman's buff anyone could kill or be killed by a chance.

And Lilly had not fetched him to Cuffwells to die like a sailor in a dockside brawl. In any case, he could tell from the rustle of dead leaves that the man had either decided that flight was the safest course or had simply lost him in the murk.

He stood still, making sure, getting his bearings, and then running on towards the fire.

HE WAS UP AGAINST the iron railings of the fence before he saw them, reaching two feet or more above his head, curving outwards into a row of barbed points that would make them impossible to climb, then fading into the smoke which billowed round him.

There would be a gate, but which way?

He peered both ways, made a guess, worked his way along the fence towards the river, and came to the gate, barred strongly between two posts, and chained and padlocked.

Why was it locked? Who had the key? How had the fire been started? The questions had scarcely formed in his mind before he heard what sounded like someone calling desperately from the boathouse.

It was hard to be certain over the hiss and crackle of the flames, with men calling to each other as they came down from the house, and the heat so fierce that it forced Justice to turn his face away. But when the cry came again, more despairingly, he could have sworn he recognised the voice of Eli Dunning.

Lilly must have posted him there to guard the boathouse. But where were Lilly and Hatherley, and what the devil were they all about, with a man choking or frying in the flames twenty yards off? He would need an axe to smash his way through the fence, and every minute of delay might be fatal.

The only way he could get in was from the river.

He groped down the fence to the water and into it, throwing off his coat as he floundered through the mud left by the falling tide.

The railings stopped, joining a wall of stone.

Reaching up and across, sliding a hand over the masonry that rose sheer for several feet above him, he felt nothing but slime, seaweed, and barnacles, and the shadow cast by the fire was so dense that he could not tell what he was facing. Probably it could only be climbed with a rope and grapnel, for the blocks were so well set that there was not even a crevice where he could drag his fingers.

He was in the water up to his waist before he realised that he was beside some kind of jetty, running out directly from the boathouse. It would point upstream towards a bend, he guessed, so that boats could be launched or recovered in a protected anchorage behind it.

He forced himself further into the freezing water, sensing the tug of the current, listening to the gurgling noise as it swirled round the end of the pier. As soon as it became deep enough to swim, he struck out with one arm, touching the stones with the other in the hope of finding an iron ladder, even a ringbolt that would give him a purchase.

Suddenly he was round, in slack water, swimming between two walls that ran out from the boathouse. Like an open-ended lock, he thought, for as he swam towards the boathouse he found himself clawing at a pair of high wooden gates. Lock gates, with slatted paddles to control the flow of water, and a long balance beam over them rising black against the glare.

Whatever boat Lilly had hidden here—and boat it must be to explain this clutter of buildings by the river—would need a dry dock when it was building and a float of water to launch it.

Justice hauled himself up on the strong lower frame of one of the paddles. It was just wide enough to give him a grip. He stretched a hand higher to snatch at a crossbar, notched himself up to a precarious footing, and with the next reach grasped the thick iron bar which ran down from the top of the gate to screw the paddle open or shut.

He clung to it, panting, cursing, then levered himself up, using the threaded metal like a taut rope on the side of a ship, arching out to press his feet inward and inch them up the face of the gate.

At the top he flung himself over the balance beam, and saw the doors of the boathouse a few feet away.

Shut doors, without windows or lattice. Doors that dropped clear from the boathouse gable to the floor of the dock, that must fit so tight that only a mouse could find a way under them. Doors that showed the care that had been taken to keep prying eyes away from whatever lay in the boathouse.

Down at Bucklers Hard, anyone could watch a frigate building. Then what kind of vessel was it that needed such care to be taken to conceal it?

Doors. He could see lanterns flashing along the line of the fence, and he thought he heard Scorcher shouting for him, but there was no way the men could help him unless they smashed through the gate or came swimming round the stone jetty.

He felt something move as he stood up, pulled at it, pulled at it again with a lift that brought it free, and found himself holding the handle that worked the lock paddle.

It was a piece of one-inch tempered iron, two feet long, bent at one end to fit the closed fist like a riding crop. It would serve almost as well as a crowbar to rip at the boathouse planking.

Or at the small door that must be used by anyone who came out to work the lock gates. He could feel its outline as he ran a hand across the wooden frame of the building.

Go for the hinges, not the bolts . . . He remembered Scorcher's shout one night when he and Justice were trying to force their way into a Breton farmhouse, and now he put his weight on the long end to lever and split the wood. Crouching, feeling for a gap near the bottom of the door, he heard a chorus of shouts that told him that Lilly's men were through the fence.

The second hinge held firmer, for he could put little pressure on the bar so close to the ground. Three times he pushed, and each time useless . . . He was going to have to risk his bones by throwing himself at the door.

But a man's life could depend on his breaking it down, for until Lilly's men began to douse the flames, there would be no way into the boathouse past the shed that blocked the way and was now blazing like a bonfire.

He drew back three or four yards to give himself pace, and heard Scorcher frantically hail him from the edge of the river.

"Dunning! Dunning!" He caught the name the second time, and looked down to see Scorcher waving a brand of flaming wood, pointing it like a torch.

So he had been right. It was Lilly's man-of-all-work who was trapped behind that cone of flames.

Now Scorcher was yelling something else. It sounded like "Louder." No, not that. "Powder." Again. "Powder store." Was there a manufactory of infernal machines in this shed, or somewhere near it?

He heard Scorcher shouting "Wait!" and saw him running. But if there was a risk of explosion he could not wait, even if Scorcher had gone for ropes or a ladder.

He felt a stunning jolt as he hit the door, then heard the wood splinter as he lurched off balance. He stepped back to give himself room to kick at the broken planks, squeezing through the gap he had made.

Then he was edging forward in the darkness. Darkness that was all the worse for the streamers of acrid smoke and the vagrant shafts of firelight.

He tripped, caught himself on a hank of cordage that was looped away by the wall, tripped again, stubbing a toe on some heavy object. He knelt, feeling for the edge, touching a length of sailmaker's canvas that stretched alongside the gantry where he was standing.

The canvas was to shroud whatever lay in the dock. So it was still safe. But Dunning?

He cupped his hands and hallooed, the sound dying fast among so much wood and the cries of the men fetching water from the river.

He called again. If Dunning lay beyond the end of the boathouse, there was little hope of getting to him before the fire was quenched. And less hope that he would still be alive by that time.

He knocked against a workbench, cutting his hand on a sharp-edged tool, steadied himself, pushed aside a sawhorse, blinked as his eyes smarted, coughed at fumes that reeked of pitch and oakum. And as he breathed he knew from the weakening of his legs that he too was in danger of suffocation if he stayed much longer. He had seen dead seamen brought

27

out from a fire without a mark on them, men who had been singing and skylarking five minutes before it took hold—and the grisly image brought back another memory that made him drop to his knees and elbows. Of old George Pildrew, the purser, who had survived the great fire that had razed two warehouses in Antigua in '98, had saved himself by lying close to the floor and covering himself with a piece of wet sailcloth.

Eli Dunning must have picked up some such piece of sailor's lore as well, for when Justice came on his inert body a minute later, his head was drooping towards the fresher air below the level of the floor, his left hand clutching a rag of soaking canvas.

He moaned as Justice took his legs, dragged him back and began to roll him over. But it was not only the foul vapours that had so nearly finished Dunning. There was warm blood on his face. And more of it oozing from a sticky, matted wound at the back of his head.

Had Dunning injured himself as he pitched forwards—been hit by a falling beam as he forced his way to refuge in the boathouse? Or been felled by a crunching blow from behind—delivered by someone who had known exactly where to strike when Dunning caught him?

One thing was sure. Dunning was no man to knock over a lantern or light a forbidden fire to warm himself or his supper when he was on duty. Justice was halfway back along the edge of the dock, hands under Dunning's armpits, when he heard a step behind him.

"Tooth here'll take him, Cap'n." Justice had tensed himself to drop Dunning and turn defensively before he recognised the voice as Scorcher's, saw him lifting a candle lantern to throw its feeble light on the man who stood beside him. The large man, Justice remembered, who had stood chatting to Scorcher in the stable yard.

And who had come charging at him as he ran to the boathouse. Even in the glimmer of Scorcher's lantern Justice recognised the curve of those bulky shoulders as the man bent to lift up Dunning. He could swear to the body of anyone he had fought so close, and a bruise under the jaw would show where he had left his marks on the fellow.

He shook himself as he followed Scorcher out onto the dock wall, where Tooth was already carrying the unconscious Dunning down a ladder. It was a habit when he was tired or worried, and Scorcher noticed it.

"You all right, Cap'n? No burns, nor nothing?" He had forgotten that the fight as well as the swim and the filthy scramble for the boathouse must have left him looking like a half-drowned mudlark.

"Nothing that won't wash, Fred," he said gratefully, with a laugh that Scorcher echoed, for the phrase was one which Mrs Roundly the housekeeper always used to make light of domestic troubles.

He waited, shipboard-style, for Scorcher to go down the ladder ahead of him, watching a man run past trailing a basket-ended length of canvas hose through the mud into the water.

That was why help had been so long in coming. Lilly's men had needed time to fetch a wheeled pump from the carriage house and to make a large enough gap in the fence to bring it close to the fire.

So long? All of five minutes, possibly, since he had looked out of Lilly's window to see the flames leap like the fuses on a fireship.

"Shall I stay, Cap'n?" Scorcher called from the foot of the ladder, after Tooth had thrown his jacket round Dunning and begun to carry him towards the house.

"No. Go on." Justice shouted and waved Scorcher away. The sooner Dunning could be put in blankets and have his wound cleaned in raw spirit, the better, but Scorcher hesitated. "Go on," Justice repeated, leaning over the ladder to make sure he was heard. "But keep close, mind you, keep close."

With Scorcher a hint was as good as an order. Before Justice met Lilly again he wanted to see what it was that lay in the hidden dock. Why it should need a score of men to watch it, and why Dunning had come so close to dying to protect it.

He picked up the lantern that Scorcher had left at the top of the ladder and went back into the boathouse. The smoke was beginning to clear as Lilly's men got the fire under control, and in the feeble light he could just make out that the canvas awning was thrown loosely over something boat-shaped.

It was bigger than a longboat or a launch. But it was like no fighting ship that Justice had ever seen, or heard of.

It had a deep draught. That much was clear as he strained to see down into the bottom of the dock, saw the wooden beams that were wedged between the dock walls and the sides of the broad-beamed thing to keep it upright and level for men to work on. In the fitful gleam of his candle it reminded him of a great whale he had once seen driven ashore, with fifty men savaging and burrowing at it to get its blubber.

He stepped down onto it, dragging back the canvas to try to glimpse its belly. It had low sides, was almost flush at the edge of the deck timbers, and then he saw that there was something more, bulging under the sailcloth cover—some kind of metal cylinder, like a fat chimney, rising from the deck just forward of the tiller. And another, up in the bows. And more tubes and knobs pushing the canvas into strange, fantastic outlines.

Yet for all its ungainly, awkward looks it was some sort of boat that lay there in the dock, and might soon lie in the water. But all these brass devices? She—it—had clearly been built for some special purpose. Some purpose which related to why he had been brought here . . . and which had to do with Lilly's prophecies an hour ago of how a squadron of ships of the line could be destroyed in harbour.

But he was still so mystified by what that purpose might be that for a moment he was not aware that Lilly himself had come up and was standing beside him.

And answering his unspoken question.

"A plunging-boat, Mr Justice. I'm much obliged to you. You may have saved it."

4

"A PLUNGING-BOAT, Mr Justice. A most terrible new weapon of war."

"A plunging-boat?" Justice repeated Lilly's words because they both puzzled and chilled him with the threat they carried.

"A vessel, God help us all, which can pass beneath the water. Can deliver its deadly blows unheralded and unseen."

Justice was silent. Now he understood why Lilly had spoken of squadrons destroyed in harbour, blockading fleets sunk or scattered to the winds.

The means to all that was the thing he had glimpsed in the boathouse.

"What I have to tell is a strange tale, Mr Justice." The light of a pair of candles lit Lilly's face, weary yet still resolute, and made the decanter glow like liquid gold on the table where Hatherley had placed the red-ribboned file. "And its main character is a man who is as elusive as a will-o'-the wisp. He was expected here tonight, and may perhaps be here tomorrow. Or then again, he may not. Or he may go instead to his friends at Wykeham Abbey.

"A man named Francis," Lilly went on, his eyes glinting with a spark of wintry humour as he glanced at Hatherley beside him. "A regular American Archimedes. The only begetter of the plunging-boat, or submarine vessel as he prefers to call it. Myself, I should have preferred a more graceful name—perhaps shark or dolphin; something classical at least, but there's such a fad for novelty these days that someone's bound to coin a word that's appropriate and ugly."

"This—this submarine vessel. It is his unique invention?"

Lilly nodded. "He's the author of a dozen things besides. And of as many damned divisions of opinion at the Admiralty as'd give comfort to the Frenchies for a fortnight . . . But that comes later."

"What manner of man is he?"

31

"A farmer's boy from Pennsylvania, though his father came from somewhere near Kilkenny. He calls himself an American, but I should say that's more of a notion than anything, for he's never been back since he first came here in '87. Most of the time since then he's been in France. Now, since Boney disappointed him, he's come back to test his luck in England."

"He was a revolutionist?" Justice had not met many Americans, but he had heard enough of their sympathy with the French. One revolution begat another, he had been taught at school, and in those days the levelling sort of men in England had been saying their turn would soon come. But that had been before the Terror; before Boney made himself master of France.

"No. Or not precisely. He wasn't like some of the Americans whose company he kept in Paris, who couldn't wait to see the guillotine set up on Tower Hill, and King George's head rolling in the basket. Though I think he believed the crowns of Europe would all go a-toppling . . . But these scientific gentry are a queer breed, and I don't know whether it was the cause that fascinated him most, or his invention. Probably his idea was that the one might serve the other. Anyway, by 1799 or thereabouts, he'd persuaded the Frenchies that his idea of submarine navigation could help them. We had news from Paris, never mind how, that the French were talking about a boat that disappeared under the water. That put us on the scent, but then it went cold again when we heard that Mr Fulton—that's his real name, though in England he likes to be known as Francis—had put a steam engine into a boat that sank under the weight of it. Playthings still, or so their Lordships at the Admiralty thought. But within the year we heard something more disturbing." Lilly sat back and turned to Hatherley, who had been softly turning the pages of his file as if he were following his master's story. "Let Mr Justice see that paper."

Hatherley got up and walked over to Justice with the file, holding on to it all the while as if he feared it might be suddenly snatched from his possession. On a larger sheet a scrap of paper had been pasted, and Justice read the words scrawled across creases that showed how small the paper must have been folded. "B. says the proposal is one that may change the face of the world. F. has promised to deliver France and everyone else from British oppression.''

LILLY WATCHED JUSTICE hand the file back to Hatherley. "I hardly think I need tell you what that note meant. If Bonaparte was taking the boat so seriously, it became the urgent business of the Board to follow things more closely. Soon after that, we received clear confirmation that a boat had actually been built. The *Nautilus*, they called it: I say 'it,' for I refuse to name these things as if they were women. By 1801, it was undergoing trials.''

Justice caught a quick exchange of glances between Hatherley and his master, that was followed by a nod from Lilly. Then Hatherley was opening the file again, so that Justice felt he was being privileged to see some private peepshow.

"*Nautilus* at Havre and Brest," he read. "Summer 1801." There followed a list of dates and notes:

3rd July	Four men. Down to 25 feet.
24th July	Thick glass window. Steered below.
26th July	Mast, mainsail, job. Tack and steer above.
	Gear struck in two minutes. 2 knots under.
	Barometer. Compass. Both work under.

"Improving all the time, you see, sir." Hatherley's bony finger traced down the page for Justice. "Two weeks after that he had a copper globe down there, full of pumped air. He stayed down the best part of an hour.''

That was the final date, but there were some more words below it. "Uncommonly manageable, F. says. 24 ft. x 6. Bomb release. Ship sunk Brest w. 100 lbs. pwdr.''

"Scientific stuff, I daresay, but damned useful. So useful it cost a man's life to get that piece of paper back to London." Lilly paused a moment. "The next thing we heard, Bonaparte had signed a contract with his American adviser.''

"What kind of contract?" Justice was seeing terrifying pictures in the fire. Burning ships, battered without a chance to defend themselves. Sleek vessels, like creatures of the depths all sailors dreaded, slipping out, breaking a patrol line. Carrying supplies, messages, bombs that could close a port. The great fleets on which England's safety depended, scattered by preying submarines.

No officer of the watch or lookout would ever again rest easy when he saw the surface of a calm sea. What Lilly's words had envisaged was not war, but horror . . .

"Quite a scale of charges." Lilly's matter-of-fact, scornful tone was curiously reassuring. "Ten thousand francs on account, and a tariff according to size. Sixty thousand for a British sloop sent to the bottom, two hundred thousand for a fair-sized brig, and twice as much for anything of thirty tons or over. What's more, he could have done it. By the summer of '02 there was no reason why he shouldn't have been making the damn things for Boney by the dozen."

"But he wasn't?"

"No. Because by then, and no credit to us, he was changing his mind. The Frenchies hadn't reckoned on his restless eccentricity. Perhaps he'd had enough of bobbing about like a cork off Brest. Perhaps he fell out with some of the French *savants* who were judging his work. Perhaps it was his fancy for Mrs Barlow . . ." Lilly spoke as though the lady were well known to him, by name at least, and stopped to explain when he saw that Justice had never heard of her. "The wife of another American in Paris. A fellow who wrote a damnable song, years ago—'God Bless the Guillotine, Which Kills a King and Queen . . .' Don't know it? Hm. Just as well. Anyway, he went off with Mrs Barlow to some watering place for months on end and spent all his time playing with little boats in a stream. Shapes, he says, and paddles, and machinery. All of which makes him seem an odd fish, but the oddest thing was the plunging-boat. Broke it up for scrap, and wouldn't even show Boney the plans for it afterwards."

"He'd fallen out with Boney?" Justice was incredulous.

"So it seems. So he says. Completely. Nowadays he curses Boney as a tyrant, calls him a wild beast, for it seems that the idea of his old hero making himself an Emperor has upset his republican digestion." Lilly smiled. "As it's upset some of our homegrown radicals. But Francis was more important. For once it came to our ears that he'd turned against his Corsican idol, there was only one thing to be done."

"To bring him to England?"

Lilly nodded. "If it was a chimera, the sooner we knew the better. If not—well, I'd have paid the price of a fleet to get him away from France. But a confidential gentleman went to Rotterdam to meet him. A Mr Smith, who saw Mr . . . Mr, er, Francis, and worked wonderfully upon him.''

Justice noticed that Hatherley was sitting so still, his eyes fixed on the orrery, that he did not need to look far for the identity of this persuasive emissary. "He was soon convinced?''

"Not soon, but substantially—if you're asking about money. And he had other reasons for wanting to come. These scientific men are like a dog on a windy day, always darting off on some new scent or other. With Francis it's been one new thing after another. One day it's a canal, or an iron bridge; and next week it's a machine for spinning flax, or twisting hemp, or sawing marble. Or a steam-driven shovel for digging ditches.''

"Steam?'' Justice kept hearing what steam engines could and might do, but like most men who had spent their lives at sea, he had never seen one of these remarkable devices at work.

"Steam!'' Lilly sounded sceptical. "Playing with fire, I'd say, and nothing useful likely to come of it. But Francis . . .'' He spread his hands. "I think that man got the smell of steam in his nose about the same time as he sniffed the vapours of liberty.'' He looked at Hatherley, who slipped another sheet of paper from the file.

"He's got an engine on order now from Mr Boulton and Mr Watt, and there's a very proper letter come to the Treasury from Mr Boulton to ask if it's right to despatch such a thing to America. Sending it out of the country when there's a war going hard against us, and the Lord knows what use could be made of it if it fell into the hands of the French.''

"For the plunging-boat?''

"The engine's not for that,'' Lilly said. "Even Mr Francis has not found a way to keep a fire burning under water. No. It's for a steamboat—he's hell-for-leather for that, as if it were the end of all his intentions and everything else but the means to it. I tell you, Mr Justice, he cares more for that steamboat than he could for a child—if he had one.''

"If he gets his permit he'll be off, mark me,'' Hatherley said dourly.

"The prospect of it certainly brought him here,'' Lilly growled, "and the nearer he comes to getting that engine in his hands the more it's the devil's own job to keep his mind on our business." Lilly looked again at Hatherley, with a hint of criticism in his glance. "I can't keep him in one place, for the man's not our prisoner. And even the men who . . . whose object is to know his whereabouts, lose him as often as not."

Justice was beginning to understand why Lilly had showed such uncertainty about the American's arrival. "But still you expect him?"

"Of course. He is contracted, and so far he's been a man of his word. Besides, he comes to see Lord William. These scientific *cognoscenti* are his cronies. But there, I'm running ahead. In May this year I saw the Prime Minister. Told him then that we'd get Francis here, and we did. Then Mr Pitt sets up a Commission to deal with him. The Commissioners sat, read the papers Francis sent them, and decided to take up some of his infernal devices—the floating bombs, the carcasses, the catamarans, that can be made easily enough at Portsmouth and run out to Admiral Keith's Channel squadron. But not the plunging-boat."

"They believed it useless?" Justice heard Hatherley smother a snort that might have been sceptical or derisive.

"I must be frank, Mr Justice. Some of my friends at the Admiralty wouldn't believe in a plunging-boat if they saw it a-bobbing up and down in St James's lake outside their windows. But that was not the case with the Commission," he said heavily. "In truth, they were convinced that it might work only too well, and in the end to this nation's grave disadvantage. Lord Stanhope told them it would be the ruin of the navy. St Vincent himself declared that Mr Pitt was a fool to encourage the building of any such instrument. 'It is a mode of war that a nation commanding the seas cannot want, for if it were successful it would deprive us of that command.' That's what old Jervie told the Prime Minister at the Lord Mayor's Banquet."

"Does Francis know of these opinions?"

"Suspects them, I think. He was angry when the Commissioners seemed to show such scanty interest—said he'd been treated like a prisoner when he first came to England and pretty much as a foolish projector thereafter. Then he was a little mollified when Mr Pitt invited him to his home. And then, when I approached him . . . nothing to do with the Commission, you understand."

36

"But with the Prime Minister's approval?" Justice realized that he had gone too far; knew before Lilly spoke that he would get no answer, for no man as grand as Lilly was going to tell a junior post-captain more than he needed to know of disagreements in high places.

"I considered, and concluded that the Board must act," said Lilly, in the plain way of a man who had long learned to take the responsibilities of office. "The truth was that the Commissioners had looked into Pandora's box, and they were so frightened by what they saw that they hastily tried to close it again."

He spoke slowly, almost to himself. "But it's too late for that. Now we know it can be done, there will always be the risk that someone else will make this fearful instrument. We must have it for ourselves, so we can take its measure. We must have Francis safe, where we can see him, however things turn out in the end."

"Safe from himself? Or others?"

"Hard to tell," said Lilly. "But as long as the French have their eyes on our beaches, or the shores of Ireland, they'll not leave a man alone who could help to bring them over." He gave the slight nervous twist of the wrist Justice had seen before when he wanted to turn a subject. "By the bye, your old . . . your old acquaintance and antagonist is said to be back in Dublin."

"O'Moira?" The amiably sinister blind doctor, Justice thought, would have a long score to settle since the French invasion plan had been spoilt two months before. "With what end, is it said?"

"We have no idea, as yet. But he is not a man to sit idle while Boney's boats swing at anchor in the westerlies and the hulls grow slimy."

"But there is no reason to suspect . . . ?"

"Nothing except suspicion itself. The French must be anxious to deny us what we can get from Francis, one way or the other . . . And O'Moira, well, you know the man, Mr Justice. A zealot of fierce ingenuity." Lilly sat watching the last log glow in the ashes, then got up. "It's bed for me, for I've papers to study and an early start tomorrow. Hatherley will see to your arrangements, which had best be done now." He glanced at his assistant before he turned back to Justice with a smile.

"When you went to France this summer," he said, "I asked you for a week's shooting in November. I hope I did not speak truer than I purposed."

"AND YOU MUST also leave?" Justice said anxiously as he watched Hatherley sorting papers at the desk, methodical as always, and seemingly tireless.

"For London, eventually." Hatherley gave nothing away. Lilly had said at dinner that he had pressing business with Mr Pitt at Walmer Castle, where the Prime Minister could gaze across the Channel at the cliffs where Boney's army camped, but Hatherley gave the impression that the submarine was only one of the Board's concerns that pressed on him so urgently.

"Now, sir," he said to Justice, brushing such matters aside, "your arrangements. A secondment to the Sea Fencibles will keep your place on the Captains' List. A note in the *Naval Chronicle*—detached to inspect the Dorset coast defences will do well, I fancy. An authority signed by Sir George . . . who will meet such disbursements as you may have." Hatherley broke off, scribbled on a paper, sanded it, and handed it to Justice. "That is all that can be done officially, for your employment here is a private matter."

"You mean I am not in the employ of the Board?" asked Justice.

"Not of the Board. But of its master." He gave a keen look at Justice. "There are many men in these times who risk their lives for their country. Not so many, I think, who would stake their private fortunes for the same cause."

"Sir George . . ." Justice began to understand the arrangements. Cuffwells, so ideally situated on the Beaulieu River. Close to Portsmouth, yet discreet. Skilled shipbuilders at hand in the nearby village. Boathouse guards . . . And all paid for by Lilly.

"Just so." Hatherley was speaking in such a flat voice that Justice could not tell whether he admired or doubted the enterprise. "Sir George believes this to be a desperate matter for the country. When the Commission rejected the . . . that vessel—" He jerked his head towards the boathouse. "Well, Sir George took the matter on himself, for all the risk. That is why, though the Board has enough urgent business elsewhere

38

to keep every man jack of us on the run, we are here on a piece of wizardry at Cuffwells.''

"You are not persuaded?" The edge of irony in Hatherley's tone was the nearest thing to criticism that Justice had ever heard Hatherley make of his master.

"It is not for me to be persuaded," Hatherley replied with what might have been mock modesty. "I may be persuaded of the argument. Of the result? I am not so sure. It may be better if Mr Francis fails, or is convinced that the venture is too ambitious, or loses heart for some other reason. I am not a sailor, nor a maker of policy, as you must know, Mr Justice, but I am driven to confess that the prospect of completing this affair is no less appalling than the risks we run by entering upon it. We may well be doing Boney's work for him, or putting a rod in pickle for some other enemy to beat us. I have letters in here . . ." He seemed to consider for a moment, then drew out a paper from his file and handed it to Justice.

It was dated 1798 and signed Robert Fulton.

"The Idea is yet an Infant," Justice read in a clear sloping hand that looked as though it were accustomed to drawing up specifications and inventories, "but I think I see in it all the nerve and muscle of an Infant Hercules, which at one Grasp will Strangle the Serpents which Poison and convulse the American Constitution . . . Are not all the American difficulties in this war owing to the Naval Systems of Europe and Licenced Robbery on the Ocean?

"This was the plunging-boat? So far back?"

Hatherley nodded as he took back the letter. "Even then he conceived it as a means of plaguing both our houses. When he breakfasted with Mr Pitt at Putney in July, he told him his aim was the annihilation of the existing systems of marine war. You see, Mr Justice? We may be obliged to give him refuge and bend his cleverness to our advantage. But there is plain reason here"—Hatherley tapped the file—"why we should never trust him."

"But surely he is at risk? The fire . . ."

"I wish I knew how matters stood." Hatherley seemed genuinely puzzled. "Is Mr Francis in danger? That's for you to judge now. Is his boat threatened? I'm not so sure, for there's something damned peculiar about these harassments—"

"But the fire?" Justice tried again.

"More spectacular than those that came before it. But oddly halfhearted if real mischief was intended. Two men beaten as they walked home to Bucklers Hard, and another bribed to run off, perhaps, for we've seen neither hide nor hair of him for a week. There's talk of gold passing in the village, but no proof. Tales of lights on the river at night, of men scurrying through the dark on forest ponies. Some say it's just the gypsies. Or wretched rick burners with a grudge against anyone who owns lands. That's the real peculiarity—it's all half serious, and then again half rubbishly gossip. Sir George inclines one way, and I incline the other."

He gave Justice the flattest of looks. "That's why you were fetched, sir. 'Send for Captain Justice,' Sir George says. 'If there's anyone can bring trouble to a head, it's him.' "

"A doubtful compliment," Justice said with half a laugh. "You make me sound like a tethered goat."

"And well said, sir, with wolves in this part of the forest."

"You mean the Romneys?"

"If you choose to name them."

"And the French?"

"They say I'm a man to see Frenchmen in every shadow, Mr Justice. But not here, sir. Not tonight."

Justice was struck by the contrast between Lilly's determination to protect Francis and the plunging-boat and Hatherley's conviction that neither Francis nor the Romneys were to be trusted.

One of them was wrong.

LILLY'S LIGHT TRAVELLING coach was at the door, high on its springs, the newly painted arms of a baronet smart on its side panels, and the silver ornaments on the harness of the champing bays catching the first gleam of morning. Hatherley had gone an hour since, scattering instructions in his wake, and leaving Lilly and Justice to breakfast together.

"How much do you count on success?" After listening to Hatherley's doubts, Justice felt bound to put the question directly to Lilly.

"A good deal, if you are asking whether this American can build an effective plunging-boat, take her down the river without surfacing, cross the Solent and blow up a ship anchored off Yarmouth, so that Mr Pitt and the rest of us can

see what we are getting for our money—yes, I count on that."
Lilly spoke so specifically that Justice wondered whether some
such trial was stipulated in whatever bargain he had struck
with Francis. "Four months ago, before I met the man, or saw
his capabilities, I should have bet at evens on him. If he had
done it once, and said he could do better, much better, given
the chance, I was prepared to believe him. He is a man who
dreams of new things all the time, Mr Justice, but he has the
wits and hands to make his dreams come true. Now the odds
are on success. That damnable fancy of his was well-nigh
finished when there was a man beaten, a fire started . . . Given
a week, indeed . . ."

"A week? So close?"

Lilly nodded. "Now you may understand why you were sent
for." He lifted a finger before Justice replied to show he had
more to say.

"If you mean something else," he went on, "if you ask me
whether Stanhope was right when he foresaw ruin in it for the
navy as we know it, I cannot answer you with any certainty.
I can only tell you that Mr Pitt tends to that opinion. That
Francis himself insists that with this weapon and the rest of his
devilments he could wreck every fleet in the world and estab-
lish what he calls the universal freedom of the seas. Sooner or
later, Mr Justice, I believe he can, and in the meantime we
must take precautions in case he is right. A man like me, as
you know, must deal in meantimes, for it is there we find the
margins between victory and defeat."

At that moment Lilly had risen from the table and Justice
stood up with him, thinking him done, and that it was time to
go. But he had merely gone across to the window to see
whether his coach had been brought round, and remained
standing there pensively, looking at the streaks of early mist
that lay across the lawn like reminders of the fire.

"If Boney had a score of such vessels," he said, so softly
that he seemed to be thinking aloud, "my restless sleep would
be even more uneasy. Give him a hundred, and I would not lay
a farthing dip on our chances of beating him, or even of keeping him from our shores."

He turned back to face Justice with a glow in his eyes.
"Francis offered him a means to victory, a device which could
have helped him drive our blockading fleets away from his
ports. If he could drive us away, take that first step across a

few miles of sea to fall on our shores, he would find it quite easy to clamber up all the rest to sit on the throne of the world. But he missed that chance that Francis gave him. Now he seeks another, and we must deny it to him, come what may."

He took his sword-cane from beside his chair, rapped on the floor, and began to pace up and down, leaving Justice uncertain whether he was conducting some argument in his head or waiting impatiently for his coachman to come.

"We may not need such a weapon ourselves." He stopped, tipping the head of his stick towards Justice.

"I'm the odd man out in this affair," he said, "as Hatherley's no doubt told you. Not one of my colleagues at the Admiralty wanted this monster, and some of them will go as far as they dare to stifle it at birth. Some of them think it risky in all kinds of ways. Others, you know, want to save money, or think it threatens some of their interests or prospects. Even Mr Pitt, I tell you in confidence, complains that experimental warfare interferes with what he politely calls the established forms of office. Established forms, my oath! Perquisites are what people mean when they say that. Patronage!"

He thumped the floor again, with the vigour of a man who knew what the system meant, and what it cost the country in stagnation and stupidity.

"There's more than one man among their Lordships who thinks infernal machines are ungentlemanly," he said. "Bah! Ungentlemanly, damn their eyes! They can keep to their codes of honour, Mr Justice, so long as Keith and Collingwood can keep Boney's fleets in port, and destroy them if they come out. But one great battle that goes against us, one lapse of judgement by Calder or Nelson, one disastrous shift of wind, and the future of every gentleman and jackass in these islands may depend upon Mr Francis and his peculiar devices. If that's what you mean by success, Mr Justice, I hope I never have to count on it, but it is no more than my business to insure against such adverse turns of fortune."

The coach had come past the window as Lilly finished and he had stumped into the hallway, where Joslin helped him on with a layered and much-pocketed coat that made him look like a coachman, slipping a silver brandy flask into one of the pockets and winding a long comforter around his neck. It would be a cold ride, with the November winds coming in from the Atlantic all the way.

42

"God speed," Justice called, as the groom folded up the step and closed the door. But Lilly opened the window for a last word.

"Be on your guard," he said. "Constantly. Be as nimble-witted as you were in France, and I'll have no fears for you. Or for the *Pandora*."

He called to the coachman. There was a sharp snap as the leather whip curled over the pair of bays, a crunch of wheels on the gravel, and then a double blast on the travelling horn.

Sir George Lilly, the member for Launceston, member of the Board of Admiralty, and Commissioner of the Board of Beacons, Bells, Buoys, and Mercantile Messengers, was on his way, and would stop for no one when he was on the King's business.

Justice gazed after the coach as it rocked away.

The *Pandora*. Only a man of mordant humour would have chosen that classical name.

Pandora. Whose box was full of the evils that would plague the world to the end of time.

And after she had opened it, Hope alone remained inside.

⤙5⤚

"A MAP," JUSTICE SAID firmly, as Scorcher came hurrying
from backstairs to meet him. "A map, and a chart, before we
set foot outside again."

He found them in a moment, rolled side by side on a chest in
the room through which Lilly had whisked him last night, and
here once more there were belaying pins, kept shipboard style
in a rack, to hold them flat on the table when they were
opened.

"The map first," he said as Scorcher brought two of the
wooden batons to him, feeling grateful that Lilly had been
careful to order a proper plan to scale, instead of the fanciful
drawing that was so common in gentlemen's houses. From the
care with which the river was mapped, indeed, it looked as
though a marine surveyor had put his hand to it.

The main features of the local landscape were penned in
clearly: the tracks that linked the farms and larger properties,
a bridge or two, the larger woods, the ruins and the Palace
House at Beaulieu, the two rows of houses at Bucklers Hard,
Wykeham Abbey, and Cuffwells at the centre of it all, probably inked in by Lilly.

But it was the river that caught the eye, running some six
miles down to the Solent, wriggling like a worm as it curled
down from the old mill at Beaulieu, where the road crossed on
the top of the weir and boats could go no farther on the tide,
widening as it came to Bucklers Hard, where a ship of the line
could turn in front of the slipways, setting on straighter for the
last half of its course before it took a sharp left-handed bend
and ran parallel to the shore for a mile to its mouth.

"Supposing," Justice said to Scorcher, taking a pair of
dividers from the table to mark off the distance between Cuffwells and the sea, "supposing someone wanted to make mischief here, or merely to come and go without leaving a calling
card . . . the way we'd go about it, Fred, if this were a French
river and we'd wicked games to play in it . . ."

"We'd make it easy, like." Scorcher's eyes were suddenly bright with interest as he laid the chart on the table and rolled enough of it back to read the soundings in the coastal water and that odd-shaped estuary. "Shifting bottom, I'd say, but a decent rise if you take the tide. Two fathoms at low water, four or more on the springs."

Justice nodded. "If they could launch the *Swiftsure* there," he said, putting his finger on Bucklers Hard and comparing the map and the chart, "well, there's water enough for anything to stand in close to the mouth at any state of the tide. Come in close-hauled on a southwesterly. Anchor fore and aft. Be ready to cut the bow cable, to swing and run for it if you have to leave in a hurry."

"You could lie there as you liked," Scorcher said, letting the thought run on, with the confidence that came from years of landing on French and English beaches at night, and never sure of your welcome on either side if you were in the contraband line of business.

"Pretty safe, too," said Justice, measuring again with the dividers. "It's nigh on half a mile to the shore from the channel along that reach, and all of it low-water mudbanks, I'll warrant. So no one will wade out to you, and muskets won't carry." He checked the distance again. "A twenty-four pounder would do it, with a lucky shot—but at night? A whole battery could miss if there was no moon."

"Cap'n." Scorcher was pointing to the thin strip of land that lay between the Solent and the river for the last mile of its course. "Gull-Island," he said, peering closer, "and nobody to go there 'cept fisherfolk, and boys after eggs." He spoke with a kind of relish that Justice found engaging and exciting. There was no companion to match Scorcher for such a venture. "You could make a burrow, like, there, in the sand and sea grass, and be as cosy as Chloe for a day or two. If you'd vittles and a bottle of rum to warm you."

"And a rowboat," Justice said, pointing to the gut between the western end of the island and the spit of marshland that ran out from the shoreline towards it. "Fast water running in or out on the tides, if you wanted to save a hauling round the end of the channel. You could be anywhere along this river within an hour or two, and nobody the wiser if it was dark. You saw how those markers moved when Dunning dropped them yesterday."

"Two knots, three?" Scorcher swung his hand as though he

was letting a log line run through it. "But you could walk as quick." He leaned over to tap the map in a number of places, making Justice realize how easy it was for an intruder to reach the boathouse at Cuffwells. "Tracks," Scorcher said. "Everywhere. And scarce a man treading them at night." He pointed at Wykeham, and then at Exbury on the other bank of the river. "Keep clear of them two places, and you could bring fifty men up here, and not a soul to say nay to 'em. And if you was a-going to 'em particular, why . . ."

"What makes you say that?" Justice asked, trying to recall what someone had said about Exbury.

Scorcher seemed aggrieved by the sharp question. "Nothing," he said, like a man preparing to keep his opinions to himself. "Only . . ."

"Only . . ." Justice encouraged him.

"Only if you was a-going to make a fight for this place . . . well, whoever's got one or other of them two . . ." He had no need to finish the sentence.

Exbury men. Justice looked at the map again as Harriet Romney's words came back to him. Sweetsea's sharpshooters. "Unless," he said slowly, "you held the river from there." He ran a finger round the triangle of land that forced the stream away from the Exbury side and round the bend at Gins Mill. "Lower Exbury House," he read, and wondered why the surveyor had drawn a hatched line around the point.

"Fred," he said. "Before we go down to the boathouse, find Joslin and ask him who lives there." He felt more confident about defending Cuffwells, now, for he could see the possible lines of attack. How one or two men might come, had come perhaps. How more might come if there was a determined attempt to destroy or carry off the plunging-boat.

But what of Francis? How could he be properly protected at Wykeham, without guards, in a house so easily reached from the river, so close to the Solent and the open sea?

The nerve of suspicion which Hatherley had touched last night twitched again.

Perhaps Francis was in no danger at all.

Perhaps men came from the sea to Wykeham.

Perhaps some day soon Francis himself might leave that way, with a manned submarine as a terrifying souvenir of his stay in England.

If there was anything wrong at Wykeham, then everything

might be very wrong indeed, and neither Sweetsea's sharp-shooters nor Lilly's seamen would be the means to put things right again.

SCORCHER WAS BACK. "Squire Sweetsea," he said, and Justice felt a fool for failing to make the easiest of guesses. Of course Lilly would have seen the importance of securing that little promontory, and done something about it at once. Hence the company of Volunteers. Hence the Brunswick rifles. Hence the drills, with Dunning to keep an eye on them.

"And Lady Harriet," Scorcher added, cutting so abruptly into Justice's train of thought that for a freakish moment it seemed that he was announcing her Ladyship's cohabitation with the Squire of Lower Exbury.

"Oh, no," he said, without thinking. "Not Lady Harriet."

"Oh, yes," said Lady Harriet herself, perkily, as she followed Scorcher into the room. "And why not, Captain?"

Dressed much as yesterday, a shepherd's sheepskin vest over a coarse linen shirt, bare at the throat, cord breeches and high boots, she might have been taken for a groom at any distance. And yet, as she came towards him, Justice saw the lively grace beneath the rough mannish clothing, and found himself responding to the fresh-cheeked intelligence in her face.

"Saw the fire," she began, putting a hand self-consciously to her tousled hair, less at ease indoors with a stranger than on her own ground by the river. "We . . . well, I couldn't tell . . ." She broke off with a disarming shake of the head. "Damn it, I was curious. Would've come then if I hadn't been sat to whist, in all m'finery." She looked inquiringly at Justice. "Sir George here?"

"No. Left at first light." He was unsure how to go on, uncertain how much she might know of Sir George's various enterprises; then, assuming it must be a good deal, for Francis was at Wykeham all the time, consulting her brother, and grand neighbours gossiped as freely as fishwives, he made an oblique comment. "Not much damage. One man hurt."

"And no one was seen?" Harriet looked so closely at Justice that he wondered whether some chatterbox among the servants had told her of his brief mistaken fight with Tooth; and taking his silence as an answer, she put her hand to stay him as he pushed the heavy belaying pins aside and began to roll up the map and the chart on the table. "There's more ways of getting about here than ever a map will show." She spoke seriously, as if she were about to tell him some, and thought better of it. "You'll see that for yourself at my hedger-and-ditcher, Captain." She gave him a challenging, almost disconcerting glance. "If you're the bold man I take you for, and can stay my pace."

Justice felt a clutch of excitement as he met her gaze. He was always attracted by women who knew their minds, and spoke directly to him, breaking through the initial shyness that made him awkward with flirts and coquettes. Harriet seemed to be inviting him to deal with her as an equal.

Leaving Scorcher to find a place for the rolled-up papers, he led her out through the marbled hallway to the porch, keeping his voice level as he let her implied encouragement lie between them. "Sir George left his apologies," he said, judging from her nod that the footman must have given her the same message. "For the . . . hedger-and-ditcher." He grinned. "I must confess I never heard the phrase before."

"It's my own, that's why." There was a hint of self-mockery in her voice. "Good, ain't it? Four miles round, all hedges and ditches, like a run after the cleverest fox in the county. No gates, no stopping to draw, no need to wait for the whippers-in. Twenty guineas stake, but no side wagers, and the stake money goes to the Lymington poorbox."

"Nothing for the winner?" Justice felt he had missed something in her account, unless this was simply a charity race which offered nothing but the chance of breaking your neck.

"The winner takes any horse in the race." She grinned wickedly. "Makes 'em keen, you know, for there's many as fancy a mare from the Lymington stables. Makes me keen, for I don't want to lose any one of 'em."

"Not that one, certainly." Justice looked admiringly at the fine hunter which fretted on the drive by the mounting block, its flanks steaming and quivering as a stableboy pulled off the rough blanket which covered them.

"Who knows?" Harriet spoke carelessly, taking the bridle. She looped her free hand under Justice's elbow as if they were old friends, and began to walk slowly down the track that led to the boathouse. "I'll mount you, of course, for that cob of yours will go all day, saddlebags and all, but two miles of a hedger-and-ditcher would finish him. Robert says it's cruelty to any animal."

"Robert?" Justice caught the charred smell that hung on the air despite the freshness of the morning; and the sight of men working around the boathouse set him thinking how he was to get Harriet to leave.

"Robert? Bless you, Robert Fulton, who so perversely calls himself Francis to please Sir George. Silly old Sir George, for London's full of people who've known Robert for years. People like us, too, who knew him well in France."

There was an edge of warning in her voice that made Justice reluctant to follow up that tantalising remark: time enough to talk of that French connection when he saw more clearly how matters stood with the Romneys and their American friend.

"Did you come together?" he asked, looking round in case Francis was close by, or down by the boathouse.

Harriet's answer surprised him. "Ain't seen him for a week," she said. "Ten days, even. But that don't signify, you know, for he comes pretty much as it suits him."

She slipped her hand from under Justice's arm and seemed about to mount when she sensed that he expected something more of her.

"Promised for Saturday, anyway," she added before a sharp look at Justice told her an obvious reason for his interest. "Oh, I see. You've never met him?"

Justice was content to leave it at that. "I've been wondering what he was like." It was the simple truth, he told himself, for so much now depended on the man. "Looks, character . . ."

"I think he's a handsome man," Harriet said without any embarrassment at her frankness. "Tall, curly-headed, large dark eyes that seem always to be looking past you. A straightforward sensible face, and it doesn't deceive, for he's lively, mild-tempered for all he's impetuous, hard-working, ambitious to get on, as Americans are . . ."

"Impetuous?" Justice picked the one word that seemed incongruous in this catalogue of virtues.

"His greatest weakness." Justice was tempted to smile at her sweeping judgment, and was glad he refrained. At twenty-two, possibly twenty-three, for she spoke like a woman of experience even though she looked so youthful, Lady Harriet Romney was clearly able to size up a man convincingly. "He starts so many things, and then wonders why people don't immediately see how they will work and how useful they could be. Canals. All kinds of clever machines. Steamboats . . ." She hesitated, and went on. "Whatever it is that he's doing here and at Portsmouth. One disappointment after another, so one feels sorry for him. Nothing he starts is ever properly finished."

"You speak as if you have faith in him," Justice said kindly, wondering whether her words betrayed some deeper attachment between her and the American.

"I have, indeed, Mr Justice. I have known him since I was a child—here, at our London home, in France when I spent two years there with my brother, for he is my brother's friend, you understand; and I've seen enough of him to be sure that one day he will succeed, and that the world will somehow change as a consequence."

Her forthright way of speaking matched the vigour of her thoughts, and Justice felt envious of a man who could evoke such conviction in her. "That is what Sir George said to me last night," he said, thinking that she and Sir George might have very different opinions about the consequence when it came.

"Sir George said much the same to me a month since," she said, surprising Justice once again with the easy way in which she spoke of such matters." 'Mr Francis may be ahead of his times,' yes, that's it; 'he may be ahead of his times,' Sir George told me, 'but if the times ever catch up with him, sparks will fly.' "

She spoke so warmly, and in such contradiction to everything Hatherley had said about Francis, that Justice hoped she would say more; but she was clearly finished, for her mood changed again, and she broke off with a jest. "As they did last night, it seems." She pulled off a glove and held out her hand, as Scorcher came towards them. "You are called to work, Captain," she said agreeably. "But remember you are pledged to come on Saturday."

Justice took her hand, held it for a long moment, and looked at her so directly that she coloured slightly.

"Come, Captain," she chided, buoyant, breaking into the quick smile that came so naturally to her, withdrawing her hand and swinging herself easily into the saddle. "Time enough for gallantries when you've earned them. Forty hedges, a dozen ditches, and a clear furlong uphill to the finish!"

• • •

SCORCHER CAME HURRYING over. "It's the wake as tells you where you're heading," he muttered as Harriet rode away, and then gave Justice a folded piece of paper. "Dunning's pocket," he said. "Caught in the lining."

"And nothing else?"

"Nothing."

The paper was a flysheet, printed on one side, and it was simply a set of moral exhortations drawn up for the crew of the *Diadem* by Captain Sir Home Popham, a stern foe of dirty, disorderly, and blaspheming sailors, a friend of Lilly's, and a named supporter of his Society for the Distribution of Improving Tracts for Seamen.

But on the back someone had roughly scrawled two words. Justice tipped the paper one way and another to decipher them. "Carcass," he read first, and slowly, letter by letter. "Carcass Shed." He had no idea what the note meant: it was probably no more than something Dunning had scribbled as a reminder.

"Nothing else?" he repeated. "Not even the key?" When he had sent Scorcher to look through Dunning's clothes he had expected him to find the key to the boathouse gate.

Scorcher shook his head with as much impatience as a captain's servant could allow himself.

"I told you, Cap'n. No key."

Then where was it? Dunning must have had it to get through the gate and lock it behind him. He would have been careful to do that if he was working alone at night: he was the kind of man who thought safe was better than sorry. But if the gate was locked . . . Justice could not see how anyone could have got in to start the fire, and he could not believe that a man running to get clear would have stopped to padlock it again even if he had Dunning's key or a copy of it.

So Dunning must have started the fire. By accident, or design, and then been injured by a falling beam.

That was the logical conclusion, and he found it incredible.

This fire, like the others, must have been lit by someone who knew exactly what he wanted to do, and how to do it.

And Dunning had been trapped as he watched.

IT WAS TOOTH who discovered how it had been done, though his discovery left as many questions open as it answered.

51

As Justice and Scorcher walked down to the boathouse, two men were shoring up the railings where a gap had been forced for the fire engine. Another was sorting through the charred timber and white ash that showed where the burnt storeshed had stood, so close to the rear door of the boathouse that Justice could see why Dunning had blundered that way to escape the flames. And Tooth was twenty yards away, picking at the ground outside the fence near the edge of the wood.

He was rolling something into a ball, ready to stuff it into a pocket of his blouse.

"About here, wasn't it?" Justice asked with casual good humour as he came up, and the man turned round, his cringe of embarrassment passing as soon as he saw that Justice was proposing to make light of his brutal greeting last night.

"And you're the strong one, sir, if I may make bold to speak." Tooth rubbed at the bruise below his chin with a rueful grin, and then held out a ball of dark-tarred twine.

"I thought it might have been a piece of fuse," Justice said as he took it.

"Sailmaker's whipping," Tooth replied. "Near twenty yards of it. Dropped off, or similar." He seemed to take very little interest in what he had found now that Justice and Scorcher had come up, and his face had slumped into the mulish expression which Justice had often seen when quite able seamen felt they were being drawn into an officer's business. "Hoses, p'raps," he offered grudgingly. "Couldn't say, really, sir."

While Tooth had been speaking, Scorcher had unravelled the twine, looking closely at it, and he held out the end, burnt off, with the tar sticky for the last yard or two, and pieces of ash clinging to it. "Must have been run through the fence," he surmised. "Could've been used to tip over a lantern or a candle."

"Or pull a bundle of burning rag into a pile of shavings and sawdust." Justice pictured how it might be done, if a man looped the twine round a piece of wood or iron spiked into the ground, left the ends ready outside the fence, tied his flammables to one of them, and then dragged at the other to bring his crude fuse to the point where he wanted to start the fire.

He remembered the first flicker of light he had seen from his room. It could have been the gleam of a lantern as a man set his lines, just like a fisherman at low tide.

And the second—the first pinpoint of flame he had seen through Lilly's window. That could have been a piece of sailcloth primed with pitch and turpentine.

It had been simply done, anyway. Whatever means had been used to light the fire, it was clear that the line had been laid by someone who had been inside the fence before the gate was locked for the night, or had an accomplice on the other side. And as Justice thought of two men, taking their chance in the darkness, he remembered the half-seen figures he had glimpsed in the wood before Tooth charged at him out of the smoke.

"How long had you been on patrol when . . . when you ran into me?" It seemed a tame way to describe that short, savage fight, but he had no desire to scare the man out of an honest answer.

"I came on right after the dogwatch, Cap'n," Tooth said, shifting uncomfortably from one foot to the other. "Last dog, that was."

"Two hours, then." Tooth had set off at eight. It would have been close to nine when they finished supper, and Lilly had talked for the best part of an hour before they saw the flames. "And you saw nothing? No one?"

Tooth shook his head. "Only you, Cap'n," he said miserably, and looked to Scorcher for support.

Justice sent the man on to the boathouse and turned to Scorcher. "Come on," he said impatiently. "Out with it."

"He won't say for himself, Cap'n," Scorcher said in the same voice he had previously used to plead Tooth's case. "That's as how he's already afraid on account of fighting with you. Fact is, he ought to have seen something. Ought to have seen that Dunning, at least, and he didn't."

"He expected to find Dunning at the boathouse last night?"

"Not exactly." Scorcher had clearly not wasted his time backstairs. "Seems he was his own master. Came and went, following his nose where the fancy took it." Justice suspected that it was Scorcher's antipathy to the pious Dunning which was making him so sympathetic to Tooth. "Must have gone in when Tooth was off, so he never saw him."

"Off where?"

It was Scorcher who looked uneasy now. "It was a cold night, Cap'n, and there's a fire in the carriage house, where a man can make a toddy. Nice little mess they've got there . . ."

His excuse faded as he saw the rising anger in Justice's eyes. "Only a quick toddy," he said, making a last attempt to defend Tooth's serious offence.

"You'll be telling me next that it was only a small one." Justice kept his irritation in check. Everyone knew what sailors were like when they got ashore and there was gin or rum to be got for the asking.

"It wasn't a regular thing, you understand, sir. Dunning used to creep around a bit, him being a prayers-and-water sort of man, but last night no one saw him. Tooth noticed it special, 'cos he asked after Dunning when he slipped in for the toddy, him not wanting to be caught out of place, like."

And Dunning had been caught instead, without any help from the man who was supposed to be on guard. No wonder Tooth was so uneasy. On a ship at sea he would have gone to the grating or the rope for less. It was altogether a depressing story.

"Anyway," said Fred encouragingly, "I'll pass the word. If they knows what you want, they'll have it all Bristol fashion in an hour or so." He grinned at Justice. "Proper tiger of a captain, I'll tell 'em. Makes me scrub the grass every morning, when he's home, and no rum ration if he finds a dirty blade in it."

"You do that, Fred," Justice said grimly. "Tell them there'll be no rum ration for any of them ever again if they let the Frenchies come up the river."

❧ 6 ❧

"THE *PANDORA*?" They were through the gap in the fence and picking their way over the muddied ground where the fire party had dragged its pump close to the river. *"Pandora?"* Scorcher asked again, and his manner reminded Justice of his own puzzlement before Lilly told him what was hidden in the boathouse.

"It's a plunging-boat," he said directly. "A boat that goes under the water."

Scorcher looked crestfallen and disbelieving. "That's what the lads were a-claiming, Cap'n, and I was for havin' none of it, being too old a bird to be caught by chaff."

Justice was irritated by the loose talk, coming after the other signs of free-and-easiness among Lilly's servants, yet there was no point in berating Scorcher. Every seaman was born with an itching ear, and sometimes the watch below seemed to know where a ship was bound before the captain had opened his sailing orders. Anyway, with men coming in to work from Bucklers Hard, and Francis staying at Wykeham, it would be astonishing if the secret of the *Pandora* had been well kept. "It's hearsay for me, too," he said consolingly, "for I got no more than a glimpse of it in the dark, and I know no more than Sir George has told me."

"You've seen it work?" Scorcher, still sceptical, spoke as though his master was reporting some mountebank's trick at a fair.

"No. But I hope we shall." Justice turned towards the ladder they had used to bring Dunning down from the top of the lock and left standing overnight. Though he was eager to see the mysterious vessel and to discover how it worked, he had been reluctant to go into the covered dock before Francis arrived. Now, with the clock on the carriage house striking nine, and a surprisingly strong sun for November driving the last of the covering mist away, he could wait no longer. Courtesy was

55

a luxury that could come too dear in such an urgent line of business.

"And if the sky falls, we'll all have larks for supper," Scorcher grunted, unconvinced, holding the ladder for Justice and then following him up onto the wall.

THOUGH JUSTICE COULD hear a lot of hammering and shouting at the far end of the boathouse, the large doors that opened towards the lock gates were still closed, and the only sign of life was a man on his knees repairing the wicket through which Justice had forced his way to rescue Dunning.

"Morning, Cap'n." The man put down the hinge he was trying for size against the newly fitted frame of the door, and touched the creased tar paper hat which told Justice he was a carpenter. "Forced it proper," he added, standing up to look so knowingly at Justice that it was clear everyone who worked at Cuffwells knew what had happened.

And the part he had played in it.

He was still looking for Francis as he squeezed past into the gloom of the long windowless shed.

He stood on the side of the dry dock, peering into the deep shadow, seeing little more than he had glimpsed the night before—the shape of a hull, half covered by the awning he had thrown back to reveal the odd metal fittings on the deck; and then he sent Scorcher scampering down and across the dock to join him in pulling at bolts and bars, tugging at the doors which would let the morning light flood into the boathouse.

The *Pandora*. Now that he saw her clearly for the first time he was amazed.

From what Lilly had said he had expected her to be remarkably different from anything he had ever seen before. To be like . . . like . . . like . . . As he fumbled for a comparison he realized that he had not thought clearly about it at all.

Now here she was, running almost the full length of the dock, shored up to keep her in place until the lock was opened to let in the water to float her.

And so like an ordinary launch or jolly-boat that he could not bring himself to believe that she was designed to sink and rise again.

To carry a store of weapons that could sink a whole squadron in an hour.

The impressions came fast, and confusingly.

It was the strong, stubby mast, set in a tabernacle about a third of the way back from the bow, that made her look so innocent.

A mast that could easily be swung down by removing the locking pin. She would have a foresail and a simple lugsail, then, carried by the gaff and boom that were lashed to the mast and awaiting canvas and their rigging lines. A mast. He remembered the note that had been smuggled from Brest, saying that Francis could strike the mast and sails of the *Nautilus* in two minutes when he was ready to plunge, and decided that this gear would take no longer. And rigged, she would look quite normal on the water. A low freeboard, perhaps, so that the men who sailed her would perch with little shelter on that shallow deck. Rigged fore-and-aft, she would be sluggish, hard to bring up into the wind, for she was broad in the beam and . . . yes, so far as he could see, round-bottomed.

He was on the edge of the dock now, crouched, screwing up his eyes. She was like . . . he had it now . . . a longboat he had once seen on an American whaler that had put in at Antigua on her way home from the South Seas. Diagonal built, for he could see the strakes catching the light at an angle, and probably double-skinned for strength, as the American boat had been made to bear the crushing ice.

That was it. He recalled Verney of the *Indomitable* telling how the weight of water drove in the sealed hold of a sinking ship as it sank below twenty fathoms; and while some part of his mind was wondering how Verney could have learned this interesting fact, he was also reckoning that this plunging-boat must be strong enough to survive at five fathoms, ten, perhaps more, without collapsing or springing such disastrous leaks that the crew would drown and the whole device would sink to the bottom.

He had no more idea of the pressure the submarine would have to bear as she dropped into the depths than he had of the means that would take her down and bring her back safely to the surface. He was only sure that, for the first time in his life, he was looking at something so genuinely new that he did not have any idea how the vessel was constructed or how the complicated machinery it must contain would be worked. And yet its shape seemed so familiar that he was still thinking in terms of caulk, pitch, and the stoutest timber . . .

The more he let his speculations race the more he marvelled, as any man would who had spent his life at sea; and the more perplexed he became, as any sailor would who had to answer questions he had never considered before. How could men breathe in such a craft? How could they drive it forward, as they must, for Lilly had been clear that it would not be wholly at the mercy of the tides? How could they despatch their infernal machines, and what could such things be like, if they were to explode beneath the sea? It was all so bewildering that if Francis had not done these things in his *Nautilus*, three years since, Justice would have been tempted to dismiss the whole enterprise as the fraud of an ambitious and unprincipled projector.

But Francis *had* done it. Hatherley had said that one life at least had been lost in proving the truth of his claims.

And one day soon . . . Justice thought he had heard a knocking sound within the hull . . . soon the lock gates would be opened, the water would pour in, and Francis . . . yes, the sound came again, close to him, and distinct from the noise outside . . . Francis would discover whether his gamble on this far larger vessel had succeeded.

JUSTICE HAD BEEN so taken aback by the appearance of the *Pandora*, and then so caught in his chain of questions, that he had made no attempt to board the vessel; and a sudden movement under the stern, changing the cast of light, caught his attention.

It was not the long tiller that was moving, nor yet the rudder, hanging straight from its pintles, but something between, something with four large blades, set like the sweeps of a windmill, which was turning with gathering speed, turning with a sound of metal grinding and clanking, like a small mill, which came up through a large circular hole on the deck.

There was someone inside the *Pandora*, working that machine.

Justice gave a hail, and jumped across to the deck, looking down into an unlit space where he could just catch the gleam of reflected light on bars and revolving wheels.

"Cap'n." It was Scorcher who answered, coming back to the wicket with Tooth and the carpenter behind him, leaving the men at the door and climbing across a piece of planking to join his master. "Cap'n, there's . . ." He broke off, to touch Justice on the shoulder, pointing to a part of the foredeck that lay in the shadow of the mast, changing his sentence in his surprise. "The chimney," he said.

There, rising from the deck and glinting now as a shaft of low sunshine flashed off the water in the lock, was the wide brass tube he had seen last night, a tube that was the size of a chimney stack, and from it a man was unfolding himself, stiffly, like a jack-in-the-box.

"I was a-testing the flyer," he said, almost defensively, as he walked along the deck towards Justice, wiping his oily palms on a fragment of cloth, nodding as he passed, and climbing off the deck onto the gantry, where Justice had stumbled into his workbench in the darkness. He reached for a piece of copper tubing, clamped it into a vice, and took a file to it without saying another word.

"Harry Warren, the mechanic." Tooth had come down to join Justice and Scorcher, leaving the carpenter to go on with his work, making it quite plain that there would be no argument about Justice's right to inspect the *Pandora*. "Curmudgeonly," Tooth said, "from Birmingham way," letting the emphasis fall as if the second piece of information explained the first.

More confident now, his usefulness demonstrated, Tooth was eager to make a good impression, and Justice let him rattle on with bits and pieces of gossip.

Three months they'd been working, he said, and a dozen men on it at times, though all the shipwrights had gone now, 'cepting the Cowleys. He glanced at the carpenter mending the door. "Joshua." And old Zech and the boy Jeremiah, who were in the sail-loft next door—and Warren, here, of course. For the boat were done, near enough, 'cepting the second hatchway. He talked on as he pointed to the circular hole on the afterdeck; 'cepting this, 'cepting that, she were ready, sails and all.

Everything that Tooth had said showed that there was very little to be done before the *Pandora* could go into the water. Then why was Francis so dilatory? When would he test the boat? Who would serve as his crew? Who would call out Sweetsea's men to cover her when she edged out of the lock into the river? What trials would convince Lilly, Pitt, the sceptical men at the Admiralty . . . ? He caught himself anticipat-

59

ing, hoping the boat would prove herself, when he had not even seen more than her deceptive appearance.

Tooth had stopped, sensing that Justice's attention had wandered, and Justice was content to let him fall silent.

Scorcher came over, jerking his thumb at Warren, now hammering away so loudly that the blows made it hard for Justice to catch what was said. "Deaf," Scorcher added, tapping his ears, "so he don't mind the noise." He followed Justice across to the squat brass tube from which Warren had just emerged and looked down. "Going below, Cap'n?"

Justice ran his hand round the rim, noting how snugly the hinged lid would fit the grooves, and how the wedge-shaped bolts would secure it tight when it was closed. Precious little water would leak through that seal, he decided. It looked as close as a watch-case.

He stared down the tube to see what lay below, for Warren had left a lantern burning there; but he could make out little save a short iron ladder leading down from the hatchway, and the light reflecting from polished brass beyond it.

He could no longer contain his impatience. Whether Francis liked it or not, he was going to see for himself what the *Pandora* was like below her innocent-seeming deck; and he would do it alone. The last thing he wanted was to have Tooth chattering explanations at him or to be chaffed by Scorcher's sceptical quips and queries.

IT WAS LIKE going down into a new world, and he did not want the moment of discovery spoiled. Even as he swung his legs into the mouth of the tube, he found himself recalling all kinds of boyhood tales—long-forgotten stories his mother and his brother must have read to him—of caves lined with gold, of dwarfs labouring magically at wondrous things, of men who could make themselves invisible and gods whose thunderbolts could strike presumptuous mortals dead. It was a world of new men, like Warren, mechanics who were like the machines they made and worked, all sinews and joints, and quite unlike the old craftsmen who had cut wood and beaten iron as their grandfathers' grandfathers had done.

And as all these notions came whirling at him he realized that he had stopped at a small platform, that his head and shoulders were still above the level of the deck, that he was

squinting out through a small thick circlet of glass set conically
into the brass, that Francis, like Hatherley, was a man of a
systematic turn of mind, for here was the peephole the commander of the *Pandora* would need as she lay almost awash,
searching for her prey.

He stepped down. Another three feet. Another proof that
Francis was thorough. A flanged lid, closing the bottom of the
tube. If there was a leak above, if there was damage, Francis
had no intention of being drowned like a rat in a flooded
drain.

Now he could see better, for the light from the lantern fell
directly on the curving brass bulkhead that cut off this compartment from the rest of the bow. He rapped at the metal.
The space beyond must contain a cable locker for the anchor.
And what else? For it was large enough, and there were two
wheels on the face of the bulkhead, with shafts running on
from them through stuffing-boxes; and there was a pump-
handle, too.

A wooden box with a pendulum in it, and two scales at right
angles.

A pendulum that quivered as Scorcher and Tooth paced
overhead. That would tip one way as the bow dropped and
another as it rose. That would swing to the left if the *Pandora*
rolled to starboard, and to the right in a larboard roll. That
would tell Francis how his plunging-boat lay in the water, for
once he was sealed in that tank-like space, he would have
nothing to go by except the untrustworthy evidence of his
senses. That . . . Justice peered closer as he thought of the pendulum swinging so wildly that there would be no telling
whether or not the boat was listing to danger point, and saw
that Francis had been before him. Four strong threads ran
from the pendulum over small running blocks to four dangling
weights; and they were so neatly made that he was sure that
Francis would have calculated exactly how much was needed
to steady and reduce the swing of the pointer.

He could hear the rumble of voices as the men above him
talked, like old shipmates, and for a moment he wondered
why Scorcher found Tooth so congenial.

The pendulum. He brought himself back to his search. And
a compass. And a barometer, the quicksilver tube glinting
sharp against so much brass and copper.

Francis had tried them at Brest, Hatherley had said, and

61

found that they worked under water. Found how to hold a course. Found how to tell the depth at which he lay.

Then here, by this bulkhead, was what would pass for the quarterdeck in a submarine, and there, somewhere close by, the helmsman must stand.

Justice looked round, but there was no sign of a wheel, nothing but handles, and connecting bars, a large box that might be some kind of pump, heavy crossbeams, the gleam of another bulkhead at the far throw of the lantern light—a kind of cage of metal inside a cylinder of brass, and all of it crammed, like a large cask, inside the wooden hull of the *Pandora*.

It was this circular tank that would take the strain when the *Pandora* plunged, and not the timbers of the frame which carried it.

The thought of clamping oneself into such a cribbed space made him feel awkward and uncomfortable. Six feet across, maybe three times as long. He could guess only too easily at the bruised foreheads, the pinched fingers, the barked shins; at men tripping and cursing in the darkness; men trying to keep a footing on the narrow walkway that seemed to serve as a fore-and-aft strengthening beam, and as a base to which all the working parts of this strange machine were bolted; men listening for orders over the clatter; men retching for air; men afraid, men feeling desperate for room to move; men longing for the light and the feel of wind on their faces again. He had once, as a boy of ten, squeezed himself into a cave in the cliffs near Dover, when the tide was rising, and he could still remember fighting the panic that made him gasp for breath until he discovered he could force his way out.

He took the lantern in his hand the better to see where the rods and pipes might lead. A handle and a windlass, a cable dropping through a box that rose from the floor. Some kind of anchor? Another box, a small cylinder, that must be a pump. Copper tubes sprouting off, running to the bulkheads. And now, amidships, a great two-handed bar, like the handle on a fire engine.

Justice touched it gingerly, rocking it backwards and forwards until he could be sure that it turned, and then making it revolve with a grinding noise that echoed all through the brassy cylinder, like the sound Warren had made, and told himself that this must be the machine which worked the . . .

the flyer, Warren had called it—the four-bladed device that must drive the *Pandora* forwards when the mast was struck and she was below the waves.

Forwards. Or backwards. The logic of the device came to him exactly as he found he could move the handle as easily one way as the other.

It was such an astounding revelation that he almost let the lantern fall as he loosed his hand from the machine and stood motionless in wonder.

If the wind could drive the sweeps of a stationary windmill, the reverse must be true. If there were a means of driving the sweeps from inside the mill, and it was free to move, they would cut into the air and pull or push it along.

And Francis had seen that the same principle must work in water, would work even more effectively in the denser medium.

Justice had a disturbing sense of exhilaration as he saw how such a thought might be applied. How sweeps . . . how something like the blades of a water mill might be used to push a boat instead of the clumsy oars which no machine would ever fit. How a mechanical device would free ships from the vagaries of wind, of current, and of tide. How a man such as Francis might be gripped by the symmetry of his ideas and in some kind of way fall in love with his own projections. It had never occurred to him before that science might seize a man's imagination quite as powerfully as art, or the beauty of a sunset on the tropics, or the sound of a woman singing a farewell from the quayside as a ship stood out to sea.

Excited by his discovery, he held the lantern to light beyond the space where the handle-turners must stand to their task. Here, fastened securely to the curving side, was a wheel which moved easily, though he had no notion what it might move; and two levers that slid to and fro, reminding him in their action of the relieving tackles below deck which must serve when the wheel of a ship was shot away, making him certain that these things must lie handy to the helmsman's grip.

And beyond again, gleaming in the darkness, was a curving end to the compartment, a means of dividing it for extra strength and safety from flooding, of making a space for more men to stand or work the deadly weapons the *Pandora* would carry into action.

"Cap'n! Cap'n!" Scorcher was calling to him, the Kentish

voice reverberating sharp and resonant through the brass, and he realized that even now he had no idea how the *Pandora* was to be plunged deep and then brought up again.

"Cap'n, there's a gentleman . . ."

Justice pulled at the lever he had found just as Scorcher shouted, deciding that it must be some other kind of pump, almost ignoring Scorcher's cry, and then starting for the hatchway as he caught the words properly.

Had Francis come at last?

He caught himself a glancing blow on the scalp as he clumsily swung back from putting Warren's lantern on its hook, and felt the blood suddenly warm on his face. He levered himself up through the tube, lifted his legs together as if he were skipping, and set himself down on the deck.

There, between Scorcher and Tooth, was an odd-looking man who seemed to be about his own age, and quite unlike his mental picture of the American inventor.

"Robert Francis?" he asked, and held out his hand, wondering why Scorcher was shaking his head so vigorously.

❧7❧

"HIS LORDSHIP." Scorcher had no time to say more before the man stepped forward and gave a jerky bow.

"William Romney," he said, as if he found titles and formal introductions tiresome and preferred to come to business at once.

He was odd, Justice decided as they shook hands, because he was so angular that his body could have been cut out and fastened together by a cabinetmaker, and everything he wore hung from him haphazardly, like lengths of cloth thrown over a tallboy. There was a family likeness—he had the same puckish mouth as Harriet, the same dark hair that lay close to the head; but where his sister had a vigorous natural grace, Lord William Romney had a peculiar awkwardness of movement, and it was set off as much by an abstract look about his eyes as by an earnestness of manner that would have done well for a ride-about Wesleyan preacher.

There was a box in his left hand, of the kind barber-surgeons used to carry the tools of their gruesome trade, and since he was trying to set it down on the deck as Justice greeted him, he bobbed so curiously that it added to the oddity of his appearance.

"Remarkable," he said, as he stood straight again and caught Justice's name, staring so hard that it seemed his distant eyes were searching for some resemblance or the recollection of a previous meeting. "I thought Harriet might be mistaken." But he left his cryptic remark unexplained and sat down abruptly on the rim of the brass hatchway, rummaging in his box to produce a glass flask, with two tubes of gut running down through the cork, and a second flask which was apparently full of water.

"Guyton's idea." He spoke to Justice as though he was on calling terms with every savant in Paris. "But Robert will have none of it."

"Did Francis not come with you from Wykeham?" Justice asked immediately, putting his question for the second time that morning, and hoping doubtfully for a promising answer before Lord William veered off into some chemical demonstration he was sure he would not understand.

"No. Why should he?" Lord William seemed more surprised at the inquiry than Justice was by his offhand reply. "If he comes from London on the Dorchester coach, he puts down at Cadnam at eight and takes a hack from the livery there." He fished in his fob for a watch and held the dial close to his face. "It lacks five minutes to ten," he said. "Therefore the coach is late, or he will not come today."

As he completed his pedantic catechism, Lord William put his watch away and took up the full flask with an air of disappointed contemplation; he shook it, lifting it against the light, so that Justice could see that the fluid was actually the lightest of greens, like a Portuguese wine, and remarked regretfully that he had wished to make his point.

"To Francis?"

"If you call him that." Romney gave him an appraising look. He might not see too distinctly, but his face was full of expression. "Do you come from Commodore Owen? At Portsmouth?"

"No." Justice had heard of the man, but could not place him.

"Or Lieutenant Robinson?"

"I'm afraid not," Justice said, although he recognised the name, and began to realise that Lord William must know a good deal about the submarine enterprises on which Francis was so busily engaged, for there had been a young man from Portsmouth called Robinson in Hatherley's office in Richmond Terrace, in June, when they had been talking of ways to attack Bonaparte's invasion flotilla. Justice still remembered one remark that had puzzled him at the time. "If we cannot get at them from above," Robinson had said, pushing his hand under the map of Boulogne harbour to match a dramatic gesture to his words, "we must get at them from below"; and he had made some other observations to that effect before Hatherley cut him short with the reminder that it was better for Justice to go to France in ignorance of such secret ventures.

Twice denied, Lord William did not seem inclined to press

his questions, for he rose from his sharp-edged seat, letting Tooth set a piece of planking across it to form a makeshift bench, and getting Scorcher to hold one flask and Tooth the other while he measured a length of gut between them.

"Do you . . . ?" Justice was about to ask if Lord William knew how men could breathe in the *Pandora* when the hatches were shut, but he was unexpectedly forestalled.

"Fresh air's not enough." Romney spoke as though he were halfway through an argument rather than at the beginning of an explanation, and then, sensing Justice's bewilderment, he leaned over the front of the brass entrance hatchway and showed him two fair-sized tubes rising beside it, and clamped to it, before they turned through a swan's neck to end in a pair of perforated globes. "Fresh air." Romney tapped one of them. "Mephitic air." He shook his head. "But it won't really do."

Justice saw Scorcher looking as puzzled as he felt. He could understand how Francis might use such tubes to draw good air into the sealed chambers below, and he guessed that one of the pump handles he had touched might force the foul air out again. Without some such device, the crew would soon choke. Mephitic air. He had heard a surgeon use the phrase, long before, as they watched the hatches being knocked open on a slaver, and they saw a line of chained and lifeless creatures who had perished in their own stench.

Romney was saying something about floats and valves, as he fingered the tubes, so that Justice grasped that they would close as the *Pandora* plunged under the water; and he caught the words "compression" and "tank" and "fifty atmospheres" . . . Francis must have constructed some means of storing more air than the great brass cylinder would normally contain . . . enough for six men or more to breathe for half a day . . . to keep lanterns burning so there was light to work by . . . to support a songbird—the memory of a Cornish tin mine came to him, and in his mind's eye he saw a group of sturdy miners going to their work with a finch in a little cage. It would be like a deep mine down there, when the hatches were closed and the outside world was shut away. Like a mine, or a burial vault.

In his own way, he had come round to Romney's point, and he saw it as Romney felt obliged to explain it, like a teacher talking to a laggard pupil.

"The fresh and foul air mixes, you see." He tapped one of the swan-necked tubes. "He must pump out the good and the bad together." He stood up, as if he had been pulled straight on a puppet-string, and pointed to his flasks. "But I can remove mephitic air," he said with some pride, "and near double the time he can stay below. See."

Justice could not imagine how he proposed to prove his claim with two flasks and some pieces of gut, and he watched with amazement as Romney picked up his first flask, which had two tubes leading from it. He had fastened one tube to a bladder, and he offered the other to Scorcher.

"Hold your nose, there's a good fellow," he said with cool kindliness, "and breathe only through the gut." He turned to Justice, ignoring Scorcher's startled grimace and Tooth's smug smile at escaping this peculiar duty. "Would you count for me?" he asked. "Quite steadily." He came back to Scorcher, tapping him on the shoulder and saying "Now" as he began squeezing the bladder, timing his actions to fit the slowly increasing pace of Scorcher's breaths.

Justice had so often counted the number of guns in a salute that he had no difficulty in calling as steadily as Lord William desired, though he had to curb his smiles at the sight of Scorcher huffing and puffing on his length of gut. He was soon to ten, to twenty, to forty. At eighty Scorcher was showing signs of distress. "Eighty-eight. Eighty-nine." At the count of ninety-two, red in the face, Scorcher spat out the tube, let go of his nose, gasped an oath, and stood blowing as hard as if he had run a furlong.

"Thank you," Romney said with prim courtesy. "Now rest until I am ready again." While Scorcher glared at Tooth and wiped his mouth with the back of his hand, Lord William pulled the bladder and length of gut from the empty flask and slipped it on to the other. "Simply limewater."

He lifted the flask and shook it, so that Justice could see the greenish fluid—and see also that both the piece of gut that ran from the bladder and the piece through which Scorcher would breathe were now fastened to some kind of valve. From the valve one tube ran down into the limewater, and another stopped just above it.

"As you see" (Lord William pointed to the valve) "when the man breathes out, the mephitic air will be bubbled through the beneficial fluid, and the noxious elements will be washed

68

from it. What remains will be drawn out by the bladder, here, you will notice; and then the refreshed air will be blown back into his mouth by the bladder. In short, the foulness remains in the flask." He clapped his hands, as if he had just completed a problem in logic and wished to show that he was pleased with the reasoning.

The argument was clear enough, though Justice made no attempt to grasp the chemical principles involved. Romney had found some means of cleansing the air, and Scorcher should thus be able to breathe the limited supply in his lungs and the bladder for much longer. Twice as long, Lord William had said. And if the demonstration proved the point . . . well, he would see it first. "I am ready," he told Romney, and gave Scorcher an encouraging grin.

Scorcher blew. Romney squeezed the bladder. The bubbles frothed through the limewater. And as Justice counted beyond fifty, sixty, seventy, he looked closely to see how Scorcher was managing. No doubt, he was breathing more comfortably. He looked back at the flask to see the water clouding, as if to justify Romney's prediction. At a hundred Scorcher was beginning to pant. At a hundred and twenty it struck Justice that he was scarcely holding on, out of a kind of pride. And at a dozen more he threw up his hands and took a great gulp of air as the gut fell out of his mouth.

"Well done!" Justice had found himself drawn into Romney's demonstration, like a round of forfeits, and was keen for Scorcher to come home triumphant.

And he had done so. If Romney could rig up some such device on a larger scale and attach it to a pump inside the *Pandora*, the vessel could stay below water . . . for how long? Where Francis reckoned on six hours, he could now count on eight, maybe more. Almost a whole tide, the hours between dawn and dusk in the close part of the year, the time it would take to put a man ashore and wait for his return . . .

"Can it be done easily?" He had scarcely formed the question before he realised how he was falling into a kind of sympathy with Romney, and Francis, whom he had never even met, and becoming eager for the *Pandora* to be a success; to be a success as a great problem solved, and not only because she might strike deadly blows at Bonaparte.

He was beginning to understand how Francis must feel about his ingenious projections, and why he was willing to change from one paymaster to another in the hope of bringing them to a pitch of perfection.

And he immediately felt the pall of frustration that Francis must often have known when Romney shook his head. "It is only the principle," he observed, as though that were more important than anything else. "In practice?" He spread his hands, gawkily uncertain. "The limewater is less active than one would wish . . . the quantity carried would be large . . . the valves liable to fail . . ." Justice could tell how often he and Francis must have argued over such practical details and found the solutions evading them.

"But in principle, yes," Lord William said, brightening. "That is what matters most to me."

"THE WHOLE VESSEL is nothing more than the systematic application of principles," Lord William said with surprising clarity, as he walked Justice about the deck, shambling, squinting, pointing, yet never losing track of his explanation, and showing a warmth of interest that Justice found engaging. "That is what I call science."

He began by answering the question that had been plaguing Justice ever since he heard of the plunging-boat.

"The weight of the vessel is almost as great as that of the water she displaces," he said in a schoolmasterly voice which fluted clearly now that Warren had ceased his hammering and left the boathouse on some unreported errand; "She will float at a hundred pounds less, or thereabouts. Pump water into the tanks which run the length of the vessel, in place of a keel . . . voilà; she sinks. Pump the water out again . . . voilà, she rises, and the principle of buoyancy is vindicated."

"It would be a clumsy business in shallow waters," Justice said thoughtfully. "Too fast, and you are at the bottom. Too slow, and you will be at the mercy of the waves on the upper water."

Lord William smiled at his pupil's progress. "That is why there are wings to the plunging-rudder." He took Justice aft to peer down towards the flyer's sweeps. "That is the principle of control." He pointed to the iron frame which jutted out above the flyer, and Justice could see that a large hinged plate was fixed to either side of it, each worked by a rod which ran from inside the *Pandora*—the pair of rods, he guessed at once,

70

which he had fingered and thought similar to the relieving tackles on the rudder of a man-of-war. "Up or down. To one side or the other." Lord William flapped his hands in imitation of the action. "Nothing more is needed—though Robert wishes to put such wings on each side of the vessel, and another flyer in the bow, for speedier movement." He shook his head. "Unnecessary. But Robert is such a logical fellow that he always carries things too far. He forgets the principle of simplicity."

While Romney had been describing the workings of the *Pandora* he had begun to seem less distant in his manner than he had been when he was making Scorcher pant to prove a scientific point; and Justice realized that, for all the shyness which intensified his physical oddity, he was actually a man of practical bent, who was quite capable of distinguishing between one of his beloved principles and its possible utility.

He had come to the man with a prejudice, planted in his mind by Lilly's gibes at the Earl of Lymington and both his children, and with a sense of suspicion as well, for after his experience with O'Moira that summer he would distrust anyone who went to Paris on supposedly scientific business in these years of war. Bonaparte certainly did not encourage such visits merely for the advancement of knowledge. Those who went would serve some French interest, or be sympathetic to French policies, and he had expected Lord William to fall into both categories—to be, in short, something of a dupe and a firebrand, and probably a hippish shatterpate as well. Yet within the hour he had found the man to be unaffected, amiable, almost as childlike in his simplicity as he was severe in his intelligence; and he was beginning to wonder whether Lilly had rightly read the character of his neighbours at Wykeham.

"And the means of attack?" Justice was aware that it was a more delicate question, but Romney had been so forthcoming in other respects that he felt free to put it directly to him. This time, however, there was more reproof than explanation in Lord William's reply.

"I don't greatly concern myself with such things, you know." A tremor of agitation in his voice made him sound tartly defensive. "I'm a man of science." And then he came out with a sentence that was so pat that Justice could tell he must have said it many times. "I devote myself to Man, not Mars and Mammon."

There was no way to respond to such a sententious sentiment except by arguing that Lord William was blind to his own paradox—and Justice had never thought that much could be gained by telling a man he was either a fool or a hypocrite. He would have to accept that his Lordship could commit himself enthusiastically to the principles of the *Pandora*'s construction, and at the same time earnestly disapprove of the deadly purpose she was designed to serve.

All the same, he pressed his point strongly enough to get a testy answer.

"Carcasses," Lord William said. "Floating bombs. In lockers." He walked some way along the low bulwarks of the *Pandora*, stamping his foot. "Here. Here. And here. A dozen or more each side, I'm told."

He stopped, staring angrily at the deck, as if he did not wish to know what it concealed, beyond the wonderful machinery that so fascinated him; and his posture made it clear that he would be drawn no further.

"I SENT FOR VITTLES." After a few moments Lord William had recovered his temper, explaining Scorcher's absence with a wave towards the house as he climbed up onto the side of the dock, seating himself on a block of wood as if he were settling for a picnic. He patted the space beside him. "If you would join me?"

Damn Romney! Condescending as though he were the host! But Justice was coming to like this eccentric and most democratic lord. And he sat down the more willingly for that.

"Captain Justice," Romney said with such familiarity that he must have known who Justice was from the moment he clapped eyes on him. "My sister said she thought you an honest man, if you'll forgive that rare compliment." He gave the sudden grin that Justice had seen light Harriet's face when her mood changed. "I have the same impression." Then he looked back at the *Pandora* and his face darkened again. "If you are to understand what that boat means . . . to act accordingly . . ." He broke off, looking so conspiratorial that Justice thought for a moment this hesitation was the prelude to an attempt to subvert him. But Romney was merely judging how to begin.

"Go on." Justice could tell he needed some slight assurance that he would not be rebuffed.

"I think I must talk to you about my friend, Robert Fulton." Lord William gave a nervous laugh. "Or Robert Francis, if you must speak of him thus, in your official capacity."

Justice kept silent now, afraid he might discourage this curiously fretful man, who vacillated so quickly between aristocratic condescension and the uncertain confidence of someone who found intimacy difficult.

"It is because I judge you to be honest that I think you may help him." There was real anxiety in the way Lord William spoke. "I fear he does not appreciate the risks he is running for the sake of his ideals."

"Risks?" Justice was so astonished by the word that he could not see where Romney was leading him. "The risk of drowning if the *Pandora* sinks, never to rise again?" He spoke the thoughts as they came to him. "The attacks? The fires?"

Lord William shook his head. "No. Such things might be expected. No, Mr Justice, it is not the threat to my friend's safety that troubles me. Nor even the possibility that some day soon the shipwrights may be scared away from this place, or that this boathouse will go up in flames. It is the risk to us all." He paused, looking towards the smoke-blackened timbers by the rear door, where Justice had found the unconscious Dunning. "It might be no bad thing if the arsonist had succeeded," he said, with a gleam in his eye and such a peculiar emphasis that Justice recalled Lilly's hint at a fanatical streak in the family. "To us all," he repeated. "To us all, who believe in peaceful intercourse between nations and prosperous freedom for their peoples. That is what Robert believes, too." He spoke regretfully as he stood at the edge of the dock, pointing to the *Pandora* below them. "The boat is aptly named," he said.

⤙ 8 ⤚

SCORCHER WAS BACK with a basket of provisions from the Cuffwells kitchen, and Lord William let his remark hang ominously unsettled while he and Justice unpacked the hamper. There was a cold fowl, crusted bread, chutney, a wheyish cheese, crisp apples, a flask of claret, and a pitcher of water for Lord William. "No faddist," he said, taking a long draught of it after refusing the tankard of Bordeaux that Justice had poured for him. "It is merely that I find the vapours of spirits and wine addle my wits and sour my stomach." He broke off a piece of bread and dipped it in the whey with relish. "Robert's the same, you know. Dyspeptic."

It was a new word for Justice, who was often bemused by such novelties in the speech of surgeons and other learned acquaintances: the best course, he had decided years before, was to nod sagely, say "Quite," and guess at the meaning.

"Quite," he said, thinking how strangely Romney shifted the direction of his talk, as though he were tacking a boat, taking advantage of each freshening in the conversation and yet holding to some line of thought. With a man like this, as with Lilly, it was better to let him pick his own course, and Lord William immediately showed how erratic that could be.

He said nothing more about Francis, or the *Pandora*, while they ate contentedly, veering off into anecdotes about his scientific friends in London and Paris, vigorously explaining his notion of making a gas from coal that could light the public rooms at Wykeham and talking of its possibilities for the public streets. Could this be why people were talking of "lights on the river," Justice wondered, his head spinning with the marvels that Romney was conjuring up for him like an old wizard in a fairy tale?

On the deck of the *Pandora*, just out of earshot, Scorcher was clearly feeling bemused, for Tooth had returned and taken it upon himself to display the mysteries of the submarine: and as Scorcher scratched his head and mumbled inaudible oaths, Justice was struck yet again by the casual way everything seemed to be done here, compared to the tight regularities which made life on a crowded ship both possible and rigorous.

"An American." With a start Justice perceived that Romney had come round to speak of his friend once more. "And Americans are different from the rest of us. They are not a particularly creative people, in my judgment, but they have a knack of seeing the effect of things in combination, so that they may be made to work." Lord William spoke with warm satisfaction. "They believe in principles. In their mode of government. In the development of their manufactures. In the conduct of their trade. They are Newtonians to a man!"

Justice could tell that this was the best compliment Lord William could pay anyone, though his own knowledge of Isaac Newton went little further than the schoolboy tale of the falling apple and the law of gravity, a few mathematical tags, and a vague sense that the whole science of calculation had been the work of the old sage in his Cambridge study.

William Washington Romney. His Lordship had come to such an admiration of Americans at his father's knee—at the font, indeed; and it was clearly the spring of all his thoughts and actions. For he was a man of systems himself, like an American as he described them, seeing good in every man who promised to make the world over, so that the movement of each person in it could be foreseen and regulated like the wheels of a clock.

And the *Pandora* had its place in that scheme of admiration. Romney could not take his eyes off this mechanical masterpiece, though he knew that it was less likely to impose peace on the world then to begin a new and terrible form of warfare.

"Near enough done, then?" Justice saw Romney's face brighten as they watched Warren, old Cowley, and his grandson manhandling the second brass hatchway to its mounting aft of the mast.

"Almost ready," Lord William said, confirming Lilly's estimate that the vessel had been within a week of completion when the disruptive attacks began. "Ready for trials, whenever Robert comes."

And that answer, Justice thought, makes the continuing

absence of Francis all the more curious. At such a time, surely, the man would be impatient to see his remarkable craft taking final shape and to see whether it would really do what he expected of it.

Yet it was now well after noon, and still no sign of him. Lord William, it was clear, had ceased to expect him, for his Lordship was packing up the equipment he had brought for the breathing experiment, and breaking off to give Warren some kind of instructions about the seal of the hatchway. He was quite at ease here—astonishingly so, it seemed to Justice, who found it hard to understand why Lilly let a man of such doubtful opinions have the run of the *Pandora* and even play some part in her construction. No doubt Francis had persuaded Lilly that he needed Romney's help and had vouched for his discretion.

No doubt, though Justice suspected that Lilly had many doubts, and no option. Once Francis made a condition of Lord William's help, there was no more to be said.

But in that case Romney might well know enough to complete the submarine if Francis still did not come, if he never came, if . . . Justice could feel Lilly's vague anxieties beginning to unsettle him, and he was already speculating what might happen if Francis had a last-minute change of heart about working for the British, and decided to go home, or back to France; if the French should come to carry him off, or make a murderous assault on him . . .

"Could you manage to . . . ?" As Justice began to frame his request, he hesitated over a word. Did one speak of sailing a vessel which was specially built to sink?

Lord William was a quick man, for all his awkwardness and his jumps of thought, and he saw at once what Justice was about to ask.

"To work the machinery? Yes, I think so." He shrugged his angular shoulders so sharply that Justice could almost see his arms at work like levers. "With some practice, of course, but we should all need that for a start. Only Robert or one of the men who worked the *Nautilus* in France could do better." He looked thoughtful. "But navigate? No." He seemed very sure of his incapacity, and his next words explained it. "I have never been a man for boats, Mr Justice. I am so indisposed at sea that they are at best a necessary evil."

In five minutes more Lord William had packed his bags and

gone, leaving Justice to sit and watch the men at work on the *Pandora*, to notice how they had come to take all its novelties for granted, and to wonder how he could muster a crew of sorts if Francis had not come by the time she was ready to take the water.

There was Lord William. He might know nothing of navigation and suffer miseries from seasickness, but his scientific curiosity would take him out and down in her if he was given the chance. The taciturn Warren would probably feel much the same: he was a skilled mechanic who would want to see the results of his work. One of the younger Cowleys, Tooth—well, Tooth was clearly fascinated by the machine, to judge from the vigorous way he had been explaining it to Scorcher.

And one more. He saw that he would have to take command himself, and he shook his head at that unpleasant prospect.

He had no knowledge of mechanics. He would lack any of the assurances that a captain normally found in strict observance of Admiralty regulations and naval practice: from what Lilly had said, and hinted, the construction of the *Pandora* was so much at odds with Admiralty policy that he could be ruining his career the moment he got her afloat. And he hated the idea of clamping himself inside that brass sarcophagus.

Yet he was now in charge of the *Pandora*.

As much in charge as if he had walked out onto her deck with a commissioning warrant in his pocket and the Articles of War in his hand.

JUSTICE STOOD AT the end of the stone pier, watching a neat, bright-painted pinnace come down the river, running with the last of the ebb and yawing as a fresh westerly gusted between the trees.

That was easy, light and lively, and he could almost feel the pull of the tiller as she came across the channel for the bend.

But what would it be like to take a submerged boat down through that murky water, without any means of judging how she was being turned by the ebb or carried towards the stretching banks of mud?

No doubt it could be done, and done better each time one attempted it, and he began to see for himself why Francis and Lilly thought so much could be achieved when such a boat was manned, and armed, and fully tried.

One could creep up a river like this, or slip under a boom into a seemingly safe harbour, where the lookouts would be slack, and one might cut out or sink the richest prizes almost at one's leisure. One could set an agent ashore, as he had often done so chancily on the steep wave-beaten beaches of Brittany . . . block the entrance to a port . . . cause the kind of confusion which could make the ships in a convoy of merchantmen run upon each other in the dark.

"Captain Justice! Captain Justice!" He stopped midway through his catalogue of possibilities as he heard a horseman come up to the boathouse and call his name; and before he could walk back to the door a burly, agreeable-looking man came bustling to greet him, holding out his left hand because the right sleeve was empty and pinned across the uniform coat of a captain in the Volunteers.

"Sweetsea," he was saying. "Amos Sweetsea." He shook hands warmly and then made the slightest of gestures to his missing arm. "*Queen Charlotte*, First of June," he added, and Justice knew at once he had been maimed in Howe's epic fight with Villaret ten years before.

It was the kind of naval introduction that both men found comfortably familiar, and they were soon talking of mutual acquaintances, exchanging the names of vessels in which they had served, and coming easily to the business of the *Pandora*.

"No serious damage, then?" Sweetsea had met Lord William on the way and heard the news from him, and now he looked about him with the confident air of a man who was trusted with the secrets of Cuffwells and had his part to play in guarding them.

"Only to Dunning," Justice said. "Taken off to Lymington by the surgeon." Scorcher had brought that disquieting news when he had fetched the basket of victuals at noon. And as he spoke he remembered the flysheet that Scorcher had found in the man's pocket.

"What's the carcass shed?" he asked Sweetsea as they walked out of the boathouse to look at the pile of burnt wood.

"There." Sweetsea nodded at the largest of the remaining sheds, which Justice saw had a thick bricked wall at the end of it. "Carcasses. Bombs. The Magazine . . ."

So that was why Scorcher had been shouting a warning about the powder store. It was only a few yards from the fire, and if the flames had spread, everything on that spit of land would have gone to glory. The *Pandora*. Dunning. And John Valcourt Justice.

"It is kept locked," Sweetsea said as Justice strode to the door.

But he had turned the handle before Sweetsea spoke, and found it answered. There was a clatter as he pushed at it, and as soon as he was inside, he saw the key ring hanging from the lock.

Four keys. And one of them must be for the padlock at the gate, he decided, sending Scorcher to try it and explaining to Sweetsea what had happened.

Sweetsea nodded, as if he had heard the half of the story already from Lord William. One-armed, he used his head to gesture like a model mandarin Justice had seen brought back from China.

"That could have brought Dunning here last night," Justice said, holding out the little tract with the scribbled words on it. "Suspecting some mischief."

"Unless it was a remind-me for some work." Sweetsea clearly had a straightforward mind and preferred the simple solution to a problem, it seemed. "And if he were working here . . ." Sweetsea looked from the door and past the heap of smouldering ash to the boathouse. "He could have seen the fire start," he said, "run to douse it, and left his keys. Got caught." He gave Justice a sharp look. "Did you say there was an explosion?"

"I didn't," Justice said, wondering how Lord William could have learned that fact and why he had passed it on. "But there was."

Scorcher was back with the keys and the expected answer before Justice could say any more. So Dunning had locked the gate behind him. So the fire had been started from outside the fence.

"What was in that hut?" he asked Sweetsea.

"Nothing much, I believe. A barrel of pitch, oakum, some turpentine, the usual shipwright's stores."

"And the other fires?" he asked, aware now that Sweetsea must have been given the run of the place.

"Much the same. Bonfires, really. A pile of sawdust and shavings against a wall. A length of sailcloth wrapped around a block of tar."

Fires that would damage but not destroy, as Lilly said. And all lighted by much the same means, Justice guessed.

It appeared that Sweetsea had no more to say on the subject. "The carcass shed," he remarked, opening a shuttered window so that Justice could see what it contained. "He could have been doing anything," he said. "Dunning, I mean."

He could indeed, Justice thought as he looked at the fantastic array of weaponry that filled the long room. There must have been samples of every device that Francis had fabricated since he came to England, and Sweetsea was obviously familiar with them all.

"Carcasses," he said, using the same words as Lord William but with admiration instead of anxious anger in his voice. "Explosive carcasses. Floating bombs, torpedoes, catamarans."

Justice let his eye run over these appalling novelties as Sweetsea rattled off their names like a shopkeeper displaying his wares.

There were carcasses that looked like pairs of barrels joined by a bridle of chain. There were square boxes covered in lead and coffin shapes in sheeted copper. There were globes and cylinders, boxes with floats and boxes with anchors.

"Clever, you know," Sweetsea exclaimed as he rolled out a large copper sphere with striking arms that ran through seals in the shell, and got Scorcher to open it so that Justice could see how the flintlock fired in the powder chamber. "Devilishly clever. And deadly. Anchor them to the seabed and let them ride a fathom below the surface so that small boats can pass and ships of war will strike and blow their bottom timbers out. Set pairs of them adrift to catch the cables of a fleet. Tow them behind a line of longboats. One bump's enough to finish a first-rate."

"But why are they here?" Justice asked, guessing that Francis had fetched them from Portsmouth dockyard, where he was making infernal machines with the Admiralty's approval and the King's money.

"For trial, I suppose. With the plunging-boat." Sweetsea spoke absently, for he was looking at something in the far corner so shadowed in the afternoon gloom that it was hard to make out anything in detail.

But Justice caught the word *trial*. That was what Dunning had been doing when he and Scorcher rode down to the river last night—tipping carcasses into the water. Not buoys or markers, but carcasses, so that Sweetsea's sharpshooters could discover how best to sink them. So that Francis might learn how to make them less vulnerable. So that the cycle of trial and improvement could go on until the *Pandora* herself was ready to be tried.

"Do you see, sir?" Sweetsea spoke respectfully, as if he had just remembered that he had been invalided as a lieutenant and that the younger Justice outranked him. "This is new, Mr Justice. New since I was last here."

As Scorcher helped the crippled squire drag the curious object into a better light, Justice saw that it was a gun.

A gun of sorts, that was a cross between a duck gun and a blunderbuss. And beside it, with a running line neatly furled in a box, was a barbed harpoon of the kind that whalers used.

It was the simplest and most menacing weapon of them all. With such a gun the *Pandora* could drive a line into the side of any ship and pull a hundred-pound carcass of powder home against her hull.

No ship would be safe against such an instrument of war.

No wonder Lilly was alarmed. With this gun and two dozen carcasses a submarine could destroy Keith's blockading squadron off Boulogne in a night, make it impossible for ships to clear Plymouth, Portsmouth, Chatham . . .

No wonder Lilly was so ambivalent about Francis. For this was only one of a dozen devilments that the *Pandora* could use.

England might profit from any or all of them. Might use them to fend off Bonaparte for a decade. But in the end they would be turned against her.

By Francis—if he fell into French hands again, or went home to give his discoveries to his countrymen.

If not Francis, one day it would be someone else, and then the whole of England's navy would be outmoded and in danger of destruction.

For Pandora's box was truly open.

THAT DAUNTING THOUGHT was never far from Justice's mind for the next two days as he laboured to get everything Bristol-fashion, as Scorcher had put it.

After Sweetsea had left he had summoned all Lilly's men into the stable yard, like a captain calling the hands aft to address them, and left them in no doubt of their duties. "Regular patrols," he had said to the seamen who served about the place, the grooms, the gardeners, and the gamekeepers, mixing them on the watch-bills so that the sailors and landsmen shared the work. "No man leaves his post without an order from me." In the flickering light of the stable lamps he saw nods of agreement.

But there had been a murmur of protest when he had insisted that there would be no more warming tots in the small hours. Ever since Scorcher had told him that the seamen had access to grog and that such a senior man as Tooth was party to it, he had been certain that the slackness which had permitted the attacks on the boathouse had begun around that cosy fire in the carriage house; and tongues set wagging by ardent spirits could easily be heard by anyone with a sinister interest in the *Pandora*—anyone who was employed at Cuffwells, or was hidden close by, or was lodged among the shipwrights at Bucklers Hard.

So he had sent Scorcher into the village that night, with half a guinea in his pocket and orders to spend it in the two inns while he listened and looked. But Scorcher had come back at midnight, his money gone and his legs a little unsteady, to report that he had heard nothing and seen nothing suspicious. "Been in the water so long that the fish got tired of me," he said, shaking his head despondently.

Thursday had gone quickly. In the morning Warren and the Cowleys had completed the work on the hatchways, battening them down and opening them until they were sure they were watertight. He had been inside the rear compartment when Warren was adjusting the screws and latches, and as the sudden slam of the tight-fitting lid put out their candle, he had guessed with quickening pulse at the terrible death that would come to anyone trapped in it. Even Warren, a godless man if ever he met one, had been superstitiously moved to take out a lucky rabbit's foot and rub it.

And in the afternoon, his spirits restored, Warren had gone over all the working parts and satisfied himself that they were in order. Justice had to take his grumpy and grudging word for it. The labyrinth of metal in the *Pandora* was immensely more confusing to him than all the ropes and spars of a full-rigged ship had ever been, and the more he saw of its parts the more he was amazed that Francis could have foreseen how they would all come together before one rod of brass had left the foundry.

Friday had been the day for the Cowleys, for he set them to rig the *Pandora* and try her sails—work that he understood and enjoyed watching. Warren had begun the day by complaining that the Cowleys were getting in his way, and that Mr Francis had never given orders to rig the boat, but after he had cussed a little under his breath he had gone below to fiddle with his rods and levers.

By midday the Cowleys had made the shell of the *Pandora* look like one of the lug-boats that Justice had so often seen work off the beach at Hastings and made him eager to see her in the water. She might not handle so well, with such bulk and weight below the waterline, but she was perfectly disguised for work anywhere along the Channel coasts.

And in the afternoon he had taken Scorcher back to the carcass shed, to puzzle over each of its infernal devices until they knew how each would work and to what effect—they had even gone into the magazine and loaded a couple to be sure. If there was a real French threat to the *Pandora*, as Lilly suspected, and the peculiarly feeble attacks and fires were mysterious heralds of worse trouble to come, they might well need to set carcasses floating in the Beaulieu River and go hunting with that extraordinary gun.

They were troublesome thoughts because they were so speculative, and Justice returned from that strange armoury in an anxious mood. He sat alone for hours, brooding over the fire in Lilly's cabin-like study, spinning the little orrery as Lilly had done, and letting his mind run over questions he could not answer.

Questions that teased him into wakefulness several times that night. And each time it was doubts about Wykeham and the Romneys that disturbed his sleep.

At six he was up and giving orders for the day. At seven he breakfasted lightly, for he had that wretched race before him and the prospect of a heavy dinner after it. And then he stared moodily out of the window until the dawn showed through the early mist and the chime of the carriage house clock told him that it was time to leave.

"Boots," he said sharply to Scorcher, and as soon as he had been jacked into them he sent his man off to make his own way to Wykeham.

"Listen and look, Fred," he urged again. "One of us at least should learn something from the day."

83

❧ 9 ❧

For a November morning it was crisp and clear, the best of weather for riding.

"It be her Ladyship's birthday," the groom at Cuffwells had said to Justice, surprising him as he mounted, since Harriet had said nothing to him about such an occasion for her hedger-and-ditcher. But everyone else along the Beaulieu River seemed to know about it. Long before Justice glimpsed the octagonal tower of the great house rising above the trees, he had found himself crowded on the track by people making their way to Wykeham Abbey.

At the sides, where the grass was firm on the sandy soil, he passed whole families on foot, craftsmen from Bucklers Hard who were making a rare holiday of the event, cottagers, men in seagoing clothes who were probably fishermen, labourers jerkined in moleskin against the early frost. On the track itself, already cut up by a succession of vehicles, he came up with several red-cheeked farmers, with their wives hitched pillion behind them, as his neighbours often rode to Tenterden market. And as he tried to press on he had to edge his way past chaises filled with gentlefolk, staring ahead as though they were going about some private business that had nothing to do with the common crowd, past tradesmen's carts from Lymington, the men jolly, the women leaning inward to keep their finery from the splashing mud, past a pair of sharp-looking men trailing spare mounts, who were plainly intending to ride in Harriet's race, and past little groups of gypsies, carrying baskets with their wares and letting their tribe of dark-faced children tumble among the wheels and the clumping hooves to call for ha'pence or a crust.

It was just like a country fair in the making, and apart from a handful of Sweetsea's Volunteers, smart in their green uniforms and evidently due for drill or duty that afternoon, there was nothing in this cheerful scene to suggest that England was fighting a war for survival, nothing to remind the pleasure-seekers that beyond the narrow waters of the Channel, glimmering in the distance, there were powerful French armies which had learned to fight and plunder and burn in a dozen campaigns, and would go on the same kind of rampage in England if they could once get a footing ashore.

Nothing sinister at all, on the face of things, but for all the holiday mood around him Justice felt the chill touch of anxiety as he came out of the woods and saw Wykeham against the sky. If he was a Frenchman, sent by Fouché to lure Francis away, or to wreck the *Pandora*, or to mount some other and as yet unguessable combination of villainies, this was where he would come. He had no proof of it, and the festivity would make the discovery of proof more difficult, for it would provide the best of concealments for anything or anyone that might be hidden here. Yet he was sure, suddenly sure, because no other answer to the questions that kept him awake made sense.

He touched his heels to the flanks of his cob to catch the burly figure he saw ahead of him, and found Amos Sweetsea pleased to see him, and full of things to say about the great house as they came to it, four square, at the head of a drive of oaks and beeches.

Wykeham was a massive block of masonry, only two storeys high, except for the sturdy medieval gatehouse at the centre, yet running for forty yards on either side of that imposing entrance, its stone slates steep-pitched, its narrow windows mullioned and latticed behind the creeping ivy.

Most of the race-going crowd followed the drive round to the left, past an odd-looking belvedere that Sweetsea said covered an old pilgrim well, past the long wall of the kitchen garden, and past the stable block which lay across from it, making their way to the little knoll where the Romney family standard flew from a flagpole that must mark the start and finish of the race. But Sweetsea led him over the wooden bridge that crossed a half-dried moat, and they clattered into a cobbled courtyard that was still sufficiently like a cloister to recall its monastic origin, and still so ancient in its structure that on three sides of the square the upper rooms were reached by sets of stone stairs on the outside wall.

It was the fourth side, however, which dominated the whole house. In one corner the high tower Justice had seen from a distance rose up to remind the visitor that the bells of a great abbey had once rung out through its slatted sides; and beside it, as high-roofed as a cathedral nave, there ran a long hall. "Once the greatest tithe barn in England," Sweetsea said knowledgeably.

It was an impressive sight, and though Justice had been to other fine mansions as a guest he had never yet seen a property so old, or so vast, and he gazed in amazement at its scale.

"An odd place," Sweetsea said in the manner of a man with more modest domestic tastes; and Justice agreed with him, though he let the remark pass without comment as they gave their bridles to a groom and walked towards the doorway of the hall.

Odd for the Earl of Lymington, rich, second cousin to the Tory Prime Minister, and yet so given to levelling opinions and to deprecating tradition in the name of progress.

Odd for Lord William, too, who must be using some part of it for his experiments with gases, and other mysteries that would have earned him a burning in the years when the abbey was built. Odd for Lady Harriet, of whom all kinds of irregular behaviour were reported. Odd for Francis, so long and so far away from his American home, who seemed to be welcomed as one of the family. Odd, and even odder, perhaps, Justice thought, remembering how his suspicions had begun to run, for a man could squirrel himself away in the corridors and closets of such a rambling house and never be found.

It was this arithmetic of oddity that had added to doubt in Lilly's mind and uneasiness in his own.

"A MIRACLE OF ACCOMPLISHMENTS," Sweetsea said as they waited to come up to the earl and be welcomed.

Justice was not surprised by the hint of sarcasm, for the earl looked like the oddity he was. He was a brisk, raw-boned man, with a nose like a parrot's bill and a face like a frost-bitten leaf in autumn; and he was dressed in strong colours, as though he was about to set off for Epsom with a party of bucks from Tattersall's or White's. But his costume was reasonable enough for a man playing host to a horse race, and it was only as Sweetsea continued that Justice realized how indulgently he viewed the eccentricities of his eminent neighbour.

"Cuts oranges into caricatures. Tears paper into dancing mannikins." He shook his forefinger as Justice gave him a sceptical glance. "Seen him myself at dinner," he insisted. "Travels a lot. Collects antiquities." As Sweetsea nodded away at the walls, Justice noticed that classical busts and statuary stood before each of the windows in the great hall. "Thinks he's been here before, too," Sweetsea went on. "Been a senator in ancient Rome. Crusader. Things like that. Reads Cicero with one eye and the Turf Register with the other."

"You exaggerate," Justice said, laughing at the man's whimsy, and looking past the earl to see whether he could pick out Harriet among the guests who stood about in clusters, drinking the tankards of mulled claret that a butler was filling from a large silver bowl in front of the fire. But there were too many people there, moving about and greeting each other, and chattering so loudly that he could scarcely hear what Sweetsea was saying.

"Not much," Sweetsea replied, blowing out his cheeks as if he found the Earl of Lymington the most amiably preposterous of men, and then stopping to chaffer with his Lordship while Justice was passed on with a casual nod and a how-d'ye-do.

Harriet was so surrounded by well-wishers and admirers that Justice had wandered past her, looking further into the hall, before she called to him; and then, taking his birthday wishes as a politeness of no great consequence between them, she smiled and drew him towards her friends.

"You are to have Robert's mount," she said at once. "Since he has not come, the best . . ."

"Not come?" Justice was so dismayed that Francis had not kept his promise that he cut into Harriet's explanation, hearing his voice betray his disappointment before he could control it.

But Harriet took no notice. "So like Robert," she said, turning for confirmation to the group around her. She was wearing what Justice took to be a long black dress, until she swung back to face him and he saw the gleam of boot leather which told him it was only a full riding cloak over her customary shirt and breeches. "I told you the other day that he comes pretty much as it suits him, and today, it seems, don't suit."

There was just enough bravado in her voice to make Justice

suspect that she might be hurt, possibly jealous that the American had found something better to do on that special day, but she was too busy with introductions to show her feelings.

"Mr Breney brought the news last night," she said quickly, indicating a comfortable-looking man with a fine set of whiskers framing his face, but first bringing forward a dark-haired woman of about thirty. "Mademoiselle Gérard de Rougemont," she said; and then, as if to avoid any hint of patronage, she was more familiar. "Marie-Louise to her friends."

Justice bowed, and was about to pass on to Breney when he caught the Frenchwoman looking so searchingly at him that he felt they must have met on some previous occasion and that he was rudely forgetting. It was only a fleeting impression, and yet it was enough to remind Justice that he had felt much the same when Harriet saw him for the first time, down at the river, and when Lord William had stared at him as he climbed out of the hatchway of the *Pandora*. To remind him, and yet to make him shake off the notion as a silliness, easily explained if the people at Wykeham had been gossiping about him.

"Robert's lawyer," Harriet said as Breney stepped up, so much the affable professional man of the old school that he at once began asking Justice whom he knew in London, seeking common acquaintances, as if any post-captain sufficiently acceptable to be found in a great country house would have influential or notable friends. But Harriet cut him off in mid-enquiry. "Parson Berdmore," she said, taking Justice over to a tall man in clerical black. "Vicar of Minstead, and if he'll forgive me, the devil of a rider to hounds." Mr Berdmore smirked, as if he were forgiving her, and she bobbed at the two men next to him. "Mr Pocock, who owns the Sowley ironworks. Mr Wort, of the New Inn . . ."

As she rattled away, Justice saw there was certainly no snobbery about the Romneys—a parson, an ironmaster, an innkeeper . . . there was a haw-hawing military man with some kind of title, a substantial farmer, and then he found himself shaking hands with a weary-faced man of fifty, who appeared to have some connection with the Romneys, though Justice could not exactly catch what Harriet said for the hub-bub around them. It was something about a cousin of cousins, as they say in Ireland, and a word about her father's politics, but the man was repeating his name clearly enough.

"Kibbie Fanshawe," he said, as though his unusual first name needed spelling.

"Who brings us Marie-Louise," Harriet said with a curious edge to her voice. "And such a reputation for chasing the Wexford foxes that he'll press us all hard today, I'll be bound."

Justice saw that the man was about to speak when a small girl ran out of a tangle of legs and clasped Harriet with a delighted squeal.

"My ward, Emma," Harriet said. She bent to catch what the child was whispering, shook her head, and stood up again to notice the attractive young woman who stood modestly apart. "And Miss Botting, her governess."

"Until today," Fanshawe put in, with an insistent sharpness that Harriet did not seem to notice, though Justice thought he was hinting that the governess should take the child away; and he tutted irritably when little Emma made a dart at him and then gave Justice a teasing push.

This time Justice heard what she said before she ran off with Miss Botting in chase.

"Play hide-my-eyes again."

He had no idea what she meant, and there was suddenly so much talk that nobody bothered to explain.

"I WAS SORRY to be the bearer of disappointing news." As more guests had come to greet and distract Harriet, the group had broken up, and Breney had taken the chance to introduce himself again, quite formally, as Brazear Breney, attorney-at-law, of Clifford's Inn.

"Not at all," Justice said, seeking to minimize his first reaction. "But I had expected to meet Mr Francis here. Lady Harriet and Lord William have spoken so much to his credit."

"Understandably." Breney seemed to require no other explanation. "He is a remarkable man, as I should know." He gave Justice a shrewd look, like a man trying to decide whether to speak freely. "I am his man of business . . ." He hesitated. "In his dealings with the, um, the officers of the British government, if you follow me."

For some reason, Justice could tell, Breney was sounding him out.

"I do," he said tersely, giving nothing away that Breney

could not have known or guessed from the gossip at Wykeham, but conceding enough to encourage the man, whether
the soft-spoken lawyer was talking only of the Admiralty contract or was hinting at the separate and even more secret arrangement with Lilly. Could he have learned of some threat to
the *Pandora*, or to Francis himself, and be seeking to pass on a
warning—to find someone to trust in this house of ques-
tionable loyalties, where everyone seemed to be a friend of
liberty and nobody was a friend of Mr Pitt? Justice suspected
that Breney had come to see the place for himself, when business at Winchester brought him so close, even though he had
known that Francis would not be there.

"Why did Francis not come when he promised?" Justice
put the honest and most simple question. If Breney was really
close to Francis, he would know the answer and put Justice's
mind at rest. No one else seemed to be in the least concerned
about the American's absence, taking his irregular movements
for granted, but Justice was getting more concerned with each
day that passed. He had the fidgety sense he had sometimes
felt at sea when nothing appeared to be wrong, and yet he had
caught a distant shift in the wind, or in the set of the sea, or
seen some slight sign that told him that the ship he was ap-
proaching was not all she seemed to be.

And more than once his life had turned upon it.

"If you ask my opinion," Breney was saying in his measured legal voice: "well, it would spoil Lady Harriet's day if
she knew it, but I think he has no taste for riding breakneck
across country, even to please her. I think he values his bones
and his wits above any woman's opinion of him."

Once again Breney was speaking in a way that seemed to im-
ply more than he said; and though Justice at first took his
remark as a gentle gibe at his own folly in agreeing to race
across Harriet's hedges and ditches, without any chance to try
out the horse she had offered him and without any idea of the
lie of the course, he soon saw that Breney might be making
some oblique comment on the relationship between Francis
and Harriet.

Francis. Francis and Emma. It was the child that came into
his mind as Breney prosed on.

"If you ask me as his man of business, of course . . ."
Breney paused for effect. "If you ask me confidentially, that
is, I should say that Mr Francis stays in London because he

impatiently awaits the arrival of a steam engine he has ordered from Birmingham—or at least the parts of it, as I understand the matter.''

How like a lawyer, Justice thought. To have two explanations of the same event, and be quite content to offer both of them. ''You thus understand the matter,'' he came back sharply, his desire for a definite answer pushing him a little beyond the normal courtesies. ''Do you know?''

Breney looked about him, as he might have done in court, treating the company to the impassive glance he must have practised on a hundred difficult witnesses in his time.

''I am an attorney, Captain Justice,'' he said, with reproving impatience. ''I therefore distinguish between what I think, what I hear, and what I know with enough certainty to stand up and swear to it. Now I have told you what I think.'' He pedantically raised a finger for each of his points. ''Next. What I heard from Mr Joel Barlow, who is a particular friend of Mr Francis, and ventures with him in the business of a steam vessel for some river or other in America. Before I left London for the Winchester assizes, he told me he confidently expected to see Mr Francis in London this very week.''

''Though he was promised here, to Lady Harriet?'' Justice came back to his first question, finding it hard to accept that a man could let his obligations so multiply and contradict each other.

''Perhaps he is too pressed.'' Breney was obviously reluctant to criticise his unreliable client, and he came back to the last of the points which justified what he had said, raising a third finger. ''Evidence? Ten days ago I wrote to Mr Francis to say that the government had at last given him permission to ship his engine when he pleased, and that the necessary papers were being drawn at the Treasury Office. Add that to my suppositions and I say that he is now in London.''

Though Breney spoke as if he were describing a simple business transaction, Justice was astonished at his news. It was only four days ago that Hatherley had spoken so disparagingly about Francis and the steam engine, insisting that the American was interested in the *Pandora* solely because of the money it gave him—''to build his precious steamboat,'' Hatherley had said in such a tone that Justice could not tell whether he considered it a mere toy or something that must be kept from the French, come what may. For Hatherley had gone on to say that Matthew Boulton himself had doubts, and had written to ask if it were right to despatch such an engine to America "when there's a war on, and Lord knows what use could be made of it if the French should lay hands on it."

Breney was waiting while Justice considered what he had said, as if some conclusion might be drawn from his remarks. But they had left Justice in a state of racing puzzlement.

How could anyone in Whitehall have given such permission at this time, unless there had been a flow of guineas into the pocket of a well-placed official or even a minister without too many scruples? It happened all the time, he knew. But to let Francis have his engine. Perhaps to let him return to America, leaving so much unfinished, so much at risk . . . He could not believe that Breney, who struck him as a straightforward man for a lawyer, could be a party to a deception that would be the ruin of all the work for which Francis had been employed.

Breney. A lawyer. A man who would know secrets and never reveal them, except by nods and winks. Could this, perhaps, be the reason why the attorney had sought him out—to convey a covert warning?

"WE HAVE SUCH THINGS in Wexford every autumn," Fanshawe said, joining them to ask Justice whether he had ever risked his neck in a cross-country race before. "Your Irishman is born to harum-scarum enterprises of all sorts, and the wilder they come the more he likes 'em."

"No matter whether they are sporting, political, or insurrectionary?" As Breney scored his point Justice sensed a sudden tension between the two men—a political difference, possibly, for Breney had spoken up like a Tory and Fanshawe was both an Irishman and a radical like the earl.

But Fanshawe was not ruffled by the gibe. "Some men are born to liberty," he said evenly, as if he were underlining some argument in an earlier acquaintance. "And some have it thrust upon them, Mr Breney." He saw Breney purse his lips with condescending indifference, and turned back to Justice. "If you haven't done it before," he said, "well, it seems simple enough till you try it." He looked out of the window as if he could see the course running away to the west of the house. "Two miles out. You'll find a gentleman there to see you go round. But it's coming back you've got to be wary."

He broke off as Breney excused himself and went over to join Mademoiselle Gérard and Miss Botting, with little Emma tripping beside them, as they came coated and wrapped on their way out to the race.

"It's ourselves must be going as well," Fanshawe said, with a last word of advice as the guests and other riders began to drift out of the great hall. "Stay close to me when the fun begins, Mr Justice, for I saw it all when they were flagging it. Flags going out, that's to say, but you find your own way home. Hedges, gates, stiles, anything will do. Head for the flagpole, damn it, hang on, and let your horse bring you in or throw you as the fancy takes him." He stopped as if his last remark had put him in mind of something. "Must see to my mount, my dear fellow," he said, nodding himself away.

There was something that grated in this patronising humour, Justice decided, watching Fanshawe greet a dozen guests on his way to the door, wondering what the man was doing in the house and how long he had been staying there.

Kibbie Fanshawe. The name told him nothing, though the man's manner suggested that he was some kind of poor relation—a person who had learned to dissemble, to seem amiable and amusing for his own ends without wholly concealing his resentment at his equivocal position. For resentment there certainly was beneath that easy Irish charm, and Justice felt that some of it was inexplicably directed at him. Fanshawe was a shade too ingratiating, and all through their brief talk his eyes had belied his helpfulness, given Justice the impression that he was being inspected as if he might be a rival claimant on the charity or goodwill of the Romneys; and as that notion came to him Justice recalled the sharp way the Irishman had glanced at Harriet as she introduced him.

He shook the feeling away as casually as it had come. It was ridiculous. It was none of his business if the man was a sponger. Every great house had to bear with such people, as hedgehogs bore with fleas.

"THE FRENCHWOMAN?" Justice asked as Sweetsea rejoined him, and saw that his question caused some embarrassment.

"The new governess," Sweetsea began, looking across to where Mademoiselle Gérard and Miss Botting were still talking to Breney, and changing his answer as he spoke. "On account of Eliza," he started again, and rushed at his point. "The fact is, Justice, Miss Botting's betrothed. To me. And has named the day."

"My felicitations," Justice said, smiling at the bashful forty-year-old bachelor as he told of his courtship. A year or more since the first asking, Sweetsea reported. Miss Botting, it seemed, had been loath to leave her small charge. "Cared for her since she was an infant in France," he added, "and could not be persuaded."

"Until now?" From the way he was telling his tale Justice sensed there had been a sudden change.

"Until Mademoiselle Gérard came." A most fortunate arrival, he declared. "French, you know, and therefore quite suitable."

"But she came as a guest?" The Frenchwoman and Fanshawe were beginning to interest Justice.

"Not exactly." Mademoiselle Gérard was looking at them now, as if some trick of sound had carried the use of her name to her ears, and she gave a cold smile as Sweetsea bobbed to her. She had the air of an actress, Justice thought—like an actress who had been hired for a play and arrived without seeing her part. "It's a romantic tale," Sweetsea said in the tone of a man who had been touched by romance himself.

"She came with Fanshawe from Ireland, Lady Harriet said."

"But before that—a castaway." Sweetsea warmed to his story when he saw that Justice knew nothing of it. "On her way to Quebec from . . . I can't remember. Rochelle, Rochefort, perhaps, and the ship sprung a leak in a storm. She got ashore with two sailors and a boy. Near Cork, I think. Lost everything, of course, and was quite destitute, she says." He glanced at Justice as if he were unsure of the details. "Then she met Fanshawe, and found that she'd known a mutual friend in France, years before. Happy coincidence."

"Indeed." Justice was not so credulous as Sweetsea, who was ready to accept any chain of events that led to his own good fortune.

A shipwreck. A fortunate meeting.

Well, it was possible. People did lose all their property at sea and rely on charity to set them up again. Mutual friends— well, again, there were so many contacts between France and Ireland, what with exiles, and rebels crossing to plot with

Bonaparte's generals, and family connections.

And it was plausible, no doubt. But if it were not true it was exactly the kind of story that one would invent to account for an otherwise unexplained arrival in Ireland, a landing at some remote beach between Kinsale and Skibbereen . . .

"I think . . ." Sweetsea broke into the run of his thoughts so hesitantly that Justice thought he was about to be indiscreet and suggest that Fanshawe had brought the Frenchwoman to England as his *bonne amie*. In an unconventional house like Wykeham such an ambiguous relationship would probably be accepted. But he was wrong. "I think they were on their way to London," Sweetsea said. "Where she had more friends, and might find employment. Nothing was said precisely, not in my hearing anyway. But Fanshawe came here on the road, to visit the earl on some political business, and there was an opportunity . . ." His voice tailed away, and Justice saw that he had no real idea of what had happened to make Eliza Botting change her mind.

And something had happened since Fanshawe and the Frenchwoman had come to Wykeham.

For the first time since Lilly had confided his anxieties and suspicions, Justice began to feel that he had touched the outer filaments of a web of intrigue that was being woven to snare the *Pandora*, though he could not begin to guess at the full shape and size of it. But if he was right, the next move would not be long in coming.

With a dull boom the bell in the tower summoned the riders to the race.

❧ 10 ❧

THE EARL HAD CERTAINLY done things in style for his daughter and the whole countryside.

Under the last golden leaves of the elms clumped near the starting place, his servants had set out trestle tables loaded with barrels of the best Wykeham ale, with baskets of bread and whole sliced cheeses, and there were two boiling pans bubbling with faggot puddings and pig trotters.

There would be a rush for these tempting refreshments once the race was over and the fiddlers and hurdy-gurdy men began to draw groups of dancers round them, but for the moment all the spectators were crowded close to the flagpole or strung out loosely on the run down across the home paddock to the first of the fences.

"It's as lively as a launch!" the ironmaster from Sowley was exclaiming as Justice came up to the improvised saddling ring and found himself swept into a new round of introductions.

"Here's Mr Dickson from Brockenhurst," Sweetsea said, presenting a lizard-faced man, whose skin hung loose at the throat, and whose habit of darting his tongue between his teeth increased the likeness. "And Captain Dodd, I believe."

The captain seemed as bold as his friend Mr Dickson was nervy—a travelling half-pay blowhard, Justice judged, who would cadge a ride from anyone's stable and bore everyone to death with his bullyragging anecdotes.

But there was only trickery there, he was sure, not treachery; and not even trickery in Mr Baitup, a prosperous-looking farmer, heavy from jowls to thighs, who was clearly asking too much from his horse. The beast was already lathered, and it staled as Sweetsea brought Justice up to get a pleased-to-meet-you from its owner.

Two more soldiers, whose names Justice did not catch, claimed some kind of cousinship to the Romneys and said they had come over from the garrison at Dorchester "to have a dash," though Justice suspected that they might be more interested in carrying off one of Harriet's fine horses than in paying her a birthday compliment. Parson Berdmore was the last man in the world to be doubted. "Thinks of nothing but God and horses," Sweetsea sais as the Vicar of Minstead settled his fretting animal. "And *he* thinks of nothing but himself," Sweetsea added, nodding at a man he called Cropland, who was some superior kind of steward in the New Forest and as supercilious as though he were its Lord Warden. "Chicken-hearted," Sweetsea mumbled, and as he led the way to the last of the riders in the enclosure, Justice had come to the conclusion that they were all the kind of men one met at an unfashionable hunt. Odd, perhaps, but not to be suspected.

The last of them was the oddest, at least in appearance, for he was dressed in a baggy half-buttoned coat, a starched cravat with a jewelled stickpin, green worsted gloves, poorly cut breeches, and boots so sloppy that the spurs fell back from his heels; and to top his bizarre costume, he wore a smoking cap and carried a longish bamboo cane instead of a whip. He looked so peculiar, Justice observed, that you paid more attention to what he was wearing than to him.

His name was Bland, Sweetsea said. Henry Bland, "and something of a nabob, from India." A neighbour, too, since the summer. "At Lepe, a little beyond my place."

Only another oddity in a mixed bag of a dozen, as Justice reckoned up the horses, for he could see that the twelfth rider would be Lord William, who was preparing to mount as Harriet passed him with a sisterly slap for good luck.

"You can gallop, of course?" she asked, giving Justice a look that implied a sudden qualm about his skills as a rider.

"I can try." And since that sounded like false modesty he gave Harriet a grin in return. "Or die game," he added, and felt a clutch of unexpected feeling. She was dressed as he had seen her that first afternoon, in a short thick jacket, shirt and breeches, and she was all eagerness and energy, as few women were, with a freshness he found irresistible.

"I would prefer you to survive, Mr Justice," she said in a cool voice. "Our acquaintance might otherwise be disagreeably short."

A small grizzle-whiskered groom stood behind her, holding two magnificent roans, so matched that they might have been twins.

"Hero," Harriet cried, taking one of the bridles and letting the groom pass the other to Justice. "And Leander." She gave

Justice an odd look. "Let us hope, sir, that history does not repeat itself."

She was mounted and away as a huntsman blew a rallying cry on his horn, leaving Justice trying to recall what fate had befallen Leander in the Greek myth.

THE HUNTSMAN BLEW another long gurgle, making the horses restless as they were coming into a rough sort of line, for they were all hunters who knew what the sound meant—Mr Baitup's weight-carrier, in fact, was so keen to get the day over and the burden off his back that he threatened to bolt and had to be coaxed back into place by a pair of cursing grooms.

While Mr Baitup and his mount were being settled, the earl was calling over the simple rules that Fanshawe had already reported to Justice, crying into the rising wind so feebly that only those closest to him caught the words, and looking a little apprehensively at the long dark bar of cloud that was beginning to blow in from the west.

Justice paid little attention to the earl, or to the threatening change in the weather, for his mind was on the course ahead of him. It was hard enough going out for a day's hunting in fresh country, when you could count on the most docile horse from a friend's stable or a patient old hack from the liveryman's stable, but this race was a very different matter. He could already feel the power of Leander beneath him, and he could barely contain the horse as he looked at the first hurdle—a clipped fence of beeches which seemed an impossibly high jump at the end of a pell-mell dash down two hundred yards of slippery grass.

He kept catching glimpses of his rivals. There was Captain Dodd fortifying himself from a flask, liquor and wind together giving his face a purplish flush. Lord William was trying to back his horse between Dodd and Fanshawe, and Mr Dickson was making unhelpful comments without noticing that his own horse was going round like a top. Behind him he heard one of the military gentlemen say "clever as a cat, and never puts a foot wrong," just as his horse stumbled and his companion gave a raucous laugh. The Vicar of Minstead, a little farther off, had his hands clasped, as though he were about to lean out of his pulpit and give the text. And when Justice turned to Harriet, close by him, there was encouragement in the smile she gave him.

He took a deep breath and looked to the flagpole, where the

earl now stood with his hat raised in his right hand. His arm swept down, and they were off.

With the screech the huntsman always gave when a fox ran clear from cover.

THEY WERE OFF. Suddenly they were thirty, fifty yards down the slope, all in a cluster, with the vicar at the head, and Mr Baitup wasting himself at the tail with shouts of "get-along-forrid" and other cries affected by hunt servants and followers.

There was a wild excitement about it all, reminding Justice of a day when he had been overtaken by a troop of cavalry at exercise, and had been so carried along by them that he ended the charge in the first rank, yelling and waving his riding crop like a sword.

Fanshawe was shouting now. So was Harriet. But he could make nothing of their words over the thunder of hooves. They were all packed close in that first rush, for no one wanted to waste ground by spreading to right or left; and in the last twenty yards before the line of crisp brown leaves came at them, it seemed to be the horses rather than their riders who made room for the tangle of legs to stretch, to flick at the rise, and go over in unbroken strides.

There was scarcely a slip as they came down like a brown cascade onto the meadow that would take them to the first of the streams, meandering so erratically that it only left odd places for a horse to jump it clear and steady before facing the hedge beyond it.

For the first time, as they came to the loops and curves, the field was beginning to break into smaller groups.

Justice saw the vicar still ahead of him. Harriet was on his left, Hero and Leander matching muscle and stride, bits jangling together. Fanshawe was on his right, and a little beyond Lord William was overreaching him, doing surprisingly well. For all his clumsy manner, Justice saw, the man could make his horse go, and as they cleared a couple of light hedgerows Romney was already beginning to move out and challenge the vicar, elbows and feet splayed, so that he looked at a disadvantage, but moving out all the same.

Ten fences out Justice began to enjoy himself. He knew enough about horses to be aware that Leander was a magnificent creature, far better than any hunter he had ever been given the chance to ride, and that, provided he could keep in the saddle, he would be brought round to the finish all up and going.

And then the twelfth jump reminded him that pride can go before a fall. Trying to let Leander choose his own way over a nasty row of hawthorns, with only a few sheep hurdles placed to mask their tearing spines, he let the horse get too close, and there was a moment of pitch and stumble that almost un-nerved him as they landed and Leander half-footed to pick up his stride again.

Glancing back to see where he had so nearly come to grief, he saw that one of the officers from Dorchester had gone head over tip as his horse refused, and that Mr Baitup had seized the excuse to pull up his wheezing nag and drag unmercifully at the wretched man's legs.

That left ten of them in the race, and before Justice could bring himself straight he felt Fanshawe bump, and bump again, the rump of the horse pulling uncomfortably at his calf, then forcing Leander away towards Hero. Though Harriet saw what was happening in time, she had to swing wider, almost to the white marker flag, and Justice caught the hiss of an ostler's curse as she looked across to Fanshawe.

They were all over, safe enough, and running over patches of sand and heather across a low hill before Justice could think about that casual collision. It might have been his fault—it was easy to pull at a horse when you turned. And yet he had an odd sense that it was deliberate. Could Fanshawe be so keen to win that he would seek a petty advantage of that kind? He had certainly taken his chance to go up two lengths, and now Justice was finding it hard to see through the veil of mud he threw up as they plodded more slowly through damper meadows and a succession of gated fields that might give them an easier ride home.

The vicar. Lord William. Fanshawe. Away to the left Dickson and Dodd were level-pegging. Cropland and Bland were out of sight. And Harriet was close, biding her time, it seemed, though Justice could not guess whether she was simply pacing Hero until she was ready to bid for the lead or whether there was something else on her mind, holding her back.

They were up and over, with Harriet pointing to a tall copse which must stand close to their turn for home. Justice pushed almost unwittingly at his stirrups to reassure himself, and Leander responded, lengthening his stride.

Coming to the marker, now, past the stand of larch and

bir... a wooden fence where a cottager and his family sat to see them all go by, a dozen yards of boggy land, a stretching rise to the far bank of the second stream, and there was the earl's steward, sitting impassively on his horse, his hat raised to greet Lady Harriet as she reached the flag. Beside him, Justice saw as he headed Leander round to recross the stream and go down to the little wood, there was a farm dray, with the carter ready to follow on and sweep up anyone who had fallen by the wayside on the way out or the way back.

Between the trees they rode one after another, for the track was too narrow for passing, and as they came out into a large field Justice saw the vicar, Lord William, Dickson, and Dodd going left, picking a line which would take them round the end of the monstrous hedge which Harriet was facing, with Fanshawe at her heels.

It was all spears of thorn and bramble rising from a bank of brown bracken, and from the way it lay back towards the stream Justice guessed there would be a running ditch soaking the ground in front of it.

For a second or two he could not make up his mind, and then he let Leander go after Harriet and Fanshawe. If she kept at it she must expect to save a good deal of time, and to cut in before the vicar; and the notion had no sooner come into his head than he saw her snatch a glance at him, lean forward, and then take Hero half a dozen strides clear of Fanshawe to give him and herself ample room.

She lifted well, and over, and was gone with a hoick and holler that showed she could no longer contain herself, whatever might be troubling her.

And at that moment Justice was astonished to see Fanshawe pull right in front of him, as though he had suddenly changed his mind and decided to go the other way, or had lost his nerve and was dragging his horse to refuse.

He could do nothing to check at that speed, and Fanshawe's horse hit Leander a staggering blow on the chest, as Fanshawe shouted what might have been an oath or an apology. Then, in a blur of browns and greens, with whinnying horses and the sensation of pounding hooves about him, Justice felt himself clutch vainly at Leander's neck and spin over, thumping into the bank, cradling his arms to protect his head, feeling the sharpest of pains in his knee as he tried to roll clear.

"Up. Up if you can." Half blinded by mud and bracken fronds, half winded, and sickened by a dragging blow in the groin as he went over the saddle, he could barely tell which way was up. But the words of his grandfather's groom came back over the years from childhood, driving him to stand, though he swayed like a drunkard when he put his weight on his injured knee.

He heard himself shout. The ground spun and heaved around him, and when he cleared his eyes he was astonished to see Fanshawe pelting away towards the gate over which the vicar had led the rest of the field.

He seesawed for a moment, cursing Fanshawe for bringing him down, cursing him for carelessness or worse, cursing him for riding off without a word or a helping hand . . . He had scarcely done cursing when he realized that he was on his feet and that Fanshawe had gone on with the race.

He heard hooves, turned to look for Leander, sensed something dark rearing above him as everything turned cold and colourless, and tipped forward into a foot of muddy water slopping through the nettle-bound ditch.

HE SEEMED TO be slung over a saddle like a rolled cloak, and a voice came and went as he bumped along, his head swinging. He vomited, and it was all blackness again.

There was the voice again. He could make no sense of the words, but they came from close to him, now. His face was wet, as though he had been crying, and he was being carried like a child.

Stunned. Sickeningly stunned, with a deep throbbing misery in the head wound he had brought back from France, and his only clear thought was that the cuirassier was carrying him away from the beach where he had been struck down.

But the knife was the first thing he saw as he forced his eyes open. It was only a few inches away, and a gleam of light caught the whole blade down to the reddened tip.

He grabbed at the knife, saw it float away from him, blinked, saw that he was looking at a long cheroot wrapped in slivered paper, and that the strange-looking man called Bland was puffing it with every sign of satisfaction.

Before Justice could think of anything else, with the waywardness of a man regaining his senses, he found himself wondering what kind of man carried a tinder-box when he went racing.

And a cheroot.

"Coming round?" Bland spoke gently, in a straightforward

voice, with only a trace of accent that meant nothing to Justice in his mazed condition. He had kept himself aloof in the saddling ring, like a stranger, but now he was all consideration. "It's a hut," he said, as he noticed Justice staring about him.

A charcoal burner's hut, for sure, to judge by the charred smell of it. But what was he doing there with Bland beside him? "Where?" he asked, fully conscious at last. "How long?" And then: "Leander?"

"One thing at a time, Mr Justice." Bland held out a flask. "Here. From Antigua. I'm told they call it the Sailor's Friend."

Justice coughed as he splashed the fiery sweetness into his gullet, covering his surprise at Bland's cool remarks. It was not so much the casual use of his name that had taken him unawares. What had touched a nerve, and alerted his fuddled senses, was the intimate, almost calculated tone in which Bland had offered the navy rum and referred to Antigua.

Even in his wretched state, plagued by bangs and bruises, he read some kind of signal into those two naval images. Rum, Antigua rum, which took its name from the great dockyard in the West Indies.

A signal that there was something wrong here at Wykeham and that Bland was aware of it, even if he was like Hatherley, who also came at you slantwise, hinting without saying anything you could hold him to afterwards. For every sailor knew that Jamaica, not Antigua, rum was the lower deck's usual ration. Then why mention Antigua? Unless Bland knew enough of Justice's own story to make an oblique reference to the place where his career was nearly wrecked.

He said nothing, and let the rum do its reviving work. Bland might be nothing more than a good Samaritan. But if he was not what he seemed, if he had some special mission here, and was simply letting Justice know where to turn for a friend if he needed one, well, it would do no harm to ignore that gambit and offer one of his own to make sure. For if Bland was another of Hatherley's eyes, or watching in some other way for some other purpose . . .

"That man Fanshawe is a fool, a damned fool," Bland said with surprising vehemence. "He could have killed you." He settled Justice to rest more comfortably on his folded coat. He was clearly exasperated by the accident. "Saw you go down from four fields away," he said. "Head down in the ditch when I got there, and bubbling your last breath away."

He stood up and went to the rough door, opening it to peer out, and Justice saw the rain that was now driving across the Wykeham fields. He must have been senseless for ten minutes, maybe more.

"If that carter's gone by he'll not be back for half an hour," he said, craning out for another look. "If he comes this way at all." He sat down on a rough bench by the door. "You were better in here than lying out to soak in it."

"I'm grateful," said Justice, holding up a hand to decline another stiff tot of rum. He raised himself, finding that he had taken no real harm from the fall—no bones broken at least, and he was about to suggest that they start walking back when he tried his legs and found one knee numb and painful.

Bland noticed his effort. "So we'll wait," he said, and sat silently, puffing at his cheroot.

"They say you were in India." Justice spoke easily, with no more emphasis than Bland had put on his reference to rum and Antigua.

"Do they, now?" It was Bland's turn to be reserved. "Yes. There and elsewhere."

It would do no harm to press him, Justice decided. If what he said meant nothing to Bland, it would seem no more than a busybody's enquiry. But any man that Hatherley trusted would know that Lloyd's had become the chief means by which marine intelligence from all over the world reached the Admiralty.

It was the underwriters at Lloyd's who insured friend, neutral, and sometimes foe, whose agents reported what ships sailed and what they carried, and paid all kinds of moneys in foreign ports.

"In insurance, perhaps? Ship insurance, by any chance?"

"That's a prosperous occupation these days," Bland replied, avoiding a direct answer as he heard the cart creaking towards the hut. He paused before he looked out into the rain, which was beginning to slacken into a heavy sea mist.

"And risky, too, Captain Justice. As you may know."

Justice's low-hung spurs scraped on the ground, and he almost tripped.

"Careful does it," Bland said, coming back to give Justice a hand to the door, and standing aside as Scorcher ducked in to help him.

❧ 11 ❧

JUSTICE LAY BACK on the sofa and looked round the apartment which Francis occupied whenever he stayed at Wykeham.

"Robert's rooms," Harriet had cried as soon as she saw him limp away from the cart. "Of course you must stay. But the rest of the house is full of guests and you'll be quieter there."

He had only twisted his knee, Justice protested, and duty called him back to Cuffwells.

"What nonsense!" Harriet had brushed away his objections. She was a young woman who was accustomed to get what she wanted, and before Justice could insist on leaving she had instructed Scorcher to help him up to this fine set of rooms overlooking the great courtyard, to get fresh linen and a robe from Lord William's valet while his clothes were being scrubbed, to get the fire blazing, to order a tray of the best dinner dishes from the kitchen, and to do anything else that was needed to make his master comfortable. "Thirty guests for dinner," she pleaded, "or I'd have seen to it all myself."

And comfortable was the word for it, Justice admitted, stretching out lazily and watching the play of the fire and candle flames on the panelled walls. Three hours of sleep, a fresh trout, slices of beef, a game pie, and a fine bottle from the earl's cellar had much restored his battered frame.

Scorcher had come back from the kitchen with very little gossip. There was talk about Fanshawe and the Frenchwoman, he said, but the servants were close. Loyal to the family, he added, and perhaps money passed—he'd heard nothing out of the ordinary, except . . .

"Except what?" Anything that caught Scorcher's sharp ear might be important.

"Except . . . well, meals at odd hours," Scorcher said. "Grumbling. About the madame. Faddish, finicky, and hungry was what one of the maids was a-calling her till the housekeeper came across with a quietener." He shook his head in disappointment at his failure to winnow more from the backstairs chaff.

But Justice saw a grain of significance in what he had gleaned. If Mademoiselle Gérard was eating alone she was a fusspot. If Fanshawe was spending irregular hours in her room . . . or if she was feeding an unacknowledged guest . . . perhaps more than one . . . If only he could make a thorough search of the place, question the guests, chivvy the servants . . . His sense of frustration was making him wish for powers he did not possess—the kind of powers a police agent would have in France, where a minister would issue a warrant on mere suspicion.

A wish that was new to him, for he was not by nature a man who found it easy to pry into another person's affairs, and it was only necessity that had brought him to accept the distasteful part of his clandestine work for the Board of Beacons, Bell, Buoys, and Mercantile Messengers. The necessity of survival—his own, and his country's.

But whether he liked it or not, the work had to be done, and accident had given him a chance to start on it. This was the room that Francis used at Wykeham, and some clue to the mysteries of the house must be found in it.

In a few minutes he had realized that there was precious little to see, short of breaking open cabinets and drawers, or forcing the lock into the adjoining room which Harriet said Francis used as a studio. There was nothing that belonged to the American in the bedroom, apart from a wardrobe of clothing and a pair of watercolour portraits entitled "Joel" and "Ruth," and signed by Francis with his initials; and the dressing room was equally impersonal. There was a chest of drawers, two of which were locked, an empty sea chest, and one of the long copper-sheathed boxes which Justice had seen in the carcass shed, with cushions set on it to make a low seat by the window that looked across to the gateway.

The main room, however, was dominated by a large cartoon over the fireplace. "Here's a rum thing," Scorcher said, catching sight of it as he went to replace a pair of guttering candles, and then holding them up so that he and Justice could see it better.

Drawn in brown ink on draughtsman's paper, it was a vast panorama of towns set in a fertile countryside criss-crossed by canals and divided by a river running from the mountains to a prosperous ship-filled harbour. "America," Justice said, pointing to the spread-winged eagle at the centre of the design and the pattern of stars and stripes which framed it. "And Columbia, no doubt," he added, for there was a figure descending from the clouds in a blaze of glory, torch in hand, and girdled with the words "Universal Peace." Justice looked closer. To the right of the harbour, where vessels flying the flags of several European nations were sinking among puffs of powder, he could just distinguish the figure of a man looking at the whole scene with evident satisfaction.

"There's Mr Francis for you." He pointed to the tiny self-portrait. "And all his own work, I'll be bound."

Scorcher gave a sceptical grunt, and stared hard at the drawing.

"Oh, yes." Justice swept his hand up to it. "That's the world as he dreams of it, Fred." He bent to warm himself at the blaze. "Listen to Lord William for ten minutes and you'll never doubt it." He stood straight to take a second look. "Here, you see." He pointed to a few lines sketched in the centre of the river. "Unless I'm mistaken, that's his precious steamboat, blowing itself upstream from New York."

"Let him cut and go there." Scorcher was clearly not impressed by this republican vision.

"And so he might," Justice said severely, "for he's an impetuous man by all accounts, and full of grievances. Yes, Fred, he might well cut and run for his own country. He's an American, when it comes to it."

"The which means he'll make money where he finds it," Scorcher growled. "First from Boney, as I hear it, Cap'n. Now from us. I ask you, who's to trust a fellow like him?"

"That's the question, Fred, and I fear we've little choice about the answer. We need him, Sir George insists. So we must trust him to do what he has been paid to do. Until he does make a bolt for it or starts new dealings with the enemy.

"I've no notion what the night will bring," Justice said, settling himself on the sofa, giving Scorcher his instructions for the night, and ordering the ponycart to fetch him in the morning. "But, no," he added, as he saw Scorcher stand anxiously at the door. "No. Be off with you, Fred." He waved his hand in dismissal. "Who would come prowling here if you were lying outside the door like Cerberus?"

• • •

JUSTICE LIMPED INTO the window recess beside the fireplace, feeling the pain in his knee begin to fade now that it was rested. A writing desk took up most of the space there, and he stood idly pulling at the drawers with little hope that any of them would be unlocked.

It was the kind of desk his grandfather had owned, and he remembered the tricks about such things that had fascinated him as a boy. You pressed a drawer instead of tugging at it and some simple mechanism released another which fitted unseen into the kneehole. Nothing remarkable: many desks had something like it. Yet it was enough to slow a sneak thief's hurried fingers.

He tried each of the drawers without result, before noticing that they had knobs rather than the customary drop-handles. Knobs that might turn—but did not seem to. He was still investigating the desk, and wondering what the knack of opening it might be, when there came a light tap on the door, so light that at first he thought it was only the creaking that so often seemed to whisper from the timbers of old houses . . . But definitely a tap, for now there came another.

He went to the door and opened it. It was little Emma.

A small, vulnerable creature she looked as she stood there framed by the big scrolled and ornamented doorway; dressed in a pink, high-waisted dress with white puff sleeves, a sash at her waist, and a wisp of hair straying from a mobcap tied with lappets. She was holding a tiny basket such as she might have used to gather flowers in.

"They said you weren't well," she said gravely, and he sensed the independence of mind and manner of a child who spent much time with adults.

"Thank you, Emma. I am almost recovered now."

She still gazed at him solemnly, holding out the basket. Laid in it was a piece of something frilly, on which half a dozen or so sweetmeats had been prettily spread out.

"These are for me?"

Emma seemed so overcome with her achievement in having brought herself to knock on the door that she only nodded shyly, pushing the basket to him.

"That was very kind, Emma. Will you be so obliging as to stay and eat a bonbon with me?"

She took one and put it in her mouth, still without a word, still not taking her eyes from him. Deep violet eyes, he noticed, that in those petite features would some day mesmerise a man as her namesake was said to have mesmerised Lord Nelson.

Till now the little girl's every word and movement had been hesitant and studiedly correct, but now, to his surprise, she seemed to shed formality and become more naturally child-like, for with a sudden swish of her dress and pantalettes, she had darted to the desk he had been investigating when her knock came.

"May I see King Louis's head off?"

There was something both ludicrous and eerie about the way the words were so innocently spoken, and for a moment Justice was half inclined to laugh and half to shiver. Yet she was smiling so gleefully now that he had the feeling that the sweetmeat basket had been only a device to get into the room, to get at the desk.

To see something she had seen there before, or played with. He wondered if it had been Francis or someone else she had seen at the desk . . . perhaps had surprised him there, in the act of searching in it.

At any rate there was something in the desk she cherished, for now she was at the drawer which he had failed to open; was turning the knob, then adroitly applying an extra pressure on it. That must be the trick, for as she pressed, the drawer came open, and Emma brought out a small rectangular frame which she placed next to the candle he had taken over to the table.

"Will you make it happen?" She gazed at him with such trust that Justice, who was not in the way of playing children's games, felt uncomfortably at a loss as he bent to examine the thing she had brought out from the drawer.

It was not much bigger than a cambric handkerchief fully opened. A sheet of glass with a narrow frame around it; two thin sheets of some transparent paper that looked to be partly painted; and a small lever that projected from the left-hand side of the frame.

But he could not see what the device was meant to do. Not until Emma, with a small, brisk touch of impatience, took it from him and placed it in front of the candle so that he saw now that another image showed through. "See. Now we have the scaffold," Emma whispered to him conspiratorially, as if the pleasure of the toy was something dark, secret, and forbidden . . . As well it might be, Justice thought, as he saw the scene lit by the candle, for what the light revealed was a crudely sketched outline of a guillotine mounted on a scaffold. Below it, his head on the block, was a figure presumably meant to be Louis XVI, his coat and breeches dabbed in with red and white paint. Beside him was a masked executioner, and at his feet a basket.

Mort de Louis Capet 1793, Justice read in minute script below the picture, and even in the crudely painted toy the words produced a shudder in him.

Emma seemed to take it for granted that he was accustomed to the toy, for she waited expectantly for him to work it, to make something happen. Justice pressed the lever lightly with one finger. Immediately the sheered-off knife of the guillotine came down, detaching the head, which slid into the basket.

"Again!" Emma clapped hands happily, her trust complete now he had shown his ability to work the device. It was simple enough, he saw: the movement of the lever brought down a second sheet of transparent paper to replace the first—but on the second sheet, the king was headless. Such a piece of sleight-of-hand would be child's play to a man like Francis.

And it was through child's play that he had found this odd clue to the nature of the man he was meant to be protecting . . . He pushed the lever back to return the first transparency to its position, then repeated the performance. Half a dozen times or more he must have done it, before it occurred to him that Emma's governess might be looking for her. "I think the poor King has been killed enough times, Emma."

"Why poor King? Was he not wicked?"

"Perhaps no more than those who killed him," said Justice cautiously, for he guessed that Emma would have picked up some of the received political opinions at Wykeham Abbey. "But it's a long story—and Miss Botting will be worrying where you have got to."

"Tell it tomorrow . . . Promise?" Emma was doing her best to prolong the magical half hour until bedtime.

"If I'm still here. But you must go. And thank you for the bonbons . . ." When she finally closed the door he went over to the desk, at first only thinking to return the grisly game to where it had come from. But as he put it back, his fingers seemed to touch a small division in the upper panel of the drawer, as if there must be some extra space concealed there.

He pushed it once each way, then slid it. This time it moved with a click that dropped a flap in the inlaid marquetry, so that Justice could feel into the space and touch a soft leather folder and a chamois key bag.

He opened the folder first, and saw at once that it was a letter from the Prime Minister to Francis, sent from his private house at Putney in July. Justice still felt a dislike of reading private correspondence. But in matters dealing with Robert Francis he was the servant of George Lilly, who in turn derived his authority from the man whose signature was on the letter.

It was a persuasive pair of paragraphs, the first telling Francis how much Pitt hoped to gain from his experimental means of war and pledging support in their manufacture. Then there was a politeness or two, an invitation to Walmer Castle if Francis ever found his duties taking him to nearby Deal or Dover.

The second paragraph had more of the Prime Minister's ring about it. "We are called to struggle for the destiny, not of this country alone but of all the civilised world, including the Americas," Pitt had written, echoing the celebrated speech which had brought him back to lead the country. "We have a duty of self-preservation, and for that we submit to unexampled privations. But amid the misery and wreck of nations, and all the terrors that despotism flaunts against us, we have a noble and a higher duty. It is to show nations now bending under the yoke of tyranny what the exertions of a free people can achieve."

Francis had drawn a pencilled line beside the last words; it was the kind of rhetoric the American would like, and Pitt, Justice thought, had judged cleverly in seeking to win him with words as well as money.

He closed the folder, laid it back in the dark slot where Francis had put it for safety, and opened the chamois key bag.

A key, but not one designed for a door or drawer. It was more like a piece of machinery—something Francis must have made himself, but for no obvious purpose. It was like a flattened cog, a row of teeth with a stubby handle to them.

The thing was useless to Justice unless he had some notion where it came from. He put it back, thinking it might serve as bait for whoever came next.

It had been an odd, incongruous trio of objects in the

drawer. The key, the letter from Pitt with its resounding pronouncements on the liberties of Europe. And the tawdry, gruesome toy that had so delighted Emma.

But what did Francis really want? Liberty, Equality, and Fraternity—but not at the price of despotism? Infernal machines and plunging-boats, sold to the highest bidder? Canals and steamboats to carry his countrymen on ever more prosperous waters?

It was a weird muddle of enthusiasms that seemed to engage the American's magpie mind.

"THERE'S A PLEASURE as well as a shame in a good apology," Fanshawe said, "if you'll forgive an Irish way of saying it. I'd have come anyway, for the pleasure of putting it handsomely, but that fellow Bland was so fierce with me at dinner that I'm covered with shame as well."

It was handsome enough, Justice thought, and the man's style had been disarming from the moment he had come in ten minutes before.

Yet the smashing collision in the race could have crippled or killed him.

How like an Irishman, who could knock you down and pick you up with a smile.

With the best of intentions. Or possibly the worst.

"We're an odd set of creatures," Fanshawe was saying as he helped himself from the decanter of brandy that Scorcher had left on the table by the fire; and it seemed that he had caught what Justice was thinking. "And there's really no one this side of the Irish Sea that likes or understands us, whether we're Papists or Protestants, and for that reason alone we'd be better running our own affairs."

Justice had paid little attention to Fanshawe's first remarks, taking them as a courtesy and nothing more, but as Fanshawe spoke more seriously he began to feel as he had felt at their first meeting—that Fanshawe was not so simple as he seemed, that he dissembled, perhaps because he was a sponger by habit, perhaps for some other reason. There was certainly a depth of cold calculation in the man which he had not yet plumbed. For some reason, it was clear, Fanshawe had come tonight to talk about Ireland.

"Dublin, now," Fanshawe said. "The Union ruined the

city, for none of the great people wanted to stay when the Parliament was closed. There's still talk, great talk in the place. You'll hear as much wit in Merrion Square as you'll hear in London, if you're content with doctors or lawyers, or the artists and authors you'll find at their dinner tables. But there's no style now, none at all.''

If the man was trying to draw him out, he was talking too much, Justice thought; and then thought again. Somewhere in this flow of words there would be a purpose, and he would have to watch for it. A request for money, maybe, or the catching of a careless word of sympathy that could be turned into money by a hint at exposure. He mumbled some platitude that kept Fanshawe talking while something that had already been said pricked at his memory.

"I wouldn't want to answer for the consequences, you know.''

"The consequences?'' Justice knew it was the mention of Merrion Square that had distracted him and made him miss the change in Fanshawe's subject.

"If the French should come.'' Fanshawe repeated his last remark. "It's not as bad as it was in '98, for there's hundreds dead, or fled, or jailed since then. But it's bad enough.'' He came across to stand by Justice as he spoke with a vigour that sounded rather strange for a man who had previously seemed no more than an agreeable talker. "Go down towards Cork from my house,'' he said, "and you'll see so many gibbets and burnt-out hovels that it will sicken you. People dressed in rags. Grubbing for potatoes. Begging in the streets of every town in Ireland. No wonder they'd welcome Boney's men if they came.''

It was odd talk, when Fanshawe must know that Justice was a serving officer, but it was not even close to sedition, let alone treason: and as Justice listened to the man, coming to feel more doubtful with every minute he spent in his company, he was aware that such apparent frankness might be the best of distractions from some other purpose. "Tell the truth as near as may be,'' Hatherley had said to him before he left for France that summer, and it was possible that Fanshawe was doing the same.

"And appalling debts,'' he said, making Justice wonder for a moment whether this was the prelude to a borrower's touch, but going on in quite a different direction. "Debts everywhere. You ask Breney. He knows.''

"About Ireland?" Justice was puzzled by this sudden turn in the conversation. "Does he have business across the water?"

"You could call it that." Fanshawe spoke bitterly. "He's a collector," he said, before he saw that Justice was not familiar with the finer points of Irish administration. "A nice piece of patronage that the government hands out to its friends in the law, and few questions asked," he explained. "When an estate's confiscated from a rebel or taken in for unpaid fines or taxes, it's men such as Mr Brazear Breney that assess it and transfer the title. Little more than legal robbery, in fact, for part of the property sticks to each pair of hands that touches it."

The plight of Ireland. Justice wanted to hear more about Breney, who seemed too well-natured for the role in which Fanshawe had cast him. But as he felt a stir of compassion for the unhappy Irish people he realized why Fanshawe's remark about Merrion Square had touched a nerve of memory.

Doctors, Fanshawe had said in passing.

And the last person he had heard recite such a catalogue of Irish woes had been Dr Declan O'Moira, late of Dublin, and more recently of Paris, Verdun, Boulogne, and other places where the blind Irish rebel could help bring Bonaparte's invasion flotilla to the point of sailing—preferably towards Cork, but in any direction where it might do the Irish cause some good.

For a moment Justice was tempted to ask Fanshawe outright whether he knew O'Moira. Whether he had seen him lately in Dublin. And he let the impulse pass. Perhaps that was the very question for which all this talk of Ireland had been the bait.

"You are hard on Mr Breney," he said, wondering why Fanshawe was so keen to discredit the lawyer.

"He is part of an evil system," Fanshawe said as caustically as Lord William spoke of government and their means of war.

At that moment Justice would have given fifty guineas for the right to shake and bully the man into admitting his real purpose. He could have come for so many reasons—merely to make sure that Justice bore no grudge that would damage his standing in the house, to see how much he had been hurt and how long he might be confined to this room, to sound out his

114

political opinions, to discover what he knew about O'Moira's plans and movements, to discredit Breney, even to distract attention from something or someone else. And there was no way of choosing one of this hierarchy of suspicions from another.

No way, indeed, of being sure that any suspicion was justified. Not all Irish patriots were rebels, or secret sympathisers with the French. And there were other than sinister motives for travelling with an attractive Frenchwoman without means or prospects.

And yet. There was something wrong with Fanshawe and his companion. He was so sure of it that he was tantalised by his inability to guess what possible connection they might have to the attacks on the *Pandora*.

He fancied Fanshawe was about to say something more when he heard a key slide into the door from the studio. It was a slight sound, but Fanshawe caught it too, and with the easiest of goodnights excused himself.

The key turned, more loudly, as if Fanshawe's departure had been heard beyond the door, and as it opened, a draught caught the candle flames and blew them out.

❦12❧

JUSTICE SWUNG ROUND and reached for the decanter, instantly alert. But he had relaxed his grip before he touched the bottle. It was Harriet who stood there, candle in hand, and through the rooms behind her Justice could see the gleam of another light.

"My own rooms lie beyond," she said, confirming his guess that she had come through from some other part of the house, and at the same time setting him to wonder again about her relationship with Francis. If they both lived in this wing of the building, if she had access to his workroom, his paper, his private apartment . . .

It was the first time he had seen her in a dress, and she looked remarkable in it, though it could not have been more simple. Low cut, in a black velvet which showed her rounded shoulders to advantage, it fell straight from its high, gathered waist to the floor. It gave her a classical appearance, and the effect was enhanced by a single gold chain around her neck and a large cameo pendant which rested on the opening curve of her breasts.

On the instant, she paused. "I came this way . . ." she began. "It is easier, more discreet." She blew out her candle and spoke more boldly as the shadows deepened. "To be frank, Mr Justice, I would be glad of your company." She stepped across to the fire and motioned him to sit once more. "That Breney makes himself so disagreeable when he is in his cups. And my distant cousins. Ugh! Using a birthday as an excuse for fawning compliments and sly innuendoes. Let them go back to their barrack women, who give themselves to such false servilities." She slapped one palm disdainfully across the other. "I am sorry to speak with such vigour, Mr Justice, but you were well spared my party."

He was unsure how to respond. Her irritated remarks made it difficult to begin with polite conversation, and in any normal household she would have been compromising them both by such a visit to his room.

"If I may be of any help." He had the impression that she had come for some stronger reason than a desire for his company, or distaste for the roistering crowd she had just left.

"I am out of temper," she said, "for the day has been one bother after the next." She put up a restraining hand as Justice seemed about to commiserate with her. "Please do not say you are sorry, Mr Justice. It is for me to apologise. It was I who invited you, teased you into racing, gave you a scarce-broken horse, left you to be tossed and trampled by that fool Kibbie Fanshawe. You are put up here, your day spoilt, a very patchwork of bruises I'm sure, and I come disturbing your rest because I'm a martyr to uneasiness."

"I think you are concerned about Mr Francis." He was afraid such directness might annoy her, but she was clearly labouring under some unexpressed anxiety; and even if she was not ready to tell him more than the half of it, he had learned enough since he arrived at Wykeham that morning to be sure that there was something she wished to say and could not bring herself to.

Fanshawe had given the same impression, though he might be dissembling for a reason, rather than from uncertainty. And Breney, too, seemed to have some inkling that there were secrets in this house that could not be mentioned to outsiders.

So Harriet's next words did not come as a complete surprise.

"Not for Robert in particular. No more than I am anxious for my brother. And for you as well, perhaps."

"For me? Why me? Why any of us?"

"Because there is something sinister going on here."

"At Wykeham?"

"Yes, at . . ." Justice saw that she had slipped, and changed the direction of her answer in a trice. "No. At Cuffwells. It . . . it has to do with Sir George, and the work Robert does there." She stopped as though she did not expect to be believed, then blurted out her accusation. "It is that man Hatherley. He will ruin Robert if he has a chance, if it suits him. And you. I do not know what end he serves, but you are all being drawn into a trap, like innocents who cannot help themselves."

"That is ridiculous!" Justice snapped out the denial so

sharply that she was upset, and even in the poor light he could see the flush spread from her face to her shoulders.

Justice saw at once that she was in no mood to be interrogated, and for a moment he thought she was about to leave him, for she put her hand to the hem of her skirt in an angry movement; and then she softened. "Let us not quarrel, Mr Justice."

SHE WALKED PAST the desk into the bay of the window and stood staring down into the courtyard as though she might see something there that displeased her. "I would like to go away from here," she said, speaking so softly that Justice decided he had misunderstood her.

"Please," he said, rising. "Do not let me detain you, Lady Harriet."

She raised her hands to pacify him. "Do not be angry with me, Captain Justice, for I wish you well, and came because I thought I might find it easier to talk with you tonight than with my family, and friends, and the besotted celebrants who will not go home till morning. Away from it all."

"You mean away from Wykeham?" He was vexed with himself for misunderstanding her.

She swung round the desk and came across the room as though she was putting the great house behind her.

"I was happy here as a child, you know, though I was so young when my mother died that I can remember nothing of her except the night when I was woken, crying, to be taken in to see her on her deathbed. For afterwards my father spoilt me, in his own fashion." She hesitated over the next words. "My brother William, you see, was a disappointment. Oh, yes, he liked William's opinions, for they were much like his own. His intellect. All those gems, as he so quaintly puts it, that William finds in the mines of science. But William, as you may have guessed, is not . . . is not manly; and my father, for all the oddities which people ridicule in him, is a conservative at heart—in matters which affect Wykeham, at least. So he wanted a son who could be raised as heir to this great estate if my elder brother died in India. And that son, in default of William, had to be me! I was brought up to shoot, to fish, above all to ride, for my father cares more for horses than any other living creature. To be, in short, a wild romping girl whom they called a tomboy when I was young, and a hoyden now I am marrying age and show no desire for what everyone would consider a good marriage.''

She was speaking with such frankness that Justice had to let her continue, whatever her motive.

"And then it took my father's fancy to send me to France, when William went to study chemistry and mechanics and such things at the Sorbonne.''

"In the years of the Terror?'' Justice asked, incredulously.

"After that,'' she said. "When Bonaparte was Consul, and in the peace. And you must believe me, Captain Justice, though it may be hard for a man who has spent his life fighting the French—that was a happy time for me as well, though with a difference. Here, let me confess it, I am wild, because I fret under the burdens that Wykeham lays upon me. In France I could think of anything and do anything.'' She came over from the window to where Justice lay on the sofa and grasped his arm with the strength of a man. "I was infected by the idea of freedom. It may seem strange to you, to speak of it, when French armies tramp across Europe and threaten our own country with the rule of the tricolour.''

"And the guillotine,'' Justice added, and could not resist reminding her where her family's levelling beliefs might lead. "Wykeham and all it stands for would get short shrift if Boney's men came up to the Beaulieu River one misty morning.''

"I know. I know now.'' She surprised him by accepting the point with a fierceness that matched his own feelings about Hook. "I would set the house on fire rather than see them rampaging through it. And yet my opinions have not changed one whit. In France I felt like a free spirit, without any of the two-sidedness that I know bedevils my nature. For a year or two I could mix with William's friends and talk to them like another man, about all the ideas that were discussed in this house in the years when I was a-growing, about the books I read and the things that William had taught me.'' She smiled in spite of her distracted state, as though she were remembering this time of happiness. "I was also a woman, who was free . . .'' She broke off suddenly and released her hold on his arm. "Do I shock you?''

"Who was free as a man might be?''

"You understand, then.'' She seemed relieved that he took

119

her meaning at once. "Exactly. As a man is free to choose his own life, and . . ." She did not need to say more.

"But you would not go back?" Despite the war, someone with her background would still have been more than welcome in Paris.

Harriet shook her head. "That is why each day I become more desperate. Since Napoleon took it into his head to make himself an emperor I see less hope in France—as William does, and Francis: only they are disappointed by the sight of a new crown, and courtiers around it, while I . . . well, I see less hope for women like me, for the Corsican is making a new empire in which the martial values are exalted and women must become what they have always been, dutiful creatures, domestic or decorative according to their station, and without a will of their own. And I am wilful, Mr Justice, so I would feel stifled in France today. As I am suffocated here at home, where there is no better prospect for me than to become a spinster, aging into eccentricity like my father, or becoming the mistress of a great house with all the daily duties I find so tedious here."

Justice was astonished by her eloquence, for he had never heard a woman speak with such bitter energy, and as he watched her pace about the room he felt a deep pity for the conflict that wracked her—though he could not begin to guess why she had come at this time to confide in him.

"Do you wonder that I am restless," she cried, with an anguished note in her voice. "That I ride till my bones ache and sleep only when I am exhausted? And that I dream of flight?"

Justice could think of only one explanation of her distress. "You are pressed to marry?"

"Among other demands," she said enigmatically.

"To Francis?"

"In Heaven's name, no! To Robert? Oh, God! That is the last and not the first of chances!" But before Justice could ask what she meant, she had run on with a hint of hysterical protest in every word. "To a drunkard a month ago. To a bully, I expect, within the year, or a rich nincompoop. And every time it becomes more difficult to refuse because I have no other reasonable prospect in life." She stopped her pacing and stood silhouetted against the glow of the fire, her arms outstretched.

"Where can a woman go to be free?"

It was the first time that Justice had ever heard that question, and he did not know how to respond to it.

"I sometimes think I must become a traveller." Harriet was a little calmer now that she had released her despair, though Justice could tell she was still much distracted. "To find relief in weariness and danger. To see the Turkish bashaws strut through the ruins of Athens or ride with savage horsemen across the sands of Araby. Or find where Marco Polo went." She dropped her arms and gave an ironic laugh. "And die of fever before I'm thirty, I expect."

"They say America is a land of new ideas and opportunities." Justice felt it was a weak thing to say, but he did not know how to cope with this flow of propositions that sounded so bizarre in a woman.

"They say!" Harriet's irritation was sparked again by his remark. "Robert says, and does not persuade me." She prinked herself before the fire in such a comic imitation of a farm woman that Justice could not help laughing, and his reaction brought her own humour back. "Do you see me, sir, in a bonnet, going to the meetinghouse of a Sunday and spending my days boiling hams in a kitchen? If I was to go to America I should run to the woods and find a tribe of Indians who would let me live with them."

"From what I hear, a squaw lives worse than the princess of the preserving pans," Justice said. "Or the queen of the canals." He lifted a finger towards the panorama displayed on the wall above her head.

She was laughing more easily now. She glanced at the figure of Columbia descending from the clouds. "Do you see the likeness?"

The idea had not occurred to Justice at his first casual glance, and he rose to hobble across and make the comparison more closely. She put out a hand to steady him, and then tucked it under his arm as they stood side by side and looking up at the drawing. "From the life," she said. "Only a few weeks ago." And then she gave Justice one of those searching glances that set his pulse racing.

"You think I am his mistress," she said as if such a comment were the most natural topic she could turn to after such a confession of emotional torment. "And that Emma is his child."

Her frank perception of his thoughts disarmed him. "Yes," he said simply, feeling that honesty was the only course with such a woman.

"Oh, no." She had not released his arm as they turned to

face each other, and he could feel her hands tremble. "He has always had a way with women—and made the most of it. But I am William's sister, and the daughter of an earl . . ." She spoke in a curiously disappointed tone, and her next words left him in no doubt of the reason. "In some ways these Americans are a very conventional people, you know, and someone as methodical as Robert likes even the irregularities of his life to conform to a pattern. We are both impetuous, but in our own ways. He is only impetuous with his ideas, and I, well, I with my feelings."

She looked up at Justice with no guile in her eyes and a strong emotion in her face. "And so I am only Robert's friend," she said, and let her hand fall away from his arm.

THEY STOOD SILENT for some minutes, each seeing different pictures in the fire. She seemed to be calmer, but more concerned again, and Justice had been so fascinated by her account of her life that the notion of asking her why she had come to see him had quite gone out of his head.

"And Emma," she said, with what struck Justice as an effort. "She is not, in fact, my child, though I love her as my own and wish to God she were. It is only the feeling I have for that child that keeps me half tamed and attentive to my duties here." For a moment Justice felt that she was about to weep, but she recovered herself. "It is that child to whom I look for any lasting happiness in my life, for I see her as my second self."

This sudden and most moving declaration of love for Emma surprised Justice as much as her implicit avowal of unrequited love for Francis. Both emotions seemed much to the fore of her mind as she stood there, trembling slightly for all the heat of the fire.

She nodded. "Her mother has entrusted her to me," she said, and seemed on the verge of a fresh confidence before the sadness came back into her face and she spoke quite differently.

"There are people here who say I am a witch, you know. Like the gypsy woman that someone found in the crowd today and brought in to tell our fortunes before dinner."

"A gypsy read my palm as I came into Hampshire," Justice said, remembering the woman whose child Scorcher had found in the barn. "And yours?"

"It was a silly rhyme. About Emma. And yet it troubled me. 'Child's game, look again.' That was it. 'Lost and found. Under ground.' "

"It is a silly kind of thing," Justice said, laying a reassuring hand on her shoulder.

"Can they foretell the future?" Harriet put up a hand to touch his fingers. "William says they come from India. But my father insists they descend from the ancient Egyptians."

"Then they should know most about the past," Justice said lightly, trying to ease her anxiety. "It's simply explained. They know something, or guess, or invent some gibberish that we make fit our facts." He paused. "How could our lives be so ordained for us that others may see what day upon day will bring us?"

Harriet gave a low cry that was between a laugh and a sob, and as she put up her face Justice felt her arm slip round his back and cling to him, her fingers working through the loosened robe.

He was given to sudden attachments. Ever since he had let his pride come between him and Kitty Rawlings, had let her marry his friend, the underwriter Edward Holland, because he had no prospects to offer an heiress, he had known what it was like to be drawn to the unattainable; and time and again he had found himself falling headlong into a short-lived intimacy with a woman who could give him passion but not love.

He put his hand behind Harriet's head and bent his face towards her, stirred by the way her body shook, and suddenly feeling certain that this was the comfort she had come to seek.

Or the means to delay and distract him from whatever or whoever was hidden in this house.

As he stiffened with that suspicion, Harriet misread his movement.

"With me there need be no reserve," she said quietly, settling herself closer to him, and as his arms closed and pressed on her he knew that he had gone past the point where doubt could restrain him.

She slipped her free hand through the folds of his robe. "Oh . . ." she began, with a catch in her voice, and as Justice felt her yield in his arms he heard the sound of an argument on the steps outside.

There were muffled shouts, a ragged rapping at the door,

and then Scorcher was calling "Cap'n! Cap'n!" and trying the latch.

JUSTICE HAD NO DOUBT of the urgency in that surprising cry. Nor had Harriet.

"Damn it," she said roughly, releasing herself and turning away from the fire, while Justice limped and shuffled to open the door.

Outside, dripping with beads of mist, Scorcher seemed to be struggling to free himself from the dragging clutch of the watchman, but as soon as Justice appeared he stepped back on the stairs with a mumbled complaint about his duty.

"Cap'n." Scorcher was panting heavily, though Justice could not tell whether it was excitement or the tussle with the watchman that had made him breathless, and he gasped a couple of times as Justice hurried him into the room.

"Cap'n," he said again, as though he were to blame for the news he brought. "The *Pandora*."

"Afire?" Justice had already begun to feel shamed for staying at Wykeham. "Quick, Fred. Out with it, man!"

Scorcher coughed out his answer. "No. No, Cap'n," he said. "Afloat. *Afloat!*"

❧ 13 ❧

SCORCHER TOLD JUSTICE the gist of the story while he was pulling on his clothes, which had the musty and meaty odour of things which had been hurriedly dried in front of the kitchen fire.

"As I got back," Scorcher said, looking about for a boot-jack while he talked, and finding one in the dressing room. "You know how it is, Cap'n, you see the shape of the sheds from the track. Poor enough on a night like this, but I'd have swore there was movement. You sometimes feel it as much as see it, if you know what I mean. Like on the marsh at night."

Justice did know what he meant, though it was never explicitly mentioned between them. Scorcher sometimes gave a helping hand to friends who ran brandy barrels up from the beaches between Rye and Dymchurch, and had to depend on that sixth sense to keep clear of revenue men in the dark.

"Go on."

"Well, I thought it was Honeyman and Small, them being on the watch, and thought nothing of it." He paused.

"But it wasn't them," Justice prompted. Scorcher had an irritating habit of dragging out a tale for effect, and Justice had never been able to break him of it.

"No, it weren't, though it were two hour or more before I found so." Scorcher looked shamefaced, and before Justice could quiz him he came out with his excuse. "I'd come up with them Cowleys, near to the house," he said. "And went on with them, friendly-like, for an ale in the village." He gave Justice an apologetic glance. "Thinking, as you wished, I might hear something said there." He shook his head. "Nary a word. Good beer, bad talk, for my money."

"Come on," Justice said testily, stretching his painful leg for Scorcher to force the boot on it and hoping he would not have to use it much for a day or so.

"It were when I got back." Scorcher grunted with the effort. "Them two skivers was in the kitchen, a-chewin' of the fat with Joslin. 'Who's at the boat?' I asks. 'Warren,' says Small. 'And them Cowleys,' says Honeyman. 'They never is,' I tells them sharpish. 'But they are,' that Joslin chimes in. 'Cap'n sent 'em hisself.' "

Justice was shouldering on his coat as Scorcher became lost in this involved tale about the Cowleys. "Tell me later," he said anxiously. "The *Pandora*. Is she safe?"

"Safeish. And afloat when I left her."

"In the river?" Could that have been done so quickly after the change of the watch? Was she nearly so ready to launch?

"In the dock, still, with three feet of water in it, and more coming in one the tide."

So the doors had been forced open, the lock paddles raised, but whoever had made this attack had been surprised an hour too soon.

"And guarded now?" Justice asked as Scorcher put out the candles and they found their way to the door by the glow of the fire.

"Joslin. Tooth—I roused that sleeping bastard from his bed. Honeyman. Small."

"Armed?"

"Cutlass and pistol apiece."

At least the *Pandora* was saved, Justice thought gratefully as he and Scorcher stood shivering in the drizzle and waited for sleepy ostlers to bring their horses.

"The attack," he said, now that he had heard the worst. "Tell me what happened."

"As I knowed they wasn't there, for good reason," Scorcher began, "I turns to Joslin and the others sharpish. 'Look alive,' I says. 'Run,' I says, and run they did. But we was heard, and too late."

"You saw someone?"

"Two men. And another in a boat, maybe. I only sees them atop of the lock, by them big handles like a tiller, and they was gone."

"Into the water?"

"No. They had a boat, all right." Scorcher spoke with certainty. "There was a rope a-hangin', you see, and I heard 'em drop. But it were as black as Newgate's knocker, and no chance to see 'em."

"One thing more, Fred." Justice caught the clop of hooves

on the cobbles and was anxious to be up and away. "Joslin said I sent a message?"

"Right, Cap'n." But Scorcher sounded doubtful as he said it. "By two of them men as was off watch and come for the race."

"To say what?"

"That the first watch could stand down, seeing as Warren and the Cowleys was to work tonight, having been give a day's holiday."

"They claimed that I said that?" Justice could not believe it.

"I asked 'em." Scorcher had been equally astonished, it seemed. "And they swears to it. 'Only Cap'n was to give orders,' they says, 'and he give 'em. He come up to us in the crowd when the rain druv in, and we was a-shelterin' under the trees.' " He scratched his curly poll. "Happens neither ain't spoke nor seen you afore, Cap'n, so . . ."

It was an explanation of sorts. But the men were lying—to protect themselves or a pair of their mates who had failed in their duty. After too much of the earl's home brew. They must be lying. Must have been bribed. So that anyone could have come in to take the *Pandora*. So that it could all have been done quite simply if Scorcher had not had his wits about him. So that the *Pandora* would now be well down the river, or sunk somewhere at the bottom of its twisting channel. "That was well done, Fred," he said. "Most admirably done."

As they came into the stable yard at Cuffwells and dismounted he noticed that Scorcher looked at his leg and offered help as he hobbled towards the house. "No, thank'ee," he said, and stopped to give his orders.

"Double the guards," he said. "I want Warren and the Cowleys here at first light. I want two trustworthy men I can send to find Sir George and Mr Hatherley. And I want every man on the estate who can row a boat, or hold a gun, or flush a bird from a covert."

Scorcher looked puzzled.

"Limp or no limp," Justice said flatly, in the tone that Scorcher knew brooked no argument. "Limp or no limp, tomorrow we all go a-hunting."

THE WEATHER CLEARED by morning, and it promised to be a

cold and brilliant day. There was frost on the fronds of grass in the marshy patches by the river, and ice crackling in the puddles as Justice came down to the boathouse—favouring his knee and well aware of his bruises but able to take whatever the day would bring.

Warren and the Cowleys were there already, the surly mechanic complaining at his early summons and the two older Cowleys a little the worse for the ale they must have drunk with Scorcher; but despite their glum moods the men were soon put to work.

"Before you drain the dock, see how the *Pandora* takes the water," Justice said, noticing how stable she looked afloat. "Warren can try his pumps and cranks and any other working part. Check the hatchway seals. And then report what else must be done before she is ready to be risked in the river."

After last night there could be no more doubt. The earlier attacks might have been mere mischief. This attempt to steal the *Pandora* was proof that they had only served some preliminary purpose, and that a cleverly planned and much more serious operation had now begun.

And the orders for it must have come from France, whatever hands had actually touched the plunging-boat last night.

As Justice came out of the boathouse to face the growing crowd of men on the river bank, he felt that at last he was coming to work he understood.

THE SERVANTS AND SAILORS had come down from the house in a body, waved off by the cooks and housemaids as if they were going to the war—in a sense they were, Justice thought, peaceful though the river looked in the reddish sunrise; and the gardeners and gamekeepers were coming in one after another as messengers fetched them from outlying cottages. There were even a few men from the village, who had heard of the excitement when the Cowleys were summoned at dawn and had tramped along after them.

Two dozen already, and a few more to come.

"I need a pilot," Justice said, finding himself among strangers from Bucklers Hard. He would go down the river in a boat, keeping in touch with the men spread out to search the banks and coppices on either side.

"Here be I," a voice cried from the back, and a stubby man

in a tarred jacket stepped forward. "Harry Ainsworth, sir, from the yard." Anyone who knew the river well would have done, but Justice saw that his request had been taken literally. Of course, with such large ships building up at the Hard there would be one or more pilots to work the shifting channel down to the Solent.

"Can you find me a gig, or something like it?" Ainsworth had knuckled his forehead and was already turning away when Justice called after him. "And a pair of rowboats." He would need them to run over the shallows or serve as ferries if he had to move men from one bank to the other in a hurry.

And while Ainsworth and some of his cronies were finding the boats in the little anchorage beyond the spit, Justice counted heads again.

Thirty now. Tooth had already formed up the sailors. "Exbury side," Justice said, glad to see that he was checking their weapons. Ainsworth and the others he would need to crew the boats would account for most of the villagers. That would leave the ground servants to work the right bank, and he had no doubt who would be the best man to lead them across the Cuffwells land and past Wykeham to the sea.

"Is the head gamekeeper here?" If anything out of the ordinary was to be found, he was the man most likely to notice it.

There was a murmur of chafing good humour, and the largest man in the group put up his hand. "Mr Grimshaw, sir," he said, announcing himself with a sense of his own importance, and seeming to think the invitation no less than his due.

"Come closer, all of you," Justice cried now the sorting was done. He had been surprised at the way they had accepted his authority when so few of them knew him, even by sight; but he owed them an explanation.

"I'm a captain in the Sea Fencibles," he said in a loud voice, "and I need your help." That caused a stir, and his next words had even more effect. "We are going to search for three men who attacked this boathouse last night . . ."

"Not the first time, neither," a rough voice broke in. "Who beat my bruvver and druv 'im from 'ome?" There were some angry shouts of "That be right!" and "About time too!" that showed Justice why the village men had turned out to help.

"Three men," he repeated. "Or some signs of them."

"Be they spies?" someone called, and he was reluctant to answer. People seemed to lose their heads when they caught spy fever.

Far better to say precisely what he wanted.

"Spread out from each bank. Look for the mark of a boat run in since the last tide. For footprints in the mud, or leading away from the river. Hail if you find anything, or send one of the small boats out to fetch me."

"What else are we a-looking for, sir?" Grimshaw put the question bluntly.

"These men have been hiding somewhere. Look for dead fires. Rough shelters. Search barns and stables. Ask anyone you meet if they've seen strangers."

"Mr Grimshaw'll find you a poacher or two, sir," one of the groundsmen from Cuffwells said to raise a chuckle. But as the man spoke Justice saw that Grimshaw looked uneasy, and he drew him aside.

"Joseph's got a point there," the gamekeeper said good-naturedly. "Yet it's not that, sir. It's the Romanies."

"The gypsies?" Justice was anxious to make a start and he failed to see what the gypsies had to do with the search.

"Aye, sir." There's a score or more between here and Wykeham, and more away to the forest edge. You see, it's the drive time, sir, when they roam across, bringing the wild ponies in afore the winter."

Justice now saw what was worrying Grimshaw. A small tribe of gypsies could leave so many marks as they camped and travelled that there would be little chance of distinguishing any that had been made by the fleeing intruders. They might even have given shelter to the men. Gold would have talked their language.

"You think the search worthless, then?"

"Nearly, sir, begging your pardon. Not quite, because I and my men could tell where a Romany's been, though them sailors . . ." He paused. "We might find something, and it would be a scare, for what that's worth."

Justice had been coming to the same conclusion while Grimshaw was speaking. At the very least this sweep across the approaches to Cuffwells would make things difficult for anyone who was on the run in the few square miles between the boathouse and the sea.

It might even forestall a new attack.

He had to wait a few minutes while Ainsworth's boats ferried the sailors across the river, and he took the chance to scribble his notes to Sir George and Hatherley to tell them what had happened and what he proposed to do. "I've no idea whether Joslin and Small can find 'em," he said to Scorcher. "But let 'em try. Let 'em damn well try."

As soon as Scorcher had despatched the two messengers he was ready to start.

"Mr Grimshaw, if you please."

While the gamekeeper spread out his men in an open order that let each keep a sight of his neighbour, Justice stepped into the neat four-oared gig that Ainsworth had found for him and settled himself in the sternsheets. "Now," he said to Scorcher, who yelled at Tooth on the Exbury bank. There was an answering cry, and Justice saw the sailors begin to move south like a line of beaters.

"They'll be putting up birds as they go," Ainsworth grinned. "And the pity of it. Not a single gun firing for the pot."

IT WAS HARD GOING for the men who were stumbling along the river banks, which the wash of the tides left gullied and muddy, and it was almost as difficult for those who were farther away from the shore and had to make their way across ditches and through coppices of willow and hazel.

It was probably a fool's errand for them all, Justice thought, trying to contain his impatience, yet it had to be done; and since Tooth and Grimshaw were too far away to keep under his direct orders, he was glad to see they were both using their common sense. After a few hundred yards of slow progress, both parties began to stick close to the rough paths and cattle tracks that ran fairly near the water.

Both men had clearly come to the same conclusion as Justice. If the intruders were moving at night along an unfamiliar river, they would never stray far from it, for fear of getting lost or of blundering into a farmyard and raising the roost.

"Over there, sir." Justice had been watching some of Grimshaw's party go into the woods when a word from Ainsworth directed his attention to the other bank, where Tooth was arguing with two men carrying guns. Fowling pieces, Justice judged from their length; and as the search party moved on, with a cordial wave from the men who had stopped it, the inshore rowboat came skimming over to report that they were gamekeepers from Exbury House who wanted to know why so many people were tramping across their preserves.

"No," the oarsman said, "ain't seen nobody they couldn't account for." He gave a sly grin. "And kep' watch pertickler, they 'ad, this bein' poachin' time, if ever it was."

And of course, Justice said to himself as Ainsworth put the gig against the incoming tide again, that is what any of the country people would think if they caught sight of anyone skulking through the dark. And they would keep their mouths shut. Nobody wanted to put a neighbour in jail or help the hangman slip a noose round a decent man's neck.

And that, Justice guessed as the thought came to him, might explain why no one had said anything helpful about the earlier attacks on the boathouse. At a time when hungry labourers were burning hayricks and farmhouses in their desperation, no one wanted to notice mysterious fires or to run telling tales about them.

"It's a funny tide here, sir, if you don't know it." Ainsworth broke into his thoughts, speaking like a sailing master to his captain. "Runs for six hours, sets a bit, then runs for a couple more. An hour's slack, and then, whoosh, she clears in a rush. There's not another I know that's like it." He looked back over the river with an expression of approving pride. "So there's good water most of the time, clear to Bucklers, and when you want to go down you've got a clean channel and a fast ebb. Couldn't be better for boat builders."

He grinned as Justice took his point and saw why Lilly had decided to construct the *Pandora* in his own boathouse. There were few places where it would be easier to launch the vessel and count on a long stretch of tide-free high water, few places where the craft would be better screened from curious eyes, for the trees here came right to the edge of the river and Grimshaw's party had been forced out of sight.

"Salternshill Copse." Ainsworth was naming the landmarks as they moved slowly downstream. "You'll see the river curves here, and you've got to get in closer to the left bank if you want more than a couple of fathoms. Then there's Gins Mill, at the start of Fiddler's Reach." He swung his arm in a sharp gesture. "You come round sharp there, whichever way you're going, or you'll swing into the Wykeham jetty. And the earl ain't so keen on ships of war, sir, that he'd forgive easy.'' He was still chuckling at the notion, when Justice heard a hail from the right bank and saw the boat coming out with Grimshaw in it, his bulk giving the man a hard row.

Scorcher grabbed a hold as the rowboat came alongside the gig, sending both craft spinning and drifting upstream, and Grimshaw leaned over so far that water began to slop into them.

''Sorry,'' he said, passing something that looked like a small metal box, ''but the captain'll want to see this, I expect.''

Justice took it from Scorcher. It was a dark lantern, with a slide that could cut out the light—useful if you wanted to keep the wick burning without being seen, or to send any kind of signal.

''There's an old oak with a hollow bole just into the woods, there,'' Grimshaw went on, while Justice examined the lamp. ''You could see it from here, sir, if'n you knew where to look. Used often enough by folk who want to put a thing away temp'ry.''

''Like a rabbit, or a pheasant?'' Justice asked, turning the lamp in his hands and trying to decide why it had been left there.

''Right enough,'' Grimshaw said, leaning over again, and making Ainsworth snap a warning against capsizing them all. ''If you'll forgive me, sir, but I had a good look at it . . . Here.'' He pointed to some small marks and scratches on the bottom frame.

Holding it at an angle to the light, Justice could see what he meant. There had been a fleur-de-lys stamped into the metal. And someone had tried to erase it.

You could see the same kind of attempt to wipe out the past on any French ship that was more than fifteen years old.

For it was a French naval lantern. No doubt of that.

And for the first time since he had come to Cuffwells, and Lilly had set him speculating about French agents, he held a piece of tangible proof in his hand.

''I'm obliged to you, Mr Grimshaw.'' He did not wish to give away the excitement he felt at this discovery. ''Keep your eyes skinned.''

''If I may be bold to speak, sir.'' Ainsworth broke in before Grimshaw was rowed away. ''There could be others.''

Justice wondered whether the pilot's thoughts were running in the same direction as his own, and found they were. "Bearing lights?"

Ainsworth nodded. "If you was a-coming through here at night, and wanted marks." He pulled at his whiskers as he paused. "Then there'd be one somewhere near Gins Mill. And another at Needs Ore Point, where the river comes round behind Gull-Island."

Justice looked at Grimshaw. "If they're there, we'll find 'em," the gamekeeper said confidently.

"But you'll leave them," Justice said to the man's astonishment. "And put this one back where you found it, if you'd be so good. There's no point in telling all we know, is there?"

And no point in letting either Grimshaw or Ainsworth know that he was expecting another attempt to bring the *Pandora* down the river. And if that happened, the lighting of these lamps would be a warning—if Sweetsea's men were told to keep a watch for them. He passed the lantern back to Grimshaw and released the wallowing rowboat as the mention of the Volunteer company reminded him of Dunning. And the first sight of him on this reach of the river.

There had been no more news from the Lymington surgeon, and Justice feared the man must be sinking. Could already be dead, perhaps, if the surgeon had bled him too savagely.

Even here, on this splendid morning, when the clearing sun was making the water dance with sparkles, one could feel the hand of the enemy was close. Too close for comfort.

Close enough to strike a man down in his prime, or to place a lantern where the *Pandora* might pass to seal the fate of a navy.

"THE OLD FORT." As Ainsworth jerked his head back over his shoulder, Justice could see the straight grass-covered dykes which ran out on the promontory ahead, forming an angle to the bend and rising a dozen feet or more above the muddy shore. "Cromwell's time, some say, but older as my name's Harry."

Justice had been looking at Gins Farm, before Ainsworth spoke, with the Wykeham landing below it and Wykeham itself a dark mass among its clumps of elm and oak. Should he go over to the farm? Nowhere could be more convenient for anyone who wished to lie up close to Wykeham and Cuffwells. Or leave it to Grimshaw, who would know better what and how to ask? He was still tempted when Ainsworth spoke, reminding him that he had proposed to land at Sweetsea's jetty, which must be just the other side of the fort though still out of sight.

"Older," he said politely to Ainsworth's comment. He had seen Roman forts like that on the little rivers of Kent, and guessed that the Romans had merely improved the ditches and walls they found when they came storming over from France.

And now, no doubt, Sweetsea and his men would have put it back in commission again, to keep a new invader out of their river. It wasn't much of a fortification, if troops were to make a set at it, but it could stand the fire of any vessel small enough to work in close—stand it long enough, anyway, for the Volunteers to get in some telling blows of their own if Lilly had found them a pair of 24-pounders.

Two guns. If Sweetsea had them he would certainly have measured all the ranges and marked them for the gun layers.

"Guns?" he asked Ainsworth, and the pilot grinned. "A pair on 'em." He gave another of the nods he used to point when his hands were at the oars. "You'll see the embrasures as we go round."

Facing seawards. Well, no one would expect to fire on a vessel coming down the river, and if they were well sited, they would serve. Justice had just begun to be relieved by the thought that Sweetsea could close the channel if needed, by day or night, when he was chilled by the succeeding thought that he was wrong.

Very wrong. The *Pandora* could pass that critical bend if she was ever brought so far.

But under water.

That was what she had been designed to do in some French harbour. To creep up the Goulet at Brest or under the boom into the Liane at Boulogne.

"Cap'n." Scorcher scrambled over to sit beside him on the sternsheets and bring his wandering ideas back to the moment. "Seems that Tooth has found something, too." He pointed to three figures waving them in towards the bank, about two hundred yards above the fort, where it began to curve out into the river.

"Pull in," he commanded, and as the gig turned he saw the

face of Lower Exbury come into sight beyond its lawns and shrubbery. "It's a handsome house," he said to Ainsworth, surprised that Sweetsea should live in such style. "I shall like to see it."

Ainsworth took his remark as a hint that he would prefer to go round and land dry-shod at Sweetsea's jetty.

"No. Put me in where Tooth wants me," Justice insisted against Ainsworth's protest about the mud. He could not believe that the sailors could also have made a find, unless it was another lantern, but having sent the men to search, he would have to go where and when he was summoned.

It was a quick step from the gig to the rowboat, and an unexpected lift on a seaman's shoulder to the point on the bank where Tooth stood. Scorcher grunted, as though such courtesies were his business, but Justice thanked the man and looked to Tooth.

"Here, sir." From the smooth line left in the mud by the last high water, the sharp cut of a small keel ran straight into the hummocky grass; and here and there beside it, a toe under pressure had dug into the soft soil. Within the last few hours two men had pushed a boat up this bank, and . . . He looked inquiringly at Tooth, whose heavy features shone with pleasure at his discovery.

"In that gorse thicket, sir." The seaman led the way, pushing the spiny branches aside for Justice to follow. Well hidden from any casual glance, and turned over as though it might have been used for a few hours as a shelter, the blunt-nosed pram must have been the boat that Scorcher had heard splashing away from the lock.

Justice peered underneath. "Only one oar?"

"We've searched, sir . . ." Before Tooth had finished, Justice had an idea.

"Could they have lost one in the dark?" Tooth was bright enough. Justice could see that he had already considered that possibility and not wished to speak out of turn.

"With that bit o' a spit, sir, the current might bring 'em in close. An' one oar, dory fashion . . .see, sir, there's a notch for it in the stern . . ."

"Well done." He considered what order to give. "Send half the men back across the river here, and back to Cuffwells," he said. "Keep the others and strike across here to see if you pick up any more traces. It looks like rough sandhills and heather, but you never know."

Tooth hesitated. "How far, sir?" and as he asked, Justice tried to remember the chart he had looked at in Lilly's map room. "South of east," he said, "for a mile or two until you come to the water again. Be cautious, though two men aren't going to tackle a boat's crew unless they're desperate. And ask at each house you come to if anyone's been seen, or a boat taken." He thought for a moment. "You may come upon a Mr Bland. Out riding, or at his residence—though I'm not sure where you'll find it. Give him my compliments, and tell him that he can find me at Mr Sweetsea's place or at Wykeham. The same goes for you and your party. But if you find nothing, make your way home before nightfall."

Tooth seemed to like being given definite orders, and Justice wondered whether the man knew what a relief it was to give them. For the past few days he had lived in a whirl of such uncertainties and speculations that he never knew where one possibility ended and another began.

He watched Tooth's party divide and the two groups go their separate ways before he began to limp up to Lower Exbury.

A lantern. And a boat. There had been more to show for the morning's search than he had expected at the outset.

But where had the men gone?

He had sent Scorcher with Ainsworth to look at Gull-Island. If that drew a blank . . . then there must be some closer hiding place . . . somewhere the search parties could not have looked.

From the slight rise he looked across the river and saw smoke rising straight from the Wykeham chimneys into the clear air.

If not Gull-Island, there could only be one place . . .

❧ 14 ❧

WHEN JUSTICE HEARD carriage wheels crunch on the drive, he remembered that it was Sunday and decided that he should let the churchgoers get comfortably into the house before he went knocking at the door.

A hundred yards away the men from Cuffwells were having an argument with the ferryman. He could tell from the man's irritated gestures that he was not objecting to carrying them over for Sabbatarian reasons. No. The silly truth was obvious even at a distance. He had forgotten to give the sailors money for the crossing, and they were no more willing to pay out of their own pockets, if they had a few pennies between them, than the ferryman was ready to take them for nothing.

The sun was quite warm as he stood in it, watching the dispute with idle amusement, but it was soon interrupted by the sound of the calling bell on the Wykeham side. Looking across, Justice could make out a woman's figure on the far landing stage. Now the ferryman would have to make the journey after all, and grudgingly let the people from Cuffwells go free.

"Captain Justice. Delightful." Sweetsea had seen him through a window and come out to greet him, offering morning pleasantries before Justice pointed to Ainsworth's gig running out towards Gull-Island and cut in with news of the attack on the *Pandora*.

Sweetsea was stunned by what he said. "My men saw nothing, heard nothing," he said, looking towards the entrance to the fort where one of the Volunteers was doing a solitary sentry-go.

"I do not think they came from the sea," Justice said, as Sweetsea turned his gaze to where the Solent made a glittering line in front of the hills of Wight. "Nor have they gone back to it," he added, telling Sweetsea about the finding of the lanterns and the boat. "Nor do I now think they meant to steal the plunging-boat. Not this time."

And when Sweetsea seemed puzzled, Justice dredged at his thoughts to be sure what lay in them.

There was more to this game than the simple theft or destruction of the submarine. Whoever had struck against the *Pandora* could have done either already—and had chosen not to do so. Had chosen to tease, even though such feints would provoke a stronger guard on the vessel. And that meant whoever was playing the game was cunning, subtle, confident, and knew exactly what he wanted to do and when to do it.

Justice grunted with frustration. He still had no idea what the ends of the game might be.

"I can't say more," he said, telling the truth, and mystifying Sweetsea all the more by it.

Then they were talking about practical matters. Guards. Messages. Signals. "There's a fine beacon." Sweetsea nodded towards the fort. "Packed with wood and thatched to keep it dry."

He gave a wry grimace as he turned to go into the house.

"Built in case the French should come," he said. "Perhaps they have."

They were in the fine circular hallway when a sharp-featured lady in billowing black bombazine swept out of a doorway in such an obvious dudgeon that Justice suspected some domestic embarrassment.

Her appearance in this mood clearly upset Sweetsea, for he stammered an introduction. "Sister. Miss Augusta. Captain Justice. Honour. Pleasure." He could not get all his words off, indeed, before the virago gave a curt nod and spoke in an acid tone that matched her expression.

"A disgrace, Amos. A perfect disgrace. Coming here, when she knows . . ."

"Who? Eliza? Where?"

"Miss Botting." Augusta Sweetsea drew herself up. "The lady governess is in the library," she sniffed. "In a distressed state." She swept off with a cant of the head which left her brother in no doubt of her state of mind.

At the sound of Sweetsea's voice Eliza Botting came running out to join them. "Amos, Amos," she cried, with tears running down cheeks that were already red with weeping, and her dress muddied where she had run across soft ground in her haste.

"It is Emma," she said, breaking down completely as Sweetsea put out a questioning hand. "Lost. Quite lost."

Justice stepped back to ease her discomfiture as she threw herself on Sweetsea's chest. Lost. It was the word the gypsy had used that had so upset Harriet last night.

Lost? But how? And where? And why?

WITH A QUICK WORD of excuse Sweetsea took Eliza into the morning room to comfort her, and though Justice could hear her voice raised in lamentation, he could distinguish none of her words. It seemed odd, he thought, for her to come hurrying over from Wykeham to report the disappearance of her charge. A servant could have brought a message if Sweetsea's help was needed. And, as Miss Augusta had noticed, she did look to be excessively distressed. It sounded as if in some way the loss of the child were her fault, and she had fled from Wykeham in fear or disgrace.

While Justice waited indecisively in the hall, looking at a large painting of the *Queen Charlotte* in action on the Fourth of June, the servants began to carry dishes into the dining room, with Miss Augusta coming behind them like a frigate in full sail, chivvying the laggards of a merchant convoy. In this strictly regulated household Sunday dinner was obviously served almost as soon as the sound of the Sunday sermon had faded.

Miss Augusta stopped as she saw Justice. "I knew no good would come of it," she said darkly, "and the banns read the last time this morning."

Justice was sure that the formidable Miss Augusta would have kept a look of martyred patience on her face all through that little ceremony in Exbury Church.

"A lady governess," she said again. "In this house." And then she sailed on, having fired two shots to show that she had not yet struck her colours in this domestic engagement.

Justice watched her flick her hand at a dilatory footman before she swept away into the fine room that looked towards the river, and he wondered how long it must have taken the diffident Sweetsea to assert himself and go courting at Wykeham. Why the marriage was now being hurried on. Why Emma had been lost at the moment when everything at the great house was in a state of suspicious confusion.

Sweetsea came into the hall with Eliza, who seemed calmer as she told her story.

It was simple enough. She had watched the nursemaid put

Emma to bed, next to the room where she slept herself, and looked in on the child when she came upstairs after dinner.

"After I left," Sweetsea said, unnecessarily, as though his departure had somehow thrown too much responsibility on Eliza. He was clearly very attached to her, and Justice could see why an aging bachelor should find her so suitable—especially a man who had long lived under the militant supervision of such an elder sister as Miss Augusta.

For Eliza, nearing thirty he guessed as he got a close look at her, was still an attractive young woman, with golden hair pulled back so tightly that it gave her a look of wide-eyed surprise: and now there was fear in those eyes, and all the time she was talking, she was glancing at Sweetsea for support.

She had heard a cry in the night, she said, had gone to Emma's door and listened, had thought the child was calling out in a dream. No, she had not gone in to look at her, as she seemed to hear her settling again in the cot.

"That was when she went, it seems." Sweetsea had obviously heard the gist of the story already.

"Sleepwalking?" That was what Sweetsea must mean, hoping that the explanation would take the blame from Eliza, but Justice could not believe that a child of four would wander where no one in that big household could find her next morning. "Perhaps she is playing a jape," he suggested, remembering how the little girl had come wandering into his room before bedtime to play with that grisly toy.

But none of these assurances comforted Eliza, who shook her head and started to weep again. "Taken. Taken. Taken." It was a piteous cry that hinted she must know more than she admitted.

"By whom?" Justice could not tell what her last words meant.

"Gypsies?" Sweetsea was clutching at straws, and for a moment Justice considered whether he might be right. It was often said that gypsies . . . the gypsy fortune-teller had certainly been in the house last night . . . no gypsy would be fool enough to take a child from such a great house as Wykeham . . . unless there were a purpose and money to speed it . . . as the thoughts seesawed in his mind, he hoped that Grimshaw's men might stumble on the child or some sign of her whereabouts.

It was the feeling that Eliza wanted sympathy without being wholly frank that Justice found unsettling, and he began to catechise her. "When was Emma missed?" At eight, or so, when she usually ran in to be dressed. "And the house was searched?" Bit by bit, it seemed, as it became clear that Emma was lost. Eliza was sobbing heavily now. "Lady Harriet?" Distraught. And then there was some muttered remark about the Frenchwoman.

She said several words that Justice could not catch, because Sweetsea was consoling her, and Justice had to hold up a finger to silence him.

Emma, he finally heard her say, did not like Mademoiselle Gérard, was afraid of her, could have run away at the prospect of being ruled by her.

Justice thought she was talking nonsense. A child might resent the coming of a new governess, might throw a few tantrums, might even hide for an hour or two. But it was only a few moments since Eliza had cried "Taken" with such conviction. And as he found himself asking why she was so ambivalent, he recalled something Harriet had said to him about the child. "Her mother has entrusted her to me."

The child was fair-haired too.

"How long have you known Lady Harriet?" The question seemingly had little to do with Emma, and he only put it on a sudden inspiration. Yet it struck home. He saw her look more wide-eyed and startled than ever, as she saw he had come close to guessing her secret.

"Five years," she whispered, covering her confusion with another sob.

"In France, then?" Justice could now see the cause of her distress. She had come to seek comfort in Sweetsea's affection, and yet she could not speak frankly to this kindly man who was about to offer her a new station in life.

A future husband whose sister would succeed in wrecking her marriage if the truth were known.

A home that would be near the child she had borne in France and come back to nurture at Wykeham when Harriet had given them both her protection.

"I shall go to Wykeham at once, if you'll come with me." Justice had made up his mind, and he saw that Sweetsea was of a mind to go too—if only, after such a scene, to avoid any recriminations from that termagant in the morning room.

"If you'll be so good, Mr Sweetsea." The quarterdeck phrase brought Sweetsea back to the matters they had been discussing before Eliza's dramatic arrival. "Four Volunteers to Cuffwells, if you please. Four more to relieve them tonight. Armed, naturally. A regular watch on the lower river, especially at night, but no lights to be shown near the water.''

"Crews for the guns, sir?" Suddenly Sweetsea was recalling what the prospect of action was like, and an old zest was returning to make him forget the years of invalidity.

"On call," Justice said crisply. "But some drills in the dark would do them no harm, I warrant. And check your ranges to the whole reach of the channel as they bear.''

Justice noticed that Eliza was looking relieved at this display of naval discipline, as if she was glad that Sweetsea was called to duty, as if she was afraid that, in all the excitements of the day, someone might let slip the one disclosure that would be the ruin of all her hopes.

"And one thing more," he said, as Sweetsea rang for a man to fetch the carriage to take them round the curving drive to the ferry. "Mr Bland." He saw Sweetsea's quizzical reaction. "Yes, your odd neighbour, who is far from being the gauche and self-made India merchant that he makes out." He stood closer to Sweetsea to make sure that Eliza did not overhear him. "It is possible that he, too, is a friend of Mr Hatherley, and as such . . ." He was hesitant to go any further.

Sweetsea looked put out, almost as though Hatherley might have slighted him by doubling up the watch on the entrance to the river. "Sound him out if the chance occurs. I suspect he made overtures to me yesterday, when I was in no state to respond.''

"To what end?" These new instructions had left Sweetsea uncertain what was expected of him.

"We may need him, if things come to a crisis. We are spread so thin, and we have no idea where the next blow might fall. Before we are done, we may need every man we can trust.''

THE GYPSIES WERE DRIVING forty or fifty of the wiry little ponies out of the soggy saltings as the ferryman brought his boat in to the landing, driving them with whoops and calls in the Romany speech that pitched high in the clear air, driving on though a dogcart from Wykeham stood across the track.

"They have seen us from the house," Eliza had cried when she saw the groom clatter down the gravel drive and turn to wait for them, and she had rushed forward to ask the man for news. And fallen despondent again as he shook his head.

Justice could not make out her changes of mood. One moment she was beside herself with anxiety, and the next she seemed to be playing a forced and uncongenial part in a mystery which even she could not understand.

The ponies were all round them now, snuffling and jostling to get past the wheels, jumping as the groom casually flicked a whip over their backs; and the gypsies were coming up behind them, the women in the bright-coloured dresses, all saffron and green and gold, the men elegantly shabby in dark velveteens.

Could they have taken the child? Darkened its face and hidden it with their own brood, as the old wives said in their tales? He looked at the brown faces as they came, jolly with their own kind, guarded with other people, and knew that if they had a secret they would keep it better than anyone.

They were almost past now, ignoring Justice and Eliza, when he heard a screech, felt a clutch at his arm, and looked round to see the woman fortune-teller on the back step. As she saw him she cried out again, in a different tone, and put up her hands to feel his cheeks as if she were blind. "Brother's face!" she called, as if it were a name for him, and reached out to pull one of the men beside her as she lapsed into a flow of angry Romany.

"She says . . . she says . . ." The man spoke slowly, as if afraid of giving offence. "She says your money is not money."

"My shilling?" Justice wondered what crazed notion the woman had carried away with his piece of silver from that first meeting on the banks of the Test.

The man shook his head and listened while the woman spoke again. "It is not money," he repeated, holding out his hand to show the coin she had rummaged out of her clothes and laid on his palm.

Justice had only the quickest glimpse of it as the groom slapped the reins and the light carriage jolted forward, throwing both the gypsies off the step to a chorus of execrations.

They were coming up the drive to the gatehouse, where Harriet stood to meet them, before Justice could bring himself to believe what he had seen.

Someone at Wykeham had paid that gypsy woman money to tell a fortune or carry a message or hide a child.

Someone had paid her with a gold franc.

❧15❧

"WE HAVE BEEN THROUGH the house twice," Harriet said. "Through rooms I've never seen before. Pulling back curtains, shifting chairs and beds, ransacking closets . . ." She sounded tired, and as depressed as though she knew the search was futile. "Through everything. Attics. Haylofts. Barns. Even the chapel, which hasn't been opened since my father came into the title."

"And no sign? No word?" Eliza grasped unhappily at Harriet's hands, and Justice sensed some cautionary glance between them.

"Mr Grimshaw?" He was about to offer the help of the head gamekeeper and his party when Harriet interrupted.

"Here an hour since, and now gone to scour the ditches by St Leonard's Farm." She was comforting Eliza as the governess broke down. "He has something to tell you," she said tartly, as if she were slightly annoyed at having to carry a ground servant's message.

Whatever it was would have to wait, for the hours of daylight were slipping away, and the shadow of the great hall was already falling cold and wide across the courtyard from the gatehouse where they stood.

"What do you think, now?" Justice spoke bluntly to Harriet. If there was one corner or cranny in Wykeham that had been overlooked, she would know of it. "Could she still be in the house? Or taken?"

"Taken?" Harriet looked startled when he used Eliza's word. "Who would take the child away? For what reason? And where?"

Justice was no more able to give a definite answer to these questions than when they had first occurred to him after Eliza's cry of "Taken" at Sweetsea's house, but since he had thought of Eliza's predicament, and seen her now with Harriet, his notion of what that answer might be had grown clearer with every passing minute.

Eliza was so bewildered that she could only know that she was threatened by some fateful disclosure, and that her child had been taken from the nursery to make that threat more potent. Harriet was not confused. She had known what had happened to Emma from the moment the child had been taken, or very soon after: had been told why she had been taken, and even where she was being held: was well aware what might happen if she was found too soon.

For some bargain had been struck. Justice could tell that from Harriet's manner and her readiness to waste time in fruitless searches. Emma would be safe, if that bargain was kept, but she would not be returned before all its terms were met; and any attempt at premature rescue might put the child at risk.

It was then that Justice knew beyond doubt that it was some French hand that was pulling the strings in this sad puppet play—the same French hand that had carelessly passed a franc for a guinea, that had been the prime mover in all the alarms and excursions of the past few days. There was a figure of evil in the shadows at Cuffwells and Wykeham, who was working to an elaborate plan and had now made the child the means to keep his presence and his plans a secret until he was ready to strike.

Who had discovered the facts of Emma's mysterious parentage. Had seen how to use them to his advantage. Had forced Harriet to remain silent to protect those whom she loved.

Justice did not know whether to be angry with Eliza and Harriet because their fears made it impossible to find a child who might be crying her heart out in despair, or to feel a deep sympathy with a dilemma so painful that he hoped he would never face the like of it.

But however he felt he would have to shock them out of it, for he could do nothing useful until Emma was found and free.

Eliza seemed about to leave when he put out a hand to detain her, feeling her quiver with anxiety as he put the question which had been teasing at the edge of his memory ever since he heard that Emma was lost.

"Did you play hide-my-eyes with her?" He could still conjure up the child's guileless face, smiling and chattering as she had played with that grisly toy last night.

146

She hesitated, looking at Harriet before she replied. "Often."

"Lately?"

"Not for some days."

"Then who did?"

"The Frenchwoman." Before she could say more, Harriet brusquely interrupted.

"Marie-Louise has nothing to do with it. She is so upset . . ." Harriet, too, became distressed as she spoke, and Justice barely caught her last words. "In her room all day."

Justice was tempted to ask why the new governess had not joined the search, but there were more urgent things to be done. He turned back to Eliza. "When?"

"Two or three days ago. I forget." She anticipated his next question. "In the gatehouse, I think. And in the picture gallery." She gestured to the wing of the house which ran away towards the stable block.

Before Justice could say more, he heard voices across the courtyard and peeped round the gatehouse tower to see a group of men filing down one of the outside staircases.

"Are they armed?" The question surprised and upset Harriet.

"Armed?" she asked. "To search for a child?"

"Or three determined men, for whom time may be running out." He spoke so forcefully that Harriet's protest died on her lips. "I at least need a pistol. If Miss Botting . . ."

"Go to Mr Grinton," Harriet said. "The steward," she added to Justice as Eliza hurried off without speaking, and then she waited, seeing that he wished to speak privately to her—though her ambiguous expression showed she was uncertain whether he wished to speak of the lost child or come back to that moment of intimacy which had been broken by Scorcher's arrival last night.

"Emma is her child, of course," Justice said without preamble.

"She said you had guessed."

"And I might also guess at the father?"

"So you might." Harriet was regaining some of her natural vigour now that they were speaking frankly. "But it would be wiser and kinder if you did not." She gave Justice a pleading look. "It is a secret that I have given much to keep. Until now, until . . ."

147

"Until someone came from France who knew it?"

She nodded in mute misery, and then grasped his arm with great force. "Let it be," she cried. "It is none of your business."

The appeal touched Justice but did not deflect him. "It is all my business, I am afraid, though you tell me only the half of it." He disliked speaking to her so harshly but her words left him no option. He knew as surely as if she had told him that Francis, whom she loved in vain, was the father of Eliza's child, and that love and pain combined to make that child precious to her.

And blinded her to the facts. The threat of exposing Emma's parentage would be enough to make both women keep silent about dubious visitors to the house, or goings-on they could not quite understand—an anonymous word to Miss Augusta would ruin all Eliza's hopes, and reveal the secret that Harriet had kept so long.

Yet they had not seen how Emma might be used more dramatically and dangerously. What would Francis do if he learned the child was missing, in French hands, perhaps. Could he be forced to abandon work on the *Pandora*, to turn over her secrets or the vessel herself to the French, or to accept an offer to return to France and work for Bonaparte again?

He had no means of knowing. He was only sure that both women knew more than they had yet revealed, and that he must compel them to help him to Emma, to break the spell that hung over the child before greater and worse use was made of her.

"Mr Justice." Eliza's voice gave her away. As she gingerly handed him the pistol he could tell that she was on the verge of another collapse into screams and weeping. He led the way to the tower.

"We shall find nothing," Eliza said despairingly.

"Not unless we look." Justice hated what he was about to do. "What did Emma see? Who did she see?" They had climbed into the room where all the winding gear for the portcullis rose in a dusty jumble from the floor. "And where?" It was getting difficult to see in the light from the slitted windows, but in a dark corner, where the ends of the hauling ropes were bundled, something light caught his eye, and he bent to pick up a piece of pink hair ribbon. "The French governess?'' he asked, swinging round to face Eliza. "Or Emma's?'' And as she snatched it with a low moan he looked at Harriet. "Is there another entrance?'' He had the impression that she was delaying, as if she was unable to make up her mind to speak.

"Above,'' she answered in a distracted sort of way, pointing to a ladder that rose through a square hole in the boarded ceiling. "Into a corridor that opens into the picture gallery.''

There was nothing concealed up there: he could tell that by the easier way she spoke, as if she was satisfied to see him waste time searching rooms that the servants had already examined.

"Did you see Mademoiselle Gérard come here with Emma?'' he asked Eliza, and knew she spoke the truth when she admitted it. "I was in the gallery,'' she said, giving her secret away again by the unhappy tone of her confession. "Watching them. They had been walking outside. By the kitchen garden, I think.''

Justice caught the slight gasp from Harriet before she could quite stifle it. "She had been playing hide-my-eyes out there,'' he said, ignoring Harriet's reaction. "Could it be that Mademoiselle was meeting someone . . . someone she did not wish the child to see . . . to pass a message . . . ?''

"I have no idea,'' Eliza said miserably. "I have told you. I have told you.''

"I believe you.'' Justice could grant her that, knowing how much worse the next few minutes would be for her. "But I do not believe Lady Harriet. She knows where to look for the child. But she will not look. And you both know why.''

The three of them stood so silently for a moment that Justice heard the creaking of wood and the sound of mice scurrying about on the floor above. But before Harriet could answer him he heard Scorcher crossing the bridge and coming towards the gatehouse, chattering loudly, and asking some servant if he knew where Mr Justice was to be found.

It was not the moment he would have chosen to release Eliza and Harriet from the pressure he was putting upon them both, but the news Scorcher brought might bear on what he proposed to do, and importantly, and he could not let him pass.

"I think you will wait,'' he said earnestly, but not too unkindly, feeling sure that only the most forlorn urgency would make them scramble up the ladder to evade him, and hoping besides that some reflection might induce Harriet to think differently.

But her last remark as he went down the steps to meet Scorcher was not encouraging.

"I hope you know what you are doing, Mr Justice." She went close to Eliza and put a protective arm around her. "I hope for the sake of the child and the mother that you are not playing a game at blind stakes."

SCORCHER LOOKED DISAPPOINTED, and all the more so because Grimshaw had come in with him bringing news that another lantern had been found near Needs Ore Point, where the river made its right-angled turn and left the fast-running gut between the point and Gull-Island to fill and empty at the top of the tide.

"And nothing else," Grimshaw said.

"And Gull-Island?" Justice had hoped Scorcher would find signs of some makeshift encampment there—fire ashes, possibly another pair of lanterns, a box with blue flares or a chart, even bottles of brandy or the remains of food.

"Nothing." Scorcher was really despondent. "Blown sand everywhere, and you wouldn't spend the night there and stay dry, well, not at this time of year."

"Spume cuts right across when there's any kind of wind and sea," Grimshaw added, and got a glare from Scorcher for his helpfulness.

"Or warm." Scorcher was determined to finish his report. "Unless you put kindling and firewood ashore, and there's none of that."

The more Fred Scorcher said the more Justice realized that since he had first looked at the map he had somehow counted on finding traces of a landing on Gull-Island. It was where he would have made a temporary lodgement if he had been seeking to work his way into the river. And then, immediately, he saw why he was wrong. A place like Gull-Island could only be used for a night or two, on the kind of operation he had carried out so often with the Breton rebels. It was not simply discomfort that made it unusable. It was too difficult to get to it. And impossible to hide on it, if a fair-sized vessel was in the river, or fishermen landed to set night lines, as they did along the similar beaches where the Rother ran out to the sea near Rye.

One of the cottagers by the point, Grimshaw was saying, had seen a brig close inshore about two weeks ago, apparently searching for the entrance but turning away to sea after reaching the mouth of the river beyond Lepe.

There could be a connection, Justice conceded. But Grimshaw's comment showed him what was wrong with all his speculation about Gull-Island.

The plans against the *Pandora* were well laid, and time had been spent on them. It was most unlikely that those who were to set and spring the trap had come all at once, or, he now saw, that they had come from the sea at all. The French would have sent one man at a time, as he was needed; and each of them would have found some excuse to be near the river, or some better hiding place than a windblown island with no water and no cover against the weather or suspicious eyes.

Then where? Where had the men gone who had vanished near the Old Fort? And which of those he had met since he had come to Cuffwells might prove to be their accomplices?

"Fred," he said hurriedly, for he was eager to press Harriet before she found some strength to resist him, "you'll find four Volunteers at Cuffwells tonight. Make good use of them. We want no second mistake with the patrols."

"And you, Cap'n?"

Justice felt uneasy in saying that he planned to stay at Wykeham, especially as Scorcher had surprised him with Harriet the night before. Yet he had no choice. Emma had to be found.

He had no idea what might follow. He only knew, in his bones, that the whole of the *Pandora* affair might turn upon that discovery.

He saw that Scorcher was looking at his hand, and remembered that he was still holding the pistol that Eliza had brought him.

"Yes," he said, to Scorcher's puzzlement. "Yes, I may well need that."

HARRIET WAS LOOKING out of one of the narrow windows when Justice returned, and as she heard his step she swung round with a look of defiance on her face.

"Stay still, Eliza," she said to the girl sitting dejectedly by the windlass. "This is my affair."

But Justice was in no mood to argue with her. "Will you take me to the child?" he asked, coming at once to the point at which he had gone off to speak to Scorcher. "Or shall I go back to Lower Exbury?"

She was about to make a fierce retort when Eliza rose to her feet, ashy-faced and hand to mouth, and ran to her. "To Miss Sweetsea, to be explicit," Justice said harshly, knowing and regretting how bitterly Harriet would resent what he was doing.

"Have you no honour? Have you no pity?" Harriet's unguarded exclamations confirmed what he had suspected.

"I have my duty, too." It sounded pompous as he said it, and he did not expect that argument to weigh much with one of the levelling Romneys, but it was true, and the only justification for the cruelty of his threat to Eliza.

"I do not know where Emma is to be found, God help me!" Eliza almost screamed at him, the tears starting again from her eyes, with such evident truth that Justice could feel for her desperation. Both her future and the fate of her child lay in the hands of others over whom she had no control.

"But Lady Harriet does, you see," Justice insisted. "And she will not tell me for a very good reason—because she is determined to save your promised marriage to Mr Sweetsea from shipwreck."

"Is that right?" Eliza stepped back so sharply from Harriet's embrace that Justice's remark about her child was clearly a shock to her. "I knew . . . I was told . . ." She floundered for words to explain. "That there was a secret . . ." As she began to speak Harriet gave a gesture of impatient resignation, as if all her efforts to help Eliza were now to be thrown away. "But only that . . . that Miss Sweetsea would be told . . . unless . . . unless . . ." She sobbed. "There was no reason to take Emma. I would have kept my promise. No reason . . ."

"Until I came," Justice said. That would mean nothing to Eliza, but it would tell Harriet how much he had already guessed.

She reacted at once. "Why do you persecute Eliza?" It was a last attempt to distract him, and even as he tried to beat down her resistance he admired the way her eyes flashed as she confronted him. Whatever else might be said of Harriet

152

Romney, no one would accuse her of lacking courage.

He laid the pistol down on the great beam that secured the windlass to the wall, and saw her eyes follow his action.

"I am not concerned with the domestic battles of the Sweetsea family," he said deliberately, but as kindly as he could. "I am fighting a very different enemy, Lady Harriet. A hidden enemy, who lives and strikes in the dark—at Miss Botting, at you, and through you at me, and through me at our country. It may seem strange, but at this moment, when so much turns on what we do in the next few hours, Miss Botting's . . . er, circumstances, are as much a weapon that is being used against me as this gun."

He lifted the pistol and saw that it was properly primed and loaded. At least Miss Botting had played fair with him over that.

"You are speaking in riddles," Harriet began, countering his attack. "Out of all proportion." There she stopped, badly shaken and bewildered by the force of his words, as if she was at last beginning to see more of the web of intrigue in which she, Eliza, and the child had become entangled; and the glint of light on the blue barrel of the pistol was the first proof to her that Justice was in deadly earnest when he proposed to pull them out of it. "If you believe . . ." She found it hard to believe that Justice had now guessed the secrets which she and Eliza were so reluctantly and so unhappily obliged to protect.

"Forgive me," he said, laying down the pistol so that she should not think that he would use violence to persuade her. "Believe? I know." He went across and put his hands squarely on her shoulders. "I know so much, Lady Harriet, that we waste precious time in argument. I have known for the past hour why Miss Botting is frightened half out of her wits. I know why you are equally afraid that the truth about Emma's parentage may be revealed." He felt Harriet stir angrily away from under his hands and throw a glance at Eliza, warning him to be discreet. "And I know why Emma was spirited away, why a bargain had to be struck over her safekeeping . . ."

She was becoming more dismayed with every word he spoke. "It was because . . ." she said defensively, and then let Justice go on remorselessly.

"Because someone heard what she said to me yesterday morning before the race. Because of what she saw when she played hide-my-eyes with Mademoiselle Gérard.'' He remembered how the child had been hurried away after she had looked at him with mistaken recognition and asked him to play again. "Or was it *who* she saw?"

Harriet's expression told him that he had struck home without having to explain what he meant in front of Eliza, who was barely able to listen sensibly or comprehend what was happening around her; even as he paused she stopped sobbing, gave Harriet the most reproachful of looks, and said savagely, "*You* could find her!" before lapsing into hopeless weeping again.

"Do not mistake me," Justice said in a way that made Harriet stiffen. "I can do nothing until that child is set free again, and to find her I am prepared to use my knowledge as ruthlessly as whoever it is who has threatened you with exposure." He swung round to take up the pistol. "As ruthlessly as I will use this gun if I am forced to it. You must tell me, or . . ."

"Or what, Mr Justice?" Harriet spoke fiercely. "The case is hopeless when you threaten, too. I have only a choice of evils. This enemy you speak of, though I have yet to learn what his affairs are to do with you . . . If you do what you propose, Eliza will be betrayed whatever happens. By you, or by him. And at least he is not walking about Wykeham flourishing a pistol in my face."

"Perhaps not. Perhaps the danger is to us all, though you cannot see it. But you have no choice. If you defy me, I go at once to . . ." He did not finish the sentence out of compassion for Eliza. "If you take me to Emma you have a chance." He went across and stood looking down at Eliza. "For her sake, for your sake as well, do not drive me too hard. We can save her if you will help, and if we act quickly. Leave her now, and take me."

Harriet hesitated for only a second, then shrugged her shoulders. "I wondered what sort of man you were, Captain Justice," she said enigmatically. "Where I should find the iron in you."

ᗒ 16 ᗕ

HARRIET STEPPED IN under an arch that was only a short distance from the tower where Eliza sat weeping, and led Justice down a short flight of stone steps into a passage that looked as though it might run under the whole front of the building. It was cavernous and gloomy, but even in the dying hours of the afternoon there was enough light filtering through gratings set high in the wall to see one's way without stumbling.

Every few yards they passed an old and padlocked door, with a metal grille in it, mouldering with age and a green dampness that told Justice they must be close to that half-drained moat.

"Dungeons?" Justice realized that this house would go on astonishing him for days if he was ever to be shown all of it.

"Cells, yes." Harriet paused for a moment to let him peer into one to see that it was quite unused. "But for the monks, not prisoners, Mr Justice." She gave a dry laugh. "Unless you consider, as does my father, that they foolishly imprisoned themselves. It makes him angry to think how their lives were wasted."

There was a door, a narrow stair, and they went up to squeeze through a shortcut between two massive stone walls. "We do not know what lies under there," Harriet said, almost conversationally, as though the decision she had just made had given some relief to her anxiety. "I say it's where the Abbot hid all the treasure, but William thinks it was a secret chapel." She glanced at Justice as though he might not understand. "In the time when they were chasing Catholic priests. As traitors. And they had to hide."

He understood very well, remembering his own family history on the French side, his mother's side, where the Valcourts had been harried for their Protestant beliefs. There had been a hiding place, too, in the mill at Recques, where he and his

155

cousin Luc had played Huguenots and Catholics when they were boys; he had used that chamber behind the mill race only a few weeks ago when he was himself on the run in France.

But he said nothing of it, for he was learning caution in the hard game to which Lilly had apprenticed him, and he was already finding his relations with Harriet more complicated than was comfortable.

For both of them, he thought, with a twinge of regret for Scorcher's dramatic interruption last night.

They went through two more doors, down a stair where a lantern was burning to light the lower lobby. It looked like any other lantern, but Justice could see that the flame burned without a wick, and that an iron pipe came round the wall to it, and joined another which then ran on upwards, and then through the rafters above them. Justice had an idea what Harriet would say before she spoke.

"It is William's special place." She came to a stop in front of a door and turned to face him. "No one else is permitted."

"So it was not searched?" The way she explained the underground chamber, it sounded as if she were doing him a favour rather than bringing him there more or less under duress. She shook her head.

"It is for . . . for his work . . . his chemistry," she said, uncertain how to account for what her brother did there, and pointed to the pipes. "Now he makes lights." She raised her eyes. "To use in his library." And as she lowered her gaze again, Justice noticed that she was looking at the pistol in his hand. They had only taken a minute or two on their way from the tower but she had cleverly cooled the tension between them there, as though she feared some evil consequence of his impetuousness.

No doubt little Emma was somewhere behind that door. But from Harriet's expression she clearly expected to find someone else there as well.

He checked the lock of the pistol and saw Harriet look at him as if she was caught in a nightmare and could not wake out of it.

He put out his hand to move her gently aside so that he could listen at the door, and felt her fingers, cold, grasp his knuckles for a fleeting moment.

There was certainly someone in the room that lay beyond this door, as strong as a house entry, and another, baize-fronted to deaden sound, which lay beyond it. But he could hear only a low murmur, and he decided that the muffling effect of the baize would give him a chance to lift the metal latch and burst onwards with as much of a rush as a man could manage with a dragging knee.

He put his hand to the latch and found to his dismay that Harriet's arm was stretched between him and the jamb of the door.

"No," he said in an urgent whisper. "No," and he tried to ease her away without using so much force that they would be heard.

"But Emma . . ."

"You are sure she is here?"

"Since you left last night. Or soon after."

"She will not be harmed." Justice would have been happier if Harriet had been more forthcoming and told him what he might find beyond that green-faced door. But he saw that she had become stiff and fearful again, and he could only explain such rapid changes of mood by a state of anxiety so acute that she was having to make a great effort to control herself.

He could delay no longer. "Stand back," he said, as he plainly heard a voice from within the room, and then a child's cry—though he could not tell whether it was a laugh or tearfulness. Whatever deep game was being played with Emma he must now put an end to it, and let the secrets that were locked in with her come out into the light of day.

He got the latch raised with no more than a snap of metal, shouldered his way through the baize door, and almost sprawled as it swung easily and left him not knowing whether to duck or fire if he got a clear sight of the man.

He staggered upright and it was well that he had a steady finger on the trigger.

For it was Lord William who sat there, quite at his ease, with Emma at his side, filling soap bubbles with some gas from a pipe and using a burning taper to pop them into flame as they slowly drifted upwards.

His first reaction was that Harriet had made a fool of him. And then, as she came into the room, he saw that she was equally surprised.

And very much relieved, as Emma climbed down with a little cry of delight and ran straight to Justice, touching him, and then running away to an inner room where she stood with her hands covering her face.

Justice followed and gently lifted her up.

"Did you play hide-my-eyes?" he asked. "With a man who looked like me?"

EMMA STARED AT HIM for a moment before she nodded, looked at Harriet, and nodded again. She had given away the secret she had been taken to hide.

Luc. Lilly was wrong, Justice knew as he set Emma down. Luc was not dead. The report that Lilly had received was simply a routine deception to cover his journey to England. For Luc was here at Wykeham, as he should have guessed already. Here to seize Francis. Or the *Pandora*. Or both of them.

"You saw the likeness of course," he said to Harriet and Lord William, using the question to control his racing thoughts, remembering the starts of half recognition when they first met him, the stares from Fanshawe and the Frenchwoman, the gypsy's fingers tracing across his face, the two sailors who had sworn he had given them a message after the race.

"I thought . . . I thought it one of those rare coincidences," Lord William stammered, but Justice cut him short with a curt gesture as he looked round the little room in which Luc had been concealed—for a week, two weeks, was it?

It was large enough to be comfortable, but there was nowhere to hide except a clothing press which stood slightly open as though someone had snatched a coat from it before leaving in a hurry.

Justice nosed it open with the pistol.

Nothing. Nothing in the drawer in the bedside table that he opened in the hope of finding a revealing scrap of paper. Nothing except a rumpled bed.

He turned to face Lord William. "How long?"

"An hour," Romney said reluctantly, after he had turned to look at his sister and been given a confirming nod. "But . . . all the same . . ."

Justice had noticed that nervous uncertainty when they had talked beside the *Pandora* and was determined to make the most of it.

"No buts, if you please," Justice said, all the more curtly for his disappointment. If Luc had been here all the time he had been beating the bushes along the river, talking to

Sweetsea about setting a trap in case there was another attempt on the *Pandora* . . . if Luc had slipped away while he had been questioning Scorcher and Grimshaw by the gate . . . He was tempted to go after him at once, instead of bandying arguments with Lord William and harassing Lady Harriet to do things she would resent and regret.

And yet he knew that it would be a waste of effort to go haring off, with no better idea where his quarry would go to ground than those which had failed to produce results all day.

Slow now might mean surer later.

"Emma?" He had been about to press his advantage with Lord William when Harriet spoke, putting the child down with that note of enquiry in her voice so that he could guess what she was about to ask. "May I take her to Eliza?"

It was so unlike Harriet to seek permission for anything, or to be so evidently dispirited, that Justice could tell how profoundly she had been affected by that unpleasant scene in the windlass room, and he regretted the necessity of cowing her into what she undoubtedly saw as a breach of a promise, however it had been extracted; he could easily understand how she would wish to get away from the risk of more bullying of that kind—especially if she did not properly understand the reason for it. He felt for her, and for Eliza as well. It would be hard to refuse this request when the wretched mother had no idea why or where her child had been taken, and whether indeed she was safe.

Yet so many peculiar things had happened at Wykeham that he was reluctant to trust anyone, or consider feelings, or manners, or personal convenience. He had spoken the hard truth when he had used the word *duty* to Harriet in the tower. He might be in England, among agreeable people, who had no idea of the exigencies of war, or any sense of wrongdoing in their relations with their American and French acquaintances. That made no difference. The danger was as great, and his obligations as clear, as they would be on his own quarterdeck.

So it had to be a matter of honour. If an Englishwoman could not pledge her word and stand to it the world would indeed be in a sorry state. "If you give me your word."

He was still holding the pistol and he searched for a place on the table to put it down among Lord William's flasks and tubing. Then he tapped it as a reminder that all this drama was no mere play-acting for effect. Emma might still be in peril. "See the child is put to bed,'' he said, still fearing some new attempt to make her hostage if Luc saw that situation would turn to his advantage. "With Miss Botting in the room, and one footman at least to keep watch outside it."

"My word?" Harriet had been so distracted by that request that she still seemed uncertain what was expected of her.

"To speak to no one else," Justice said firmly. "To pass no messages. To return here as soon as possible." He paused, and made a gesture that included both brother and sister. "I wish I could believe you innocents, and no more." He spoke in the earnest voice he normally used only for shipboard defaulters.

He paused again, to emphasise the gravity of his next sentence.

"What you have done could be a hanging matter."

Harriet gasped, and clutched at Emma, and Lord William's nervous fingers snapped the tube of glass he had been twisting in his fingers since he had lifted it to make room for the pistol.

"For what?" Lord William seemed as much surprised as anxious.

"Treason, for one thing," Justice said harshly, "and there are judges and juries that would not give a Romney the benefit of much doubt." He saw Lord William flinch at his words. "Harbouring an enemy, for another. Conspiracy to commit arson." He looked directly at Harriet. "And kidnapping. I expect the indictment would run to a score of pages before the lawyers were finished with it."

"This is nonsense." Lord William seemed defiant, but his voice was quavering, and Justice recalled that Harriet had said that he was not manly. "You cannot be serious. You have no cause to frighten us in this way. My father . . ."

". . . is best kept out of it, if he is so far ignorant." Justice was waiting for Harriet to protest but she seemed stunned by the savagery of his charge. "Go," he said to her, feeling the infliction of such misery much against the grain of his character. He would not have resorted to such stern methods if he could have found any other way of quickly bringing them to realize that they had been playing with fire; and he hoped his words would worry at her while he was examining her brother.

"Only the utmost frankness can help you now," he said. "Or make it possible for me to help you."

"There is no truth . . . no evidence, witnesses, nobody saw." Harriet was a resilient young woman and she was making a last attempt to conjure his accusations away and put some resolve into her agitated brother.

"There will be, before I am done," Justice said, feeling miserable in the harsh role in which he had to cast himself.

"If you would leave me with Lord William . . ."

"THE FRENCHMAN CALLED himself Charles Gérard. Her brother." It had not taken Justice long to bring Lord William to a full explanation. He sat there, cracking his long fingers, looking around at the well-appointed room as if it were truly a cell instead of a modern alchemist's laboratory, blinking nervously each time Justice put him to the question.

He had rambled over Fanshawe's arrival—unexpected, he said; and he had taken the Frenchwoman's story about the shipwreck as credulously as he seemed to take everything that was not scientific in nature.

"And Lady Harriet believed it too?" Justice could see how someone could impose on her instinctive kindness.

"Until yesterday," Romney insisted, and it was then that Justice understood why Harriet had been so restlessly uneasy that she came to his room.

Until yesterday, when little Emma had so nearly given everything away at the party before the race. Until late last night, when Luc had come to fetch Emma and left a bundle of threats in her place.

"But Lu . . . the man she called her brother?" Justice was trying to imagine how his covert arrival was explained.

In danger of arrest, she had told Harriet, according to Lord William—and near to the truth, Justice said to himself. On account of debts run up when he was an exile in London. And now come over to seek a settlement of some other money due to him before he sailed again for America. It was all plausible enough, Justice supposed.

Yet he could tell that Lord William had not been deceived by it. "You knew he was not her brother," Justice said with brutal force. Lord William hemmed and hawed. He might have been deceived, after all. Why not?

"Because he was a clandestine agent from France. And you knew that from the moment he arrived."

The repetition of that charge alarmed Lord William and he started up, jerking one arm so violently that he sent a flask of some noxious fluid spilling across the table and Justice had to turn away from its vapour while he mopped it up.

"No! No! No! I had no idea. No idea at all." Lord William spoke with agitation as he swabbed away, and Justice could see that he was past telling lies. "He came to see Robert, to ask him . . ."

"To lure him back to France," Justice said bluntly.

Lord William waved his hand in vehement denial. "No! No! To America!" he cried, surprising Justice by his conviction that what he said was true, and showing how Luc must have played upon his attachment to Francis and to all Americans. "To persuade him to give up the plunging-boat. The carcasses. To stop all these designs for weapons of war and deploy his talents peaceably." He had become very excited. "That was what I wanted. What I begged so passionately from Robert every time he came."

How clever Luc had been, how well prepared, with a tale that would be immediately acceptable to a man of Lord William's opinions and credulity. Lilly had been quite right in fearing that the Romneys might be more nuisance as dupes than as conspirators; and everything Justice had learned in the last hour had confirmed that judgment.

"Did he come with any proof to support his story?"

"He was engaged in some speculation," Lord William said. "Or so he claimed," he added, caution coming late upon him. "With other Americans. A man called Livingstone. Barlow, perhaps. He mentioned others. To make Robert leave for New Orleans." He spoke as though Francis was a free agent, as if he saw nothing particularly out of the way in getting a man to throw up all he had undertaken and to set off on some quite different enterprise—and as Lilly had said, Justice reflected, Francis was quite capable of doing that if the fancy took him. "To New Orleans," Lord William repeated, finding some satisfaction in the sound of the name. "To start steamboats on the Mississippi. With French capital." He had become a little calmer when he saw that Justice was listening to him. "An excellent idea. Useful. Profitable. Exactly what should be done."

"But why did the Frenchman come? Why did Barlow not speak to Francis in London?" Justice had to check his enthusiasm.

Romney obviously failed to see the point of these two questions, for his answer was irrelevant, and revealing. "Being French, you see, he could not come openly."

"And came secretly because that was not his true purpose."

"Only from Ireland." Romney seemed to regard his route as a mitigating circumstance.

"From France, by whatever route: it comes to the same thing." Justice found it hard to make Lord William face the realities of his situation. "He must have come from France. Either he or the superior agent who sent him on this mission despatched others to assist him—Fanshawe and the woman who claims to be his sister for two of them, certainly, and probably more besides." Romney was beginning to look startled again as Justice went through this litany of accusations. "He persuaded you to conceal him." Justice looked all round the pair of rooms, thinking how much more pleasant they were than any hiding place he had imagined for Luc. "Thinking only that he might risk internment if caught, and that he could wait here in comfort until Francis arrived."

Lord William's eager assent was pathetic. For a man whose political beliefs bordered on sedition he seemed to be unaware how easily he might be compromised.

"But he was actually here to seize or sink the *Pandora*, and abduct Francis as well."

As Justice spoke a new thought came to him. "Perhaps the original plan was to seize the submarine last night," he said. "If only Francis had come."

Perhaps that was why the horse race had been arranged. Perhaps the dinner had also been planned as a distraction.

"If you had foreknowledge, gave any kind of help . . . in that case both you and Lady Harriet would have been parties to the scheme. Accomplices." He gave Romney a cruel look. "Let me remind you, Lord William. Everyone in a conspiracy suffers the same penalty irrespective of the degree of personal guilt."

"Oh, no!" Lord William seemed so astounded that Justice suspected he had never given a serious thought to the dangers of collusion with a Frenchman.

"Oh, yes!" Justice suddenly thumped the table so hard that all the flasks and bottles rattled. "That is why I said you were risking your neck on what you claim is a peaceful speculation between Mr Barlow and his mysterious friend from France. A surreptitious *commerçant*, indeed. Your neck. Your sister's neck. The neck of anyone who knew that you were sheltering this man . . . this experienced agent who works for M. Fouché and for present purposes calls himself Charles Gérard. Even the unfortunate Miss Botting is in peril.''

"Then that is why . . .'' Lord William was at last beginning to see the design of the maze in which he was so innocently wandering.

"Why you were told so explicitly to say nothing about his presence here—to me especially. Why threats were made to Miss Botting to ensure her silence. Why Emma was kept down here. Why Lady Harriet was encouraged to think that Hatherley was responsible for the troubles at Cuffwells, and that you might be in danger from him, or his underlings. Why she is so confused that she now does not know whom to trust or where to look for help or how to put your family affairs straight again.''

"HOW DID HE LEAVE?'' Justice had found that the simplest question got the simplest answer from Romney.

"By the old well, of course.'' Lord William spoke as if everyone knew of this exit from the house, and Justice had to ask what he meant.

Romney lit a lantern with a taper from the fire and led him to one of the old cell doors in the passage. Like Harriet, he had the knack of cool explanation between moments of excitement or anxiety.

"Under the moat,'' he explained, opening the door and showing Justice the damp passage that opened from the back wall, and in the flickering light Justice saw the iron pipe that ran into the dark.

He did not understand what it was at first, for as he had crouched to follow Lord William he had recalled how Harriet had seemed so curiously upset by the gypsy's words. "Child's game. Look again. Lost and found. Under ground.'' Could the gypsy have been brought here by Luc, have seen Emma, have been bribed to pass on that reminder to Harriet not to forget her bargain?

"It opens beyond the moat?''

"I cleared it for my gas pipe,'' Lord William said, as if that were the best reason in the world for crawling through the debris of this ancient tunnel. "There is gas coming continuously from the slime in the old well," he said. "It bubbles." He scrambled on ahead, talking as he went. He seemed about to give another of his impromptu lectures on chemistry before he decided that it would be wasted on Justice. "It was built long ago." He stood aside so that Justice could see a gleam about twenty yards down the tunnel. "To provide a water supply if the house was besieged. In Cromwell's time, I imagine. Perhaps as a means of escape as well, for there are rungs . . ."

He had not finished before Justice snatched the lantern from his hand and set off down the passage, feeling his way along the dripping walls and almost tripping flat over a loose piece of stone.

At the far end he came to a chamber with a capped wellhead at the centre of it; and as he lifted the lantern he saw that the pipe which ran out from the house turned down through the metal plate.

"It carries off the gas." Lord William had crept up beside him, and was pulling and pushing at an iron rod which also ran down into the well. "To stir the slime," he said. "To make more bubbles."

Justice was in no mood to listen. He looked about him for the shaft and saw it set to one side. Sweetsea, he remembered, had said something about it being a holy well, a place for pilgrimage, and pointed out the odd-looking belvedere which had once been a shrine.

That was where Emma saw the man who played hide-my-eyes.

When the Frenchwoman was meeting him to pass a message or be given instructions.

He found the rungs, rusty but sound enough to bear his weight, and climbed up some twenty feet to stand in the shelter which covered it.

At that moment he caught the sound of coach wheels rolling along the drive, and limped out, thinking that it might be Francis, or Lilly, coming at last, and found that the long wall of the kitchen garden prevented him from seeing the coach.

He hurried as best he could to the gateway, only to see the glimmer of light in the dusk as the coach reached the fork and took the turn up towards Cuffwells and the main highway.

His first thought was to get a horse and follow, for even now Luc might be making a bolt for it. But as he passed through the archway he found Harriet coming up, as if she too had heard the coach departing and run behind.

"It was Mr Breney's coach," she said a little breathlessly. "Returning to Winchester."

"Alone?" Even in this fading twilight he could tell that she was embarrassed.

"No," she said disconsolately. "Fanshawe and Marie-Louise have gone with him." She came to take Justice by the arm in a more friendly way, as if they were companions in some misfortune. "I have not broken my promise," she insisted. "The first I knew of it was when the wheels began to rumble on the cobbles below the nursery. Clean gone, and my father, as well, the footman says. Gone off suddenly, as he often does, to see one of his cronies."

"Damnit," she said with something like her old spirit. "Damnit. And I gave you my word!"

‹17›

"I MUST FIND ROBERT and warn him." Lord William had already made up his mind before Justice and Harriet returned. And as he stood moodily by the table, his fingers playing with his flasks and piping, he seemed much less concerned about his own safety, despite all that Justice had said about collusion with the King's enemies, than with the prospect of danger for his American friend. "I said no good would come of that damned plunging-boat," he cried in distress. "Oh, how wrong I was to let it fascinate me so!"

It might all be pretence. Luc's escape might be only one more move in a whole scheme of deceptions. Yet Justice found himself believing what Romney now said. "Did the Frenchman speak of him at all?"

"He spoke much of Robert, of course. But in the friendliest way. I had no idea. . . ."

"Nor would you." Justice spoke sharply to prevent Lord William starting off on one of his digressions. "Today, I mean. Or within the last two or three days."

"He spoke of many things," Lord William said, running over some recollections in such a low voice that Justice could not catch anything he said.

"A question." Justice was becoming impatient. "Any particular question that he pressed on you. Whether Francis was coming. When he might come. Where he was. Or anything like that."

Lord William's face brightened as he thought of something. "I noticed," he said. "It was odd. He asked if Robert had begun to pack last time he was here."

"Pack? Pack what?"

"Papers, I imagine. He had just been asking about Robert's papers, you see. There was something about a contract. A plan. I was not greatly interested."

"But there were papers here?" It was obvious now that

167

Romney had prompted him that Francis must have kept the working drawings for the *Pandora* close at hand—had probably kept them here at Wykeham, in the house of friends he trusted, rather than at Cuffwells, where it would be all too easy to copy them without his knowledge. He had not even let Boney see the plans for the *Nautilus*, Lilly had said.

"There were papers in the studio." Harriet had been waiting to see what turn the talk would take after Justice's tirade against her brother and herself. Now she was helpful. "I saw Robert at work on them last time he was here."

"Then we must search," Justice said, "or we may be forestalled. It may already be too late."

Lord William raised a hand to restrain him. "Search by all means. You'll find nothing but scraps and scribblings. The room is always full of them. See." He went to a cabinet and took out a drawing which Justice recognised as a sketch of the eyeglass in the hatchway of the *Pandora*, with a good-looking curly-haired man peering out. "Robert himself. I've picked a score of such things off the floor."

"So I may take it?" Justice placed it in his pocket before Lord William could nod. He would now recognise Francis if he met him, and the self-portrait would help anyone set to watch for the American.

"Scraps," Lord William repeated, but the way he said it made Justice suspect that he was making a last attempt to conceal what Francis had wished to hide. His loyalty was admirable, and most exasperating.

"That is not the truth." Justice's voice was hardening again when Harriet interrupted him.

"We must tell what we know, William," she said. "Captain Justice has threatened us with the gallows once today, and will do so again if we impede him, and though I think he would find it hard to prove his case the worst might be believed of any Romney brought to trial on such a charge."

"But you will tell." Justice picked up the phrase.

"Not because we are threatened, Mr Justice. Because we are—what was it you called us?—yes, we are innocents, truly mistaken perhaps, but not malign. And because Robert is our friend. And because you say he is in danger, and I believe you."

"Bravo, Harriet!" Lord William was delighted by his sister's spirit. "The truth, then."

"There were papers in the studio," Harriet said again. "A very particular set of papers that Robert called his Drawings and Descriptions. He told me that they were like an investment in the funds."

"A whole bundle of things." Romney was now eager to play his part, and he raised his hands as if to frame a sizeable box. "In case anything should happen to him. So that his work should not be lost."

Justice was flabbergasted. "A complete description of his designs? The *Pandora*, the carcasses . . ." He stopped, appalled by the implications of what he had just been told.

". . . Military schemes, steamboats, canals . . ." Lord William clearly had a good idea of what Francis proposed to keep. "He was going to send them home to America. Soon."

Justice could understand why Francis might try to ensure his work against his death, or some lesser mishap, or even against undue pressure when he was bargaining with the Admiralty. Nothing could guarantee him better terms than the knowledge that copies and plans of all his intentions were in safe keeping in America.

"Were they assembled?" Justice asked, recalling the question that Luc had put to Lord William. "And packed?"

"I think so."

"And the Frenchman?"

"He thought likewise. Perhaps he had news from Barlow, in France, or in London."

"So Barlow knew as well?"

"He was to take them, I believe. It was part of their arrangement, Robert said. The papers, the steam engine for the boat . . ." Romney stopped. "To America, naturally. Not to France."

"Naturally. To America." The sarcasm in Justice's voice touched Harriet's temper.

"Why not?" she asked, cuttingly. "Is everything wrong that is not done with your permission, Captain Justice? Robert is a free man, fortunately for him. His country is neutral. He may sell what he likes, where he likes, when he likes, so long as he does not break a contract."

Justice was silent while the little storm passed. The fact that she was right was no comfort. Whatever the law, what Francis knew and what he did might tip the balance of a long and terrible war, and Justice shuddered at the prospect of such a budget of secrets and schemes falling into the hands of Bonaparte's agents.

Taken together, they would be worth even more than the *Pandora*. There were enough clever men in Paris to turn such principles into practice, and Boney could call on some of the best shipwrights in the world to build copies of the *Pandora* and all the other deadly fancies that Francis had conceived.

"If they were packed, where are they?" Justice saw the change in Harriet's face as he ignored her outburst and came back to the question: she was remarkably like her brother in these quick changes of mood.

"Last time Robert was here . . ." she began, and then interrupted herself. "No. I don't know where they are. But last time I saw him he spoke of taking them when he came. They must be hidden somewhere here, somewhere safe if I know Robert."

Lord William saw Justice's eyes flick round his laboratory. "No," he said, shaking his head. "Not here. Though search if you must."

But Justice was not thinking of a hiding place. He was thinking of what might be the key to one. And what it might fit. He was about to ask Lord William if he knew of that curiously shaped piece of metal he had found in the desk, and then thought better of it. If that was what Luc had been searching for when Emma saw him, he would come back to look for it again. And until then, the less that was said . . .

"I told the Frenchman nothing at all—I said I had no idea what Robert had done with his drawings." Like Harriet, Lord William was touchy on points of honour, and Justice was inclined to believe him.

"Did he search?"

"Perhaps. He came and went as he chose."

And would come again, Justice was sure. Tonight, because he could wait no longer. Because he had already failed to seize the *Pandora*. Because he must try for the papers tonight and Francis tomorrow if he was to rescue anything from his crumbling plot.

"I shall stay, and search." Justice looked at Harriet, saw she nodded with relief.

"I should be otherwise alone." She gestured towards her brother. "For William must go. To find Robert, as he says."

It was a hard decision for Justice, who was still uncertain

whether to trust Lord William, to trust him even to carry a warning, for the man was so volatile in purpose and so naïve in the ordinary affairs of the world.

He had already been obliged to let Fanshawe and the Frenchwoman flee without pursuit, except by a messenger who would discover where they were set down and what direction they took—and precious little use that would be. They would be half way back to Ireland before he could raise a hue and cry, and safe away to France or America before there was a chance of catching them.

But Lord William it would have to be. He could not go himself. Not while Luc was at large at Wykeham and the papers were at risk.

"If Robert is not at Portsmouth, he may be at Langstone Point," Lord William said, displaying a sudden and disconcerting knowledge of the secret naval establishment on Hayling Island. "And if I find him not . . . ?" He gave Justice an enquiring glance. "Deal? Dover?"

"London first," Justice said firmly. "If what Mr Breney tells us is true, he will be in London."

"At his rooms, then. He lodges with Barlow."

"Or Breney's office."

Justice thought for a moment of asking Romney to leave word at Richmond Terrace, and decided it would be a mistake. With Dunning sick, and Hatherley travelling on other business, there was little point in sending Lord William to the Board of Beacons, Bells, Buoys, and Mercantile Messengers. Anyone who was on duty there would probably give him the dustiest of answers. Or a religious tract for godless seamen.

"Leave any message at Breney's," Justice said as Romney began to pick up odds and ends he would need for his journey. "And when you find Mr Francis, stay close. Stay close until I come."

LORD WILLIAM HAD RIDDEN away, a little fat groom behind him, and the pair of them looking like a print Justice had once seen of Don Quixote and Sancho Panza. Not the best of messengers, Justice thought ruefully. Simply the best to hand, and he had genuinely wished his Lordship well as the two odd figures vanished into the night. A life, more than a life, might depend on him.

Then the search began, with Harriet holding the candles while Justice rummaged through the studio, pulling out drawers and opening cupboards.

They soon despaired of any discovery. "Lord William was right," Justice said as he thrust the last folder back on a shelf. "Nothing but scraps."

And they turned back to the neighbouring apartment.

Harriet had fetched a key that would open the chest of drawers, and they found only a dozen shirts, a pair of breeches, and a folded and faded American flag. "Where did Robert mean to hoist that?" Harriet asked as she held it up.

Justice looked at its stars and bars, and said nothing, though he had a good guess at the answer. That flag, he was sure, must have flown on the *Nautilus* three years ago, when Francis put his first submarine in the water. And it would have been hoisted somewhere on the *Pandora* when she came out of the boatshed for her maiden voyage.

Francis, he had learned already, was a man who was strong for symbols.

And for mechanical devices. It was clear that he had installed the hidden drawer in the desk himself, for Harriet knew nothing of it: Justice had let her run over the desk in case she touched the secret spring, or another like it, but she had merely tugged at the locked drawers, and then told Justice to smash them open.

Nothing again. Two drawers empty. One full of scraps and idle sketches. One with a few childish scrawls on paper that Justice knew were done by Emma, and ignored while Harriet took them up and pocketed them.

They rapped at the walls, scoured the floor for any sign of a loose board, felt the cushions and squeezed the mattress on the bed.

Twenty minutes were enough to convince them that Francis had either taken the papers with him or hidden them beyond their reach, and the only consolation in failure was the thought that Luc would be equally frustrated if he came to search.

"It's bait, all the same." Harriet put into words what Justice was thinking. "If he comes and finds the papers, you have 'em both. If he comes and fails like us, you have him, at least."

If he comes. "Is that door normally locked?" Justice asked,

172

pointing at the entrance from the outside stair. Unless Luc came through the nursery, as Emma had come, or through Harriet's rooms and the studio, he would have to come that way, for all the risk of being seen.

"We should never be able to turn some of the keys again if we locked every door," she said. "Age. Rust. Damp wood."

So it would be easy for Luc to enter. And hard to watch. As Justice sized up his chances, he saw that he could not stay in the three rooms which Francis occupied. There was nowhere to hide, and in any case he had to give Luc the time and the chance to search for the papers. Nor could he conceal himself in the studio. Luc was likely to run through the drawers and boxes there as he and Harriet had just done.

And yet he had to remain close at hand—near enough to hear what was happening and to surprise Luc at the right moment.

He had walked across the doorway which gave into the studio, trying to judge lines of sight and distance, when he heard the scuffle of sound as Harriet picked up the pistol he had laid on the desk.

And cocked it.

JUSTICE TURNED, to find Harriet holding the pistol muzzle upwards, like a duellist, and laughing at his look of consternation. Had he been wrong to trust her, he would now be at her mercy.

"Shall I call you out, Captain Justice?" There was a hint of meaning in her rough humour. "Shall I make an affair of honour out of all your impertinences today?"

She swung on her heel, took four paces away from him, and came round sharply as though to fire. "Pistols, at dawn? Or swords? Or would a singlestick be best for a country bumpkin like me?" She put the pistol down and chuckled at her macabre jest. "There is a man called Tooth at Cuffwells who is a champion at wrestling and singlestick, and such games. Did you know that?"

"I had no idea," Justice said truthfully, remembering the burly sailor's charge at him, and counting himself well out of any further education in that line.

"He comes here. He has a friend among our servants, and one day I found them battling among the hay in the stables."

Harriet gave the first of her boyish grins that Justice had seen that day. "So now he teaches me."

"You aren't serious?" Justice was not sure whether it was annoyance at such familiarity or plain jealousy that made him feel uncomfortable at the idea of Harriet engaging in knock-about with a common seaman.

"Indeed I am. Should a woman not know how to defend herself? In case the French should come?"

She was quite serious. Justice could tell that from the way she spoke. But there was a flicker of a smile on her lips that showed she was teasing him at the same time.

"And so I'll keep watch with you," she exclaimed, as if that conclusion followed from all she had just said. "In my room."

Justice was about to protest when he saw that she was right. Her room was the only place that was near enough for the purpose. And before he could say anything about the risk she might be running, she anticipated him.

"You'll insult me if you refuse, Mr Justice." Now she was plainly in earnest. "You would be willing to take help from my brother, just because he is a man—though quite useless in a fight. Take it from me, I beg of you." She came up to grasp his arm with a power that revealed her passion. "Strength, you see. Courage, you can count on it. But above all . . ." She broke off as though she was unsure whether the card she was about to play would take the trick or lose it. "Repayment, if you like," she said with quiet emphasis. "If William and I have done wrong by . . ."

Justice suspected that she was about to say "by our country," and had found that patriotic phrase too stiff for one of her upbringing to utter.

"By . . . by being innocents." She smiled as she repeated Justice's phrase. "Well, then, we must make amends."

"It is not customary . . ." Justice heard his voice slide into masculine pomposity, and saw that Harriet had caught him.

"Damn you!" she cried in frustration. "Damn you for a stuffy fool, Captain Justice. What is customary here? To sit waiting for one of Bonaparte's men to break into my house? To have a naval officer, pistol in hand, prowling about my bedroom? Either this is some black comedy, sir, or it is a real drama, and I will have my part in it."

She sensed that Justice's resolve was weakening, and fell

back on argument. "You need my help," she said, as if it were merely a practical matter that now had to be settled. "You cannot watch alone, and you have no time to send to Cuffwells for your servant, or any other man. And you cannot turn out the watchmen here in case that scares your . . . your quarry."

Justice had never had to deal with such a woman before, and he did not know how to cope with her startling indifference to the conventions. He had mastered her at the moment of crisis earlier in the day because he had known exactly what he wanted, and how to get it. Now she had turned the tables on him.

"Very well," he said, letting her have her way, less because he was really persuaded than because he felt himself gripped by a force he could neither fully understand nor resist.

"Very well, then. Together."

They would share the danger. Whatever it was, and whenever it came.

"I NEVER KNEW my mother," Harriet said sadly as they sat before the fire in her room, talking the hours away, knowing that Luc would have to wait until the great house was quiet and all the servants sleeping.

They were comfortable enough, for Justice lay resting his leg on a chaise longue, and Harriet had fetched the large cushions which Francis had used to turn one of his carcasses into a window seat. And in this companionable mood, with the brandy decanter to hand for Justice and herself, Harriet's agitation had faded to the kind of melancholy which Justice also knew when he remembered how early in life he had lost both his parents.

"And my stepmother was a misfortune for us all." Harriet stared into the fire as though she saw pictures in the flames. "She married my father on an impulse, I think, as one might choose a groom at a hiring fair. He was never handsome . . ." she laughed, "as you may see, poor man! But he was amusing, well-connected, rich, and so he could pay her debts." She spoke with contempt. "She was never home, you know, for each night she was at a ball, or out playing cards or faro, and I saw so little of her that twice I passed her in the street without recognizing her. Truly. But it didn't last. Only a couple of seasons, and then she ran off to Italy. Died in Rome, they say, of a colic.''

They had sat quietly after that, until Justice felt so encouraged by what she had said that he had talked a little of his own mother, of what it was like to have the loyalties of an Englishman and the feelings of a Frenchman at war within oneself, of boyhood memories, of Luc—very little about Luc, though she was naturally curious about him, for Justice found it hard to speak of the shame of the Valcourts. He told her how Luc had turned his coat. How he had gone back to France. How this. How that. How his life would be forfeit if he was seized tonight. How his trial would mean ruin for a navy captain with Valcourt for a middle name.

But no more than that. Nothing about the Cadoudal affair. Nothing about O'Moira, Luc's companion in the evils of espionage and treason. The less the Romneys knew of such things the safer they were.

''But you would kill him?'' Harriet had asked the one question that mattered as they sat waiting for Luc to come.

''I would,'' Justice said grimly.

''Even you?''

''Especially me.'' He felt a ripple of cold hatred that was far more murderous than the killing fever which raged through a man in the heat of action, for it was a family matter, a matter of honour as well as duty. ''We were once as like and close as twins,'' he said, thinking he might meet Luc for the last time before the night was over, and Harriet heard the break of tragedy in his voice. ''And now, now I am owed this death.''

''By God, I envy you!'' Harriet cried so unexpectedly that Justice was startled by her jealous vigour. ''The harshness of it. The power to compel.'' She turned quickly and kneeled beside him; and even as he puzzled at her words he felt a very different shiver run through his body, for she had put one hand to his cheek and with the other she had loosed his cravat to reveal the rugged scar that ran to his throat.

She gasped a little as she saw and touched it, and he thought she would ask how he came by it. But she said nothing, for her free hand was pulling his face towards her, and her lips were moving eagerly, searching for the kiss that would bridge the distance that the tensions of the day had set between them.

He felt her passion stir him as her tongue found his mouth and her fingers ran the length of the scar, making his flesh prick and tingle as they teased it into life. In a moment she had brought back the hot flush of intimacy which had been ended by Scorcher's arrival the night before.

And then, just as suddenly, she broke away, releasing him as though she were shamed by her own urgency, and she went to stand before the fire, her arms clutched across her bosom like a person overwhelmed by emotion. The hesitation that broke in each time they met was there to torment her even when she was in the grip of sensuality.

"I am not a normal woman, Mr Justice," she exclaimed, as if she had read his thoughts. "I cannot submit. I am not winsome, like the heroines in Mrs Edgeworth's romances. I must take what I want from life, as a man does, and to the devil with the consequences."

Though Justice could not see her face, it seemed that she was weeping with frustration.

"Damn! Damn me for it," she said as if she were ashamed of her confession. "There is such a hunger within me, a raw hunger that is hard to appease and has nothing to do with love or liking." She was silent for a moment, coming to some decision, and then turning back to face Justice. "It is struggle that appeals to me, Captain Justice, as you may have learned by now. I must find the iron in a man, so that I can feel myself ring against it."

As she spoke so vehemently, Justice clearly understood the springs of her feelings, and those she aroused in him. It was the prospect of danger which excited her, as he had seen it excite men on the eve of battle; and the more she challenged him, the more his own excitement grew.

He had never taken a woman who had not come to him as an equal, and in Harriet he had found one who craved that equality of passion so fiercely that he no longer had the will to hold back the desire she aroused in him.

She had stopped on that note of exclamation, like an actress, waiting for his response; and as he swung himself upright and threw off his coat, she pulled her hands roughly from her shoulders, ripping her shirtfront open to the waist, so that Justice could see the swell of her breasts.

He was beside her, hands reaching to cup those nipples as they hardened, and feeling the tautness of her body as she stretched her arms upwards. "And for all that, I am a woman, John Justice," she half whispered in a husky voice, "and you must win me to bed on my terms.''

She meant every word of it, Justice discovered, for she taunted and teased him with her quivering body as vigorously as she had spoken, letting him touch her where he chose, offering her breasts to his mouth, turning so that her buttocks pressed his straining thighs.

"Oh, John," she cried, in an ecstasy, as he took the last of her clothing, to leave her gleaming gold before the leaping flames. And as he fumbled at his breeches, she tore his hands away to do the work herself, pushing his shirt aside and falling to her knees as she dragged breeches and drawers together from his loins.

"The iron, sir, the iron!" Her voice was coarse with desire as her fingers felt for him and brought him down beside her on the spread of cushions. And even then she could not be still to receive him, rolling over to sit astride and taking him in great gasps as her knees gripped and her hands tugged at his shoulders.

With his hands at her breasts and her nipples working between his fingers, he could feel the surges of energy that went on until she flung herself down on him, bringing her mouth to his in a final cry of satisfaction.

"And now to bed," she said later, as she lay beside him, caressing him back to strength and desire. "If the navy can spare Hero another hour."

It was that mercurial change from hardness to humour that made her so tantalisingly attractive, Justice thought, as she now came to him more gently, as if the passion of their first encounter had appeased her hunger for his body and set her free to enjoy its pleasures.

And then, as she slept, he slipped away from her, dressing himself, setting a chair behind the half open door, so that he could see through the studio into the apartment beyond, putting his thick-barrelled pistol on the floor beside him, hearing the old house creak and settle into the night, and seeing the glow fade in the room with the last spit and crackle of the embers.

It was a year since he had parted from Luc on the surf-beaten beach at Biville, where his cousin had led Cadoudal and the rest of his party into a trap.

Now it was Luc's turn.

The trap was set, if he would walk into it.

～18～

It was a sound, half heard, and Justice was on his feet. It was the slightest snap of sound, and the musty smell of burning lamp oil, carried on a draught as a door opened.

He reached for the pistol he had placed on the floor, moving his hands with care lest a careless knock gave him away, kneeling as he failed to find it . . . he would throw his hand away if he stayed scrabbling until some chance noise betrayed him.

He touched the brandy flask, long-necked above a strong bowl, and took it gratefully in his right hand. That was better than facing Luc unarmed.

In the room beyond, as he looked through the studio, he saw the gleam of a shaded lantern like those that Grimshaw had found in the woods, heard the click as a half-seen figure bent over the desk and sprung the hidden panel.

Luc had come to try again.

Now he was reaching farther into the space, as Justice had done, and this time he too was lucky. Justice caught the different noise as the inner compartment dropped free, and then Luc had that curiously shaped key in his hands, its brass winking briefly in the lantern light.

Luc. It was so like the games they had played as boys that it was uncanny—that sense of having seen everything once before that the French called *déjà vu*.

He had no idea how Luc had known where to search for that key, and might never know more than he could guess: something that Francis must have said in all innocence to a man he trusted, perhaps, only to have the confidence betrayed. But Luc knew, all right, and the first time he must have missed it because little Emma had surprised him while he held that grisly guillotine device in his hand.

Luc had crossed the room, now, going towards the bedroom, and Justice tried to think what he had missed in his search. A panel in the wall? A false back to a cupboard?

But Luc had stopped in the dressing room, by the window, and the lantern flashed from the glow of copper.

Of course. A hiding place so obvious that it was easily missed. The carcass. The copper-sheathed box that had served as a window seat.

And if Francis had made it as a safe place for his papers, waterproof, capable of resisting hard blows, it would certainly have a most ingenious fastening.

That was what Luc was trying now. At that distance Justice could not see exactly how it worked, but from the way Luc's hands slipped to and fro before the lantern, he thought it might be some combination of lock and hinge, that allowed the lid to slide and open.

He thought he heard Harriet stir in her sleep and paused. If she could sleep on, she was safe, but if she woke suddenly . . . He put her out of his mind, for he was coldly alert now, making up his mind how to tackle Luc.

A rush, that would give his cousin vital moments to turn and defend himself? A challenge out of the darkness, with the threat of a pistol shot to follow? A lucky cockshy with the brandy bottle? He had never been trained in that kind of fighting, like thieves and thief-takers, but Luc would have learned it in the hard way of the secret agent, the dirty way, with all the tricks of a man who would maim or kill without question.

So the voice from the darkness would be best, giving him time, distance, and the advantage of uncertainty.

And there was only one way to find out if he was right.

"Luc! C'est moi." And as he saw a hand pull back past the face of the lantern his voice sharpened into the Picard slang they had both picked up knocking about the stable yard at Valcourt. *"Voilà, que tu fais des foutaises, comme toujours!"*

"C'est toi, alors. J'attends, Jean."

Luc was as cool as he had ever been, giving no hint that he had been taken off guard as he slipped to his feet and stood back from the glow of the lantern. Now he was as invisible as Justice, safe, except from the flukiest of pistol shots.

And as they stood face to face, but unseen, Justice felt the old affection seeping back, sweeping away the tense hatred with which he had thought of Luc for the past year, making him wish for the brotherly embrace with which they had always greeted each other. It unnerved him, would have unnerved him more if he had not suspected that Luc was hesitating for the same reason.

But he was wrong.

"Have you come to offer me a bargain?" Luc's voice had the familiar ring of mockery. "My life against the papers, Captain Justice? Or the papers against your life? Have you come alone to take me, or are the brutes of your press gang waiting somewhere out there?"

When Luc was in such a mood of taunting vanity it was possible that he might make a mistake, and Justice kept silent, waiting for a chance to strike. "The first blow's half the battle," Scorcher often said. And he was right.

"Or perhaps they, too, are being entertained by the Lady Harriet. Such an energetic young woman, Jean. In all ways."

The sneer told Justice how much Luc must have seen and heard in the two weeks he had been hidden at Wykeham, told him that Luc was hoping to tease him into error, was for some reason playing for time. Told him, too, that Luc was truly a blackguard, now. And as these words touched the memory of Harriet in his arms, as surely as though Luc had watched their lovemaking, they brought back the cold fury which nearly drove him into an impetuous attack.

"In the King's name . . ." As Justice rattled off the formal words of arrest, he knew they would have no effect. And Luc's derisive retort proved it. But there might come a time when a man who had turned his coat once would do it again—when the offer of money would make Luc talk, or the threat of the rope would persuade him to turn King's evidence. And the act of arrest might be the beginning of the bargaining.

"*Pauvre Jean. Pauvre garçon.*" As Luc spoke, Justice thought he heard a board creak or a foot scuff on the floor, and he thought their voices must have woken Harriet and brought her creeping to join them. "Poor Jean, spare me all that," Luc said patronisingly. "You have so little idea what I am about, and I have no intention of telling you. What am I doing here, you are asking? Where is the man you so stupidly call Francis, as if it deceived anyone? What are my plans for him after I have been forced to kill you? Poor Jean, you will never know."

The taunts were leading to some kind of trick, Justice knew.

"And what will the Emperor do with these infernal machines?"

Luc kicked the carcass ironically, or so it seemed to Justice, but the gesture must have been some sort of signal, for it was followed at once by so clear a step behind Justice that he had time to duck, to twist sideways, and throw himself forward as a bludgeon swept moaning through the space where he had been standing.

THERE WERE TWO of them, at least.

In the same movement as his fall Justice had smashed the brandy bottle on the floor, had kept the jagged stump in his hand as he tried to guess where his hidden assailant had gone. And for one chilling moment, as he drew his arm back in a stabbing swing, he recalled what Harriet had said about learning singlestick and wrestling from Tooth the sailor.

It could not be. It could not be. But the hesitation that sprang from that instant of suspicion was almost the end of him. He sensed the next blow coming, in a long searching swipe at floor level which caught him on the shoulder as he lunged with his makeshift dagger, heard cloth tear, and a muffled yelp of pain as he ripped long into flesh.

Then Luc was upon him, grappling in a wrestler's hold which would have left him powerless if the response had not come back to him instinctively, so that he could roll over Luc, letting the broken bottle go so that he had a strong right hand to cut edgeway's at his cousin's throat and knock him away.

But the relief was momentary, for Luc's accomplice was on him again, getting a lucky purchase on an arm, and kneeling at him in a way he could not resist, for his weakened leg gave him no leverage against a pressure that would surely break bones unless he could worm out of it.

He heard, through the blinding pain, a stream of French obscenities, and realized that it was his own voice that was panting, grunting, and cursing like the angriest ostler in France; and then, scratching desperately at the man's leg, he found the wound he had made with the bottle and tore at it to get a scream of agony and a sudden release that let him jab twice with his head, sending the man scuttling away with low moans.

As Luc came at him again, kicking hard to find his legs and knock him off balance, he backed off, trying to reach the lantern; at the worst, he could set the papers ablaze by smashing it among them, and he would have the advantage if he could use the beam to find the men he was fighting.

But suddenly, there was light coming from the studio, and as he saw one figure stagger across its glow and lurch towards the door, getting away while the going was good, he knew the odds were turning in his favour.

For it was Harriet, in the scantiest of shifts, like a figure in a tableau, candle in one hand and pistol in the other.

Aiming at him.

For she could not see Luc, and he was standing by the open trunk of papers. And he had been cursing in French. Still, from habit, spoke in French as he pointed at Luc, somewhere in the darkness beside her. *"C'est lui! A droit!"* In a moment she might fire.

But before she had time to tighten her finger or to look round, Luc had come out of the shadows to knock the candle to the floor, to seize her arm, forcing it up with one hand while the other stole round her body, grasping her so roughly that her shift ripped with the snatch of his fingers. And that careless move gave her a chance. With a speed and power that astonished Justice as much as Luc, she dropped to her knees, using the arm he held as a pivot to swing him round and over, smashing hard on the floor as she swung the heel of her free hand in a sharp and confusing blow to the side of his face.

Even then he had wind enough, as he kept tight hold of the pistol, to shout an obscene gibe at them both.

And there was no mercy in the way he dragged at Harriet, tugging at her tattered shift to lift himself, twisting her arm to bring the gun barrel round as Justice came at him, pulling at the trigger without effect, letting the pistol go, and rising fast enough to catch Justice a cruel kick in the ribs before they clutched and fell together, and Harriet slipped free.

Luc was on top, and Justice had too little breath in him to fight back as a knee forced at his groin, a hand strained at his throat, a fist pounded at him below the heart; and then, as he felt the last of his strength too little, he saw the white shape of Harriet loom beyond his cousin's back, and heard him cough with pain as her foot swung between his spread-open legs.

"Should not a woman know how to defend herself?"

Harriet's words came back to Justice as she tugged at Luc's hair, giving him room for a raking and jolting blow that forced Luc back; and as the Frenchman's knee slipped, so that

Justice could retaliate in kind, she clasped her hands together to deal him a double-fisted backhander that sent him reeling between the sofa legs.

He had no chance to recover before she was beside him, matching his obscenity with another that came out in a terrifying cry of rage and revenge.

Whoever had taught her must have learned his trade in a dozen alehouse brawls, for now she held the jagged bottle poised to slash, as Justice had done, and her words left Luc in no doubt where she would cut at him.

And that threat put an end to the fight more dramatically than any blows or bruises or broken bones could have done.

So far as Justice could tell, in the reflected gleams of the lantern, Luc scuffled under the sofa to protect himself, with all the bravado knocked out of him at last; and while Harriet turned to see what had happened to Justice he tipped it over against her, and ran for the door.

Justice cursed his own failure as he saw Luc go. Even if he had saved the papers, he had missed his chance to close the trap, and his evil cousin was still at large to cause harm to Francis or the *Pandora*.

"The pistol, John."

Harriet had fetched the lantern to find it while Justice was still crouched on the floor, fighting for his wind; and he saw it only a yard away.

At half cock.

That was why Luc had failed to make it fire.

And the powder in the priming pan scattered, no doubt, after so many bangs and shakes.

Yet he took it in his right hand as he dragged himself to the door that gave on to the courtyard, cocking it as he went, and coming out on to the stone staircase to see a flicker of movement as Luc made for the gateway.

It was a long shot. A useless shot even in daylight with an unfamiliar gun. And if he fired it, if it would fire, he and Harriet would be left defenceless if Luc came back. If he had more than one accomplice close by.

"Thanks to you," he said to Harriet, who had come out on the porch, shivering, with the remnants of her nightgown gathered about her; and he put an arm about her shoulders as they turned and went indoors, feeling her as strong and taut as any youth he had ever known, and yet alive with all the physical attributes of a woman.

He bolted the door, as Harriet went to clothe herself and fetch brandy and more candles.

Even if there were no chance, no chance at all, of catching Luc and his companion in the darkness that lay beyond the walls of Wykeham, he had found the papers.

He had saved the papes.

He dragged the copper box into the sitting room and crouched beside it to go through the treasure chest of mysteries that Francis had left behind him.

❧ 19 ❧

"DEALINGS WITH THE Admiralty," Justice said, as Harriet took the first sizeable bundle of papers to retie them and stack them neatly on the desk.

They were mostly manuscript copies, not letter press tissues, of the letters that Francis had sent to the Admiralty about his recent settlement in England; and they were neatly arranged, with the replies of the various officials to his requests and complaints—all much as Lilly had said, and some were indeed the same as items he had seen in Hatherley's secret file.

There was nothing to detain him here, though he paused for a minute or two over the minute details with which Francis had embroidered his plans in the thick paper Bond and Contract which he had signed with the British government in July.

The date particularly caught his eye. The twentieth day of July 1804. One week from the day on which Lilly had first sent for him to serve as a Mercantile Messenger, and to go to France on business that was closely related to the inventions of Robert Francis.

He noticed that Harriet watched him closely while he stared at that document, but she said nothing as he passed it over.

Then there was some old correspondence with Lord Stanhope, about canal improvements and steamboats, all of it going back to the years when Francis first lived in England. And letters from the painter Benjamin West, and from Joel Barlow and Ruth Barlow, who both wrote in such extravagantly affectionate terms that Justice guessed he would have been embarrassed to read on.

There were business notes from Barlow as well, almost all dealing with the arrangements for shipping a steam engine from Boulton and Watt's factory at Birmingham—a most complicated affair, as Hatherley and Breney had already made clear. And there was a phrase in a copied letter to Barlow that Justice found worrying. Writing early in September, when he was expecting his friend to arrive in London on his way to New York, Francis had admitted his suspicions of his British employers. "I have come to believe that Pitt and his friends may never give a fair trial to my most dreadful engines, in case success should attend them."

In case success should attend them.

It was a suspicion at which Lilly and Hatherley had already hinted. It was a reason to suspect that Francis might be planning to bolt, listening again to the blandishments of the French or succumbing to American speculators who would like to see him conducting his experiments on the banks of the Hudson.

He looked at Harriet, wondering whether to ask her opinion, and decided against it. She had got a fire going in the great hearth, and wrapped herself in a blanket, and as she sat on a stool gazing into the flames she seemed lost in a reverie.

Justice would have wagered a good deal that she was thinking of her unrequited attachment to the American—the raw hunger that she had shamelessly confessed to him.

It was just as that thought came to him that he found a small packet that it would be unkind to pass to her—letters from women, mostly in French, and intimate drawings that gave him an idea of what Francis seemed to expect from their sex; and to distract Harriet while he surreptitiously slipped the papers among some other sketches, he laughed and handed her a paper that amused her, too.

"How like Robert," she said, running her eye down from the heading and reading out some of the entries from this exact inventory of clothes.

"Twenty-three fine shirts, eleven night ditto," Harriet exclaimed. "My word! Fifty cravats, thirteen white waistcoats, nine pairs of white silk stockings." And then, after running through a list of coats, pantaloons, boots, and shoes, she seemed to recall something painful about the man who wore them, and threw the memorandum on the fire so impulsively that for a moment Justice feared she might tip all the other papers after it. Might destroy a collection of confidential material more valuable than any French or British agent could have secured by bribery, robbery, persuasion, or intrigue.

And Francis was proposing to ship it all out of the country, in this sealed bomb case, without a by-your-leave to anyone.

But Harriet had fallen silent as the paper burned to ash, and

Justice went on with his search, flipping over draughts to letters he longed to read in full. There were a couple to President Jefferson in Washington, half a dozen to Bonaparte, more to a scattering of French *savants*. There was a scheme for a canal from Paris to Dieppe, beautifully mapped and sketched in the meticulous style that marked everything that Francis drew. And there was page after page of equally painstaking estimates of the cost of his projects and the economies his weapons could achieve in war.

"Your Mr Francis is a great calculator," Lilly had said. "Give him a penny a foot or sixpence a pound, or any such figure, and he will prove you a profit on its multiplication as good as any speculator in the land. But he is honest, and he does his sums well."

Dozens of sums, Justice saw, all ruled into neat tables, and though he had no time to work the numbers as they flashed under his hand, even the quickest skim across them left a staggering impression.

Here was the annual cost of the British navy—£13,547,613, or, as Francis precisely computed in his own currency, $60,684,502.40. He brought it down to the last forty cents.

Here was a list of every ship in that navy, down to the last slow gunboat and sluggish hoy, down to the last ton of displacement, down to the last cannon and the men to man it.

And here a suggestion that his submarine bombs could effectively defend the ports of Boston, New York, the Delaware, the Chesapeake, Charleston, and New Orleans, and all for less than the cost of one ship of the line.

It was remarkable. It was even more worrying than remarkable, as Justice realized what dangerous marvels Francis had hidden away in this box and understood why Luc might well have counted its contents more valuable than the *Pandora* herself. For here, now, in one folder, were all the sketches, measurements, and description that would permit anyone to fabricate such a vessel.

And much more, very much more.

Francis had kept old notebooks crammed with extraordinary plans for using balloons to drop explosives, for making cannon to fire under water, for new kinds of telegraph, iron bridges . . . Justice could do no more than look at the titles scrawled on the covers. There was a folder describing the harpoon gun that he and Scorcher had seen in the carcass shed at Cuffwells.

And then he came to several files, wrapped together in oiled cloth, which all seemed to deal with the construction of the floating bombs and a dozen means of deploying them in action.

That was the Admiralty's business, Justice thought, for these were the weapons that were being made at Portsmouth and tried out with Lord Keith's squadron off the Channel ports of France.

He was about to straighten the papers and fold the cloth around them again, when he caught sight of a few words written on a protruding sheet.

In a hand he had seen only once before, and was unlikely to forget.

Written in the round, looping, and wavy script of a blind man.

IT WAS THE HANDWRITING of Dr Declan O'Moira, who had pursued him half across France. Who was so deeply involved with Bonaparte's plan for a simultaneous landing in Kent and in Ireland. Who was determined to recover Francis for the French cause, or so deal with him that he would be of no use to the British.

O'Moira. Who must have sent Luc to Wykeham, by way of Ireland. Sent Fanshawe and Mademoiselle Gérard to help him, in some devious fashion. Found other helpers among the Irish rebels and their levelling friends. Devised the whole scheme of intrigue which was now beginning to emerge from the shadows.

Justice was so shaken by this sudden proof of what had so far been no more than a nagging suspicion that he sat very still, thinking about O'Moira, who combined charm and a touching dedication to the Irish cause with a ruthless determination that nothing—*nothing* was his word—that nothing should be allowed to hinder it.

Harriet caught the change in him, as the busy shuffling of papers gave way to silence; and she was about to come over to see what he had found when he motioned her away.

Anything written by O'Moira must be of such a confidential nature that it must be kept from her eyes.

But to occupy her he gave her the remainder of the papers to tidy and pack while he drew out O'Moira's note and the large sheets that were attached to it.

There was no date, no address at the head of it, though it began quite formally.

"Dear Mr Francis. I write to you as a friend of liberty, and the son of an Irishman—from Kilkenny, I'm told." Justice found this beginning ominous, and the ensuing sentences were even more disturbing. "American and other friends who wish to renew their acquaintance . . . make sure his genius was properly rewarded . . ." Anyone who knew what company O'Moira kept in France, as Justice knew, would read those apparently innocent words very differently from a person who cast a casual eye over them. "The steamboat, now . . . on the Liffey and the Shannon . . . prosperity brought to a hungry people . . . visit to Dublin to discuss a speculation . . . and . . ." Here Justice felt so foolish that he almost tore the page in his frustration. "And a gentleman will come soon to discuss the arrangements . . ."

Fanshawe! Fanshawe, not Luc. For Luc, with his long experience of clandestine war, would have come to attend to the darker side of those arrangements, if Fanshawe's persuasions failed . . . arrangements which sounded so harmless as O'Moira proposed them . . . which could lead Francis to Paris rather than Dublin . . . coul lead to an unpleasant captivity and even an early death if he refused to do what O'Moira and his French master wanted. Justice had seen men when the Service des Renseignements had finished with them, and the memory still chilled him when he thought of anyone falling into the cruel hands of its interrogators.

But, of course, there was not a word on the paper to compromise Fanshawe, or Luc, or Mademoiselle Gérard, who might well have been brought over to beguile Francis with the ease and peculiar nature of her charms—if those drawings he had made were a guide to his tastes.

There was only a single sentence, at the end of the letter, which would make it look to a careless reader as though the final page had been lost.

"B. will of course know and vouch for me."

"B." It could stand for anyone, even Bonaparte. Or Bland. Or Parson Berdmore. Or Brazear Breney. Or Barlow.

Surely it was Barlow, so recently come from France, so close for years to the French revolutionaries, so much a figure in the American group in Paris which had supported them.

The reference to American friends must be proof of that,

proof for the moment, if not proof positive. For as Justice thought about Barlow his attention strayed to the larger sheet to which O'Moira's letter was pinned.

He was so startled and dismayed by what he saw that he pulled it right up to the candles to make sure of it.

A chart of the Channel between Dover and Calais, small in scale but drawn precisely.

With a date on it that was only three weeks old.

IT WAS A GOOD deal else than a chart, and most sinister. Francis had drawn on his knowledge of the Channel squadron to note the normal stations and movements of Lord Keith's ships—the ships that would be unable to prevent a crossing to England if they were driven off, or for any other reason prevented from getting at the French during the crucial hours when their army was being ferried across twenty miles of sea.

And more. For here were the distances to Portsmouth and Plymouth and Chatham, and estimates of the times in various winds that it would take to bring the heavier ships from those ports to the aid of Keith's blockading force.

And more, again. For on the chart the careful Francis had marked the places for row upon row of floating bombs between the French and English beaches. Ten rows, forming a deadly carpet over which no ship of any draughts could pass without an explosive collision, though the lighter vessels which Boney would use would sail or row over it without any risk of striking the infernal machines tethered a dozen feet below the surface of the sea.

Ten rows of the very carcasses that Francis was now constructing at Portsmouth for use against the French.

Ten rows, laid at intervals of thirty yards, laid so that no one could detect them, laid by just such craft as the *Pandora*—as Justice read through the notes that accompanied the chart the phrases hammered at him, and he remembered how Lord William had shown him the compartments in which the submarine would carry her deadly stock.

Ten thousand bombs in all. Denying the British fleets the most vital parts of the Channel. Preventing any junction between them.

Yes, ten thousand. The French would have powder enough. The means to build them. The money to pay for them, too.

For here was another of those damned calculations. "A cost of only £168,000, which would render it impossible for any vessel to pass without certain destruction, and thus forming a blockade of the whole Channel . . ."

And thus. Here were the deadly words, which made Justice realize that he held the key to a secret which made the dangerous prospects of the *Pandora* a dozen times more dangerous. Here they were, starting up from the page. "And thus the revered British sovereignty of the seas would be for ever lost . . . commerce cut off . . . colonies abandoned . . . whole influence which Britain holds in the scale of nations destroyed . . . obliged to submit to any terms Bonaparte might dictate . . ." All this—if Luc carried this paper back to O'Moira, back to France. It was worse than Lilly had imagined. The threat these infernal novelties offered to his country's safety and prosperity was like the terror that sometimes came on a man in sleep.

But was Hatherley also right, in suspecting Francis of double dealing? Was this the evidence that Hatherley would want to make his case—evidence that would be enough to send Francis to the gallows if he were an Englishman?

Justice could not tell. He only knew that he must get this whole collection of papers to London, where they would be safe, would be looked at by men who could weigh the balance of dangers within them . . . and that O'Moira's letter and the chart, above all, must travel in his own pocket, from which Luc or any of his accomplices could tear them only by killing him first.

IT WOULD BE LIGHT in an hour or two, and there was much to be done before he could take the road to the capital.

He looked at Harriet, drowsing half bent, hands on knees like a weary traveller, and felt the kind of gratitude and admiration that no woman had ever evoked in him before. Without her help, her vigour . . . he scarcely liked to think of his earlier suspicions about her, let alone what might have happened if she had not come so bravely into the fight . . . And he went over and stood behind her, placing his hands gently on her shoulders.

"It is time to be going," he said, and felt her body lift and stretch as he touched her, felt her hands come up to take his own and draw them down so that he held her breasts and she could lean her head back where the crotch of his legs could cradle it.

He went to draw back, fearing the warmth of his response, but she held him more firmly while she spoke.

"It is a parting, John. For both of us. We shall meet again. Often, perhaps. Often, I hope. But not like this. I have struck and rung against you, John, and there would never be such a night as this again."

She stirred against him, and sighed. "I think you love another woman, as I . . ." She did not finish the sentence, and turned it. "As a marrying man may love. But there would be no iron there, John. None of the struggle and strength that has coupled us tonight and would drive us apart in a week together."

She had unwittingly hit the mark, Justice said to himself, her words touching his hidden feelings about the wife of his best friend; and that remembrance silenced him as she rose, throwing off her blanket like a shawl, taking his arm, putting up her face for the briefest of kisses before she murmured her farewell.

"And so, John, to all that, goodbye."

Straightening herself, standing back, she was once more the Harriet Romney the world knew, brisk, self-possessed.

"Now what must be done?" she asked, as if Justice were simply a normal guest, making an early departure after an agreeable weekend in the country.

WHILE HARRIET ROUSED servants, called for an ample breakfast, ordered up the basket carriage to take Justice and the precious papers to Cuffwells, and went to see how Eliza and Emma had passed the night, Justice wrote a note to Amos Sweetsea.

The most urgent business took him to London for a few days, he wrote, without further explanation, and Sweetsea must be responsible for the watch on the river until he returned, or Sir George or Hatherley came back to relieve him. "If there is an attempt by sea, light the beacon, turn out the Volunteers and the gun crews, and send to have the great bell rung at Wykeham. If there is an attempt at Cuffwells, you know your duty. *At any cost* you must keep the vessel safe from an outrage, or a cutting out.''

He disliked laying such a burden on the one-armed squire of Lower Exbury, but he knew he had no choice. During the small hours, as he scanned page after page of the Francis drawings and descriptions, he made up his mind that he must put their safety first—put it before the safekeeping of Francis himself, wherever he might be found or the security of the *Pandora*, lying almost ready for sea in her dock at Cuffwells.

For if they fell into the hands of O'Moira, if they should reach France . . . He did not care to think too far in that direction. Only when they were truly safe could he turn back to the duty which Sir George had laid upon him.

Less than a week ago, though it seemed like the most crowded week of his life.

"I will take it myself," Harriet said, coming back as he folded the paper and took up a wax taper to make a simple seal. "At once, if you are ready to leave."

"If you let the steward or some other guard go with you," Justice replied, rather grimly, and was glad when she did not protest.

The game had become dangerous for them all. "Armed," he added.

He primed the pistol as two grooms carried the heavy box down into the carriage and settled themselves in it to go with him as far as Cuffwells. It would be only too easy to stage an ambush in the mile or two of dense beech and oak he must traverse before he reached Lilly's house, and he had no intention of letting Luc have one last try to lay hands on all these secrets.

Then the carriage wheels grated on the cobbles, and Harriet was only a solitary small figure, standing still in the grey dawn, watching him out of sight.

⚜ 20 ⚜

"GET THE BEST PAIR of horses in the stable," Justice said as Scorcher came running out from Cuffwells to greet him, all talk and questions that would have to wait. "Strong saddlebags. Padlocks. And a pair of horse pistols." And when Scorcher had given him an enquiring look he had been explicit. "Prime and load them yourself, Fred. Large buckshot." If they were surprised along the way the scattering pellets would be better at close quarters than a hit-or-miss ball.

"And put that box in the hall, with a guard on it until you can repack the contents into the saddlebags."

While Scorcher had been busy with these preparations, there had been a letter to write—to Lilly, or Hatherley, as the case might be, for he had no notion which of them would first come back to the house. A letter to say what had happened at Wykeham, to describe the Francis papers, to explain why he had galloped off to London. An extremely cautious letter, even though he would entrust it to Mr Grimshaw, who seemed the steadiest man about the place, and unlikely to start lifting the seal to learn what he had written.

Then there was only one thing more to be done. He had to take one last look at the *Pandora*. What he used to call a look-for-luck when he was a lad going off to school and leaving his boyish treasures behind—ship models, one of those wonderful sea atlases his grandfather called a Neptune, a telescope that had once been his father's, his own pony in the stable.

And as he and Scorcher trotted away from the house, down to the boathouse half hidden in the trees, so thick and sombre before the sun broke through to gild their bare branches, he recalled Lord William's gloomy doubts about the submarine.

"It is a risk to us all," Romney had said. "Aptly named."

The same could be true of the papers folded in the saddlebags that flapped at his horse's flanks. There were risks to them all, indeed, in that deadly inventory of warlike schemes and instruments that the pacifically intentioned Francis had so paradoxically devised; and the sooner they and their inventor were in safe hands in London the better. For the risks were to them all, not merely to the single enterprise that Lilly had sponsored on this Hampshire backwater, but risks on the scale that Francis himself had sketched in his plan for closing the Channel, ruining the mercantile trade of the country, and making it easy, as Lilly had put it, for Bonaparte to take the first step that would lead him up to the throne of the world. A plan that was disturbingly crisp and fresh to the touch.

But of all these infernal ingenuities the *Pandora* was still the prize, he thought, after they had passed the guards at the gate and gone in to look at the vessel lying in her dock.

Afloat again. Afloat this time by choice, for the Cowleys had let the water in to check her trim as they tested the mast and rigging, ran up a set of sails, scampered about the deck to see how she could best be handled. They were cheerful enough, proud of what they had done, and gibing at Warren, who sat by his workbench watching them, nursing an injured foot.

"Caught it on his blamed rods and levers, yesser'day," Cowley had said with a grin of an old craftsman's satisfaction at the discomfiture of a rival with newfangled ideas; but the gibes made no matter to Warren, deaf as he seemed to be, for he made no retort to the shipwright and his sons, and said nothing to Justice as he scrambled past to see what the Cowleys were doing and give them instructions that would last for a few days. The glum mechanic might be a master of his trade, Justice had decided the first time he saw him, yet he was a disagreeable and dissatisfied man, for all that, and he might well be the worst kind of arguing sea-lawyer if he thought he had a grievance against his superiors.

Francis was welcome to him, Justice thought, as he left the boathouse and stopped for a last word with the guards, who had let him pass in with no more than a friendly bob and fingers to forelocks.

"You must challenge everyone," he said firmly, noting with dismay how quickly the men sloughed off naval discipline when they were ashore. Hatherley might have his own strict standards for confidential work, but he had clearly failed to grasp the essentials of sentry-go; and there had been no time since the fire to break the men of all the sloppy habits they had acquired since Lilly had taken them from the sea and brought them to Cuffwells.

Each day he had seen some evidence of this weakness in the defences of the *Pandora*, and that feeling left him with a feeling of discomfort he could not ease as he and Scorcher mounted and rode away, along the boggy track beside the river that they had missed when they first came, picking their way through the piles of timber seasoning by the slipways at Bucklers Hard, pausing to watch the men at work on the new brigs, giving a wave to old Mr Adams as he sat watching at the window of his house, and going on through the riverside woods to make their crossing at Beaulieu Mill.

THEY HAD TO REST their horses three times on the road to London—at Winchester, at Farnham, and the last time at the Star and Garter on Richmond Hill, long after dusk, when they came to the hostelry in shivering cold; and here, as the effects of a bruising fight and a wearying ride began to tell on Justice, so that he started to sway in the saddle, Scorcher had insisted on a longer rest.

They snatched a few hours of broken sleep, and then hurried away through the little villages along the Thames, so that the first light was gleaming leaden grey on the water as they saw Westminster before them, the towers of the abbey still dark against the sky.

"Storey's Gate Coffee House?" Justice hailed a watchman, asking for an address he had seen on one of the letters that Francis had written to the Admiralty, and with a grunt he was pointed to one of the entrances to St James's Park, where a pair of windows gleamed gold through the morning murk.

Even as they tied their horses in the narrow yard and Justice realized that Scorcher would have to take his breakfast there, keeping guard on the saddlebags he dare not risk taking into a strange place, he wondered whether he should search first for Francis or for Luc.

Francis would be the easier quarry, for they could begin here, while Luc might be anywhere in London. It would be useless to go looking in his old haunts . . . the smarter streets in St Marylebone where the richer exiles had settled . . . the Rose of Normandy, where the pothouse plotters spent their days . . . the French House in Lisle Street, where he had dined

197

more than once with Luc . . . the meaner lanes of Lambeth and Southwark where the poorer French people eked out a living as seamstresses and translators . . . No, Luc, if he had no other safe place to go, would surely find a temporary refuge in some no-questions house, like Hockley-in-the-Hole at Clerkenwell, where men had eyes only for the fighting cocks and the coins they bet on them . . .

"Mr Francis?" The landlord was watching a potman tidy the room from the muddle left when he had closed the house in the small hours: pots, dice, torn cards lay across the table at which Justice had sat to order a chop and coffee for himself, a rasher of ham and four gills of Jamaican rum for Scorcher in the cold outside. "Gone these six weeks," he said unhelpfully, and then made some amends. "But I saw him last week. Thursday, I should say. Came with some of his parliamentary friends." He leaned over, a man with time on his hands, talking while Justice brushed some of the drying mud from his clothes and sat down to eat. They were all Whig gentlemen here, the captain would understand, and lively at that, and Mr Francis was a game 'un, too, though more partial to the ivories than the cards, if it came to it . . . He rattled on, saying almost nothing, and it was only when Justice asked him directly that he went back behind his counter, opened a drawer, and pulled out a scrap of paper on which Justice could just make out the characteristic slant in which Francis wrote.

"Bedford Street," the man said, holding up the paper to squint at it in the lamplight. "Number Nine." He looked even more closely at something that was written below the address. "Next the corner of Bedford Square," he spelt out slowly, and took the coin Justice slid to him with a nod that showed some irritation that this early morning chat had come so quickly to an end.

Justice was about to ask if anyone else had come looking for Francis when he saw that the man's slothful and garrulous manner told him what he wanted to know: if Luc had been here, the landlord would have mentioned it, or else could have been bribed into giving nothing away.

But there were other things to be done before he could set out for the smart squares that had lately been built on the Bloomsbury side of the Oxford Road.

Richmond Terrace was only a stone's throw away, up Whitehall, and the saddlebags would be safer in the office of the Board of Beacons, Bells, Buoys, and Mercantile Messengers than anywhere else he knew, except the Admiralty; and he would prefer Lilly, or Hatherley, or someone under their authority, to see the papers before the officials could hurry them up to Mr Secretary Marsden or bury them in the muddle of files you could see every time you went into the Admiralty, with men burrowing hopelessly for documents that had been lost for years.

They turned right off Whitehall into the single line of houses that ran across the end of Scotland Yard towards the river, and Justice ran up three flights to find the door of the seamen's mission locked, the door of the Board on the floor above closed just as firmly, the silence that showed no one had yet arrived for work.

"Clarence Row," he said to Scorcher, mounting and leading off into Whitehall, threading his way through the maze of little streets at Charing Cross and then west for half a mile to St James's Palace, and the discreet little square beside it where Lilly had his London home.

A fine property, close to the Palace on one side, backing on to Clarence House, a few yards from Pitt's town residence when he was out of office, it was a mark of Lilly's standing in public life, and Scorcher was duly impressed. "Comes it as fine as fivepence, don't he?"

But Lilly had not come at all, as it turned out. It took half a dozen raps to bring a sleepy-eyed footman to the door, who would only open it on the chain and give surly answers until he saw the gold on Justice's shoulder. In frustration Justice left him, trailing Scorcher back towards Richmond Terrace. The sooner he could get rid of those bulging saddlebags the better. Luc or any of his accessories could easily have kept watch on Richmond Terrace, or Storey's Coffee House, or Lilly's elegant establishment.

Could still be there, looking like any of the crossing-sweepers and horseholders who hung about the corners of Whitehall, or the clerks who were now scurrying about the entrances to the fine stone houses as the working day began, but that was a risk that Justice could do nothing about; and so they tied up outside Mercury House, in the centre of the row, where a set of columns ran up past the offices of the Commissioners of Crown Lands and a branch of the Tax and Exchequer Department to the pediment, running across the face of the building just below the floor on which the headquarters of the Mercantile Messengers could be found.

Still closed. Justice and Scorcher flung the bags on the landing outside the door, and were settling on the stairs for a long wait when they heard someone coming up below them, and Justice did not even need to glance at Scorcher before he took his pistol out of his travelling coat, cocked it after a quick check of the priming pan, and looked over the iron balustrade.

The tread was slow, deliberate, with no attempt at concealment, and, as Scorcher turned with an expression of bewilderment to beckon him over, Justice assumed that it was simply someone coming to open up the office of the Board, or the door of the Mission for Seamen on the floor below.

All he could see in the poor light was what appeared to be a white beaver hat, a pair of shoulders that had a familiar look about them, an unbelievably familiar look, for as the climbing figure stopped outside the Mission office and the light from the landing window fell on him, Justice saw quite clearly who it was.

Who was putting a key to the lock as easily as if he did it every morning. Who was not wearing a beaver hat but a bandage.

Dunning. Of course it was Dunning.

Who was supposed to be lying sick to death at the surgeon's house on Quay Hill in Lymington. Who must have left the little seaport days before and come to London on other business.

Come on Hatherley's orders. Come to watch Francis, if Justice knew his man.

BUT DUNNING WAS as short as ever on explanations, confessing himself as surprised to see Justice and Scorcher in London as they had been to see him clambering up the stairs below them. Even now, as he greeted them, he kept up the pretence that the Society for the distribution of Improving Tracts for Seamen was the prime concern of his life, and that his involvement with Sir George Lilly's other enterprises was an unwelcome distraction from it.

"The Lord moves in a mysterious way," Dunning murmured, and went on with the words of the evangelical hymn that Justice thought were peculiarly apt to his business. "He plants His footsteps in the sea,'' Dunning sang as he waved them to an inner room piled with bundles of tracts, "and rides upon the storm.'' And as Justice and Scorcher followed him he gave them the impression that he wanted to busy himself with the despatch of his parcels, rather than with visitors, for he went on whistling the tune through his teeth as Justice ground at him with questions about the movements of Lilly and Hatherley.

He answered, but grudgingly, making Justice wonder again whether Hatherley was playing a deeper game than he had admitted. And that doubt was increased by the offhand way in which Dunning was treating them—more like a pair of men who had left their posts without good reason, and would soon have to account for their blunder.

Dunning could well be speculating on what had brought them, trying to decide how Lilly or Hatherley would wish him to respond.

They would all make fools of themselves if they went on like that, Justice decided with a flick of irritation that was directed as much at himself as at Dunning. The caution that made Lilly keep each of his Mercantile Messengers in ignorance about the work the others were doing was understandable, sensible, and a damned nuisance when the chances of their strange trade threw them together.

"Here,'' he said, pushing aside some packages of tracts on a trestle table to make room for one of the saddlebags, unlocking it, and preparing to pull out some of the Francis papers. "This is why we have come.''

But before he touched any of the papers he had a different idea, and thrust a hand into his coat to take out O'Moira's letter and the small chart attached to it, wrapped together in a folder of oiled cloth to protect them against the weather on his long ride. "And this is why we have come most urgently.''

Dunning took the two documents as though they were tinder and he held a fuse in his hand, and whistled all the more as he looked them over.

"From Francis?'' he asked, screwing up his eyes at the lettering on the chart, and saying nothing about O'Moira's rounded script, as if he neither wished nor was able to recognise it; and when Justice nodded he seemed to shake off the self-deprecating manner which made him look like a lawyer's clerk or a wandering preacher, and by some intangible change of presence he suddenly became a person of substance and authority.

"All of these?" He hefted the other saddlebags onto the table, feeling at its packed pockets, patting them both with the satisfaction of a man who has had his doubts confirmed.

"A man cannot leap straight from the lap of Delilah into Abraham's bosom," Dunning said, enigmatically, but with enough emphasis for Justice to see that he shared Hatherley's doubt about Francis—shared the worry whether the conversion from French to British service was as complete as the American professed. And Justice was just about to protest that he had no reason to suspect Francis of double-dealing when he realized how little he knew of the man, and how much more Hatherley and the men he employed might know.

Hatherley had only shown him part of that secret file. Hatherley had never told him whether he had men watching Francis, or what they might have seen and heard. Hatherley had used the excuse of Dunning's injury to spirit him away from Cuffwells.

But Justice knew things that Hatherley did not know. He knew about the attempt to float the *Pandora* out of the dock. About Luc's hiding place at Wykeham, the flight of Fanshawe and the Frenchwoman, the attempt to steal the papers: and none of those things seemed to incriminate Francis.

"So. So. So." Dunning did not ask for details, but at each crisp sentence he nodded, as though he were trying to fit these pieces of fact into a pattern that was already formed in his mind. He was clearly as eager to see what the saddlebags contained as Justice was to be off in search of Francis.

Now if Hatherley had been there. If he had said plainly that Francis was under surveillance, for good reasons. If he had hinted that some of the admirals had a devious intention of proving the *Pandora* and the other submarine weapons worthless, as Francis clearly believed was the case. Even if he had been told exactly where the limits of his own authority lay . . . As Dunning extracted one packet after another and placed them on the table, Justice was aware that there were so many ifs without answers that he had no intention of bandying guesses with Dunning—and being snubbed for his interference.

Dunning would go his own way, whatever was said.

And Justice would go his way.

For he still thought that Francis was more in danger than a cause of it.

He looked through the window at the dome of St Paul's, rising out of the grey blanket of haze and coal smoke that ran from the river over the roofs of the City, and he remembered how the magnificent golden orb which capped it had gleamed that morning, only a few months back, when he had stood in Lilly's office on the floor above and heard the Commissioner call him a man of character and intelligence—"clever, practical, and effective" were the words Lilly had used so flatteringly.

It was an encouraging memory, enough to make Justice feel that any talents he might possess should be applied as much, and with equal ingenuity, to a situation of danger and confusion in his own country as in France.

And he was sufficiently impulsive to trust his own judgment when there was a need to act without knowing all the facts.

"Scorcher will stay here," he said in a level voice that he hoped gave nothing away, and he laid his own pistol on the table to give Scorcher a second weapon, brushing aside Dunning's protest that the papers were safe enough in his hands. "He stays until Mr Hatherley comes," Justice insisted. "Or the papers are in a vault. Or there is an Admiralty guard on them."

He saw that Dunning did not greatly care for these proposals and wished only to be left alone to rummage through the collection of secrets; and that eagerness made him add another proviso. "And there must be an inventory," he added. "A hand list. So we all know what we have, and what may have to be returned to Mr Francis as his property."

Dunning merely shrugged his shoulders, but Scorcher looked sharp, and Justice knew he could count on him to see that these things were done before nightfall.

"I go to Mr Holland at Lloyd's," he said to Scorcher.

It was his friend Edward Holland, he was sure, who had first mentioned him to Lilly as a possible Mercantile Messenger—though Holland had never admitted that he was more than a patriotic underwriter at Lloyd's, with an understandable interest in marine intelligence: and Justice thought that Holland might well know something about the steamboat with which Francis was so concerned. And about its inventor, too.

"Ask for me at Lloyd's if you should be free by noon," he

203

repeated to Scorcher. "Later at the Tavistock."

The small hotel in Covent Garden was an excellent place to leave messages, for there were so many naval officers coming there from all points of the compass, wanting a bed or a meal before they hurried on about the King's business, that the place was open day and night since the war began again, and some of the older servants at the inn boasted that they knew every post-captain in the navy by name and sight—some of them since they had been midshipmen. It was only a boast, but certainly everyone in the navy knew the Tavistock.

"I am glad to see you so restored," Justice said as he took his leave of Dunning, and remarking to himself that the man was so close about his business that he had said nothing at all about his accident or his rescue.

"The Lord looks after his own," Dunning said, lapsing into his role as a pious sobersides, holding out his hand for the key to the second saddlebag with a gesture that looked like an abrupt dismissal, waiting until Justice was at the door before he spoke again, as if to Scorcher. "They say that Francis is a freethinker, you know."

"And don't take an oath?" Scorcher asked.

"And can't be trusted," Dunning added, as the door closed and Justice went down the stairs to seek the man himself with these doubting words in his ears.

ᕹ 21 ᕷ

JUSTICE RODE UP Whitehall as quickly as his horse could thread through the press of riders and carriages, feeling rather ashamed at the contrast his stained and rumpled condition made to the smartness of the officers he saw heading toward the Admiralty in full fig; and he was glad that none of them were men he knew well enough to be recognised by as he hurried past. If he had time when he called at the Tavistock he would have his boots blacked, his coat and breeches brushed, so that he would look at least as presentable as any man who had just come into London off the country roads. But duty came before appearance in his book, and his duty, as he now saw it, was to find Francis. To find Francis was also the easiest way of finding Luc.

For if his speculations were correct, if Luc had made for London, he would already be very close to the American, might even have made contact with him: with Fanshawe and the Frenchwoman in flight, and Justice certainly at his heels after that inconclusive fight at Wykeham, Luc would know that he must bring off his plans within twenty-four hours.

Or fail so miserably that he would be lucky if he saved his own neck from the hangman.

And the place to begin was the address in Bedford Street which the landlord of the coffee house had given him.

It was easy enough to find. He came across the top of the Strand at Charing Cross, glanced at St Martin's-in-the-Fields —the navy's own church in London, which he never saw without hoping to hear the sudden ring of bells that would announce a victory at sea; he took the road north, alongside Leicester Square, as though he were off to Edward Holland's house up on the hill at Hampstead, waited for a gap in the stream of carts and other vehicles along the Oxford Road, turned right, and went trotting past the elegantly symmetrical houses of Bedford Square, whose façade was already taking on the characteristic grime of the city, past the beggars who almost blocked the roads running into the square, past the tradespeople sitting round the stone coping of the little park hoping for a servant to come out with an order, past a knife grinder, a chimney sweep, a chair mender, a tinker, past a woman with a tray of taffety tarts and hot spiced gingerbread, and up to a doleful muffin man, whose wares had gone so cold and stale that he was happy to hold a horse for a penny while Justice walked towards the street where Francis lodged.

The fifth house from the corner, on the left. He was at last within hailing distance of his quarry.

But as he left the square he was bumped by a flying barber, with razor, soap, and hot water in his hands, and he was so distracted, swinging round with a curse as he kept his balance, that he failed to notice the gangling figure coming towards him until Lord William touched his arm, spoke to him with such a hangdog look of disappointment that Justice could guess what he had to say and anticipate his bad news.

"He is away from home?"

"We have missed him by half an hour, it seems." Lord William had something more to say but he waited while Justice looked up at the house where the door had just closed behind him, and thought of going up the steps to enquire for himself: Romney might have been put off with an excuse, might in fact have seen Francis, and been sent out to fend off an unwelcome visit. Yet there was something convincing in the lugubrious way that Lord William complained of the cost of posting through the night from Portsmouth.

"One and sixpence a mile! Sixpence for the ostler with each change of horses! Another thruppence a mile for the postboy! Seven pounds. Call it guineas, the wretch said." The radically minded heir to a splendid fortune was shocked by such importunity. "It is what my father pays a footman for a year," he said, so busy with his aggrieved multiplication that Justice had to bring him back to the point.

"Gone to see Breney, according to Barlow's man," he replied to Justice's enquiry, and was surprised when Justice gripped his arm so hard that he winced and cried, "What now?"

"Barlow is there?"

Romney shook his head. "Staying there, of course," he answered, as though Justice should have known, and then took his words back. "But gone to Bath. Wife unwell. Back

Thursday, man says.'' He shook off Justice's arm with an irritation that Justice scarcely noticed in his relief that he had at
last run Francis to ground, and that the American had been
safe enough within the hour.

"Where then?"

"To Breney's,'' Romney replied testily. "All conundrums
today, ain't ye?'' He dropped the sharpness in his voice as his
volatile amiability returned. "In the Temple.''

ROMNEY APPARENTLY KNEW the place well, and the best way to
it, for as soon as Justice had collected his horse he led off
through a maze of crowded and narrow alleys, coming down
over High Holborn to Lincoln's Inn, crossing the Strand between St Clement's and Temple Bar, ducking through an archway, threading his way past the small circular church the
Crusaders had built to fetch up at a fine set of stone chambers
not unlike Richmond Terrace. He waited while a liveried
youth took the bridle from Justice and hitched the horse to an
iron railing, waited with some impatience while Justice looked
at the Thames, lapping its marshy edge right up to Temple
Stairs, and reflected that if he lived in London he would
choose to have rooms here, where he could smell water, see
sails, feel the sea driving upstream twice a day. He was so lost
in a daydream that Lord William had to nudge him as the bells
of St Clement's struck nine, and as he followed his Lordship
up a flight of stairs, he was thinking how easily a man might
come and go into London by ship, with no one any the wiser.

One floor up, on a black-painted door, a gleaming brass
plate declared that Breney, Breney, Bubb, Arthurvole, Trim,
and Breney did their legal business within, but as Justice
followed Lord William into the office, he felt little faith in the
corporeal existence of the earlier Breneys, or Messrs Bubb,
Arthurvole, and Trim, for there were only three rooms in the
set—one for the clerks, with a pair of youngsters perched on
their stools, and a much older man who had a desk to himself,
stacked with dusty calf-bound volumes; one, beyond him,
which was clearly an anteroom, for it felt crowded when he
and Lord William were shown into it to wait; and a third,
beyond a closed door, that had the words "Brazear Breney,
Attorney-at-Law'' painted in a flowing gold script on its
centre panel.

And Mr Breney was presently engaged, the chief clerk said,

without much necessity, for Justice could hear the rumble of voices beyond the door and hoped that Francis would soon emerge from it.

But it was an Irishman who came out, expostulating loudly, spluttering ". . . downright fraud, it is . . . embezzlement, when a man's got his back turned to other things and his mind's upside down . . . a Limerick bilker with the face of Janus . . ." and the last words Justice heard, as the two young clerks bore him bodily out of the office, were a wild shout of "coggery and gullery, to beat all tarnation."

"The poor man has been deceived and I can do nothing to help him," Breney said, standing coolly at the door of his room and welcoming Lord William and Justice as though he had been expecting them. "And like all his countrymen, so liable to prefer a grievance to a reasonable explanation." He paused. "Like my client at Winchester. Pleaded guilty out of perversity, I should say, considering His Majesty's hospitality better than the prospect of paying me a substantial fee for securing his acquittal."

Justice was on the point of asking about that hurried journey from Wykeham to Winchester, and what Breney knew of Fanshawe's intentions, when Lord William for once came straight to the question.

"Mr Francis?" Breney said with satisfaction. "In London, as I supposed, and here this morning, as concerned as ever about his blessed steam engine, and gone off to Deptford dockyard in a huff because he is urgently summoned on Admiralty business and has no time to go to collect his precious permit."

"Then it has come?" Justice did not wish to reveal how much he knew of this transaction, and even this question seemed to make Breney pause to consider how much a lawyer might decently say about his client's transactions.

"The permit? Or the engine?"

"Both, if you please to say." Justice softened his voice. "Lord William is naturally interested . . ."

"Naturally," said Breney. "And as a matter of fact, both is my answer. The permit waits in Whitehall. The engine, or the parts of it, I should say, was at Brentford dock yesterday and will be moved up the Paddington branch of the canal today. Mr Francis can send carts to fetch his puffing machine from Paddington tonight, or tomorrow, or when he pleases." He spoke as though Francis had no other business, though he must have known that the sudden appearance of Justice and Lord William in his office had in some way to do with the Admiralty contract he had helped Francis to negotiate; and he cut off that part of their talk with a polite enquiry after Lady Harriet and a compliment about the weekend festivities.

That gave Justice his chance, breaking in before Lord William, in his innocence, could get any further with what promised to be an account of the troubles at Wykeham. "But the Frenchman . . ." Lord William began.

"The Frenchwoman and Fanshawe," Justice said, with an apparent correction, "and the Earl of Lymington?"

"The Earl was much taken by affairs at the assizes," Breney said, "for there were rick burners arraigned there, and he had me fee a counsel for them—pure waste, you know, for they'll hang or go to Botany Bay. When I found my occupation gone, and came back to London, the earl stayed on. He will post on tomorrow, I daresay."

"And the others?" Justice pressed him, guessing at the excuse Fanshawe might have made and learning he was near the mark.

"I think he was in some kind of embarrassment," Breney said slowly. "He . . . he persuaded the lady to leave with him. In Ireland, you know, he has a certain reputation. So I have no idea where he proposed to go. I could only say that he is likely to lead her something of a dance before he gets to London, or Dublin."

Justice saw that Breney was either ignorant or reluctant to say more, and since he had no means to start a hue and cry after the fugitives . . . Hatherley could concern himself with that, if he appeared soon enough to give any chance of catching them.

"There is a disagreeable side to that man," Lord William said as they came down the steps to find the air thickening into the kind of fog that might become a London particular. "He has a kind of commercial virtue that I do not find convincing. As if he would swear to anything that was to his own advantage and within the law. Or close to it."

"You dislike him for a Tory," Justice said, more for a tease than the truth of it, and found that he had provoked Lord William so much that it took some minutes to calm him into an admission that he disliked all lawyers, and especially a lawyer such as Breney. "He has used his interest with the government to make money out of the misfortunes of Ireland," Romney cried, so loudly that people stopped and stared at him. "Misused his interest, no doubt," he added, as if he were quoting the kind of tale at which Fanshawe had hinted in his talk with Justice.

"Who is one to trust when everything has gone so wrong in that unhappy country?" Justice asked in a mollifying tone, remembering how O'Moira had successfully deceived him; and then turned to a more practical problem. "But Francis . . . ?"

"We could try the New England Coffee House, where all the Yankees take their breakfast," Romney said doubtfully, then looked at his watch and judged that his friend must already be half way to Deptford. "We could miss him there again." He spoke like a tired man who saw no point in another fruitless search, and he brightened as another idea came to him. "Let us go to Paddington tonight. If I know Robert's impatience he will go there directly he is done at Deptford." Then, with one of those turns of sudden practicality that surprised Justice in such an abstracted man, he made a definite suggestion. "I shall go to his rooms at five," he said, as confidently as though that was a regular hour for Francis to be receiving callers. "If he is not there and there is no other news of him, I shall meet you at the King's Head in the Harrow Road at six. You know it, I suppose?"

"I suppose not," Justice answered with a touch of asperity, for he had only the haziest notion of the villages on the northern edge of London and even less acquaintance with the hostelries to be found there, "but I shall find it, no doubt. We meet there, whether you come with him or not?"

"If I come alone it will be all the more important to find him." Lord William seemed to have been so preoccupied by the problem of finding Francis that the urgent reason for the search had apparently slipped from his mind until this moment; and when Justice remembered what Harriet had said about her brother he was far from sure that he was the most suitable companion for the night ahead. If his cousin Luc were following Francis about London, or had somehow learned that the American must go in person to Paddington, the whole affair would come to a decisive encounter on the banks of the canal.

•　•　•

210

JUSTICE DID NOT waste time looking for the New England Coffee House. Whatever Lord William might say, for he was the kind of man who could while away a morning on talk that interested him, Francis was clearly so eager to lay hands on his precious engine that he would hurry down to Deptford to despatch the Admiralty's business and get back to Paddington to deal with his own.

There was more to be gained from talking to Edward Holland than from passing the day with William Romney or hanging about with Yankee merchants and skippers in the hope of coming across one who might know Francis well or another who was expecting to take a steam engine on board in the next few days.

And so, leaving Romney to call on a friend who lived in a little court of Fleet Street, Justice rode on into the City.

He had often ridden that way, but familiarity had never staled his pleasure at the London scene that opened from the top of Ludgate Hill—the shops and churches bustling each other for space, the pigeons circling above Wren's great dome, the gloomy Mansion House, the peculiar placards on which teeth pullers and herbalists and other quacks proclaimed their trades. And there were shouting boys and ragged horse holders jostling each other as he dismounted outside the Royal Exchange. In the gathering gloom of the day, with smoke darkening the mist into a heavy fog, they all looked like creatures from a nether world.

It was a very different inside, the rooms where the Lloyd's underwriters wrote their business, for it was warmer, more comfortable. And yet here too, past the red-robed waiters who presided at the door, ran messages, and generally did the menial business of the place, there was another crowd of men clamouring and elbowing as vigorously as the mendicants in the street, brokers trying to get into the Underwriting Room as if their livings depended upon striking a bargain before the clocks on the fifty churches within earshot began to strike the next quarter. Justice saw that he had no chance to push his way up to the curious little boxes where the underwriters sat, measuring the risks of marine insurance in every quarter of the globe, and he could not see Edward Holland anywhere among the throng. All he could do was to ask a waiter to find him; and when the man came back after ten minutes, bringing word that Mr Holland was expected within the hour, Justice said he would call back and set out to amuse himself.

He seldom had the chance to stare at shop windows, and he looked at books, and hats, and bottles of wine; stopped at a jeweller's, considering whether Edward would take it amiss if he bought some expensive trinket to mark Kitty's birthday next month, thinking of a ruby brooch, thinking better of it, and taking a pair of sapphire earrings that would set off her ash-silver hair and china-blue eyes.

He stopped again to buy himself a pair of gloves, a set of pocket handkerchiefs, which recalled the inventory of clothing which Francis had left among his papers—and must now be puzzling Dunning, who would consider it the most baffling of cyphers; stopped to buy himself a new kind of burning glass, with a lanyard, which hung round the neck like a woman's pendant; stopped at last in Cornhill, peering into a gunsmith's window, realizing that since he had left his pistol with Scorcher he was quite unarmed.

He was not interested in the rack of sporting guns that Mr Edward Bond placed in his window, under a sign that told he was carrying on the business established by his grandfather when the first of the Georges was on the throne. Nor in the boxes of duelling and travelling pistols that were shelved below them. They were no doubt as fine as anything that Manton made, but of no use to him at the moment. What had caught his eye was a strange-looking weapon, with four short barrels splayed like the fingers of a hand, all of them fired at once by a single flintlock. He had heard of such a thing. Someone had called it a captain's pistol, designed to quell four mutineers or pirates at once. But he had never seen one before, and he was tempted.

Mr Bond had no shame about being a craftsman as well as a proprietor, for he came forwards in the same kind of apron as his workmen were wearing at the benches behind the shop, though he took a black topcoat from a hook before he bowed Justice up to his counter. Yes, he would be delighted to show the captain the duck-foot pistol, yes, duck-foot it was, as the captain would see for himself when he took it from the window: and while he was leaning over to pick it up, Justice noticed several other oddities set on padded trays, their steel, brass, and dark hardwoods winking in the candlelight, and an occasional plate of engraved silver adding a touch of fancy.

"The watch is little more than a toy, sir," Bond said, putting down the four-barrelled pistol and taking up a timepiece which he handled with some care, grasping one side in a crumpled leather before he pressed the turnkey and released a small knife. "All the same . . ." He wound the knife back. "The spring is strong enough to startle a light-fingered jack who reached for it. And the knife, well, who knows? Now these muff-pistols . . ." He moved to a pair of the neatest guns that Justice had ever seen, showing how they were loaded by unscrewing the barrels and brought to half cock by an ingenious slide. "Ideal for a lady," he said, "and fatal at twenty feet." He glanced at Justice, who was beginning to think how useful such a gun, or something like it, would have been in the fight with Luc, and shook his head. "I could make something like it, a sleeve gun, for instance, but these are not for sale." He handled them as if they were made of a precious metal. "My father's work, you see. Just before he died. A remembrance."

This family of gunsmiths obviously had a taste for the bizarre. Bond pulled out a drawer of guns that combined with daggers—"most popular in the Eastern trade, sir," he said, giving Justice the impression that potentates from Africa clear to Asia were clamouring for these novelties, and making him think that Francis would get on so famously with this man that they would be in partnership an hour after they met.

He was intrigued himself by the succession of odd devices that Mr Bond laid on the counter. He bought the knife-watch for five guineas, telling himself that he could not always carry about the splendid gold and crystal watch that had been a keepsake from the dying Tissot in Boulogne harbour. He was equally taken by another example of Bond's ingenuity, for which he could see many uses. It was a tinderbox, short, narrow, so that it was small enough to go into a pocket, and tightly closed, so that no damp could get at the tinder. And it worked almost like a pistol. When Bond pushed back the clasp and snapped it open, there was the click of a spring releasing and a tiny hammer struck enough spark from a flint to set the tinder glowing.

"Bibulous paper. Soaked in nitrate of potash." Bond was very proud of it.

But Justice was not really listening to the gunsmith's patter. He had walked into this shop with very little idea how best to arm himself, and it was only when he saw what Bond could do that the idea came to him.

"I would like a gun I can secrete about my person," he said impulsively, and he caught the glint in Bond's eye as the man led him into the workshop to produce the greatest of his surprises.

"If you would be good enough to remove your coat, sir? Thank you. The belt of your breeches. Thank you again, sir."

Justice went to turn round when he heard the man busy behind him, but Bond stayed him, slipping both ends of his belt around his waist for him to fasten, and as he did so Justice felt the pressure of a metal plate in the small of his back.

"A moment if you please, sir," Bond said a mite anxiously, stepping smartly aside, passing a loose cord over Justice's shoulder, lifting it gently away as he reached for the end that dangled in front of him. "It should normally run down the sleeve," Bond added, taking Justice by the arm and leading him out into a yard that was plainly used as a proving range, for the smell of powder hung in the air and there were targets at the far end.

Bond went over to prop up the black outline of a man, cut out of wood, and came back to twist Justice round so that he could not see the target.

"Put up your hands," he said sharply, and as Justice began to respond almost by instinct, the gunsmith laughed and then spoke politely again. "And be good enough, sir, to pull the cord as you do so, for . . ."

He did not have time to finish before Justice had tugged at the twine, felt a thumping blow just above his hips, heard the sharp crack of a small bore pistol, swung round to see the black target knocked flat.

"Front or back, it's all the same," Bond said, displaying a hole in the target as Justice reached round to feel a small hot barrel protruding from a thin slab of steel. "Only the backfire can be the more surprising, especially if a man's been taken at a disadvantage." He waited until Justice had released his belt to slip the device clear of it. "A belt-buckle pistol, sir," he exclaimed with pride. "Neat, simple, deadly at short range."

Justice could see that every claim Bond made was true. The base plate, on which his belt was threaded, was about three inches wide and five long; and on it there was nothing but a miniature and marvellously crafted flintlock, working at right angle to the barrel, which was exactly like those Bond's father had made for the muff-pistols.

He was entranced by it. Fired it twice, back and front, and began to feel the bruising of his muscles where Luc had kicked and pummelled him. Loaded it under Bond's careful eye, using the best powder and making sure the oversize ball was properly seated, for there were no wads to hold the charge. Left it loaded, at half cock for safety. Got Bond to put it in a small box. Bought it.

"Ten guineas," Bond asked. "Five for the work, and five for the idea."

Justice had heard that old joke more than once but he was now in such a good humour that he laughed at it, realized that he did not have enough in his purse to pay for the watch and the pistol, and wrote Mr Bond a draft on Marsh's Bank that the gunsmith accepted without even bothering to look him up in the Captain's List. In front of him, as he wrote, he saw a clever mechanical calendar, with the day and the date on it.

It was just one week since he had been riding towards Cuffwells, without any idea what awaited him, and there would be more sinister twists of fortune before his work was done. But now, whatever the next days and nights might bring, wherever his duty might take him, Mr Bond had given him the means to walk into danger without the fear that came to every man who fought alone—the fear that a sudden jab of a knife or a pistol in his back might be the end of him.

EDWARD HOLLAND WAS WAITING at Lloyd's to carry him off to split a pheasant and a bottle of port, and as they walked towards their favourite chop house, Justice quickly told him as much about the events at Cuffwells as he thought proper.

Holland was a friend of Sir George's, was certainly one of those Lilly always called "my band of gentlemen" in the City, whose resolve, influence and courage had helped to gather intelligence during the uneasy peace, who had gathered money for Lilly's covert activities before Mr Pitt returned to office, who even now were giving him all kinds of unacknowledged assistance.

Even so, discretion was the best part of such clandestine business, and Justice said nothing about the *Pandora* or the papers he had brought to London. He only told Holland that his renegade cousin was back in England, doing Boney's work for him, and got so little response to that news that he suspected Edward already knew it. Told him that Francis, of whom he also seemed to have heard, was at great risk. Told him that there might be some deception planned with the steam engine that was being sent from Birmingham for onward shipment to America. Told him that it had been impossible to speak freely to Breney in the presence of Lord William, who was far too free with his confidences.

"Have you actually seen Luc?" Holland had listened all the way up to Cheapside, and he put his first question after they had settled in their booth and sent the waiter away with their order.

"Not here." Justice felt obliged to add the briefest account of his struggle in the dark at Wykeham, though he said nothing of the reason for it or Harriet's part in it.

"So you are not sure he is in London?"

"It would be useless to search for him, Edward. Even with a dozen men. He will be disguised in some way, you may be sure, especially if he is watching Francis and waiting for his moment to strike. The only way I can come at him is to watch Francis myself."

"You go to Paddington Basin, you say? Tonight? And by yourself?"

Justice had known Holland for a cool fellow ever since they had first met as midshipmen, and his questions were put in his usual drawling voice, which gave little away: but Justice had the feeling that his friend did not altogether approve of what he proposed to do, and that impression was confirmed when Holland followed his answering nod with a more troubling enquiry.

"With no other, er, arrangements?"

The implication was clear. Holland was asking whether Justice was acting with Sir George's approval, with Hatherley's knowledge, perhaps. "Speaking purely as a friend, of course."

"Of course."

It was always a pleasure to see Edward, to hear his gossip about the war at sea, the rumours that ran through Lloyd's like a wind in April, to say nothing of news about Kitty. Today he was less comfortable, sitting glumly, wishing that Holland could be more helpful and yet knowing there was little he could do, for his friend was not directly involved in this affair and would know too little about it to give sensible advice. All he could do would be to counsel caution because he saw that Justice was acting on his own, chasing after Luc and Francis without a word to Sir George or to Hatherley and without any notion of what deep game they might be playing with either man.

He almost said as much to Holland. But what came to his mind, and he said, was a remark by Nelson he had heard from Captain Blackwood. "A man cannot go far wrong if he lays his ship alongside one of the enemy." Like all Nelson's maxims, it would do for a sailor when he was not otherwise clear about his duty.

"There is one other thing, Edward," he said, after a pause in which they addressed themselves to the pheasant. "The permit. For the steam engine. What does it say? What, precisely, is being shipped? When? Where? By what vessel? Can you find out?"

"That could be done this afternoon if the permit is ready for issue."

"For collection, Breney said. How soon?"

"Within the hour, possibly. Where shall I find you?"

Justice hesitated to say the Tavistock: he would merely call there to leave word for Scorcher to come on after him. "I am due at Harrow Road at six," he said, a little doubtfully, "and Hampstead is almost on the way."

"You will call on Kitty, then? She will indeed be pleased."

"If I may, without notice."

"My dear fellow, there can never be ceremony among the three of us."

This was the nearest Edward would come to mentioning the way in which Justice had once loved and lost the beautiful Kitty Rawlings on a voyage home from the West Indies, when his career was under such a cloud that he had no prospects at all to offer an heiress.

"And I should send a man there?"

"Until five, let us say. At six to the King's Head, where I meet Lord William."

Holland looked solemn as they walked out into Cheapside and made their way back to Lloyd's as briskly as the crowds in the narrow fog-darkened streets would permit.

"I hope you know what you are about, John," he said, as Justice took his horse at the railing and prepared to mount. "The stakes may be higher than you know, higher than you have played before."

"Even in France?" Justice was nettled at this repetition of a

217

warning that Lilly had given him days ago.

"Even in France." Holland did not smile as he put out his hand to steady the horse, champing after being tied so long. "Remind Kitty that I dine at Goldsmith's Hall tonight and shall be brought home merry at least, and as pressed with food as a Christmas goose."

He gave a wave of farewell that was more like a salute. "I think you will need all the luck I can wish you, John," he said in a warmhearted way, "and I wish I were free to go with you."

With that cryptic remark still troubling him Justice trotted away towards Covent Garden. If Scorcher had not yet come he would have to go on alone.

And it was only the prospect of seeing Kitty before he went on to his rendezvous that kept him cheerful, so that he was whistling into the swirling mists as he came up Haverstock Hill, turned for Church Row, and was knocking at the door of Holland's elegant house within half an hour of leaving its owner.

❧22❧

"JOHN! WHAT AN unexpected delight." Kitty was halfway down the stairs into the hall before the footman had closed the door, hands held out to welcome him, chattering a dozen questions as she led the way into the parlour, laughing at her own excitement, and at last letting him announce himself.

"I may look like one of Congreve's farmer squires," Justice said, knowing Kitty shared his passion for the theatre, and making an ineffectual attempt to tidy himself. "Straight from the turnip fields, it would seem, but actually from duty on the Hampshire coast."

There was no need to say more, since Edward must have told her something of his return from France, and even if that tale left her curiosity unsatisfied she would be too discreet to ask exactly what he had been doing, or what precise duty now engaged him. Her answer, indeed, made him wonder briefly whether she might know more of his occupation than he guessed, or whether there was simply a coincidence in the name.

"You are like a Mercury to me," she exclaimed, giving him a kiss on the forehead before she made him sit beside her on the window seat, where what little light the fog left in the day so caught her pale and fine-drawn features that her face looked like a cameo against the dark walnut panelling. "And what news do you bring from these darkened skies? Lord, what a day! Are the gods angry?"

"Nothing of importance, except that I am very glad to see you." He put his hand to his pocket and drew out a small box. "And these, if it is not too indelicate to remember a lady's birthday." He was about to open the box when she took it from him, laying her fingers lightly on the back of his hand.

"It is more than five years since you first remembered it, John." She spoke very quietly before she unfastened it and touched the sapphires with a cry of delight, running to a looking glass to hold them up and see the effect, and then coming back with her eyes glistening and the slightest of catches in her voice. "You are the dearest of friends. To us both." She sat facing him, and now she took his hand and put her lips to it. "To Edward, and to me, John dear. We miss you so much when . . . when you are away." She paused, changing her mood as she put the jewels beside her on a sofa table where she could see them glinting, gold and blue, in the light of the four-branch candelabra the footman had just brought to brighten the sombre room. "And when you are in port . . ." She smiled.

"I am still tied up alone in the berth, Kitty," he said, picking up their familiar joke about her attempts to marry him off to a rich and attractive widow. "But then I am so seldom home that . . ."

"But here you are." Kitty was already making plans for him. "Can you stay in London? Can you come back? What use are you to His Majesty wandering about the New Forest and staring at the Isle of Wight?" She laughed as though everything might be arranged on a whim. "Hampshire. Is that all the Admiralty can do for you? For shame, John. They will make you a Greenwich pensioner yet, for no man ever found death or glory in Hampshire."

There was something about the way he shrugged his shoulders, an involuntary movement that told her she might be wrong, that her teasing was far from the point; and she stared at him closely, seeing the rumpled clothes, the fatigue in his face, the knuckles he had skinned as he rolled on the floor with Luc.

"My dear," she said gently, "you look like a ghost, and I am prating like the silliest gibble-gabble." She stood up, to speak seriously. "Do you need help, John? From me? From Edward?"

"I have seen Edward," he said, passing on his friend's jocular message, and grinning when Kitty grimaced.

"La, those devilish dinners, John. He will be off to Bath, nursing his gout, unless he quarrels with all the livery companies in London." She came back to her question. "What can *I* do for you, John?"

"Let me rest a little, Kitty, if you would be so kind." Her words had made him feel the exhaustion of his long ride, and though there was nothing that he enjoyed more than talking to Kitty he knew that unless he slept till dusk he would have

220

neither the wits nor the energy for another broken night.

She was ringing for the footman before he had a chance to explain, and once she had given orders for a bed to be made and aired she came across to clutch Justice by the lapels.

"Are you in danger, John? Surely not, here in London?" She sounded incredulous, yet it was her thought, and Justice saw that she could not be fobbed off with a denial.

"It could be so," he replied, trying to make light of her question. "But there are many dangers in a great city. I could be struck down by a cutpurse in Camden Town. Edward could get lost in the fog coming home and be tipped into a ditch. Your neighbour's house could be set alight by a careless chambermaid . . ."

Kitty would have none of such trifling, and said so, before she added anxiously what someone had lately told her. "At supper, I forget where," she said. "A plot to do with French prisoners. At some camp beyond Cambridge. To release and arm them."

"At Norman Cross?" Justice shook his head, thinking how carelessly people talked of secrets in the drawing rooms of London. "That's an old story. No, nothing of that kind." He gave a wry smile as the footman came to summon him, hoping to reassure her.

"But it is confidential business, all the same?"

"My dear Kitty. If I told you I was likely to become a bargemaster on the Grand Junction Canal it would be near to the truth." He perceived she would let him evade the question. "But bless you. I am safe enough for any man of my calling."

WHEN JUSTICE WOKE he found it hard to place himself, for the footman was at the bedside with an apology for disturbing him, holding a pair of candles and offering him a note from Edward.

He broke the seal on the heavy Lloyd's paper, scanning the words. "A schedule of materials . . . cylinder, piston, condenser, other parts that meant nothing to my man . . . approved for shipment at once . . . Limehouse Reach . . . *Star of Salem* . . . American brig, lately from Flushing . . . application made by a J. Barlow, countersigned George William Ewing, the American consul in Nicholas Lane . . . all appears to be in order . . ."

At once. *At once.* These were the words that stood out from the page, explaining why Francis had stayed in London waiting for a crawling barge to bring his machine from Birmingham, why he would hasten to Paddington to see the parts unloaded at the basin and put on carts for the long haul round the northern fringe of London and down to the river at Limehouse. It would take all night, and the brig would be waiting to sail with the tide.

Could Francis actually have gone to settle everything with the master of the *Star of Salem* today, after telling Breney that official business took him to Deptford? It would have been easily done. If the brig was at Limehouse he had only to row across the river from the naval dockyard.

Justice could not bring himself to believe that the American was about to flee the country, though he could manage it well enough with a vessel from Massachusetts lying to hand. If he had flight in mind he would never have left that chest of papers at Wykeham.

But someone else might have it in mind to trap him, to smuggle him aboard, to sail for Ireland, or France, as neatly as setting a course for Cape Cod.

There was only one way to find out.

Justice pulled on his clothes, washed and shaved, smiled at Kitty's protest when he only pecked at the cold table laid for him in the dining room; and at five, when the clock chimed on the parish church, he was on the gravelled track down to the Finchley Road, the footman running before him because Kitty feared he would get lost in the Hampstead mists, or be waylaid, or trip and fall. Her worries warmed him in the chill air as much as her farewell kiss.

IT WAS AN EASY ride to the King's Head. Down the Finchley Road, where Justice could make no mistake about his route, for it was busy despite the weather; at this hour a good many gentlemen were visiting the discreet establishments in St John's Wood where they had settled their paramours. Down between St John's Church and the new cricket ground where he had played twice in the brief summer of peace. Down to the bank of the canal, where the towpath took him almost to the junction of the Edgware and Harrow Roads, and the lights of the rambling hostelry stretched before him.

The inn was an agreeable place, much favoured by travellers

from the north, for it gave proper measure to man and beast, and its stable was so renowned for the quality of its posthorses that a man would often choose to start his journey there; but on this foul evening Justice had no demands on its offerings beyond a stiff glass of its celebrated milk punch, served piping hot, which he sipped as he waited in the hallway for Lord William.

There was a large clock against the wall, a great-grandfather properly called, with heavy weights and a great brass pendulum that swung away the minutes, and he had just compared Mr Bond's clever novelty to its chime of six when he heard Lord William call his name in a cheerful voice.

He got up, looking about the crowded lobby for Romney's angular frame, bumped into a tall good-looking man, with a fine set of curls framing a sensible face, thought the features familiar, and found Lord William introducing the subject of the self-portrait he had carried away from Wykeham.

But it was a more vigorous, energetic face than he had expected—a face that came out to meet you; and as he smiled Justice saw how Harriet could have been attracted by that easy, indolent charm. And yet, beneath it, there was the firmness of purpose which had carried the Americans into a world of their own making.

"Captain Justice, may I present . . ."

"Robert . . . Robert Francis," the man said, introducing himself with only a flicker of hesitation about his name. Cordially. He shook hands with Justice as if they were old acquaintances. "Lord William told me . . ."

It was Romney rather than Justice who cut him off, as if they might be overheard, suggesting a private room and going off to find one.

"William is full of fancies," Francis said in a kindly tone while Romney was gone, giving Justice a clear impression that he was not in the least impressed by anything he had been told on the way. "I could scarcely make sense of what he was saying, and nearly ran down one of those beggarly fellows who hang about Bedford Square."

He paused, looking towards the door as a man might who thought he was being followed. "Excuse me, Captain." He went over to a groom who stood in the entrance and gave him some instructions. "It's a fine fast curricle," he said when he came back, like a man who enjoyed driving, "but I never saw a pair of horses so hungry. If I'm here half an hour they'll get through a bag of oats apiece."

So this was Francis. At last. Safe. Apparently unruffled. "I am famished," he said, looking around as the three men settled in front of the fire in a small upstairs parlour. "Would you gentlemen join me in game pie and cheese? No? Then if I may be forgiven . . ." He rubbed his hands. "It was cold on the river today. The English cold. That drips into your blood until you feel you will die of it." He grinned, and slapped William lightly on the shoulder. "Not the day at all for submarine men, was it now?"

At the Irish shape of that sentence Justice pricked up his ears, remembering what O'Moira had said about a father from Kilkenny, wondering whether to take the remark as a chance to talk about the *Pandora* or to speak first and directly about Luc.

But Francis broached the subject himself as soon as the waiter was out of the room.

"Now, as to this Frenchman," he began, going on so casually to discuss what Romney had told him, and taking Justice so much for granted, that it was clear that he had no idea that he was in danger; and it was also clear that he did not wish to be persuaded.

"A farrago of misunderstanding," he exclaimed, shrugging off Justice's attempt to tell him more about the fires at the boathouse and the mysterious attempt to float the *Pandora* out of the dock. "I have never seen this Frenchman, Mr Justice. I have never heard of him. I have never been approached by any of his countrymen since I parted brass rags with them and came over to England at Lord Hawkesbury's request. His express request. His official request, though you would not think so if you knew how I was treated during my first weeks in London." He was firm, sceptically disgruntled.

"Who starts the fires at Cuffwells? Who beat the workmen? Who tried to damage my submarine by flooding the dock? I don't know. Ask your Mr Hatherley. The safety of the *Pandora* is his business, not mine, and I very much doubt whether a Frenchman who came to destroy my work would be so hesitant and amateurish. If Mr Hatherley wants to find someone to blame, let him chase after rick burners and machine breakers and other malcontents who dislike such novelties as mine and will damage them if they can. There are such men, I suppose, even in the peaceful backwaters of Hampshire, even among the shipwrights who work for Mr Adams at Bucklers Hard and see my submarine as a threat to their occupation." He paused, taking a sip of the milk punch that Justice had taken and recommended, giving a sarcastic grin. "Like some of your admirals," he said.

"Not malcontents?" Justice was astonished at this off-handed explanation.

"Yes, malcontents," Francis repeated. "You have a great many of them in your country, Captain," he said in a plain-spoken way that gave no offence. "You cannot explain every sign of dissatisfaction by claiming that it is the work of French spies, you know. We Americans have heard that argument before and we are not easily convinced by it."

His forceful words gave Lord William a chance to complain about the government's attitude to political reform and to the poor, and while the two friends were busy exchanging demo-cratic opinions Justice gave the impression of sympathetic interest.

But he found himself at a disadvantage. He had no wish to bandy politics with the American. He would rather question him—and yet there were so many questions that he could not ask without letting Francis know that he was distrusted. Even now he was wondering whether he had impulsively gone too far.

What would Francis say, as they sat here so pleasantly in the parlour of the inn, if he was told that in the interests of public safety his papers had already been ransacked once, at Wyke-ham, had been carried to London, had been turned over to Dunning for a much closer scrutiny? What would he do if he knew that Justice, sitting across the fire from him, was still not sure whether it was his duty to watch or protect?

Justice had little doubt of the answers. It was plain from the papers, and from the way that Francis had just been speaking, that he was disillusioned by his British employers and that any fresh sign of distrust or chicanery on their part could be enough to tip him into flight: to America, probably, but perhaps to Ireland or France. A man who had changed sides once, out of political pique and a desire to make money, could easily change his mind again.

Watch or protect. Because Justice had no means of knowing which case applied, he could only go on as he had now begun, staying on close terms with Francis, winning his confidence by listening, trying to keep him in sight at least until his precious engine was shipped and the *Star of Salem* was on her way down the Thames to the sea.

"I WOULD DESTROY all instruments of oppression, Mr. Justice." Francis was clearly in no hurry, for he was expanding on his ideas, and as he explained his principles Justice saw Lord William nodding a satisfied I-told-you-so.

"In the meantime, however, you would make them?" Justice still found it hard to follow that piece of reasoning. "It sounds rather like Hamlet—there shall be no more marriages, save one. No more means of war, save your submarine."

"I am aware of the paradox." Francis had begun to speak like an orator rather than a practical man. "But I am speaking of two different worlds. The war system of the old world is the greatest cause of its miseries. Destruction. Hunger. Pillage. Rape. If you will forgive my saying so, in Britain you use the bottle and the lash to keep your unhappy people up to the mark, getting them drunk and butchering them before they die in what you call the defence of freedom. The defence of a king, and aristocrats, and great landed interests, I should say."

He raised a hand to stop Justice challenging him. "Hear what I say, if you please. I would hope for a new world, in which every government would adopt the simple rules of free and universal education, honest industry that gives a man the fruits of his toil, and the unfettered circulation of everything that comes from the fields and manufactories. That would be real freedom, Mr. Justice, and we are closer to it in America than anywhere else on earth."

"Because our navy, for all its rum tub and the cat, defends you from Bonaparte." Justice was stung into a sharp retort, but Francis took the point.

"Indeed, sir. You may thus see how industry proceeds apace when it is not saddled with the expense of a war system, and its institutions are not corrupted by a great and vicious military establishment. But how should we go on in America if one day your navy should once again sail into our ports, bombard our coastal towns, prey on our shipping? Only my submarine instruments can offer my country protection against that possibility, maintain the freedom of the seas, provide . . ."

Justice scarcely heard this peroration, for he was thinking

of all the paradoxes in this conversation.

England, as Lilly had said, was driven by present necessity to experiments in submarine war that might in the long run be the ruin of her naval supremacy.

Francis, a man of most pacific intent, was driven to make these warlike experiments, partly because he was an inventor with a passion for mechanical systems, partly because he needed the money to pay for the steamboats he dreamed of setting on every canal and river in America, partly because he was fascinated by the power of the instruments he had created and proposed to use them as a form of revolution to settle mankind's future according to his opinions. In his way he was just as keen as Bonaparte to mount the throne of the world, though his motives might seem more altruistic.

"You may find the means revolting, Mr. Justice," Francis was saying, as if to confirm his unspoken thoughts. "I believe they are anything but inhuman. My system is certainly the most peaceful and least bloody mode that a philosopher could imagine for overturning the system of plunder and perpetual war which has always vexed the maritime nations. I am convinced that it will at last give peace to the earth, and restore men to their natural inheritance, with a happiness till now unknown."

All these phrases verged on the fanatical, in Justice's opinion. In the world he knew best, all expediences of war, there were no perfections except the love of honour and the strictest attachment to duty. But he could see how a man of such strong levelling ambitions might end by selling his soul for the chance of fulfilling them. There was even something rather refreshing in this vision of a peaceful and prosperous condition for all humanity, as Lord William had said at their first meeting. At worst, Francis was only claiming for his system what the politicians of France and England alike were promising if their side won the war; and at best, if what he had heard about America was true, there was something to be said for a system where all men had more equal starts in life and no man went hungry to his bed.

Justice had been nodding so regularly, while his thoughts were elsewhere, that Francis had taken his silence for agreement and gone on to speak of his frustration at the Admiralty's failure to use his devices to good effect.

"I do not know why the admirals are so halfhearted. I have no doubt that they are determined to beat Bonaparte—preferably in their own old-fashioned way, and taking the credit for some great battle which wrecks a score of ships and butchers ten thousand men. They allow me to construct my carcasses and floating bombs. They spend the money they promised me when I came. They may even know and tolerate what Sir George is doing with the plunging-boat. But . . ." Francis spread his hands as though he were genuinely puzzled. "They do not give me the trained men, the vigorous officers, the flotilla of small boats I need for my plan of attack, a proper chance to prove to the whole world how deadly my weapons can be."

He gave the first grunt of irritation that Justice had heard from him, took up the poker, and leaned forward to stir the coals into flame. "Three weeks ago I offered to lead an attack into Brest, right up the Goulet." He looked at Justice. "I think you will appreciate the dangers and difficulties of that enterprise, Captain, especially in winter. Sir Home Popham favoured my scheme. He is a good man, you know, though I find his piety rather tiresome. Yet Lord Keith, I'm told, merely shrugged his shoulders and sent a disparaging letter to Lord Melville, saying that it was a madcap venture that would achieve nothing, and that it would be unwise to trust me so near to the French coast."

"He said that?" Justice knew Keith for a crusty commander, but such derogatory pessimism was plainly unfair to Francis.

"He told a friend," Francis said. "To me he was all politeness, saying that he could not ask a neutral to compromise himself in that fashion. Your damned English politeness! A man can be bamboozled out of his wits and his rights by it."

The more Francis spoke the more Justice was coming to understand why the Admiralty was so ambivalent about him, why even Lilly was uncertain whether he had been right to commission the *Pandora*. At the same time he could also understand how these disappointments were beginning to prey on the American's mind and to make him ready to look for more consistent patrons elsewhere.

"After such experiences," Francis said, recovering his humour and settling back in his chair with the mischievous grin that Justice found so much more appealing than his earnestness, "after such experiences, well, I sometimes feel like a man who has invented gunpowder at the time of Julius Caesar. I present myself before the gates of Rome with a four-pounder. Caesar sends out a commission of two centurions and two priests, and I set out to convince them that with this simple-looking device I can batter down the gates and take the city. Try, they say, giving me a half-witted slave as my gunner, and so I try, though they will not let me bring my gun within range of the gates, though their catapults are pelting me with stones, and it is raining. The first attempt fails, of course. I beg for three weeks, and Caesar graciously grants another trial, in worse conditions. Gunpowder is useless, they cry! This gun is only a fraudulent toy! This man is nothing but a charlatan! So my ideas are put off for a hundred years, a thousand years, and the centurions join the makers of catapults, spears, bows, arrows, and Greek Fire in celebrating the triumph of common sense.''

"Capital! Capital!" Lord William clapped his hands like a child who has been told a favourite story, and Justice found the fable so apt that he felt quite drawn to Francis in his tussle with the admirals. He too had suffered from stuffy and inconsiderate superiors. "There are such centurions everywhere," he said.

"True enough." They had been sitting an hour, for Justice heard the heavy chime of the hall clock come up the stairwell as Francis rose, shaking his head with sardonic resignation. "That is why I get more homesick every day," he said honestly. "I would far rather be back in my own country, making steamboats . . . if I only had the means." He gave Lord William a warm slap to go before him out of the room. "William knows exactly how I feel," he said, "though he doesn't agree with my conclusions. He wants me to abandon these weapons. But I cannot afford to do so. How else am I to finance my peaceful enterprises?" He took Justice by the arm as they stood at the head of the stairs. "You must believe me, Mr Justice. I am only a hired man, who lets out his talents on contract. I have no more liking for these terrible instruments I devise than William. I would willingly take a hundred thousand pounds to let them all lie dormant—unless my own country had need of them.''

He dropped his arm in a cynical gesture. "But who will pay me so much? Who will pay me at all unless I give them the means to destruction?"

❧23❧

"MR JUSTICE! MR JUSTICE! Do you come with us?" He heard
Francis calling up the stairwell over the babble of voices
below.

"I will be with you directly." Justice stood behind the half-
open door of the parlour, struggling to get his belt fastened
and his coat on his back. It was only as he was about to follow
Francis that he had remembered to put on the buckle-pistol
and run the firing cord down his sleeve. He had found the
American so beguiling, and the milk punch so comforting,
that he had begun to feel quite at ease, almost convinced by
the indifference which Francis had shown to his warning, that
he had been exaggerating the danger from Luc and his accomplices.

Almost. Not quite. And he had no intention of going to
Paddington Basin unarmed on such a night. It was just the
weather for ordinary footpads to be at work, let alone secret
agents with a malicious purpose.

Francis stood alone in the hall. "William has gone for the
rig," he said. "Will you ride?"

"I will follow you." Justice quickly decided that he might
need his own horse, if it came to trouble, though he would
have preferred to sit with Francis and Lord William as they
drove up to the canal office; and the thought prompted a question he had meant to ask Francis when they were talking
upstairs.

"Why must you go to Paddington at all? Surely the engine
will be passed through on the lading certificate?"

Francis gave him a shrewd look, and he recalled that the
American had made his early career as a canal engineer and
was an expert in such matters.

"We shall make a freshwater sailor of you yet, Captain,"
he laughed. "But there's a simple reason. Its name is Matthew
Boulton."

"Mr Breney mentioned a permit . . ." At the time Justice had not understood why an export permit was needed at a canal office.

"That's part of it," Francis said, looking about for William like a man who now feared he would be late for an appointment. "This means the goods can go straight to the ship. But Breney was being polite. The face is that old Matthew—we've been good friends for years, you know—now old Matthew trusts no one when it comes to steam engines. The devil a bother I had to get one out of him at all. Ever since he was cheated by the Hornblowers . . ."

"The Hornblowers?" Justice was mystified.

"I thought everyone knew about that family of plagiarists. Jonathan, Jabez, and six more brothers, each one of them with the same initial to their name and the same light-handedness with other people's property. Each one copied Boulton's engine, and he had to fight a patent action with every blamed man of them before he got his rights."

"I can see why he should be touchy." Justice marvelled at this peculiar tale.

"Even with me," Francis said, "so I grant the old man his whims. Which include payment in advance to his bank, and proof of payment at the point of delivery—which happens, in this case, to be Paddington Basin. That is how Breney arranged it all, to save wasting time at Limehouse." While Justice noticed the easy way he came out with these arrangements, as though he had nothing to hide, Francis was patting the pocket of his coat. "It's all here," he said with the pleased satisfaction of a man who had become tired of waiting: "permit, bank receipt, countersigned by the American consul, Breney's letter to the agent . . ."

"But why at this hour?" It seemed to Justice that this business could all have been transacted at a more normal time.

Francis saw nothing odd in it at all. "Because we only heard yesterday that the parts were come to Brentford. Everything to be done today if we were to catch the tide tomorrow. My friend the captain is an impatient man. Time is more than money to him. Like all venturing owners from Salem he calculates his life away in sea days!" Francis laughed. "So Mr Breney arranges carts to carry my goods, and a whole lot else from Birmingham. That's Boulton for you again. He waits until a whole bargeload of merchandise is ready for the

American trade, and tonight this convoy of brass and tin will stagger slowly from one alehouse to another along the New Road unless I am there to drive them out of Pentonville and down to the Thames." He glanced at the clock. "The carts were promised for seven-thirty."

Lord William beckoned them to the door to say that the carriage was ready.

"But not my horse?" Justice saw that William had not thought of it, or had assumed he would be going with them. "Then you'll wait?"

"We shall make poorer time than you in this miserable light," Francis said, making it difficult for Justice to argue. "You will overtake us long before Paddington Green."

They had mounted and driven off into the fog long before Justice had cursed the groom into finding his horse among two dozen of them milling and whinnying in the yard.

IT WAS IMPOSSIBLE to hurry. Justice found his eyes smarting as he peered through the smoky gloom, reining back as he came up with an open vehicle to see if he recognized it, and frightening a dozen worthy riders into thinking him a highwayman come close into London to take advantage of the foul night.

He was misdirected twice, as he tried to find his bearings in this unfamiliar suburb, and even when he rode up to Paddington Basin he seemed to stumble across the canal by accident rather than design, and let the line of the towpath carry him to the entrance.

He looked about for the carts that Francis expected, and saw none, and so went straight to the office, which was easy to find, for it had the only lighted window in the place. Inside was a man in the uniform of the canal company, obviously eager to close for the night.

"Mr Francis?" Justice was not even sure that Francis and William themselves had found the basin in such evil conditions.

The man looked hard at Justice. "Was it you, sir, as what the two gentlemen was a-mentioning?"

"Yes. Yes." Justice was testy after his difficult ride.

"Well, now," the man said reproachfully, as if he were put to some inconvenience, and scratched among some papers on the table. He pulled one out, held the face of it to the lamp and spelt out a name under his breath."

"Justice?" he asked at last, and when Justice nodded he passed over a scribbled note from Francis.

"Damnable fog," he had written. "The agent sends to say the barge is still at Brentford. We hasten on, and shall expect you. F."

Justice gave the man a coin, and turned away, quite as irritated as Francis must have been. And then he went back, getting the slowest of instructions to follow the Bayswater Road past Hyde Park to Hammersmith, and then to go down through Acton to Kew Bridge. To Brentford Dock, where the long canal that ran half across England came out into the Thames just before it began to circle like a great snake into London, and on down to the sea.

The fog was dense, clearing, and dense again, and after another mile or two of it Justice found his senses playing tricks with him. He imagined once that he saw Francis standing by the roadside and Lord William running back towards town. A little later he thought this man with a round hat crammed over his eyes rode so stiffly that he might be Dunning, that another could be Luc, or Tooth, or any one of the people who had so crowded his life in the past week that he was tired and bewildered by them.

And once started on this train of distracting fancies, he found them running away with him. When he had passed Kew Bridge and was beginning to look sharply about him for the dock, he could have sworn he saw one of the beggars from Bedford Square sitting in a carrier's cart, and when he heard the ring of a muffin man's bell through the murk, sounding like a bell buoy in a channel . . .

He shook himself together again as he saw the sign over the dock gate, pulled in by a winding hole where two men were turning a barge into another branch of the canal, threw his reins to a boy who was minding two boat horses, and stopped.

By the kind of trick that sound sometimes plays in fog, he clearly heard a voice coming from some distance away, clear but low, a voice he had heard before but could not place with so few words to help him.

"Are they all come?"

The answer was lost, but the question was just enough to make him pause before he strode along the track, following a sign that pointed to the office.

Francis and William must be there, with the agent, unless they were quite lost.

He could see very little, for the yellow vapours lay heavy over the dock and the river beyond it, and as they swirled about the line of wharves, they conjured the piles of timber, coal, and stacked boxes into fantastic shapes, lit every now and then by the glow from a brazier where barges and their boys stood warming themselves before they set off back to Birmingham, or on to Paddington, or down the Thames.

He could not even hear very much except the whiffling of their horses, standing ready with tow ropes looped on their swingletrees, and roistering cries from men who were fortified by ardent spirits and were jostling at each other in a jovial sort of way.

Justice waited a moment to steady himself, feeling the ominous pricking in his hands that always came with a sense of unseen danger, and then he began to move more slowly, picking his way from one stack to the next, trying to judge where the man had stood who asked that question.

He would have taken no notice if he had not caught that touch of accent that reminded him of someone he had lately met, if there had not been such a hard and urgent tone to the voice, as if a man were waiting to start a coach . . . to sail . . . to close a trap . . .

A long cart of cut timber went by him, the driver grumbling to himself at working so late. There was another cart, carrying bales of sheepskins. And Justice paused to watch a man who seemed to be pilfering coal in a wheelbarrow while the watchmen warmed themselves elsewhere.

He stopped, still worrying at that voice, thinking that he might first go to find the barge that was loaded for the *Star of Salem*.

And then, from somewhere beyond the stacks, he heard a sharp cry.

A cry, no, more a desperate shout of warning, down towards the gleaming patch of light he supposed to be the door of the office.

Two more cries, shouts rather, a sound of scuffling, the neigh of a horse, and then the rig was coming up the track towards him, its lamps like baleful eyes, poor enough lights for this weather but enough for him to see Lord William standing at the reins and whipping the stallions into life, to see

Francis hanging over the tailboard as if he had just scrambled on to it.

By the time Justice had run out and recognised the two men, they were past him, ignoring his yell of "Wait! Wait!" as the curricle tore on and was swallowed in the darkness beyond the gate.

At least they were safe.

For some very sudden danger must have startled Lord William to send him driving away helter-skelter.

Justice ran towards the light, wondering why none of the bargemen had taken any notice of the disturbance and realizing as he wondered that casual fights must be as common as gin in such a place.

The door of the office slammed while he was still twenty yards from it, cutting off the light, so that he could not see whay lay in his path and tripped him.

He scrambled up, feeling for something soft he had struck with his knee in falling.

It was a body. A body with little face for his hands to touch, as he fumbled in the mangle of blood and bone left by a crushing blow from the side. A body he could recognise, for all that, once the door opened again and the light fell across it.

It was Dunning, the wretched Dunning, dead. Dead because he had followed Francis too close, tonight.

Justice had just rolled the body over to search the pockets for a pistol, or anything else that might serve as a weapon, when he remembered he had forgotten to cock the buckle-gun.

He lifted his coattail, swearing at his forgetfulness, leaning backwards as he reached for the hammer, and the move surprised the man who had come up behind him while he knelt by Dunning's corpse, diverted the bludgeon blow.

It was only a glancing smash that caught the side of his head and slipped to his shoulder, but it was enough for its evil purpose.

Justice staggered, sprawled over Dunning, and did not even feel the ground as he hit it.

HE WAS COLD, so bitterly cold that he shook as they half carried and half dragged him through the dark, and beyond the haze of pain, as a lantern flashed on his face, he heard the remembered voice again.

"Will he live?"

"Come a real buster, but he'll live right enough."

Then the same voice again, so clear that he knew he would recognize it if he could get his addled wits to work.

"Damn fool. You could have killed him." Damn fool, coming like an echo. Could have killed him, like the other. Damn fool. Damn fool. Damn fool. He was just aware that his senses were fading as he caught the words "sail tomorrow . . . sail tomorrow . . ."

He came round to feel a brisk rummaging in his pockets before he was folded over the shoulder of a man going down a stair or a ladder: he could feel the movement jerk against his ribs with each step, and then the bruising thump as he was thrown onto a pile of sacks.

The pain came so fiercely that he could just ask himself whether any bones were broken before someone was roughly pulling at his arms and legs to tie them, lash them with a length of rope so that he was bent double, and he knew that he was still all of a piece.

Then it was all darkness.

IT WAS CRAMP that woke him, pricking him out of a miserable sleep that had left his head throbbing and his whole body as stiff as butcher's meat.

Still dark, though the faintest of glims from a grating overhead told him that it must be close to the late November dawn. Between seven and eight, he supposed, forcing his mind to work to get it usefully ordered again.

He was in a cellar. He could smell coal, feel it knobbly in the sacks where he had lain all night.

He was not in a cellar. Because it was moving. At a snail's pace, evenly. With a quiet gurgle of water beyond the planking, he felt, when he crawled about on hands and knees, like a rooting pig, discovering the limits of his prison.

The *Pandora*. It could not be the *Pandora*. Last night he had been in Paddington.

With Francis. With Lord William.

Very slowly, most painfully, one thought at a time, he started to construct a memory. Starting several times at the moment he left Kitty in Hampstead and stopping when he came to Paddington. Starting and stopping, with a determination that took his mind off his pain, until the idea of a canal came to him and he knew that he had been beaten and dumped in a barge.

He could not tell why, or where it was going.

He thought there should be a body beside him, snatched at Dunning's name as he searched, remembered the boathouse fire, decided that the body was only a feverish dream, remembered almost everything up to the moment he found Dunning.

In ten minutes he had scrabbled around with his tethered hands enough to know that he was in a hold, most of which was packed with barrels and casks, boxes with canvas coverings, a lot of straw—yes, there was enough of that to pull out and make a more comfortable resting place; and a load of coal, probably intended for the galley and the captain's cabin on the *Star of Salem*.

He was pleased with himself when he grabbed that thought from the shadows, because everything else then tumbled into place behind it, leaving him in no doubt about his predicament.

Whoever had beaten him, whatever the reason, whoever had killed Dunning, was taking him over to Limehouse Reach.

To be interrogated, murdered perhaps. To be carried off to France, where that job would be done very effectively and with a great deal of suffering on the way. To be shipped to America, maybe lost at sea . . . Wherever that engine was going, he would go, too.

With Francis.

No. Not with Francis. The American and Lord William must have bolted for their lives at Dunning's shout of warning.

Justice was now certain that was the first cry he had heard.

But for Dunning, both Francis and Lord William would be sharing this makeshift cell with him. All three of them had ridden into a trap.

Three of them. Then the sickening thought came to him that he was the only one who had been trapped. That Francis could have known . . . that Lord William could have known . . . that Dunning had been hit a savage blow from that flying rig . . . that even now Francis was on his way to the *Star of Salem* . . .

No. Not Francis, if he had any capacity to judge a man's character. Hatherley could not be right.

This was Luc's work. But that was not Luc's voice he had

heard last night, and now the memory of it had faded beyond recall.

Then there were shouts overhead, a clumping of boots, a bang and a creak as the barge stopped. He thought of yelling for help, and saw at once it would be useless. Boatmen were a hard lot, and the bargee had only to say that one of his mates was as drunk as a fiddler's bitch. The barge was moving on again when the hatch was pushed back a foot or so, and he could see a head peer over, dark against the band of grey sky.

He kept still, snored.

"Lying there like Ludlam's dog," the man said gruffly, and spat for good measure, but he left the hatch open long enough for Justice to see the words stencilled on some of the packages —buckles, plated wire, other gewgaws, tools: to see, from the shape of the barrels that some must contain powder and others rum. The Birmingham merchants were doing the *Star of Salem* proud.

For the first time since he had got his wits together again, he saw a possibility of escape.

AFTER MUCH STRAINING, he managed to get Bond's remarkable watch out of his fob pocket and into his right hand—in such a hurried search the man had missed it, for he was probably looking only for a knife or a pocket pistol. He pressed at the winding key, and his heart sank as nothing happened. He pressed again, harder, hoping that it was merely jammed, and this time the sharp little blade sprang out. He cut at the rope which linked his hands to his legs, so that he could stretch freely, freeing the cramp which had become almost as agonising as his bruises. He cut again, when he was able to bend without difficulty, severing the rope which was twisted round his ankles. But he found it impossible to turn the little knife on to his wrists, and he dropped it twice into the darkness and had to scrabble for it, before he thought of holding it between his teeth, the metal grating against them as he sawed at the blade.

Now he could stand erect, move easily, and while he waited for the blood to flow back and give his tired muscles strength for what was to come, he unbuckled his belt, brought the little gun round where he could inspect it under the grating, made sure of the priming, set it down where he could find it again.

The barge slithered to a stop. He could hear the boy screaming at the horse before another boat hammered and bumped against the planking, the bargee letting off a string of obscenities, and then another man beginning the kind of provocative shouting that Justice had heard so often when sailors from different ships met outside a tavern. Another barge must have tangled in the towline.

The more delay the better. If there was a danger of being hauled on deck it would take only a moment to fasten the buckle-pistol, and he might make some sort of fight for his life. Even bolt if they were so close to other boats and people walking on the towpath. But give him another quarter of an hour and he might do better than that.

The row went on, joined by more angry voices on the towpath. It gave him his chance to do the one thing that was bound to make a noise.

He tugged at one of the canvas-covered packages that were labelled as tools, slit back its covering with his knife, tested it for balance, raised it shoulder high. He panted, sweated with the strain, and then, aiming the centre of it at the corner of another crate, he smashed it down, hearing the wood splinter but not break.

Not enough. He could feel where it had splintered. Not enough. He would have to risk it again if he was to make a large enough crack to lever it open with his fingers.

The barges bumped, and there were fading shouts as they began to move again, as he felt the dead drop which meant that the frame of the case was broken, and he reached forward with desperate haste to tear back the boxwood panels.

He had no idea how much time he had left before they would come for him.

Hammers? Jemmies? Chisels? It did not matter what he found. Any of them would be a makeshift weapon or do what he wanted.

He needed something that would open a powder cask or a barrel of rum. And though the sets of bootmaking hammers and punches were not what he would have chosen they would do.

The rum would be easy. Powder best, but more dangerous, especially if it were the high-proof priming powder for which

239

the Birmingham mills were renowned. Much more dangerous. If his captors were slow to react they would all be blown to glory together.

Powder, nevertheless. He made a pile of dry straw underneath the grating, and hoped there would be enough draught leaking through the timbers.

The next move was the most risky. Once he opened a powder keg and let the grains trickle out he had to make sure that he caught them cleanly in his hand and carried them over to the straw. A dribble of powder through the cracks in his fingers, three or four carryings across the hold, and he would have the beginnings of a fuse.

That would flash in a matter of seconds.

And with so much powder . . . And rum . . . And the coal dust . . .

At moments of crisis Justice always felt that time slowed for him and that his actions were more rather than less deliberate. It was a habit that had saved his life more than once.

Use enough powder. Only enough. The straw would do the rest. He leaned forward, licking all round the hole he had made in the keg, getting the bitter tastes of sulphur and saltpetre, moistening his grubby handkerchief with the saliva that was left before plugging the hole with it. That was all he could do to stop the flash striking back.

That was the best he could do. Five minutes at best, he judged, and if the bargee was dozing, or looking the wrong way . . . He suddenly realized that he had no idea what to expect once he reached the deck. Were there two men up there, and a boy leading the horse? Three? Would there be some kind of cabin or makeshift shelter at the stern? All the advantages of surprise would only give him a few seconds to answer those questions.

He looked up at the hatch, knowing there would be no way of opening it from the inside, for he heard a bar slide across when the bargee closed it.

Three feet above his head? Two crates would do, one above the other, in the opposite corner from the straw. Where the air might last longest. Where he would have a chance to scramble out while his captors were looking at the fire.

If he could make the fire. And survive it.

He kept the punch in his hand. Laid the small hammer flat on the top of the crate, when he could snatch at it.

Crouched while boots stumbled close to his head and the bargee shouted a volley of oaths at the boy. He heard something about Putney, and going down the river on the drag, and decided he could wait no longer.

Everything now depended on one move. On the greatest care. If he fumbled, his chance was gone.

If he dropped the tiny flint he now extracted from the buckle-pistol's lock.

He held it firm between his fingers, worrying whether the sweat or dirt might stop it sparking. He gripped the rough steel of the punch, pushed it out over the little pile of powder on the straw, struck the flint against it.

A crude strike, too close, for his thumb got in the way. Another. Another with the first spark. A fourth, and the powder was sputtering, little blue and orange flames that licked at the straw, sent up picric fumes as he fanned them with his hand, took firmly enough for him to know that he succeeded and for him to have just enough light to squeeze the flint back in the pistol.

This time, as he hurriedly fastened his belt, pulled the firing cord over his shoulder, he remembered to cock it.

He took four or five deep breaths before he climbed up the crates to bend double in the space below the hatch. There would soon be very little air in that hold—and as he thought about choking, if they left him to it, he had a sudden image of the solemn Romney experimenting with his bottles on the *Pandora*.

Mephitic air. That was the word. And there was a great deal of it now, as the straw began to smoulder, blue and bitter, burning the throat, smarting at the eyes.

He wanted to shout "Fire! Help, fire!" He watched the red heart of it winking as it took hold, and had to contain the instinctive reaction of any man who had been to sea in a powder-filled ship.

Yet they had to catch the smell for themselves. See the smoke as it curled up from the grating. For a few moments of panic they might think only of the combustibles in the hold and not about their prisoner, and if they tore the hatch open to sluice the fire he would be out of it before they could turn.

Unless they panicked too much, jumped and ran for it, leaving him with a fire he had no means of dousing before it reached the rum and powder barrels.

Five minutes, he had given himself, and before the first was over he was fighting a cough, forcing his face to a crack in the hatchway where he could feel the faintest breath of air.

Four minutes. He found he was counting them away, trying not to think of the store of explosives stacked behind him.

Another thirty seconds gone, and then he heard the first shout for water, oaths, some words he lost in the running of feet on the deck.

". . . the bloody man's pipe, by God" was all he caught as the bar was drawn back and the hatch thrown open.

HE WAS OUT, hammer in one hand, punch in the other to give weight to his grip, a point that could slash as well as a knife; and the bargee, still bent from lifting the hatch, had no chance against his rush. Sprawled over the opening, with nothing to offer a purchase, as he put up an arm to ward off a blow; and was lost. For Justice simply put a foot under his ribs and heaved him over the sill into the hold. Even if he clambered out again . . .

So there were three of them.

Nearest to him was a figure charging with a boathook its curled iron tip aimed at his ribs, coming at him so fast that Justice sensed rather than saw that this was the muffin man who had held his horse in Bedford Square, the muffin man whose bell he had heard last night, sending a signal that Francis had arrived at the basin . . . and the third man, beyond him, trawling a bucket in the water and calling over his back for a gun . . .

Four of them, then, the fourth hidden from him in the little hencoop that served as a cabin of sorts . . . and the muffin man making things easy for a seaman who had survived a dozen fights with boarding parties.

Justice threw the hammer at his face, like a tomahawk, ducked as the pole jerked upwards when the man flinched, put out a leg, tripped and pushed him as he went past, staggering forward over the side into the water.

Two. For the moment. The odds were shortening. So long as no one could get a long shot at him.

He had run twenty feet or more before he saw that the third man was Fanshawe. Who had tried to kill or disable him at Wykeham.

Fanshawe. Throwing the bucket of water at him before reaching for the bell-mouthed pistol that was being held out of the cabin window.

Most of the water missed him, slopping at his feet, making the deck slippery as he stumbled on, trying to grapple with Fanshawe before he could level that coachman's gun.

Fanshawe. Of course. That was the voice he had heard last night. It was not Luc who had run to London but Fanshawe.

And the Frenchwoman.

Who was now in the cabin of the barge, making for the *Star of Salem* and safety.

Each thought came with a pace, bringing him close enough to drive past the pistol before Fanshawe was ready to fire it, to lunge with the hand that held the metal punch.

And to slip, as the wet soles of his boots failed to grip, giving Fanshawe the chance to strike with the pistol butt as he fell, flattened face downwards.

"I have no wish to kill you," Fanshawe cried, pointing the pistol whose charge would tear a man apart, dragging at Justice's collar to bring him to his feet again. "Not yet. But by God you are the worst of meddlers . . ." He was so much harsher, more determined, than the man who had chattered away at Wykeham that Justice wondered how he could have been deceived. Fanshawe was not a weak fool. Or a dupe. He was a trained man. One of O'Moira's men from Dublin.

Three minutes. Two minutes. The seconds were ticking away all the time as the smoke billowed about the barge, and as Justice stood straight he could see there were green fields on either side. He was not on a canal. He was going down the Thames to Limehouse.

While Fanshawe still held him, marching him towards the hatch, pistol to his head, shouting at the horseboy to come and help.

There was no sign of the man Justice had kicked into the hold, but he could hear the muffin man pulling himself aboard with a curse.

"Pick up the bucket." Fanshawe's curt order gave him the chance to lower his hands, to reach the firing cord.

Too slow. Too late.

"Get on with it," Fanshawe shouted, putting his hand round Justice to pull at his lapels in exasperation. Catching the cord as he did so.

Mr Bond's invention worked well. Fatally well.

Fanshawe grunted once after the little pistol cracked, and Justice swung round to seize his weapon before he snapped the hammer in a dying spasm . . . saw the Frenchwoman give the muffin man a hand over the side and start forward behind him . . . saw, glancing backward, that the bargee was at last climbing out of the hatch . . . saw the boy stop and begin to run in fear when the first tongue of flame leaped up . . .

It was any moment now, and he flung himself into the river with an awkward sideways twist, striking out before he surfaced to get to the bank before that stunning shock came hammering through the water.

He was ashore, the boy giving him a hand over a slippery and muddy bank. Grabbing at the boy to roll them across the towpath, over the grass that sloped towards the drainage ditch. Holding the boy, who was struggling convulsively, keeping them both as low in the water as possible.

Hearing nothing. Hearing nothing, but feeling all the earth shake, seeing the ball of flame rise above them as the fire reached the rum and powder barrels, ducking as pieces of burning wreckage rained down about them.

He scrambled up, unsure whether the river bank would hold, running towards a distant house, leaving the boy to follow if he would, glancing over his shoulder and seeing only the stern of the barge poking up from the bed of the river.

He stopped to draw breath. He was sorry that Francis had lost the steam engine on which he had counted so much.

And then the realization came to him. There were no steam engine parts in that hold. There was no steam engine. The whole story was bait for the cleverest trap.

❧ 24 ❧

"You'll be right enough, sir, in a minute or two." The waterman handed Justice a steaming pot of gin toddy. "Get that inside you and I'll see to the boy."

The cottage, set by a small bridge where a brook ran into the Thames, was small, neat, marvellously cosy, and the man himself was equally warmhearted. He had heard the explosion, run out, seen Justice and the boy staggering towards him, brought them in to strip in front of his fire and sit wrapped in coarse blankets while he hung their dripping clothes to dry.

He led the boy into another room where there was a truckle bed, sat with him while he swallowed the gin and curled up to sleep. "That'll be best for the little beggar, sir, till the constable's fetched to him."

Justice started at the words that were meant to be reassuring, for he had been so bent on hurrying to Limehouse that he had not thought of all the explanations and delays that might follow from the sinking of the barge. If he had to deal with a bumbling parish officer, who would expect to be told how he and the boy were found stumbling along, like survivors from a wreck, he could be kept hanging about all day.

Longer, indeed, if they found enough of Fanshawe's body to discover a bullet hole in it. If anyone began to talk about murder, he would be lucky to get away at all.

The sooner he was away the better.

"Stern's the name, sir," the man said amiably, holding up a pair of muddy drawers and tutting at the sight of them. "Stern in name but not in nature they allus said of the family. Well known in Brentford." He laid the drawers over a chair back. "Fair pickle you got into, sir, I must say, more's the credit to you."

Confound the man for his talkative amiability, Justice thought, and then realized the chance he had been given.

Perhaps no one had seen him jump from the barge, except for the boy, and the hot gin would knock him out for a couple of hours. Perhaps the man had marked him simply as a passerby who had rescued the boy from the water.

It was a role he could play with decent modesty.

"Not at all," he said, taking care not to be too specific, because there was always the risk that someone would turn up who had seen enough to challenge his story. "Saw the smoke. Heard a shout about gunpowder." He sipped at the last of his toddy. "Rolled the boy out of the way." All that was strictly true.

"And clever you were, sir." The waterman gazed out of the window at a barge going upstream on the tide, two men working a pair of long sweeps. "Powder barges!" He made a derisory gesture. "T'ain't right. I allus said that. T'ain't safe for them as makes a calling of the river and lives close to it. Bloody powder barges! Two or three a day, I reckon, since the war a-started again. Coming past, man and boy alike a-puffing at their pipes. Allus said there'd be trouble one day."

"True enough," Justice said as the man finished ranting. He had begun to pull on his steaming clothes, and he was so eager to leave that he would agree to anything that put the fellow in a mood to let him go without asking who he was or where he came from. Fumbling at his breeches to find half a guinea, he noticed that Bond's buckle-gun was concealed by the fold. Thank the Lord, the waterman had been too busy chatting to notice it, or to see the blackened tear in his coat where the ball had passed.

"It will be a trouble for you to get the boy settled." He held out the coin. "This should help."

The man took it, spat on his palm, clapped his hands together before pocketing it. "There's no gent like a navy gent, I allus says, sir." He peered out of the window with such curiosity that Justice could tell that he was itching to go and look at the wreck. "Quite a stir it's caused. Folks everywhere."

"I'll keep an eye on the boy if you want to go for a gander," Justice said, and saw that he had guessed right.

"Five minutes, then, sir." Stern saw all the possibilities of self-importance in a little gossip about the disaster. It wasn't every day that something like that happened by Beverley Brook.

As he opened the door Justice saw two familiar figures detach themselves from the crowd and come hurrying along the towpath. Standing back in the doorway, for he did not wish other people to see him there, he waited until they were abreast of the cottage.

"Edward!" he called. "Fred!"

Holland stopped short, came into the cottage to embrace him. "My dear fellow! We thought you a goner. Blown to bits." Holland stepped back to stare at Justice like a tatter-medalion back from the dead. "And close enough to it, by the look of you."

"Like a patchwork quilt," Scorcher said, delight and relief in his voice. "With all respect, sir, of course."

"Of course." Justice grinned, feeling himself again now Holland and Scorcher had come.

"What the devil happened?" Holland looked in at the sleeping boy while Scorcher helped Justice scramble into his torn and soggy coat.

"The story can wait," he said. "Get me away from here before people come to stare and ask questions I can't answer."

They were out on the towpath, heading towards Putney, and Justice looked at the river, flowing up strongly from the sea, and the mudbanks showed that it was still some time to high water.

"If ever I needed your help, Edward, it is now. I must be at Limehouse before the *Star of Salem* sails."

"MY GOD! WHAT A TRAIL of trouble and wreckage you have left behind you," Holland had said as they came to the White Hart, but leaving the matter there, insisting that they stop for Justice to wash and change into whatever clothes Scorcher could buy or scrounge from the servants at the inn. "You cannot ride through London in that condition, John. You will be stopped as a fleeing gentleman of the road by the first watchman who sees you. Come, be sensible. My chaise is here, and there is nothing faster in the town."

And while Justice completed his hasty toilet Holland told his part of the tale.

"I came home at midnight, half seas over," he said, "and there was Scorcher, sitting on my doorstep, demanding that I call out the watch, send for soldiers from the Tower—you never heard such a fuss . . .'' He broke off as Scorcher appeared at the door of the upstairs room they had taken to be private, lifting Justice's torn and dirtied topcoat.

"Cut off the buttons and epaulets, Fred," Justice instructed. "The rest's good for nothing but a beggar's blanket." He turned back to Holland as Scorcher sat by the window, slicing at the thread with the horn-handled sea knife he always carried. "And then?"

"He'd been to Paddington. Found you gone. Went on to Brentford. Found the canal yard in an uproar, constables everywhere, and the runners sent for." Holland spoke approvingly of Scorcher's discretion. "He had sense enough to keep mum, and post back to me at Hampstead. There wasn't a mile of breath in his horse when he reached Church Row." Holland shrugged. "The rest was easy. I knew about the shipment for the *Star* from your questions, and a sovereign got all the answers I needed at Brentford. Gone at first light, they said, as soon as·they looked up the barge certificate. We came on, stopping and asking. When we got here, they told us of a barge blown up, a furlong or two along the bank." He glanced at Scorcher. "Your rascal here knew at once that you'd done it."

Justice, dressed, took the buckle-pistol from Holland, who had been examining it with interest, decided that it was wiser not to ask at the inn for powder to reload it, slipped it into his pocket. "I'll tell my story as we go," he said, urgently. "Now. To Limehouse as fast as you can drive that damned rig without breaking our necks!" And as he spoke he had a fleeting memory of Lord William and Francis fleeing the Brentford yard as though a squadron of Ney's cavalry was after them.

"To what end?" Holland annoyed him with the question, and the restraining hand that followed it.

"To find Francis, of course. To stop the *Star of Salem* before she hauls her anchor."

"What! The three of us? A Lloyd's underwriter, a manservant, and a fellow who looks like a mountebank and says he is a half-pay captain! Stop a ship that's going down with the tide, without a warrant or a whiff of powder to back you!" Holland pointed at the pocket in which Justice had placed the little pistol. "With that popgun?"

"I don't know. I truly don't know." Justice felt the force of

Holland's sarcasm. As he tried to settle a stranger's cloak on his shoulders, and stared at his friend in moody irritation, Scorcher called him to the window and nodded down at the towpath.

"There, Cap'n."

Justice looked at a small crowd following two men carrying a body stretched on a plank. "They've found one of them," he said. "It's time we were away."

"No, Cap'n." Scorcher was pointing behind the knot of people to a tall, burly figure, as flash and fresh in appearance as ever, walking with two men who had the look of professional thief-takers.

For a moment Justice felt the chill of doubt. Would his tale make sense? Would it be believed? Then came a surge of relief. Hatherley was the one man in London who could now do what had to be done. "My compliments to Mr Hatherley, Fred, if he would be so good as to join us."

As Scorcher rattled along the passage and down the stairs Holland also made for the door. "If you would stay, Edward?" Justice was not certain how far Holland wished to be involved in this affair, and was answered at once.

"Better not." Holland excused himself, coolly, but so pointedly that Justice knew for certain that he was deeply involved in Lilly's mysterious affairs. "I am only a friend, remember." He stood in the doorway, glancing down into the hall. "I will wait in this parlour beyond, if you please, while you see Mr . . . Mr Hatherley, was it?" It was not a reprimand, Justice knew, only a reminder, and Holland softened it as he went. "But if you are pressed, afterwards . . ." Justice caught the hint of hesitation on the point. "If you are pressed, I say, my chaise is at your disposal. To go anywhere you please."

"IF IT WERE in my power I would have you before a court-martial, Mr Justice." Hatherley had sent Scorcher out of the room before he spoke with a cold anger that Justice thought might be explained by the death of Dunning. But that was only the first part of Hatherley's indictment, which he delivered in a few curt words. "Dunning is dead," he said, unaware that Justice had seen the broken-faced body at Brentford. "A man without equal for his particular work, who might still be alive if you had not blundered across his track. Yes, blundered, Mr Justice." He paused, letting Justice feel his displeasure and his loss before he spoke more kindly. "There's this to be said, Mr Justice. At least you settled the account of the man who killed him, whether or not you knew of the crime."

"The muffin man?" Justice asked, finding the name ridiculous yet lacking any other way of describing the marauder who had come out of the fog to smash at Dunning's head. To strike Justice down as well.

Hatherley nodded. "From the Ratcliff Highway, as vicious as the rats of the docklands from which he came. An infamous creature who would run any dirty errand or swing a bludgeon for anyone who paid him." He gave a grunt of satisfaction, jerking his head towards the window. "He'll run no more, though I would have liked to see him dance at Newgate instead." He saw that Justice was about to speak and stopped him with a raised finger.

"Mr Justice," he said bluntly, coming to his main complaint. "I've respect for you. Great respect. And so has Sir George." He had a habit of opening his eyes when he had something awkward to say, and Justice had noticed that it made him look quizzical rather than critical. "But now, sir, now you've got deep into matters that weren't really your business, if I may say so. That's what Sir George would say, if he were here. I know he would. Leaving Cuffwells like that. And the *Pandora*. Running up to town after Mr Francis, setting Lord William after him, making a muddle of it all just when everything was coming clear. Because you had fancies of your own." He spoke patronisingly, like a reproving schoolmaster, and Justice found his tone annoying. "By now I might have had my hands on Mr Francis and his Lordship, instead of having to make guesses where they've gone." He repeated himself, grinding the fist of one hand into another. "Gone. And I don't know where to turn next."

"If it's Francis you want," Justice said, understanding Hatherley's annoyance but considering it a waste of time when the sands were fast running out. "Francis and Lord William . . ."

"Of course it's Mr Francis." Hatherley brusquely interrupted him. "Who else? Who else is at the heart of this conspiracy to cheat Sir George, sir, to defraud Lord Melville and the whole Board of Admiralty? To scuttle off with our money, our submarine, and anything else he could lay hands on after making fools of us all. I told you as much at Cuffwells, didn't I, now? It was him as brought French agents into it, double-dealing to play his own hand to advantage—him, and that Lord William." Hatherley was working himself into a state of frustrated rage; and the more furiously he denounced Francis, Justice noticed, the more he slipped into a common style of speech that was very different from his normal suavity. "French agents as was supplied by your acquaintance, that damned Irish rebel O'Moira."

There was a clatter below the window, and Justice looked down, thinking it might be Scorcher, bringing round Holland's chaise, seeing a shrouded corpse being trundled away in a cart by one of Hatherley's sombre companions. What troubled him still was the bitter conviction with which Lilly's assistant spoke of Francis.

"I was watching him," Hatherley said, almost plaintively, recovering himself, but sticking to his case. "He was planning a clean sweep, you know, Mr Justice. The *Pandora*. The papers." He stopped, and the severity went out of his face for a moment. "To be fair, I owe them to you. I had no idea he was planning to bolt with everything drawn and in detail, and that plan for the blockade of the Channel. I tell you, as soon as Dunning saw that he sent for me, but I came too late for him, poor devil." He leaned forward and tapped Justice on the chest, like a politician arguing. "And clearing out himself at the same time. There's no denying, your Mr Francis is the most dangerous asset of the lot, if he comes to Boney's hand again. And now I've lost him."

"I can tell you where he's gone if you give me leave to speak." Justice was annoyed by Hatherley's hectoring manner, which he had been spared at their previous meetings, but they had a common interest in finding the American, and he had just realized that Hatherley probably knew nothing about the *Star of Salem*. He could not have spoken to Francis or Breney. Nor could Dunning. As he came to think of it, indeed, it was strange that Dunning should have found his way to Brentford dock *before* Francis and Lord William arrived. What had led him to his death? What dangerous secret could he have known, that Hatherley did not know, that could be revealed in one shout of warning to Francis and Lord William?

Hatherley fretted as Justice appeared to hesitate. "Where, then? Out with it." Only great anxiety could have rattled him to speak to a post-captain as brusquely as to a messenger—a Mercantile Messenger, Justice thought sardonically as he checked his irritation.

"I believe he has hurried to the *Star of Salem* in Limehouse Reach."

Hatherley was dumbfounded. "You knew that? Yet you never told Dunning? Left no word for me?"

"How could I, when I had no idea where to find you," Justice testily replied. "When I only knew yesterday afternoon."

"Then there's a chance that we may yet catch him?" The notion that Francis might be caught in the act of absconding revived Hatherley's spirits, and he was ready to leave without more argument.

And suddenly, decisively, Justice felt that Hatherley was wrong. Badly wrong.

Perhaps it was the unreasonable tirade against Francis that had changed his opinion. Perhaps. He was not sure of his reasons, but he surprised himself by the vigour of his conviction.

"Francis is innocent," he said, bringing the scowl of frustration back to Hatherley's face. "Quite innocent. And you are quite mistaken about him, Mr Hatherley."

Hatherley was about to start blustering again when Justice asserted himself as if he were back on his own quarterdeck.

"There are three possibilities, Mr Hatherley," he said. "If Francis is as guilty as you think, he will be planning to escape on the *Star*. Very well. Go to Limehouse and catch him at it. But if he is innocent, as I believe, you may still find him at Limehouse—lured there by tales about his steam engine, or some other tempting falsehood. So, in either case, Limehouse is the obvious place to go, as fast as possible."

Hatherley went to the door as if it had all been settled.

"I said *three* possibilities," Justice said, making him stop in his tracks. "Suppose I have miscalculated up to this moment in making so much of the connection with the *Star of Salem*. Suppose Francis has gone to Cuffwells after all, and has walked into the other end of a trap."

For trap it was, he was now certain.

"It is a devilishly clever plot, Mr Hatherley. So like O'Moira, who placed the pieces on the board and anticipated almost every move they would make. Two plots, in fact, in the most ingenious combination, designed to seize the *Pandora*, the papers, and Francis, *wherever Francis happened to be when they were ready to act.*"

Justice was suddenly gripped by this vision of the whole scheme as O'Moira must have planned it. "Where Francis would be—that was the one thing that O'Moira and his accomplices could not have known when they first made their plans, weeks ago, in Paris or Boulogne or Dublin. It would have been easy for them, Mr Hatherley, if Francis had come to Wykeham last Saturday, for they were ready to take all three prizes that night—as it was, they tried for the *Pandora*, and tried for the papers the next night. But the alternative plan was to take Francis in London, to lure him to Brentford with fairy tales about his steam engine and let Fanshawe collar him. They have failed in all respects so far, Mr Hatherley, because my servant accidentally saved the *Pandora*, because I found the papers, because Lord William and I had made Francis wary before he reached Brentford, because Dunning warned him, because I stumbled into that end of the trap. It was Francis, not me, who should have been shut in the hold of that barge. It is Francis who will be seized here on the Thames today, or on the Beaulieu River tonight."

In his excitement Justice had gone across to Hatherley and gripped his arm. "Timing. Precise timing. That was why the boathouse was attacked—to delay completion of the *Pandora* until they were ready, until the *Star of Salem* could reach Limehouse, until . . ."

"More fancies, Mr Justice." Hatherley pushed the detaining hand aside, obviously dismissing what Justice said as mere persiflage, wasting the time he would need to hasten down the river, calling out the men and the officials he would need to detain the *Star*. And he seemed bewildered by Justice's dramatic change of mind. "One moment you are hot for Limehouse, Mr Justice. The next for Hampshire. Do you really know what you want? Where to go?"

"To Cuffwells," Justice cried, released at last from the dilemma which had plagued him for days, and forced him to leave Hampshire for London because he could not decide where the greatest danger lay. "Cuffwells for me, Mr Hatherley. Limehouse for you."

Hatherley looked severe, yet equally relieved. "If Mr Francis has gone back to Cuffwells," he said, shrugging off Justice's notion of the double-ended plot, persisting in his conviction that Francis was guilty of some sinister intention, "you may be sure that it is to take the *Pandora* from us, and the sooner you are on your way back to your duty . . ." The sharp edge had come back into his voice as he contemplated the wreck of all his schemes to discover Francis breaking his contract, betraying secrets for which he had been well paid, from which England would suffer most grievously if they fell into hostile hands. He drew out his watch. "Three hours to the top of the flood, or thereabouts," he said, and stayed a moment before he went out to the stair.

"If we both fail, Mr Justice. If either the *Star* or the *Pandora* gets to sea with Mr Francis aboard, the saving of the papers will not protect us from ruin."

Justice could tell he was talking of the anger with which Sir George would break those who had so disastrously failed him, and of something more.

"Both of us," Hatherley said. "And perhaps the ruin of our country as well."

IT WAS A NIGHTMARE of a drive. Justice made for Cuffwells as fast as wheels could turn and take him there, finding that Holland had not boasted when he claimed his chaise was the fastest thing in town, realizing with each mile that passed that he was in no fit state to keep control of two such powerful horses over so long a distance, and that Scorcher was no man to take his share of driving in a rig like this, more suited to racing then to the rutted roads of the English countryside in winter.

They shaved walls and hedges. The great slim wheels bounced through potholes and puddles. They swerved by carriages, forced their way alongside and past the great stagecoaches, drawn by teams of eight and blocking the best of the track, while the passengers on top cheered them on and the coachmen shook their fists. They were slowed to a pace in the towns, where people crowded round barrows and carts, and groused when they were pushed aside, and they careered through villages without breaking their pace, Scorcher standing and shouting like a man demented at anyone who seemed likely to stray in their path.

They had to stop twice. Once at Farnham, to give the horses oats and a breather. Once at a posthouse ten miles from Winchester, when it was already dark, and Holland's fine horses could go no farther. Beyond Winchester they were slowed again, coming on so many wagons and companies of soldiers moving towards Portsmouth that Justice thought there might be some new threat of invasion, and asking, got such answers as made him decide that a great expedition was in the making. "Against Spain, perhaps," he said to Scorcher. "If Spain joins Boney next year."

Beyond Winchester again, ten miles more, they came to a crossroads, with a man hanging in chains from a gibbet, and for one moment Justice let his attention wander, running too far before he turned, tipping one wheel into a ditch and hearing the spokes snap before they both followed it, sprawling in the darkness while the horses dragged what was left of the chaise another hundred yards.

It took ten minutes to cut the horses loose and make improvised reins from the leathers, ten more to settle them to the unfamiliar feel of bareback riders. A distant clock struck midnight as Justice and Scorcher felt the road drop down towards Beaulieu and drove their exhausted mounts the last miles through Bucklers Hard.

They were at Cuffwells, where there were candles at the windows, lanterns by the boathouse.

"Gone, sir! Gone, damn you!"

Justice had guessed what had happened before he heard Lilly's angry cry at the sight of him.

He had come too late.

After all, they had taken the *Pandora*.

✒25✒

"WHEN WAS IT DONE?" Justice asked, once Lilly had calmed sufficiently to tell him.

"An hour ago, no more," Lilly said, staring into the darkness on the river as though he could will the *Pandora* back into sight.

"And it was done quite simply," he went on. "Your damned cousin, Justice, that's how it was done. Why the devil a Frenchman and an Englishman should be born to look so alike . . . It ain't reasonable."

"He impersonated me?" The likeness had worked to Luc's advantage again, as it had in the first attempt on the *Pandora*. As he would have known if he had considered why the two sailors believed they had seen him at Wykeham, instead of insisting they lied.

"Of course." Lilly was abrupt. "The men were told to take orders from no one but you, or me? Or Hatherley?"

"Exactly."

"So they did. From you, or so they thought, not wishing to trouble me when I had come from Deal without rest and gone straight to my bed exhausted."

"But Sweetsea was . . ."

"Captain Sweetsea . . ." Now Lilly was being acid and formal. "Captain Sweetsea was cozened away from his post. Like you, Mr Justice, if I may be blunt."

Justice felt the accusation was as unfair as Hatherley's rough criticism but he had to let it stand. This was no time to tell Lilly everything that had passed at Wykeham while he was away or to run over the murderous events in London.

With each passing minute Luc was working the *Pandora* closer to the sea.

"Yes, cozened," Lilly said, seeing Justice's astonishment. "Some message, it seems, saying that the governess at Wykeham was hurt and asking for him—though I've no idea why that was his business. Simply put the fellow who brought it in charge, and rushed off into the night.''

"What fellow?''

"A chap called Bland.''

"Bland?'' Justice could scarcely tell Lilly in his present mood that he had hinted to Sweetsea that Bland might be counted on in an emergency, that he had suspected he was one of Hatherley's men, posted out at Lepe to protect the eastern approaches to the river. "Bland,'' he said, thinking of that odd man's cordiality when he fell in Harriet's race.

"Bland, yes. For God's sake, Justice, do something more than repeat what I say.'' Lilly was getting angry again as he thought of Luc. "And then your blasted cousin turns up, hatted and cloaked in the dark, making himself out to be you with enough effect to bamboozle the guards. Bland as well, I imagine. Fooled them all, it seems for there was no kind of fight, and he had a pair of pistols on them before they could raise an alarm.''

"How many were with him?'' Justice was thinking of the accomplices who had helped Luc the night the *Pandora* was floated.

"Nobody came with him.'' Lilly stopped to listen to a sailor who came up with some request and gave him a testy answer. "Yes. Yes. Let them go on with it, though it's all too late.'' He turned back to Justice. "That precious Frenchman came alone, Justice. *Alone*, damn him for his brave impertinence. And cleared off with Bland, a man called Warren, who was working late on the *Pandora*, with Tooth, who had gone down with Francis and Lord William when they arrived. And the *Pandora*, naturally,'' he added savagely.

"Francis, too,'' Justice said miserably, guessing what Lilly was about to say. "Lord William.''

"The pair of them,'' Lilly said, and there was something in the way he spoke that sounded like confirmation of some regrettable suspicion.

"As hostages?''

"As crew, more likely. Working willingly or under duress, I've no idea. But there are six men on that blasted submarine, Justice, all it needs . . .''

"But he didn't take the guards?'' Justice asked, wondering which of the five men had in fact gone willingly with Luc.

"They were trussed at pistol point—while I'm tucked in my

bed, two hundred yards away, with twenty-five able-bodied men within call!''

Justice saw there was nothing more to be gained by this recital. ''What has been done?'' Precious little, it seemed, to judge by the scene of confusion in front of him. There were men with lanterns on the water's edge, in the trees farther down the bank; men readying a couple of boats, loading guns that were being fetched from the store.

''Nothing until ten minutes ago,'' Lilly was saying. ''When the fresh guard came on for the middle watch. When they found the other men tied like turkeys and the *Pandora* gone.''

''Gone an hour,'' Justice said, considering the state of the tide, the strong easterly blowing over from the Exbury side of the river, the difficulties Luc would face in finding his way in the darkness, in making a partly recalcitrant crew work the peculiar machinery which drove the submarine if he struck the mast and submerged.

''The *Pandora* can still be saved,'' he said to Lilly, calling Scorcher to his side and giving the first order.

EVERYTHING HAD TO be done at once. One man was sent to rouse the Volunteers, fire Sweetsea's beacon at the Old Fort. Another to Wykeham, to tell Harriet that her brother had been taken and to sound the great old bell in the abbey tower. If these alarms did little else, Justice thought, the sight or sound of them might give the prisoners hope, make Luc more circumspect, slow his passage down to the sea—he was never a man to be panicked, and tonight he had obviously been at his best. It was the kind of nip-and-tuck situation he had always enjoyed when he was working as a confidential agent for Louis and the Comte d'Artois. Even in this moment of anger Justice could not help admiring Luc's bravado and finesse, for all his change of sides.

It would be a slow passage, anyway. First, the bends, tricky at any time, perilous in the dark on a falling tide. Then the fort: he would want to pass that half submerged. Then the more open water past Gins Mill, most of it shallow, with a long enough fetch to raise a sharp chop in this wind—and he would have to turn east there, forcing his way out the last reach of the river against a rising gale. And beyond that . . . out in the Solent . . . In a moment Justice realized that Luc must have made some plan to be picked up. Close inshore. In these conditions . . . in such a novel and untried vessel . . . with prisoners huddled into that terrifyingly small brass cylinder below the water . . . he would have no hope of making more than a few miles to a rendezvous.

"Send to Needs Ore Point," he said to the sailor who had come back after attending to Lilly's order. "Keep a lookout for any fair-sized vessel standing in to the river or close to the coast. Fire one blue flare for the river. Two for the sea beyond."

A weapon. A suitable weapon. A most suitable weapon.

When the idea came to Justice he was on the wall of the lock, looking down at the small craft the men were readying, choosing the gig in which Ainsworth had carried him to Lower Exbury the other day, having it drawn into the boathouse for loading. At least he had the feel of that boat already, and it was strong in the bows . . .

"Fred," he said, beckoning Scorcher away from the pool of light round a lantern, where he and another man were loading a pair of pistols, wrapping their locks in scraps of oiled cloth for protection against rain and spray. "The harpoon gun, Fred. The gun we saw in the storehouse with the carcasses. Could we make it work?"

"Works right well, begging the liberty, Cap'n."

The man who had been helping Scorcher seemed to be some kind of gunner's mate in charge of the powder barrel, for while he worked he was giving instructions to other men who came up to load rifles and the blunder-pistols that would be deadly at short range. But before Justice could do more than nod permission to speak, Scorcher had seen the point and was off, pulling the man after him, raising a hand as Justice called after them. "And a loaded carcass, too!"

In less than five minutes they were back, struggling with the weight of the gun and its barbed harpoon, its box of running line, setting its oblong cradle between the forward thwarts of the gig, checking the action of the flintlock, priming it, loading it, and going back to help the two men who were ladling thirty pounds of the best powder into the copper-covered carcass; carrying the carcass down to the gig, resting it near the stern to balance the gun, laying its bridle convenient to the running line.

It was the longest of chances, Justice knew, but no waste of time if it worked . . . what could a pistol, a rifle, even a fowling piece do against the planking and brass of the *Pandora?*

Lilly came down to watch, a disapproving look on his face, pursed lips; and Justice mistook his expression for impatience at the delay.

"I must have some means to secure the *Pandora,*" he cried. "I cannot ram her in a gig. I cannot board her if she is sealed and below water. I must secure her if I can. Sink her if I must." He pointed to the heavy gleaming carcass.

"Secure her if you can." Now it was Lilly who was picking up a phrase and repeating it. "Otherwise . . . Sink her you must, at all costs."

Justice was so astonished at these words that he thought he had misheard them, and he looked up at Lilly on the dock. The Commissioner's mouth was set in a grim line. "Sink her, I said, Captain Justice."

"Francis. Lord William." Justice began a puzzled protest. "If she is lost, they are lost . . ."

"But all is not lost." Lilly spoke sharp and clear. "On the contrary, Mr. Justice. That may be the best course. The only course in the circumstances."

Justice still found it hard to accept the order that Lilly was giving him. To sink the submarine on which so much money and effort had been spent. To send Francis and Romney to their deaths. That was what all costs meant. And was that what Lilly meant too?

It was. *"At all costs,"* he was insisting. "Remember what I said to you when you first came," he said, striking the ground with his cane and leaning over so that Justice should not mistake his words. "I had to know whether Francis could do what he claimed. Whether he could build that damnable fancy and make it work." Lilly paused, his anxiety echoing beyond the end of his sentence.

"Now I have my answer, Mr Justice," he went on. "For the past six months this thing has haunted me like a phantom from the deep. Now it is afloat on the waters, and under the waters."

He took Justice's shoulder in a strong grip.

"It works, Mr Justice, it works! And the better it works the more dangerous it becomes, the more I shall wish it and its inventor at the bottom of the sea. If I heard they were both in

the hands of the French I should not sleep this night, or any other, knowing that I should never see the daystar of victory rise above the darkened shores of this island."

His grip tightened.

"That is the real secret of the *Pandora,* Mr Justice. Not the idea of a plunging-boat. Not the building of such a monster. *The fact that it works.* Once that fact is known . . ."

He dropped his arm in a gesture of cold despair.

"Do you have my meaning now, Captain Justice?"

"EASY, FRED." They were out in the stream, the sails filled, the water gurgling under the bow where Justice sat, peering forward, looking for the first glow of the lanterns held by the men he had sent riding forward to the places where Luc's lanterns had been found. He would take the chance of them serving the *Pandora,* for by his reckoning Luc would now have passed those bearing points.

But not by much. An hour, no more, Lilly had said. Half the time to get the *Pandora* out of the dock, waiting for the tide to turn and carry her down the river. Almost as much to learn the simplest knack of handling and driving her, with men who had no wish to crank or steer or pump . . .

Two of them at least must be Luc's accomplices if the machine was to be worked at all; and as that thought came to him Justice realized that if it came to close quarters he would have no means of knowing which of the five men with Luc would be enemies, which he would trust and try to save.

First find the *Pandora* and worry about all that when the chance came. If it came.

Justice could see the loom of the banks, more when the scudding clouds broke to give a fitful glimpse of moonlight—enough to know that he would be able to see the *Pandora* if she was running close enough to the surface for Luc to see through the glass eye in the hatchway, or to be conning her as he stood up in the open hatchway, feeling his way, hoping that he had done what most men would have considered impossible . . .

A gleam of silver from a shallow patch of water. It would be mudbank soon, Justice could tell from the way the ripples lifted in the falling tide, striking against a projecting piece of land, a jetty, a . . . It was the *Pandora,* a third out of the water, slowly turning, while a man with a pole or paddle lay on the bow to push her clear.

The *Pandora.* Aground. Almost caught helpless in the oozing mud that flanked the channel on both sides, grabbing at any boat that did not hold its course through the long bend before you came to the Old Fort on the Exbury side and Gins Mill below Wykeham.

Scorcher had also seen the black stubby shape, giving a low cry and pointing before it was lost against the dark line of the fort's foreshore and earth embankments.

Aground, almost where Justice himself had gone ashore to see the little wherry hidden in the brambles and gorse a few hundred yards from the fort, and it crossed his mind that Luc might have put a man in there, to send a signal to a waiting brig at the river's mouth, to silence a sentinel, to spike the great guns before the alarm was sounded. But that was impossible. Luc would not have any hands to spare as he struggled to keep steerage way on the *Pandora,* forced his accomplices and his prisoners to turn those cranks, sweating, cursing and slithering in that cold, dark, damp, and airless cylinder that had felt so like a tomb when he stood in it for the first time.

Aground, sliding off like a great whale making for deeper water. Justice leaned over the harpoon gun, bringing it to full cock, covering it again with the oiled cloth as the wind whipped spume and icy dollops of spray over the bow. Out in the Solent, where the waves were beginning to roar on the far side of Gull-Island, it would be blowing half a gale. More, later, from what he knew of easterlies at this time of year. And if it went round a few points, no one would get away from this shore tonight.

Another moment of moonshine, scanning over the river so quickly that Justice could scarcely trim his eyes to it before it was gone, showing no sign of the *Pandora* within a cable's length. And she could not have moved fast enough to gain more than that. Could not have moved anything like that fast, for Scorcher was calling, had seen her aft, was making ready to go about to come up to her, was waiting for the command when Justice saw a lantern flash in the fort and gave a different order.

"Take her in close," he shouted at Scorcher, intending to

warn Sweetsea's gun crew. But before Scorcher could put the tiller over, there was a rippling line of flashes, and Justice heard one ball strike the thin planking of the gig before the others whistled over and he heard the crack of a disciplined volley. Sweetsea's Volunteers were up to the mark—half a dozen of them, at least, he judged, and a gun's crew ready as well, if Sweetsea had taken his advice and the warning had reached the men on duty.

A gun's crew. Justice had no more than a couple of seconds to think what that meant before he saw the first flames lick out from Sweetsea's beacon, and a bright blue light flared on the water's edge, making the gig the clearest of targets.

A target that would look enough like the fore-and-aft rig of the *Pandora* for a trigger-happy gunner to put his match to the breech.

That would be smashed to a bloody pulp by a twenty-four pounder firing grape or langridge at point-blank range.

And there was no hope of getting away now the gig had been sighted. If Sweetsea had done what he was told, his gunners would be able to sweep clear across to Gull-Island. No means of drawing attention to the *Pandora*, for Luc would now be holding her upstream, away from the light of the flare, away from the guns of the fort. He would have known about those, of course, and expected to slip past unobserved on such a night.

As he still might, if Sweetsea's men shattered the gig in error.

"Take her down on the landing stage," Justice shouted at Scorcher, risking another volley of rifle fire, hoping he could run in under the gun that pointed to Gins Mill, run in before he crossed the muzzle of the one which pointed seaward. He had no idea which would be loaded, manned.

There were men running out on the jetty with levelled rifles before they luffed into it, letting the tide slap them against the piles with such a crunch that Justice feared for the fragile hull; and Sweetsea himself, thank God, standing among them, shouting explanations and excuses that Justice did not want to hear.

"The *Pandora*," Justice yelled back at him, pointing up the river. "Give Scorcher two of those rifles. Get the rest of your men out in the ferryboat. Ropes. Grapnels." He could not understand what Sweetsea meant, shaking his head and gesturing with his good arm towards Wykeham. And he became more confused as the great bell began to boom and echo sonorously out of the night.

"Ferryboat," he shouted again, the wind whipping the word back at him, and this time he caught Sweetsea's answer.

"Wykeham side." Sweetsea did not try to explain, though Justice suspected that Luc might somehow have made sure of that: he was too busy trying to persuade Justice to let him fire out at random into the darkness. With such guns, with charges that would spread fifty yards wide, he could be sure of hitting the *Pandora*, damaging her, sinking her . . . But damage was not enough, destruction, with innocent men aboard the submarine, too much.

"Fire only if I fail," he said to Sweetsea, as he jumped back in the boat. "If all else fails." He made sure that Scorcher had the rifles to hand, and he was about to push off when he remembered something he had forgotten in the rush at Cuffwells. "A knife, if you please, Mr Sweetsea. If it comes to close quarters . . ."

He had taken a knife from one of the Exbury men, cast off to let Scorcher bring the gig before the wind, when he heard a last shout from Sweetsea: and even before another blue flare sputtered close by, he saw a gleam on the river some thirty or forty yards away, the reflection of a beacon flame on one of the brass hatchways of the *Pandora*.

While they talked Luc was seizing his chance to slip past and away.

ALL THE SAME, the submarine appeared to be in difficulties, for it was only half under water, and the wind was making it roll heavily; it was yawing, as though its steering gear was out of control, and carried forward as much by the tide as by the flyer which was supposed to drive it.

"She's done for, Cap'n," Scorcher shouted as the gig ran across her stern and came up into the wind, Scorcher keeping her in stays as long as possible to give Justice a close look at her.

Justice was not sure. From what he remembered of the *Pandora*, the levers that worked the tiller and diving wings both ran through the rear compartment, and so did the shaft that drove the flyer. Suppose. Suppose the men cooped in the rear had overpowered their guard, had somehow interfered with those vital metal rods . . . had already swung the *Pandora* onto one mudbank and were trying to repeat that manoeuvre before it was too late . . .

He could not wait to find out, and he had already crouched over the harpoon gun, wondering whether it would fire, how well it would aim, where the harpoon would find the best of purchases: he had his hand on the cover, poised to whip it off and fire, when he saw Luc's head come through the hatchway.

There were less than a dozen yards between them, close enough for his shout demanding surrender to carry, for Luc to recognise his voice and answer with a defiant gesture.

"I will treat you as prisoners of war," he cried again, doubting whether Luc would catch his offer, aware that if he did and accepted, it would in honour have to stand, whatever Lilly said, whatever notion the French royalists might have for revenge. It would have to stand, though he hated making it, knowing all that would be said about Luc and their relationship.

It would ruin him. But it could save lives. It might save all their lives.

It would do nothing of the sort. His last shout was still ringing in his ears when he saw the flash of a pistol and heard a ball whine off the barrel of the harpoon gun. Luc was not trying to frighten him away. He was trying to kill him, and coming too damned close for comfort.

The gig had begun to pay off before Luc fired, and Scorcher was so quick to run clear out of range to windward that Justice dared not let the harpoon fly for fear he would miss, or make only a glancing shot: and there would be no means of reloading that clumsy and unfamiliar weapon in the dark. But while the gig came round to run straight at the *Pandora*, the submarine began to veer and wallow so sharply that Justice thought Luc must have regained control and was dodging him, or that any mutineers aft had chosen the worst of moments to fool again with the steering. Each time he was about to pull the firing lanyard the *Pandora* slipped out of his line of sight.

A third, a fourth time. Justice jerked the cord, felt the gun jump as the harpoon drove forward, its line snaking out of the box beside the cradle. Thought he had missed, for he saw and heard nothing; pulled on the rope to feel it tighten and the gig tip under strain. Passed a loop back for Scorcher to attach to the carcass bridle. Hesitated, unsure whether to put that deadly cask of powder where a chance collision could blow both gig and submarine to matchwood. Decided that the danger of an explosion caused by a random shot was even greater. And rolled the damn thing over the side, to float just below the surface within reaching distance.

He fumbled for the burning slow match and blue light that Sweetsea had tossed to him while he was waiting for the knife, bent over low in the boat to start it out of the wind. As it flared to show the whole of the *Pandora* bright as day, he saw the harpoon firmly struck amidships, well out of reach from either hatch. It was the luckiest of shots.

And he saw something else. The aft hatch was open, and he heard muffled shouts from below as Tooth heaved himself up, shouting and waving his hands as Scorcher hauled on the harpoon line to bring the gig within six feet of the *Pandora*.

"Don't shoot!" he cried. "Don't shoot!" And there was anguish in his voice as the blue light starkly revealed Justice taking aim at him.

☙ 26 ☙

JUSTICE LOWERED the pistol, waiting to see what Tooth's next move would be, clinging to the mast as the gig and the submarine rolled towards and away from each other on the ends of the tough rope which joined them.

Tooth was calling again, and Justice caught the names. "Francis . . . William," the man yelled, pointing below, and then there was something about Bland that was lost in the sounds of wind and water.

"I mark him, Cap'n."

In the corner of his eye Justice noticed Scorcher covering Tooth with the other blunder-pistol, which could rip anything within a circle of six feet at that range.

"Up with your hands!" He was taking no chance that this might be another trap.

But Tooth merely waved one arm, and as Justice hauled on the rope to bring the two craft closer he saw that Tooth was bending down in the hatchway, pulling hard, allowing another figure to squeeze past him and crawl over the rim to flop onto the slippery and shallow deck of the *Pandora*.

It was Francis, no doubt of that, though the blue light had guttered out and left Justice groping in the blackness to find another rope to throw across the yard or so of icy river water between them.

He thought he had missed, for the rope lay slack at first, and then he felt a tug as he gathered it in and took the strain. He heard Tooth's voice, surprisingly clear and close at hand.

"For God's sake, hurry, Cap'n."

He wondered whether Luc might be opening the other hatchway, unseen now, preparing to try another shot, crawling aft with a knife to cut the rope from the harpoon. He fought off the temptation to play safe, to fire blind in case there was some movement forward, and kept his nerve. Would Luc need to take such a crude risk as that, when every minute

267

told in his favour, when the ebb was running faster, carrying both boats away from the threat of Sweetsea's guns and deeper into the night?

Even as he calculated he felt the gig come hard against the *Pandora*, and he was taking the American's weight as Francis grabbed for a hold, fell slithering like a wet plank across the gap, gasped as a ridge of wood jammed at his ribs, scrambled in to lie huddled in the bottom of the boat with a grunt of thanks.

One.

And there had been no treachery in that move. Only the most breakneck bid for escape in which he had ever been involved.

He could hear more shouts as he released the rope which Francis had tied under his arms. Tooth again, though the noise was more muffled, as if it came from inside the hull of the *Pandora*; and then there was a distinct hail. "Cap'n! Cap'n!"

Seeing a little better, now his eyes had grown accustomed to the dark again, Justice could make out the shapes in the hatchway well enough to get the rope back to them at the first attempt. But even as he felt it tighten, it went slack again, and from the oaths that came out of the darkness it seemed that there was some kind of struggle going on over there.

There was another cry from Tooth, and he tugged, guessing from the on and off tension of the rope that it must be Lord William awkwardly struggling to make his way across. He had just made out Romney's gangling shape when the moon broke through and he heard a shout behind him, turned to see Francis seize the rifle; and he had no time to reflect why Scorcher had given that cry of warning before the muzzle swung toward him, past him, and the flash from it fused with another from the bow of the *Pandora*.

Both misses. But as Justice heard the forward hatch clang down, and Lord William cry for assistance, he knew that Luc might be able to reload below, while each of his guns was useless for anything but a club once it was fired.

Lord William. Two, now, for Romney was safe, though Justice barely noticed the struggle to get him over the side: for at that moment he realized what that rifle shot had meant.

He had been right, not Hatherley.

Francis could be trusted. Francis was the victim, after all.

And with Francis and the papers snatched from him Luc would stick at nothing to carry off the *Pandora*.

It was that thought, in which Lilly's stern words still echoed, that prevented Justice from cutting loose, calling to Tooth to jump and swim for it, making for the shore while the gig was seaworthy. For the sound of splashing among the floorboards gave him a nasty feeling that the boat was already taking water after that smash against the jetty; and with the three men rescued from the submarine . . . the thought was broken before he completed it.

He had forgotten Bland. Who had been so amiably helpful. Who had taken charge at Cuffwells at a moment's notice. Who must have brought a false message to Sweetsea, though there had been no time in that brief stop at the fort to make sure of that.

Bland. William was gasping the name, gabbling more. "Never thought of it . . . Jerseyman . . . to the French," he puffed, wanting breath for the words, as Justice's mind raced ahead of him.

Bland. At the house on the eastern shore, near Lepe. The base for the whole campaign against Francis. Against the *Pandora*.

"Tooth," William was saying. "Like a lion . . . ran us ashore once . . ." And now Justice was looking, in the broken light, at Tooth fighting again, trying to get clear of the hatchway. At Scorcher kneeling and yelling encouragement, holding up his pistol in the hope of a clear shot. At Tooth again, forcing himself up while someone was attacking him from below.

He was steadying himself to make a neck-or-nothing leap onto the submarine when the heavily built seaman gave a gasping cry, another as he collapsed backwards over the hatchway, legs still kicking, a third that died in a gurgling scream as he went over the far side of the *Pandora* and the water took him.

"Knifed, poor bastard," Scorcher said with gritted venom, squeezing the trigger as the figure of Bland loomed for a second, reaching up to snap down the hatch and seal the submarine.

The spreading shot must have cut Bland to death. His hand never reached the hatch cover, and his arm gave a convulsive jerk as he dropped out of sight.

Without thinking, Justice dragged the gig close enough to

269

risk a jump, moving so quickly that he was already over, on all fours, scrambling for a hold, when Scorcher saw what he was doing and shouted in surprised dismay.

It was the first time he had ever boarded a submarine, and with a characteristic flick of irrelevant and mordant humour he wondered what the Admiralty would say if he claimed prize money for it. Wondered, but at the same time made sure that Bland was not foxing him, creeping to the hatchway, peering down, seeing in the slightest of lantern beams the crumpled body below.

From what he recalled of the *Pandora*, there was no way aft from the front compartment of that great brass cylinder, divided amidships by a strengthening hemisphere; and as long as he kept command of the deck and the hatch open, it was impossible for Luc to dive, to take the submarine under the water and leave him to drown.

But if he stayed where he was, cutting the gig free and ordering Scorcher to take Francis and Romney ashore before it sank, it was equally impossible to do what Lilly wanted and wreck the *Pandora*. He would simply be carried wherever Luc was going.

It was a stalemate.

And there was only one way to break it.

WHEN JUSTICE WAS a schoolboy he had been fascinated by the fable of Buridan's Ass, which starved to death because it could not choose between two bundles of hay, equal in size and equal in distance. He had known naval officers like that, men who had missed chances or ruined themselves through havering, and each time he saw such a case it made him more determined that he would take any risk rather than fail in his duty through indecision.

As he clung to the cold brass rim of the hatch he could not see what was happening in the gig, but Scorcher was holding it close enough for words to carry.

"The carcass," Justice shouted at him. "Can you work it round? Ask Francis."

He had no more than the vaguest idea how the infernal machine was worked, and he doubted whether the gunner's mate had set its triggers before it was dumped in the boat: that would have been far too risky. So there must be some device that cocked it before it was used, when it went into the water.

In that case . . . in that case, it would come to the same thing when he heaved it alongside the *Pandora*, for he proposed to drag it on board and detonate it with the last of the loaded pistols.

Lord William shouted something he did not understand, and then all was quiet except for the rising sigh of the wind and the water splashing around them. There was not even a sound from within the hull: the last men on the *Pandora* were as still as the rods and cranks that drove her.

They would be waiting for his next move, knowing that their prisoners had escaped, guessing what Justice would do.

Luc. Luc and Warren, for the mechanic must have been a Jacobin sympathizer, easily suborned by the French. Just the two of them left, now, and Justice thought of the deaths their plot had caused in the past three days. Dunning. Fanshawe and the Frenchwoman. The two men on the barge. Tooth. Bland.

Seven of them, and there would be others before the night was out.

"Justice. If you please." Francis was at the side of the gig, as cool as ever, trying to explain what was wrong, saying he dare not touch the carcass.

"Three to one it won't work, for I never set it." He was making some gesture, and Justice saw a knife in his hand flash blue in a fragment of moonlight. "But if it is set . . ." He waved again, throwing his hand upwards. "Too risky. Far too risky."

There was no reason why Francis should risk his life in order to destroy the most brilliant of his inventions, no reason to blame him.

All the same, it was worth an argument. Justice shouted at Scorcher to change places with him, keeping the guard on the hatchway, while he scrambled across to plead with Francis, to see what might be done.

Scorcher was over, and he was back in the sternsheets of the gig, telling Francis to use the line through the eye of the harpoon, to draw the carcass slap up to its target, to take a chance on the explosion. He was looking at the flapping sails, thinking about the run of the rope as they pulled away, when he heard shouts, when Francis thumped him on the shoulder and pointed.

Heard shouts. Saw lanterns. Saw the ferryboat fast bearing down on them. Saw Harriet in the bow, and half a dozen men crowded behind her. Saw that the ferry was heading to come alongside, and that the carcass lay exactly in the way. Saw that there was no hope of warning Harriet with a yell or wave that would be mistaken for a welcome.

He had no choice, whatever Lilly might say.

He snatched the knife from Francis, cut frenziedly at the rope which held the carcass bridle, tugged at it, felt the current take the heavy cask, glimpsed its gleaming shape as it slid through the narrowing gap.

Five yards. Three yards to spare, perhaps. And enough.

But the ferry drove on, running too hard and too clumsily before the wind, missing the turn, crushing the gig against the submarine, swinging and sliding past. And as hands reached out to drag Francis and Romney to safety, Justice was thrown over the splintering wood to tear at the side of the *Pandora* for a hold, to feel Scorcher's grip on his arm as the remains of the gig sank under him.

He lay on the deck, panting with the shock, watching the ferryboat go down the wind, hearing shouts as the men realized that he and Scorcher had been left behind, seeing Harriet run aft as the darkness closed on her.

For the *Pandora* was moving again, moving fast in a desperate bid to escape, as if Luc had guessed what had happened. Justice could hear and feel the crank turning below him, sense the vessel swerving up into the wind where the ferryboat could not easily follow.

That was exactly what she was designed to do, Justice thought bitterly. What she could do most dangerously.

And the last he saw of the ferryboat was the dwindling glow of a waving lantern. He had no doubt that it was Harriet's gesture of farewell.

JUSTICE AND SCORCHER were trapped on the *Pandora*, to swim or sink with her.

They could stay on the exposed deck, where they would have a better chance if the vessel ran onto a mudbank or was cast away on the northern edge of Gull-Island; where they could make sure that Luc was cooped up below; where they would soon begin to feel the wind cut through their soggy clothes and bring the drowsy chill in which their brains would numb and their hands would slip. They could last two hours, perhaps, like that.

Or they could huddle below for shelter, try, like Tooth, to manipulate the steering gear, risk Luc or Warren creeping up to snap the hatch down and make them prisoners as the *Pandora* plunged to hide in the depths.

Luc had already gone down a foot or so, Justice guessed, lowering the vessel so much that it would be hard to see her even in a better light, sending water sloshing over her shallow sides.

Perhaps he was trying to wash them off, for one sharp wave caught Scorcher unawares, while Justice was fumbling to see whether there was any sailcloth wrapped around the dropped mast and boom, anything that might enable them to affect the speed and direction of the submarine; and it was Scorcher's instinctive snatch that found the tiller, still shipped, still working—for as he lurched on to it Justice felt the *Pandora* swing and roll. Swing and swing back again, as someone under the deck corrected the movement on the smaller rudder that was controlled from inside the boat.

Now began a game of pull devil, pull baker, as the *Pandora* headed up wind and down again, but all the time leaving the lights of Gins Mill and Exbury farther behind as the current drove her onwards, relentlessly, crabwise, and always closer to Gull-Island, until Justice could tell where they were going.

Where Luc must have wanted to go all the time. Where he was clever enough to reckon that such a sluggish vessel would inevitably be carried if he caught the fast rip of the tide.

Out through the gut between Needs Ore Point and Gull-Island that Justice had noticed that first morning when he looked at the chart.

Risky. That wasn't the word for it. Even a fast and easy handler like the gig would be hard to coax through such a swirling passage, especially at night. And the *Pandora*, well, Luc must be counting on bouncing her through like a cork, using the immense buoyancy of that copper cylinder to keep her afloat, relying on the spill of the emptying river to carry her out into the Solent.

Justice strained to pick up the narrow space between the low promontories: there ought to be the faintest glow of light from the open water beyond them, and if he could tell exactly when they would enter the gut, a sudden thrust on the tiller might be sufficient to set the *Pandora* athwart the channel, to roll her as if she were broaching, to let water pour into that open hatch, to give them a chance to swim for it while Luc and Warren went down with the submarine.

It was all fancy. At this tide the gut seemed wide and deep enough to let the *Pandora* wash through exactly as Luc must have intended, and Justice was already cursing at the failure of his hopes, wondering how much farther Luc would have to go to reach his rendezvous, when a blue light flared over to the right, to the left, to the right again as the *Pandora* bobbed and spun.

One blue light. One of the sailors must have caught a glimpse of a ship standing close in, even anchored within sight of the shore. A blue light only thirty yaards away, near enough to see the men standing by it—men who must have taken the *Pandora* for Justice's gig as she came down towards them, and would now be able to make out Justice and Scorcher clinging on for dear life as she swept past and out through the broken water at the south end of the gut.

She took the rising waves well, better than most vessels of her size because she was both buoyant and low in the water, and there was no top hamper to catch the half gale that was now blowing up from the southeast. "Backing south," Scorcher shouted, and Justice realized that any ship would have trouble clawing off this open shore tonight. Down the Solent there was the long point at Hurst to be cleared, beyond that the reaching headlands of the Dorset coast, Portland Bill. A wise captain would wait until daylight to run narrowly past those dangers.

And each hour's delay contained a grain of hope.

For Justice's mind had now turned to the unknown vessel that must be riding out of sight, beyond the breaking seas that were making it hard for Luc to make headway.

It would be easier if he could plunge, Justice understood, get below the whitecaps that were tossing them, use all the advantages that Francis had given his remarkable boat.

For there was no longer any doubt about her capacities. Fresh off the stocks, without trials, without a trained crew, she had done all or more than Francis had promised.

And was all the more dangerous, as Lilly had said.

Give her trials, give her improvements, give her dedicated

men prepared to run the risks of submarine warfare, and she would make those who built her and her like the masters of the world.

If she survived. If the secret of this astonishing maiden voyage was ever known.

Not even Francis had seen how Luc had triumphed over so many hazards to bring the *Pandora* to this storm-tossed meeting place.

THE BRIG WAS there all right, with three lanterns in its stern window making the shape of a triangle, and Justice began to consider what Luc would do.

He would certainly come up under her lee, where he could get help from the deck, overpower the cold and feeble men who had tried in vain to stop him seizing the *Pandora*, secure the submarine until it was getting light and he could see whether she was well sealed and dry.

Then he would start to tow her to France. A brig would find it very difficult, almost impossible, to haul such a heavy boat out of the water—especially if there was a hurry. It would be easier to tow her. Safer, too, for she could be towed below water, out of sight of any curious naval patrols that might otherwise be tempted to look at this strange craft.

It would all happen just like that, Justice knew, unless he could find some means to prevent it.

For the brig was coming nearer with each turn of the driving flyer and Luc would soon turn into the wind to come up on her. It was a time for farewells.

Justice climbed down the hatch, kicked Bland's body aside, and carefully eased himself among the spinning rods and wheels, seeing how easily the valiant Tooth could have interfered with them, thinking how simple it would be to take the *Pandora* down to the bottom if he knew which lever to pull, which valve to open.

He must have touched something which told Luc that he was there, for the grinding suddenly stopped, and in the unexpected silence he heard a triumphant shout.

"C'est toi, Jean? J'ai gagné, alors." And then, in a kinder, ribald voice. *"Tu vas mourir comme un poisson?"*

In this extremity of their lives Luc's streak of gallows humour took them back to a shared boyhood joke, which had begun one day when they were fishing at Recques and Justice had fallen into the millpond.

And the answer was always the same.

"Only a dead fish swims with the stream."

"*Tu verras, enfin,*" Luc cried before he began to crank at his gears again. "For the last time, eh, Jean?"

There was affection as well as a grim truth in the jest, and Justice felt his heart turn over as he heard the once-loved voice.

For the last time, as Luc said. In a few minutes they would both die like fish, with water flooding about them and into their lungs as they struggled vainly for breath.

"*Adieu, Luc,*" he shouted, all the enmity and contempt draining away as he put his face to the grating, finding the tears on it more salty than the spray. "*Adieu pour toujours, mon brave.*"

It was an honest parting, for all that he proposed to do as he climbed up from the hatch and squatted beside Scorcher to take the tiller from him.

"I'll let him come in close," he said, pushing Scorcher forward to give himself room for a sudden move. "Be ready to jump. They're bound to have ropes ready to pull you out of the water." He sensed that Scorcher was about to say something and took his arm. "Keep your mouth shut, Fred, and if you're lucky you'll spend the rest of the war in the naval prison at Brest."

Scorcher felt for the hand that was holding him and grasped it. "And you?" For once there was no rank between them.

Justice was silent. He was judging his moment, letting Luc come within a few yards, for the *Pandora* had little enough way on her.

Only a few yards more, moving a little faster as Luc and Warren made a last effort to pass the heaving stern of the brig, making sure it would not smash down on the submarine's hull.

Trying to make sure, and failing, as Justice pushed the tiller over and brought the bow exactly where he wanted it, under a sternpost that crushed down on it with the force of a hundred tons. Once. And again. Splitting the wooden bow of the *Pandora* and letting the sea rush into the balancing tank that lay forward of the brass cabin. And again, like a great ram, as the bow dipped forward, pulling the *Pandora* farther under the stern, to be pounded and pounded to pieces.

She was going down, her natural buoyancy impaired by the very means that were intended to help her dive.

She was going down, and the open hatch would finish her.

Justice had heard Luc shout at the sudden impact, more in desperate surprise than agony. At the very end of things, he knew that he had lost.

And Justice knew that he had done all that duty required of him. The *Pandora* was finished, and Scorcher would be the only man alive who knew the ghost of her secret.

He started to crawl down the steepening deck as the hull ground slowly under the side of the brig, hearing a man shout and hammer in frenzy on the jammed hatchway, drawn by some blind instinct to be near Luc at the last.

He lurched past Scorcher, who was fiddling with one of the ropes that had come snaking down from the deck above, yelling at him to climb free or jump, and before he could make another yard he felt a clutch at his coat and a fist thumped into the back of his jaw.

Feeling his limbs go weak, stumbling, hearing Scorcher mutter as a circlet of rope hardened around his ribs.

And Scorcher was saying it again. "You don't go this time, matey, not if I swing for it later."

Then Justice himself was swinging, drooped like a corpse from his noose, remembering nothing as his senses faded except the gypsy's words.

Over water, under water. Brother's face and hangman's halter.

⚜ 27 ⚜

"WELL, MR JUSTICE, you were the last person I expected to
see come over the side this morning. And in such a state, too.
But you can be my consolation prize. Must be, for I've
precious little else to show my friends in France." The words
were cynically jovial, the tone was grim, and the voice so unexpected that it took Justice some moments to place it.

Ever since it was light he had seen that he was bundled into
the corner of a roughly furnished stern cabin, and from the
way the boat was moving beneath it he could tell that she was
running down wind in a fairly severe sea.

Bound for France. As he had expected since he woke from
an exhausted sleep to find himself alive, and a prisoner.
Bound for whatever O'Moira and Fouché's creatures had in
mind for someone who knew so much and had caused them so
much trouble in the getting of it.

For France. As Brazear Breney had just told him.

For it was Breney who stood over him, rolled him specula-
tively with a foot to make sure he was sufficiently bound, and
sat on the window seat beside him like a man prepared to while
away a journey with a fellow passenger who was bound to listen.

"They are all dead, you know." Justice spoke boldly to
cover his astonishment. "In the wreck of their hopes."

Breney. Breney of all people. The one person among all
those he had met in the past week who had seemed beyond
suspicion. A bluff and comfortably condescending man. A
Tory by interest and reputation. A lawyer of obvious standing
in his profession. And yet . . . As Justice tried to thread
together the fragments of falsehood that must have run
through Breney's chatter, the signs that he was a knowing
party to this conspiracy, the man went on in the same self-
confident manner.

"I never had great confidence in this enterprise," Breney
said, fetching himself a bottle of geneva and a glass to improve

his spirits, giving Justice the impression that he was not an easy sailor. "I always considered it a harebrained gamble which could land us all in Newgate. Such things usually are, from all I hear. In Ireland, now . . ." He did not choose to follow that thought. "I was clearly right. You may know what has happened to my—to my, er, associates, Mr Justice. I have no idea. I can only deduce from your presence here, and mine, that we are indeed the only survivors, as you say."

He seemed so curiously unconcerned by the failure of the plot that Justice remarked on it.

"But then, I am not one of them," he answered, surprising and puzzling Justice by this disclaimer. "Not by occupation, if you follow me. I am the rankest of amateurs in such matters, and this was my first essay." He took a substantial swallow of gin. "And the last, I hope. Nerve-racking. Troublesome. Unprofitable." He gave an edgy laugh. "Dangerous, as you see."

If what he said was true, and there seemed no good reason for him to lie once he admitted his complicity, he must have been a reluctant conspirator. "It was against your will?" Justice asked, scarcely believing that a man could be forced to take such a key part in a clandestine affair that called for both courage and duplicity.

"Precisely said." Breney took another glass and gave him a decent sip of gin as though to reward him. "There are times in a man's life, Mr Justice, when his past reaches out to strangle him. When for fear of exposure he is obliged to act in ways that run counter to his present intentions and connections. When the price he is asked to pay is much less than the loss that refusal would entail." He poured himself another glass, and Justice saw that his hand was shaking despite his apparent composure. "Even so . . . even so, the pressure that is put on him does not make him an enthusiastic colleague of those who drive him, though he may do exactly what they want. It merely shows him the measure of his own corruption and the lengths to which he will go to preserve his comforts, let alone his neck."

From the moment that Breney had begun to speak Justice had been wondering whether he was hinting that some kind of bargain might yet be struck. "You could save both," he said meaningfully, "if you'll take this ship into the nearest English port."

"What! Be bribed!" Breney exclaimed in mock horror. "Be

offered the chance to turn King's evidence? When there is no one left on whom I could peach? Come, man, be sensible." Breney chuckled sourly, and gave Justice a patronising dig with his foot. "I can shop in a better market than that, Mr Justice, now I have you in my pocket. And if I should lose you, well, I would not need to go horse trading with Lord Melville's confidential gentlemen from the Admiralty. I should simply go home, if I pleased. No, you come after the fair with that notion."

"It was O'Moira, I suppose." Justice tried a different shot, and had the satisfaction of seeing that it struck hard.

"That Irish devil! I first met him in '98, and I wish that had been the last of the years he's lived to plague me."

It was clear that Breney was not going to tell what secrets O'Moira had discovered and used to extort his help in this ill-starred venture, but Justice recalled what Fanshawe had said about Breney's administration of Irish estates that had been seized from convicted rebels—thought, too, of the hanging of O'Moira's brother for his part in the rebellion.

"And Fanshawe?" Who could never have spoken as he did that night at Wykeham if he had known then that Breney was a covert helper in the plot: Justice was coming to see how skillfully the network had been woven together, and why it had been so hard to unravel it.

"He never cared for me at all," Breney said in a contemptuous sort of way. "Nor I for him." He gave Justice a quizzical look. "You say his trap at Brentford failed?"

"I didn't say, but it did." Justice thought his answer gave some perverse satisfaction, and saw that Breney could easily spin out the day with an attorney's to-and-fro. It was obviously a habit with him. And it took his mind off the seas that were hissing under the window. Perhaps he had not noticed that the brig seemed peculiarly sluggish, squatting into the troughs as though she were heavily laden, though Justice was prepared to wager she was near empty if she had come a-purpose to carry or tow the *Pandora* away.

Near empty. As the *Star of Salem* must be if her captain was depending upon the barge from Birmingham to top up his hold. Justice let his mind wander for a moment to the thought of Hatherley running a fruitless errand to Limehouse Reach; and then, before he listened again to Breney's guilt-ridden recollections, he wondered again what they had done with

Scorcher, whether his servant had actually managed to scramble aboard after saving him.

If Breney said nothing about him, it was best to keep silent. There could be some advantage to it.

Breney was talking about Francis. "A head for business," he was saying. "As good as his head for inventions, down to the last cent. But that's your Yankee for you, ain't it?" He mused over his glass for a few moments. "He'd have done better to accept the French offer, all the same," he said, nodding away the fact that he was the go-between, nodding away so that Justice saw at once that he had been the mysterious B. who was mentioned in O'Moira's letter. "They wasted him before, now they want him back. Quite the opposite of our countrymen, Mr Justice. They wanted him, and now waste him. You see. They'll keep him in their hand, sure enough, but only until they know whether they need his tricks or can safely discard them."

He paused to give Justice a macabre smile. "I forget, Mr Justice. Perhaps you won't see, after all."

Justice let the threatening gibe pass, noticing how Lilly and Breney had come to the same conclusion about the work Francis was doing in England.

His submarine novelties would be given a fair trial in none but the most fearful of circumstances, when all other means of survival or victory had been exhausted. If the war could be won by more traditional weapons, these infernal projections would lie dormant, as Francis put it. Until another generation found itself in such a pass that it would turn to them with the same desperation that had made Lilly commission the *Pandora* that summer.

For they were dreadful things that had come before their time, and like all premature monsters they aroused such fears in people's minds that men would rather strangle them and say they were stillborn than let them spawn new horrors to come after them.

In destroying the *Pandora*, Justice now knew, he had been the instrument of those fears.

No wonder Lord William had said that she was aptly named.

BRENEY HAD BEEN called away twice by a man who seemed to

be the captain and came to stand in the door of the cabin, bracing himself against the pitch and roll of the brig as she made poor sailing out of the Solent and into the Channel. He talked to Breney in a muttered and broken English that seemed to come from somewhere between Flushing and Altona, and though Justice could not catch more than an odd word at a time, he got the impression that the man was worried about something. Down here, for all the noise of the wind and water, and the creaking of the ship, Justice was aware that he had been taking in sail and that several times in the last hour he had put the helm hard over as if the rudder refused to answer properly.

And when Breney sat down between these consultations he was moodier, talking in bursts as though he was trying to keep up appearances when he was distracted. He had said something about Bland. He had only met him the once, at Harriet's birthday dinner, and liked him.

"Dead, you say?" He looked down at Justice with a saddened look, for once. "That wasn't his name, you know, though I was never told what he was really called. I don't know where O'Moira found him. Perhaps he was always a French agent—had been in the West Indies for years, he said." He spoke little about Luc, but looked closely at Justice as he mentioned him.

"Yes, my cousin." There was nothing to be concealed any more. For Luc was dead, and so much had died with him. "He was a brave man. And dishonourable." Justice thought of Luc as he had once known him. "I never truly understood what turned him."

"Perhaps he was just a Frenchman, when it came to it," Breney said with more understanding than Justice would have expected, for it touched him where his own loyalties were most entangled and obscure. Half French. What did it mean to be half French in this war? And what had Luc felt, with all the pride of the Valcourts at work in him, when he found himself so long exiled from his native land? Had it simply been homesickness that made him a renegade?

The captain was back again, speaking urgently to Breney, pointing to Justice, and going over to drag him to his feet when Breney nodded.

"I'm afraid I must trouble you, Mr Justice," Breney said. Whatever the man had done, he had at least kept his manners.

"It appears we may be blessed by a visit from your friends—or should I say your colleagues?"

IT WAS THE *Antelope*. Justice was pretty sure of that as he was pushed out onto the heaving deck and staggered, hands still bound, towards a part-open hatch. A fine ten-gun cutter of ninety tons, armed with twelve-pounders, that kept the regular patrol between Portsmouth and Plymouth, serving as a despatch boat, the scourge of smugglers and privateers, and a general watchdog along the Channel coast.

Her commander might easily take it into his head to take a closer look, perhaps board a neutral brig making towards the Atlantic: Justice took a glance at the masthead—yes, as he had guessed, the captain had broken out the Danish colours, and could probably produce papers to show he had sailed from Altona. A close look would be easy, a boarding party much more difficult in this broken sea, with the wind apparently going round a point or two every hour.

And there was nothing he could do. Long before the *Antelope* came near enough to see a man clearly, let alone catch a cry for help, he would be tucked away below, bound again, gagged probably, lying somewhere in the stinking darkness of the bilges, and no casual search would find him.

There would be no search. He was sure of that within minutes, as he tried to stretch in the narrow space between some water casks into which the captain had thrust him. He had felt the brig slacken its wallowing progress for a time, and knew the *Antelope* must have come down on her and veered away again. There would have been no time yet for Hatherley to get word to the Channel patrols, warning them to keep a particular watch for strange vessels in the Solent, and the *Antelope* must have been satisfied and gone elsewhere about her business.

Half choked, with cramp beginning to bite at his legs, Justice tried to distract himself by running over the things that Breney had told him. There were still gaps in the story. Breney had said little about O'Moira's role in planning the whole business, nothing about his own flight from London, or the way in which he had brought the brig round from Portsmouth to reach its appointed place on time. But he could guess at all that. He could even guess about Dunning's sudden and fatal appearance at Brentford. He must have followed Francis to Breney's office, seen Fanshawe there, perhaps overheard words between Breney and Fanshawe that made him follow the Irishman to Brentford and shout his desperate warning to Francis and Lord William.

It all made sense, now, like a play moving towards its climax, and he wondered darkly what his own part in the final scene would be.

And where it would be played. The brig could be bound to Ireland first, to pick up O'Moira from some safe, lonely beach, or running straight for Cherbourg, St Malo—he supposed one of the smaller ports in Brittany would be the most likely, for the blockading sloops and frigates could not watch them all continuously.

There were rats, scuttering over the boards, making strange sibilant noises. Like a man whispering. Like Scorcher, he said to himself, and thought his reason going before he felt the touch of a hand and the familiar voice at his ear.

"Cap'n?" More anxiously. *"Cap'n."* Scorcher's hand ran up to the gag, and as he cut he said, "Gave me a turn, that did, Cap'n."

He was slashing at the ties on Justice's wrists and ankles, chafing them to bring back the blood. "Creaking doors hang longest," he said consolingly, as he began to tell his tale in hurried breaths. Half a dozen ropes dropping to the *Pandora* and he took his pick. "Took the knife, too, Cap'n, seeing as how you'd have little use for it." Up and over the side. "Well, no man's better nor another in the dark, Cap'n, and there I was. Running about yelling with the rest of 'em." It was all soon told. A hatch. A hiding place. An explanation. "If I could find you," Scorcher said. "Make a fight of it. Make a fight, if we could do nor other."

Scorcher was right. A fight with one knife between them would still be a better end than a slow walk to a prison cell or the steps of the guillotine.

But it had not yet come to that. Justice silenced Scorcher's flow of anxious questions while he stood listening to the pumps, feeling how the boat moved, hearing the captain's voice raised in angry argument.

The brig was in some kind of trouble, for she lay too heavily, rolled too slowly, and there was too much water sloshing about and around her bilges.

He hustled Scorcher away when he heard a pair of seamen making their way towards him. "Wait for a chance, Fred. Who knows?"

The men were also troubled, he could tell, for they were chattering anxiously in their thick dialect, and seemed not to notice that his hands and feet were free as they took him back to where Breney and the captain were standing on the deck. Breney held a pistol, with which he fidgeted while the captain shouted and pointed away to seaward, over the white combers towards the *Antelope* still keeping company a few cables away.

Before Breney spoke, Justice took a good look round. Conditions had worsened in the hour he had been kept below, and he had a sense that as the tide ran against the wind they were being carried closer to the coast all the time, sliding northwest towards the cliffs of Purbeck. It had become the kind of day when only ridges of foam marked the difference between sea and sky.

"We seem to have the devil of a choice," Breney said. "If we turn for France, the captain says, that damn cutter will intercept us, and he refuses to be taken with a British officer on board. He says they will all hang for it."

"He might be right," Justice said, and meaning it. "And the choice?"

"To be driven inshore. Which would be the end of all of us." For the first time, Justice saw, Breney was beginning to show signs of fright, though his lawyer's calm was serving well to conceal it.

"It is no choice at all for me." Justice had taken Breney's point even before the man raised his pistol.

"I am sorry," Breney said. "I have no personal dislike for you. I shall regret depriving my . . . my principals of the chance to meet you. But I shall save my own neck, at least."

At least he has no idea that Scorcher is aboard, Justice thought, as Breney went on to explain that he would be in no danger at all if the *Antelope* took him off.

"Who knows my part in this affair, except you? I am a London lawyer, travelling to Ireland on official business. A friend of the government. A man of the utmost respectability." He glanced more nervously than he spoke at the *Antelope*, where men were lining the rail to watch the brig plunging about with only a few shreds of canvas to keep her before the wind.

"I shall simply go back to London. If I have to kill you, Mr Justice, London might even be better than Paris for me. I shall just go on with my work." He gave another of his uneasy laughs. "I do not think Dr O'Moira is likely to betray me."

"Until he needs your services again."

"As you say." Breney lowered the pistol. "If there is any last service I can do you without compromising myself—a message to Lady Harriet, perhaps?"

While Breney had been talking, the captain had left them and gone to the wheel, and out of the tail of his eye Justice saw him making attempts to bring the brig on to a more southerly course. And failing. There might yet to be something gained by talk.

"You are a swine, the worst of them all," Justice cried, taking half a step forward, making Breney afraid he might make a rush to carry them both over the side, forcing him to fire or give way. "O'Moira has his country. Fanshawe had his cause. My cousin had decided where his loyalties lay. You . . . you are nothing but a man who has betrayed his own people because he had been caught out in his embezzlements. A traitor. A party to murder. A friend to spies."

Breney was so taken aback by this tirade that he took another step backward, losing his balance as the brig shuddered and flinging out his free arm to catch at something for support.

Catching at Scorcher as he rushed out of the shadow of the hatchway, swinging Breney around so that Justice could grasp the pistol before Breney could cock and fire it.

He had no idea how Scorcher had worked his way through the ship without being stopped, but however he had done it . . . "Thanks, Fred," he grunted, as Scorcher lay across the lawyer and he twisted the pistol free to train on the captain and the men who were struggling with the wheel.

There was something wrong with the ship, for instead of putting up any show of resistance the captain made a despairing gesture and pointed to the stern.

She was lower in the water, though four men were taking turns at the pumps. She was settling, for the rising seas were now spilling over her quarter and swilling back through the open hatchway where Scorcher was leading Breney, knife at his neck, back to the cabin.

She was holed, right enough, her sternpost wrenched so that

her rudder worked erratically. Holed and wrenched by the blows on the *Pandora*, whose strong brass cylinder must have ripped at the planking and levered at the sternpost before she went down.

And the captain knew it. He was yelling in his own language as he looked at the cliffs that were looming up through the shifting grey scud to leeward.

Durlstan Head, south of Swanage? Or St Alban's, where the Purbeck hills swung away to Kimmeridge and Lulworth? Justice could not tell in the few seconds before the weather closed in again. But whichever it was, they were coming as close to destruction as he had been when he faced the muzzle of Breney's pistol.

"Worbarrow Bay," he shouted as Scorcher came back to join him, making motions to show that Breney had been secured. A few miles of searoom, that was all, and beyond that lay the stretching spit that ran out past Weymouth to the rocks and race of Portland Bill.

As he remembered that coast there was only one place that offered them the faintest chance of saving their lives—the brig was doomed, anyway. Somewhere along Ringstead Bay, where the Purbeck chalk turned away from the shore.

"Lost. Lost." The captain was so plainly convinced that nothing could be done that Justice expected no challenge from him. Or from his men, who were getting that listless look he had seen before on the faces of sailors who thought their hour had come.

But Justice was taking no chances. "Stick to him, Fred. Stick to him."

"Like a dying debtor," Scorcher replied, pointing to the pistol and making sure the man understood he would use it.

And as he did so, there was the crack of a cannon, sounding flat over almost half a mile of sea, and Justice saw the *Antelope* begin to haul her wind. It was a warning shot, telling of perils ahead, saying she could no longer stay in company.

From now on Justice had nothing to trust but his luck and his judgement.

THE CAPTAIN WAS RIGHT. There was nothing more that could be done for the moment, as the brig went down the wind, except to keep the men at the pumps and make such steerage way as the state of the sails and the rudder permitted.

Justice went to stand by the wheel.

"Here's a randy-dandy-do for certain," Scorcher said, with the wryest of nods shorewards, looking startled when Justice straightened himself and spoke in his official voice.

"I'm taking over," he said, "as you'll be my witness." And he was about to start on the official rigmarole about taking possession of the brig in the King's name when Scorcher cried out in protest.

"Don't do it, Cap'n, I beg 'ee. It'll be a court-martial job for sure, then."

It was astonishing how that prospect had raised Scorcher's hopes of survival, and Justice felt his own spirits rise until he saw that Scorcher might well be right. He could be ruined for seizing a neutral as a prize, or for wrecking the brig afterwards, or both. Odder things than that had happened in the navy.

Nonetheless, he was in charge, and by a combination of shouts and dumb show he made the captain understand what he wanted. Four men at the foremast, four at the main, cutting away at the strained and towering shafts of wood. Not much yet. Not enough to bring them crashing down before he was ready, but enough to make it a short task when he gave the order.

It kept the men busy, too, stopped them panicking like Breney, whose terrified voice could be heard under a smashed skylight through which water was pouring into the cabin.

They ploughed on through the waves, alone now, for the *Antelope* had disappeared almost as soon as she made her turn, pulling away as fast as she could from the dangers that lay ahead. Alone, with only occasional sights of the shore to give Justice any idea what speed the brig was making. He thought he had seen Kimmeridge. He was fairly sure of Durdle Door, for he had glimpsed light through the hole in the cliffs there. But he dared not go closer, for he had no idea what offshore reefs lay under the waves as they rolled towards those tiny anchorages.

The undulating line of beetling chalk rolled on. And all the time the brig was settling.

And then, unexpectedly, in a clearing of the low cloud, Justice saw the beacons beyond Bats Head, set there as markers for vessels that had cleared Portland and were making for Weymouth Bay.

It could only be a mile or two more to Ringstead, where he knew there was deep water close inshore, if he could get inside the sheltering banks to shave and scrape along the steep gravel of the beach.

He shouted for Scorcher and the captain, told them what they must do. The captain at the foremast, Scorcher at the main, where he could watch for the signal Justice would give when it was time to cut again, and again, as if their lives depended on it.

As they would, Justice thought as he went over to the wheel and told the men to steer for the shore, forced them as they protested.

They were past the great falling warren called Burning Cliff, with only a few hundred yards to go, and waves breaking outside them as they came in the lee of the banks.

When? When? They would never clear the little headland at Osmington, where he had once spent three days as the guest of Squire Lockwood, said to be the best sportsman in Dorset. They would barely come up to Ringstead Church, where someone had started to toll a bell at the sight of the brig rolling and pitching towards the beach.

Fifty yards to go. "More," he cried to the reluctant helmsmen, and dropped his arm so Scorcher could see it. The bow was swinging just enough, for the tide was working against the wind here, making him hope the impact would shock the whole frame of the brig and snap the masts over her sides.

It was a manoeuvre he had never tried before, and he had made it up from what men had told him of other shipwrecks.

He heard the axes at work, looked up at the masts, at the shore. He could have cast a line ashore on a good day. Yes, the masts should reach.

"Now," he shouted, pushing the helmsmen away in case they had failed to understand him, letting the spokes run at finger-breaking speed as the bow swung back just enough to make the brig lurch at the shore, feeling the keel bite the gravel in a long shuddering rasp.

And over the hiss and roar of the sea he heard the splintering crack of the foremast, pitching shorewards, digging its tip into the surf. Scorcher had done his work well.

And the captain? With a louder crack, and a long wrenching agony in the wood, the mainmast followed, slowly at first, then faster as the half-cut stays gave way, dropping into the water with a splash that rose high above the waves.

"Quick! Quick!" Justice saw that he had done it, but he had no idea how long that precarious hold would last. Two minutes, no more than three, with the sea dragging and pounding at the hull.

The captain needed no urging. He was there with his men, scrambling along the remains of the rigging, clinging to the masts for dear life as the waves licked up at them.

Scorcher was there, too, waiting for him.

"Go on, Fred. Go on!"

There was one more thing to do, and he turned back to the cabin. He would get Breney out to stand his trial on a capital charge of treason.

THE MAN WAS crouched on the swilling floor, weeping in terror as he held to a table leg. He gibbered, clung harder as Justice came for him, yelled the wildest abuse as his hands were forced free. "Where are you taking me?" he cried piteously, like a man terrified of taking the last walk to the gallows.

The brig lurched. The makeshift bridges to the shore would not last much longer, and Scorcher knew it as he came running back to help Justice drag Breney towards the mainmast.

Even then it was almost impossible to make the man move, though he could see the shore beyond him. Scorcher looped a rope under his arms to lead him, securing it each time he moved, and Justice crawled behind, grabbing at the mast with one hand while he used the other to push Breney's legs forward, one by one, inch by inch.

Slipping, sliding with every movement of the ship, they got clear of the hull, made a few more feet. And then Breney froze with fear. He had looked round, looked down, and scared away the last shreds of self-control.

He screamed in terror. He tried to kneel, tugging at the rope under his armpits as if he could escape if he were free of it.

And then he stood up. He had not even found a grip for his feet when the wind took him, tipping him over and down, and as he fell, the rope slipped over an arm and round his neck.

For all the noise, Justice heard the sickening snap as it came tight, and Breney swung below him, his head at a dreadful angle in a hangman's halter.

Dead. Quite dead.

"Poor devil," Justice said, as he stood with Scorcher on the shore, staring at the miserable figure that now hung like a gibbeted highwayman from the mast as it began to slide away into the sea. "Dying without a cause to believe in. Without a friend to say amen."

"Amen," he said, but he was no longer thinking of Breney. While Scorcher started to trudge up the beach towards the gathering crowd of seamen and villagers, he stayed for some moments more by the edge of the sea, and let his mind go back to Luc.

All he felt was pity and sadness for a part of life that had gone forever when the *Pandora* slid under the waves.

And as the sound of them faded, all he heard was water rippling past the mill at Recques. All he saw was a boy's face laughing in the sunshine.

Historical Note

THE AMERICAN INVENTOR, Robert Fulton, was born in 1765 and died in 1815. He is best remembered as the man who designed the *Clermont*, launched in 1807, which ran between New York and Albany to provide the first regular and commercial steamship service in the world. But he had many other technical innovations to his credit, and many of them have been mentioned in these pages.

During his long stay in France in the early years of the Revolution, with which he at first greatly sympathised, he constructed a submarine with some initial support from Napoleon. When he became disillusioned with Bonaparte he was willing to listen to clandestine offers from London, and in May 1804 he accepted a large sum of money from secret service funds and agreed to build a variety of secret weapons in England. The carcasses which are mentioned in this book were used in several ineffective attacks on French harbours—especially Boulogne, Calais, and Rochefort.

Fulton stayed in England for two years, calling himself Mr Robert Francis but making little attempt to conceal his identity: while the standards of secrecy and security in this period seem incredibly lax to modern readers, the poor communications between England and France, and the delays they caused, made efficient espionage most difficult. The troubles Fulton faced, for instance, were caused more by the attitudes of his British employers than by the chicaneries of his former hosts in France.

Letters and memoranda written by Fulton show that he felt that his devices were never given a fair trial—that the Royal Navy disliked them and may indeed have ensured their failure. It is certainly true that after Nelson's victory at Trafalgar in October 1805 the Admiralty lost interest in Fulton's array of weaponry. In 1806, after a difficult arbitration to settle how much secret service money he had spent, and how much he was still owed, he returned to the United States to the *Clermont*, to a series of attempts to persuade the American government to adopt his schemes of submarine warfare, and to the construction of the first steam frigate for the U.S. Navy.

Almost all the documents in Hatherley's file, and the remarks made by Mr Francis, are based upon the original sources. These may be found in books about Fulton, in the archives of the New York Historical Society, and in the New York Public Library. Ms Cynthia Owen Philip's knowledge of the Fulton materials has been an invaluable source of help, generously given.

When Fulton first came to England in 1804 he submitted plans for a much larger submarine than the experimental craft he had made and tested in France, and the *Pandora* is based precisely upon these plans, included in the collection of projects—the "Drawings and Descriptions" which appear in this novel—he made to send back for safekeeping in America. A commission appointed by the Admiralty considered these plans and rejected them, annoying Fulton because he was never called to speak in their support; and he long suspected that the British might actually have made some effort to build such a plunging-boat without telling him.

The Pandora Secret assumes that some such effort was made, with Fulton's knowledge and help, though all the characters are fictional save Fulton himself, known here of course as Mr Francis.

There was no Wykeham Abbey on the Beaulieu River, which was dominated by the Cistercian Abbey at Beaulieu. Readers should note that the lands of the Romney family, like Sir George Lilly's house at Cuffwells, lie across woods and fields which have always been part of the Montagu estate. The present Lord Montagu of Beaulieu has been most kind, but he bears no responsibility for the location of the Romneys between Beaulieu and the sea, or for anything else that has been said or done in this book. The archivist of the Montagu estate, Mr A. J. Holland, has given generously of his lifetime's knowledge of the river and its history, and Mr Fred Walker, of the Maritime Museum staff at Greenwich, has helped with many details of shipbuilding, tides, and weather.

Edward Bond, who shares a surname and a taste for odd guns with Ian Fleming's hero, was one of a well-known family

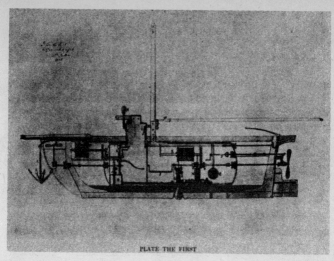

PLATE THE FIRST

PLATE THE SECOND

Two of Robert Fulton's original drawings of the submarine described in this book

of gunsmiths in Cornhill, and his shop contained some of the novelties described in these pages. Others were made by his contemporaries, such as George Goodwin, who undoubtedly made a buckle-pistol of the type used by Captain Justice. Here again thanks are due, this time to Mr Colin Strong of Brighton and Naples, Florida, who has been armourer-at-large to this novel.

It was said afterwards that 1804 was the turning point of the Napoleonic Wars. All through the year Napoleon threatened to invade England and Ireland, and failed: see *Captain Justice* for one explanation of that failure. In 1805, dragging Spain into the war on his side, and turning against Austria, Prussia, and Russia, he let his excellent ships languish and allowed the British to maintain the precarious maritime supremacy which triumphed at Trafalgar and thereafter contained the Napoleonic empire until it collapsed in 1814.

All kinds of intelligence operations stemmed from the tensions of that year, some amateurish, some foolish, and some successful. The fact that the British government was prepared to pay £30,000 to launch a series of secret weapons, and promise more if Fulton was successful, shows that the fancies of this story may not be all that far from the truth.

Bestselling Books for Today's Reader